For Rosemary Courtney.

With Kindest
regards.

Yours truly.

Oct, 1985

TWILIGHT
CHILD

BOOKS BY WARREN ADLER

NOVELS

Random Hearts

The War of the Roses

Natural Enemies

Blood Ties

The Casanova Embrace

Trans-Siberian Express

The Henderson Equation

Banquet Before Dawn

Options

MYSTERIES

American Quartet

American Sextet

SHORT STORIES

The Sunset Gang

TWILIGHT CHILD

Warren Adler

MACMILLAN PUBLISHING COMPANY New York

The author is indebted to Judge Paul Dorf, formerly of the Baltimore Municipal Court, for his valuable information and insight and to Frederika Friedman for her advice, counsel, and superb sense of craft.

Macmillan Publishing Company
866 Third Avenue, New York, N.Y. 10022
Collier Macmillan Canada, Inc.

Library of Congress Cataloging in Publication Data
Adler, Warren.
Twilight child.
I. Title.
PS3551.D64T9   1985   813'.54   85-11477
ISBN 0-02-500360-7

10 9 8 7 6 5 4 3 2 1

Designed by Jack Meserole

Printed in the United States of America

For my grandparents

Se niente va bene, chiama nonno e nonna.
—ITALIAN PROVERB

If nothing else is going well, call your grandfather and grandmother.

Chapter 1

FRANCES watched him as he stood in the patch of garden in the sweltering night, squinting into the grate on which the steaks sizzled, intense and absorbed in his task. In the air-conditioned cool of the den, she sipped the martini he had mixed with scrupulous care. It was strange and bitter to her taste. Music spilled softly from the speakers. Mozart, he had said. She whispered the name and continued to watch him.

He wore a blue blazer, light gray flannels, and a floppy polka dot bow tie, which, in Dundalk, would have certainly seemed eccentric. But in the environment of this townhouse in Columbia, it was, she supposed, perfectly appropriate.

The candles he had lit in the den cast a flickering orange glow on the books, some helter-skelter, some standing like soldiers, in the paneled bookcases. On the walls were paintings, real paintings, not just prints. Mostly, they were splotches of deep colors in strange shapes. Abstract art, he had called them, expressing the hope that she loved them. She did not give him cause to think otherwise. It was all very wonderful and mysterious and she felt transported into an environment totally different from any she had ever known.

She had, in a way, expected this first formal date to be exactly as it was turning out. No, there were no disappointments. In her life, that was most unusual.

"I know it's confusing."

Those were his very first words to her, soft and considerate, yet unmistakably authoritative. It was, after all, his department and she was hired merely as a temporary to check input forms for some computer program, of which she understood little. He did not know, of course, that she was mortified by her failure. Nor could he see the symptoms of her agitation, the sudden tightness in her stomach, the tremors in her knee joints, the dryness in the roof of her mouth.

Patiently, like some kindly teacher, he had re-explained the process, and by the time he looked up at her, showing dark brown eyes with yellow flecks, her symptoms had disappeared.

"I'm terribly sorry," she had whispered. She hadn't expected the apology to be as abject as it must have sounded. Apparently, though, it struck a chord of sympathy in him, and later in the day he had stopped by her desk, looking over her shoulder until she felt the symptoms begin again.

"Now you got it," he had told her. This time, the receding symptoms left anger in their wake. He is treating me like a child, she thought defensively. The way she sometimes treated Tray, her five-year-old, when he did something right after repeated failures.

"Thank you," she had replied, wondering if he caught the tinge of sarcasm. It frightened her to think so, and she turned to look up at him and flash him a quick smile. In that instant, she sensed that he had, in some strange way, photographed her with his mind. It was so unexpected and illogical and ill-timed that she tried to force herself to deny it. But that didn't stop her from thinking about it, and soon she simply dismissed it as a mirage.

This is ridiculous, she had told herself the next day as she hunched over the forms, feeling his gaze at her back destroying her concentration. And when she got up to drop her batch of finished forms in the collection tray, the gaze continued to follow her. To test her imagination, she turned swiftly, only to confirm her instinct. Through the glass partitions of his office, he was, indeed, watching her, too absorbed to discover his embarrassment. When he did, he grew flustered, blushed scarlet, and his hand inadvertently brushed against a half-filled coffee mug, which sent its contents onto his lap. He knew, of course, that she had seen the mishap, and now it was her turn to be embarrassed.

She must have been to him some kind of a curiosity, she decided. Certainly he was not looking at me as a woman, she assured herself, although vanity dictated that she take stock of herself, which she did immediately in the mirror of the ladies room. That morning she had allowed herself a light dab of lipstick and only the faintest touch of mascara, wondering if even that little make-up was appropriate to her recent widowhood.

Charlie, Chuck's father, still wore a scrap of black crepe on his shirt. It was as if he had dedicated his whole being to memorializing his son. Of course, she did understand his pain, the lonely agony of his and Molly's loss. Chuck had been, after all, their only child, the entire product of their long marriage. It gave her guilt feelings to assess her own grief and find it wanting. At times she wondered if Charlie wore his scrap of black crepe solely to remind her of her widowhood. It was, she knew, an unworthy thought. By then, she was having lots of those. Particularly disturbing was the eerie sense of freedom that Chuck's death had given her. Grass widowhood had actually been more lonely than the real thing was. Now there was no more apprehension, no more anxiety, no more waiting. Chuck was never coming home, ever again.

Her scrutiny of herself had proved that she was reasonably neat. She had ironed her skirt and blouse the night before. There were no tears in her panty hose. Her chestnut hair, washed, set and brushed that morning was, well, in the flattering light, nice. Her skin, if one ignored the little milky way of freckles over the bridge of her nose and cheeks, was clear. As always, she ignored the circles under her eyes, a genetic gift from her mother, destined to deepen and darken, as her mother's had done as despair over her father's loss and declining health slowly destroyed the woman's life.

Her image in the mirror had been oddly reassuring, marking what was, in retrospect, a new chapter in her life. At the time, it was impossible to acknowledge such a fact. It was too soon. Even now, watching Peter squint into the smoke, it was still, chronologically at least, too soon. Or was it?

She had squirreled away the memory of their first full-length conversation. Most of her responses had been evasions. Had she been too frightened, too conscious of her own vulnerability? He had materialized beside her in the company cafeteria. She had sidled off by herself, deliberately eschewing the company of her co-temporaries. Later she would question that contention, since she had observed him in line behind her and it had set her wondering why he was not in the executive dining room where he belonged.

"Do you mind?" he had asked, putting his tray down beside hers.

"Of course not, Mr. Graham." What else could she have said? She was, after all, not exactly annoyed. Surely curious. But she refused to give herself permission to feel flattered. She did remember, however, that she had posed to herself the inevitable question, "Why me?"

"Peter," he had said. "My name is Peter."

After an awkward silence, she had said, "This seems like a

very nice place to work." It seemed an embarrassingly trite response, and she had had to pause to ride out a difficult moment. ". . . Peter."

"Yes, it is. I am happy here," Peter said tentatively. But the message he conveyed was very clear. Happy here? He was clearly advertising a condition of his life outside of the office and scrutinizing her for a reaction. When he observed nothing definitive, he looked down at his tray and cut his beef patty with a fork. "Do you live around here?" he asked, obviously seeking a new tack.

"About forty minutes away," she said. She wasn't sure if she was being clumsy, guarded, or merely afraid to tell him Dundalk, as if it would define her as being beneath him, a thought that brought an immediate sense of belligerence. "Dundalk," she said, slightly snappish. She felt better after getting it out.

He shrugged.

"I've never been there. I live in Columbia. Just ten minutes from the office." He looked up at her, but when she returned his gaze, he withdrew his own. "I've got a townhouse. Not bad for a bachelor. I'm divorced."

There was no mistaking the approach, of course. She wasn't that naive, she told herself. She also couldn't yet quite conceive herself to be available, even for this type of conversation. Besides, she had forgotten how to participate in the ritual. No, she had never really known. With Chuck the evolution was natural, the contrivances nonexistent.

She had been working as a receptionist in a daytime radio station with its studios and towers on the edge of a marsh north of Baltimore. Chuck's job was to climb and check the structure of the three directional towers that sent out the station's signal. From the window beside her desk, she would, with her heart in her throat, watch him climb, a romantic and courageous figure in cowboy boots and tight jeans, golden hair flowing in the breeze.

It was always a relief to see him descend and move gracefully toward the little building that housed the studios. While he waited to give his report to the engineer, they would drift into conversation which, in time, turned into what she supposed people termed courtship. Then came marriage, motherhood, estrangement, and widowhood.

In her mind the chronology of events became blurred, leaving her with only the terrible memory of perpetual loneliness and the never-ending search within herself for blame. So not everything natural was automatically good, she had told herself later when the comparisons between Chuck and Peter rose more sharply in her mind.

But, in that first conversation, Peter had persisted.

"They say it's supposed to be easy for men. I can tell you, it's not. Even though I wasn't married very long." He drew in a deep sigh and offered a smile. To foreclose on his asking the inevitable question, she interjected her own.

"Any kids?"

"No, thank goodness."

"You don't like kids?"

"Oh, I like kids, all right. I mean it's lucky we didn't have any. No. I do like kids. She didn't, you see."

"I have a five-year-old," she had replied.

"That's terrific," he had said, but she had noted the considerable damper her seeming unavailability put on his initial enthusiasm. He actually flushed, and she noted that he pushed his tray a trifle forward, as if he had suddenly lost his appetite. She debated telling him of her marital status, but by the time she made her decision, he had looked at his watch as if he had just remembered an important meeting, gotten up, muttered a good-bye, and gone off. She wasn't certain whether to be insulted or relieved.

Assessing her reactions later, she had wondered why she did feel even a smidgen of righteousness. She was, after all, a very recent widow and very conscious of propriety. How could she not be? With Charlie still in deep mourning and Molly breaking into an occasional lip tremble and Frances herself trying to look appropriately grieved, although it was difficult to maintain the pose, since she wasn't feeling it. It was, in fact, awful to live with the feeling of liberation that Chuck's death had given her. Yet it was only a partial liberation, since she continued to search for reasons her marriage failed. Death could not erase her own failure. If she only knew where it lay. What were her marital sins of omission and commission? Was she destined to repeat her mistakes and relive her disappointments? On the plus side, at least she had been left with a fine, beautiful, healthy child and some semblance of family.

It took her a week to tell Peter the truth about her status. Not that he wasn't friendly after their conversation in the cafeteria, but it was in a purely office sense. He had continued to watch her. There was no mistaking that. Actually, she watched him as well, and not without some womanly reaction. It was a fact that was troublesome to admit to herself, especially at night, lying on her back looking at the endless expanse of shadowless ceiling. She took her mind off it by listening for Tray's breathing, waiting for his heart-stopping little sighs.

"A widow? Are you really?" he had said, a reaction that did not hide his elation. "You're so young."

"I don't feel so young." Somehow, twenty-five did not seem very young. Considering what she had already been through, orphaned and widowed, that quarter of a century seemed like eons. But she had hastened to put her widowhood in its accurate time frame. "Less than two months ago. He fell off an oil rig in Saudi Arabia."

"How terrible," he had replied.

What she had wanted to say was that it had been terrible for him to have been there in the first place, terrible for him to have felt this need of both adventure and distance, terrible for Tray to have been left fatherless. For her, the tragedy had been her inability to engage his permanent interest. True husbands and fathers did not volunteer to go off to die in faraway places. Not without wars or compelling and unavoidable reasons. It was odd, but the idea of his death filled her more with anger than with remorse.

Frances and Peter had begun to take their lunches together every day, and although she did feel that others in the office were taking notice, she chose to ignore their occasional odd glances and chance remarks. There was, indeed, no doubt about his interest in her.

"How does your boy take it?" he had asked. His probes were, she observed, very careful, as if he were frightened of offending her. It's all right, she wanted to say. But she had her own fears to contend with. After all, he was her boss, even though she was temporary. And he was vastly more educated, a computer engineer, an executive in a big company, a man of means and substance. Her life had been so . . . so inconsequential compared to his. Was the mysterious power of attraction able to bridge that gap? She had no trouble thinking up questions to nag at her.

She had no one to confide in, of course. No one to whom she could express her fears and doubts, or even to merely report her conversations with Peter. There had been relationships with young couples at the beginning of her marriage to Chuck, but with Chuck's long absences, those had gone out the window. She had felt like a third wheel, which also considerably dampened her enthusiasm for socializing. Then bringing up Tray alone became a more acceptable excuse for her isolation. The easy way out was to fall on the mercy of her in-laws, whose agenda was a lot different from her own. Charlie would, of course, be appalled by her growing friendship with Peter. To him, widows mourned, especially Frances, who had married his golden-haired prince. It wasn't just a matter of wearing black, which she had dutifully done for a few weeks, it was also a question of wearing an appropriate expression of inconsolable grief. She was not very good at that. For Charlie, she knew, the tangible symbols of her mourning would never, could never, be enough. And yet, he might have prevented Chuck from leaving home and dying. But he had not raised a finger to stop him. He hadn't even tried.

She might have confided in Molly. Between them had always lain the possibility of real friendship and understanding. But the opportunity always fell short of the wish. Molly, after all, had given her life to Charlie, and one could never be sure how one's confidences might be distorted.

But when Peter asked her out for the evening, she invariably refused.

"It's my son," she told him apologetically. It was only partly true. She could always have dropped him off at her in-laws'. But then they would be curious about her absence, and she was not very good at telling lies.

"What about weekends?"

"I really can't." Of course, she wanted to. And she hated the burden of fear and guilt.

"Why?" After a while, it became his refrain.

"Bring your son, then," he had begged her.

That would hardly have been a solution. Tray would spill the beans to Charlie in two seconds flat.

"It's just too soon, Peter."

She didn't explain about Charlie and Molly. Perhaps Peter would think her too weak, too dependent. He just might be right about that. Then, of course, there was the chance of familiarity breeding contempt. It was nice and safe to have these cozy little lunches in the cafeteria. She could keep herself guarded so that he might not truly know the dimensions of her inadequacy. In that way, she could avoid disappointment.

"Then when would it not be too soon?" he had asked.

"I'm really not sure."

"Just to go out. A simple date. Maybe just a walk in the park on a Sunday afternoon."

"You don't understand about Sundays. Sundays are with my in-laws."

"Tell them you're with a friend."

"There aren't any," she admitted with some trepidation.

"Yes there is," he protested. "Me."

"I can't tell them that."

"So make someone up."

She hadn't answered. But he had triggered her resolve. Despite her inability to be a truly good liar, she did make someone up, a friend at work, and she gave her a name. Sally. A nice innocuous name. When she was with Charlie and Molly, she would make sure to talk about her friend Sally. She had even given her a bit of history, a widow with one child, like Frances. They had a lot in common.

"You must bring her around," Molly told her. "It's nice for you to have friends. Especially now."

"Do you good," Charlie had agreed. "Keep your mind off things." How could she explain to him that her entire life was not absorbed by grief?

But the lunches continued. Then, as Sally became more real and her friendship with Peter deepened, Frances would spend an hour after work with him in a bar, which meant that either Molly or Charlie had to pick Tray up from school, a chore they both welcomed. There were other worries in that. Charlie never missed an opportunity to mythologize his golden prince to Tray. By then, Chuck had become a heroic figure in Charlie's view and surely in Tray's mind, a man of true courage who had risked his life and limb for his loved ones and died covered with glory in a foreign land. What protection could she muster against that? Certainly not the truth—that Chuck had been a neglectful father who had not wanted his own son, who had wished to be as far away from family responsibility as possible.

"Why can't you stay?" Peter would press. "We can have dinner."

"I've explained that." Actually her explanations had been sketchy, but he hadn't pressed her for more than she was willing to tell. She had not, at that point, painted an unflattering picture of Chuck. He was simply her young husband who had died far away from home and had left her a $20,000 life insurance policy and in-laws who doted on her son and treated her with a little too much concern.

"You have your own life."

"It's not as simple as that."

It wasn't exactly an argument. They had already begun to hold hands under the table.

"Is it me?"

"Of course not."

"Then why?"

"I have obligations, responsibilities." It was much safer to be vague and general.

He was far less reticent and much more specific than she. His ex-wife, a professor of mathematics at Syracuse University, the area where he had been brought up and where his parents still lived, had not wanted a family, had preferred childless independence. He had thought that was an idea that time would dissipate. It hadn't, and soon she was advocating open marriage, which, to him, had been a devastating suggestion.

"Imagine that," he had told her. "She had absolutely no concept about the meaning of marriage as a commitment, a solemn bond. I mean, you don't just *lend* yourself to the institution. The lines are very clear, honed by years of societal acceptance. Could you imagine advocating a group marriage? It's humanly impossible." He had winced, showing the residue of pain.

"Did she give you a bad time of it?"

"To put it mildly. One day, I came home and there she was, in bed with a student."

"How awful."

"Neither of them made any attempt to move. You know what she said? 'Stop being a child.' Imagine that."

"Did you love her?"

"I thought I did."

"And then?"

He had looked at her for a long time before answering.

"It's another thing you just don't lend yourself to. If it's there, it's there all the way."

There was no mistaking his intensity, and she had sipped her beer to avoid any further references to that subject. There was no question about his intentions. It was her own that were confusing. Despite her widowhood and the long months of loneliness

before, she still felt married, and the daily proximity to her possessive in-laws reinforced the feeling.

"There's nothing worse than being alone," he said.

"Sometimes you can be with somebody and still be alone."

"I wonder which is worse."

"They're both pretty terrible."

She watched Peter turn the steaks and cough away the smoke.
Although he was smart enough to be an engineer, he was not an
expert at barbecuing. But he was tenacious, and although dinner
at his place had taken her by surprise, she was determined to be
sophisticated about it, whatever that meant.

She sipped her martini, which was already making her slightly
light-headed, listened to Mozart, sat back in the soft leather chair,
and raised her feet to the hassock, continuing to observe him.

Peter Graham was wiry, smaller than Chuck, no more than an
inch or two taller than she. His face was round and a bald spot
was spreading on the top of his head, which was impossible to
hide because of his tight curly hair. He wasn't ruggedly handsome
like Chuck, but attractive in a neat, spare way.

She watched him come inside in a swirl of smoke and poke
around in the dining room, where he had set an elaborate table.
Earlier, he had opened a bottle of red wine to "let it breathe."
She had had no idea that wine breathed.

"Are you sure I can't help?" she called from the den. He had
given her explicit instructions to be a total guest, that it was his
party all the way, and she had obeyed them. Besides, a sense of
euphoria was taking possession of her, and the music and can-
dlelight created the illusion that a magic carpet had spirited her
away from the sober realities of her predicament.

He came into the den, bowed, and made a courtly theatrical
gesture, offering his arm. She laughed, rose, felt slightly dizzy for
a moment, took his arm, and let him lead her to the dining room.

Sitting across from him, she sipped the full-bodied red wine
and ate her charcoaled steak. She watched the flickering candles
cast shadows over his face.

"This is beautiful, Peter."

He lifted his wine glass.

"You're beautiful," he said.

She could not remember if Chuck had ever told her that.
Besides, she hadn't felt beautiful for a long time.

"And you're exaggerating," she joshed. To her mind, she was far from beautiful. Maybe pretty, in a well-scrubbed sort of way.

"Take my word for it."

"I hadn't expected this, Peter. Your place is wonderful." It was certainly a long way from her own cramped little apartment in Dundalk.

"To tell you the truth, I was afraid you wouldn't come. I know you said that you would. I trusted that, of course. But I felt that some unknown force would intervene at the last moment. Is it really you?"

"Really me." She felt a lump form in her throat. "Whatever do you see in me?" she asked.

"The future."

"Nobody can see the future," she told him honestly. She did not yet want to put it into words.

Earlier, she had told Molly and Charlie that she and Sally were going to take in a movie. They volunteered, of course, to take Tray overnight. "It will do you good," Molly had told her. She felt a sudden stab of guilt, which annoyed her. How dare they intrude? she thought.

"I'm so happy that you came," he said.

"Bet you say that to all the girls." The remark seemed shallow and stupid, which triggered the old worry about her inadequacy.

"No. No, really," he protested. "I'm not very good with the ladies." She knew he felt uncomfortable about having her to dinner at his house. She had assumed that when he said dinner, it would be at a restaurant. "Please don't feel pressured," he assured her. "I just want you to see me on my turf." A test, she knew. For her, as well.

"The steak is marvelous," she said, sensing the intensity of his inspection.

"I can't take my eyes off you, Frances," he blurted, the words expelled as if with regret. "Not from the beginning, from when I first saw you."

"Well then, you need glasses." She wondered if she had gotten into the habit of self-deprecation.

"I wear contacts," he said.

"Really?" She took another sip of wine and sliced into her steak.

"I can't think of anything else," he said, momentarily confusing her.

"You can't? But what?"

"But you."

"Me?" She smiled. "You have your work." Her hand swept the room. "Your music. Your books. Your paintings." She had none of these.

"Entertainments," he said. "To make up for what's missing."

She shrugged, secretly flattered but suddenly cautious and guarded.

"Some people are crazy," she said, deliberately choosing the light touch. She concentrated on chewing her steak.

"Why do you do that?"

"Do what?"

"Put yourself down."

"Do I?"

"All the time."

She felt a tingle of belligerence.

"You do, too," she said. "Telling me how bad you are with the ladies."

"I am. I'm all thumbs."

"Not with me." It wasn't quite true. He blushed often in her presence, and he sometimes seemed vague and uncomfortable, although she was always catching him looking at her, following her with his eyes.

"You're either very kind or very unobservant."

"Maybe a little confused," she said. It was, of course, more caution than confusion.Not to mention being frightened.

"About what?"

"You," she said, quickly averting her eyes. She finished the wine, and he started to pour more, but she put her hand over the glass. Her eyes darted around the room, as if seeking protection. She was beginning to feel defenseless.

"Do you want to get me drunk?" she asked.

"Not so you don't know what you're doing."

"I always know what I'm doing," she said. She laughed suddenly. "Now there's a fish story for you." She didn't elaborate.

"God, I'm happy you're here."

"Happy to be here."

Across the table, he watched her.

"I'm crazy about you, Frances."

He couldn't be that, she told herself. Crazy about her? She repeated the words in her mind, wondering. To put your trust in someone required an enormous act of faith. She wanted to trust him, yearned to trust him. Hadn't she lied for him about Sally? Or had it been for herself?

"It's the wine."

"There you go again."

"Well, what do you expect me to say?" The fact was, she didn't know exactly how to behave. But don't stop, she said in her heart. He seemed to have heard her.

"I'm telling you how I feel. You don't have to say anything."

"Just sit here and say nothing." I've done that most of my life, she thought.

"I don't think of anything but you. I think I've already told you that."

"What about computers?"

"A far second."

It was strange to hear these things. But it was refreshing, like a glass of water after a long thirst. Was he really talking about her?

Despite Chuck's death, she still could not shake the discipline of marriage. Hadn't she been a true and faithful wife? Had she ever known another man in an intimate physical way? Chuck, she was sure, had felt some macho sense of pride in being the first, even though it had happened before they were married. Whether or not she had felt the pleasure that sex was supposed to bring was another story. The fact was that she had felt nothing. Nothing.

"I'm courting you, Frances," he whispered. "I'm so in love with you, I can't stand it."

She looked at him and bit her lip. Her gaze drifted about the room.

"I know you must think that it's happening too fast. I mean so soon after—" He cleared his throat. "I just can't keep it in anymore, Frances. If I'm out of line, forgive me. It's a fact, and I'm acknowledging it. I know I'm taking an awful chance."

"I don't understand."

"You know. Going all out. Baring what's in my heart." He paused. "And the other."

"The other?"

"My *first* marriage." The mention of marriage pounded home the message. His candor stunned her. But he continued relentlessly. "It crippled me, Frances. I can still see them both looking at me as if I was the mad one. Eight years and it's still with me." His voice broke with emotion.

"People make mistakes," she said foolishly, wondering in what other way she was expected to respond. She knew that she was speaking for herself as well. We've both been crippled, she wanted to say, but didn't. She did sense that she was beginning to look at him in a new way.

"I'm dead serious, Frances," he said. In the flickering candle-light, his eyes seemed moist and glowing.

"I'm not questioning that, Peter," she said gently.

He smiled boyishly and showed her his palms. They were damp with perspiration.

"I feel like an adolescent. Dammit, I'm thirty-eight years old and I want to write you love notes and carve our initials in trees." He paused for a moment, and she felt pressured to respond in some way.

"It's just that I'm not prepared . . ." she stammered. Prepared for what? Had she ever been prepared for anything? "I'm a widow with a small child, Peter." She looked around the room. "And my real life is far, far away from here. Really it is. You've never been to Dundalk." It was a working-class section of Baltimore, actually a bit of a joke in some circles, which triggered in Frances a pride in it that it didn't deserve.

"Actually, I did go once. After you told me where you lived. I found your place, and I wanted to come up and visit you, but I didn't have the courage."

"Courage? You needed courage?"

"Cross my heart."

"So now you know."

"Know what?"

"That Dundalk is different. In two words, the pits."

"I didn't think so. I thought it had character. An honest place." He hesitated. "It doesn't pretend to be what it isn't. Besides, you live there, and that made it important to me."

"Really, Peter. There is a difference. I don't mean age. Thir-teen years is no big deal. But how about mental distance? Here you are with I don't know how many college degrees, and I just barely got out of high school. You know very little about me. Very little."

"I know what my heart tells me."

"How do you know you can trust it? Engineers don't think like that. Do they?"

"All right then. Let me explain the way an engineer thinks. I

know I have this need . . . to be with someone . . . to love someone . . . to share with someone . . . to love and protect and support . . . to make me live at optimum potential. I know that's my
missing link. So, subconsciously, I surely have been looking around.
Ever since . . . well, I won't go into that again. Then you cross my
path. Aha, something in my engineer's mind reacts. Even engineers have instincts. That's it, I acknowledge to myself after giving
the matter a great deal of thought. . . . I have found the bit of
machinery, the device, that eliminates the missing link."

Yes, she thought with a sudden burst of emotion, that's it
exactly. The missing link. Was it possible for her to find it as well?
In Peter? Yet she had been deprived of love and sharing and
friendship for so long, she distrusted her own sense of need. She
did not, however, distrust her growing feeling of confidence. She
had, after all, seriously engaged this man's full attention. Considering her long history of disappointments, that was no small
achievement.

"How can you be so sure?"

"I've been programmed to know."

"People aren't computers."

"Thank God." He reached out and took her hand. "So there.
I've declared myself and my intentions. So that's my half of the
equation. What's yours?"

"Mine?" She rolled the question around in her mind, watching
him as he waited eagerly for her answer.

"I want the best for my son." She had expected some sign of
discouragement. None came.

"Granted. But what about you?"

Whatever was happening, it was going too fast for her to comprehend. She felt slightly disoriented by the speed. So far, except
for Tray, life had been a maze of dead ends. Nothing had turned
out in even the remotest proximity to her dreams.

"Let's postpone me, Peter," she sighed. "For the time being."

"When you're looking at forty, things go much faster," he said.
"Time gets more precious. I've just stood up to be counted. Could
you at least tell me where you stand?"

"I'm not sure," she said honestly. With Chuck it had all seemed
so simple. There had seemed to be less at risk. She had been living
with Uncle Walter and his family, hating the sense of obligation
and charity with which she had had to contend. He had a bakery
in Timonium, and she had worked long hours there all through

high school for room and board and spending money. She had felt like an indentured servant, and the job at the radio station had meant freedom and independence. Then Chuck had come along, offering more promise, a home of her own, a family. That disappointment dulled the promise of Peter's words. Still, she had to think beyond the lessons of bitter experience. She felt like a cork on a wave. Go with the tide, she begged herself, wondering if she could muster the courage.

They finished their dinner in silence. Then he led her back into the den. He poured two brandies in snifters, and they sat on the floor and took off their shoes. He reached out and caressed her arm, and she felt the rise of goose bumps on her flesh.

"I've been very empty for a long time," he said. He bent over, brought her free hand to his lips and kissed it. So she was not the only one in the world in desperate need, she thought.

"I'm very frightened, Peter," she said finally, after she had let him kiss her deeply.

"You're not alone in that regard."

Again she let him kiss her, responding. Was it wrong? Suddenly, she stiffened and turned away. She had felt the tangible presence of her in-laws, Molly and Charlie, cursing her descent into infidelity. Leave me alone, she cried within herself.

"What is it?" Peter asked.

"Nothing."

"You won't tell me?"

"Not now."

He kissed her eyes, the tip of her nose, her cheeks. He found her lips, and she felt his hands caressing her everywhere.

"Stay the night," he whispered.

Her mind whirled with objections. She had promised her in-laws that she would come over early enough the next morning so that they could all go to the Boat Show in Annapolis, and they were sure to call her apartment at an ungodly hour to remind her.

"I'm totally unprepared for this," she said hesitantly.

"I want to love you. That's all."

She felt surrounded by him. Not that she offered any calculated resistance. It had been so long since she had been in a man's arms—Chuck's arms. And there had been no feeling in that, no sense of protection. No pleasure at all.

She was surprised to feel Peter's hard, corded muscles. His

hands were gentle and knowing. She felt alive, wanted. Someone was loving her, someone was caring, someone was pleasing her. Her alone.

When she awoke, she did not feel as if she was a stranger. There were no where-am-I's or lapses of memory, nor did she feel that what she had done, what she was doing, required a rebuke, from herself, from anybody. She lay in his arms, and it was, she felt, her natural place. In their haste they had not drawn the blinds, and the sun streamed into the room, a perfect lighting counterpoint to her feelings.

For the first time in years, burdens had been lifted. In her mind, she felt a calm serenity. Her body felt light, replaced, as if she had been transformed. A miracle had occurred, she decided.

She felt him stir. His voice surprised her.

"Up?"

She nodded, nuzzling his chest.

"I know what it means now," he said.

"What what means?"

"To find that lost piece of yourself. The missing link. I found it." He kissed her earlobe. "You."

She put a finger on his lips, stopping his words. What she feared most was that it would go away—the way it had with Chuck. Comparisons had intruded all night, and she had fought them away like someone chasing bats in an attic. Finally, she had won. In the light of morning the fear had less power, but it was no less annoying. After last night, Chuck would always seem nothing more than a boy, a beautiful boy. His body had been tight and wonderful, without blemish, wrapped in a down of golden hair, a statue, equally as cold to the touch.

But Peter was fire. Behind the scholarly facade, the nervous beginning, were feeling and a mind that gave depth to his passion. Peter had made her rise from the dead.

Then she remembered, noting from the face of the digital clock on the dresser that it was nearly ten. She reached for the phone beside the bed and dialed her in-laws' number. Molly answered.

"We were worried," she said. "No one answered at your place."

"I slept out." Brave words, Frances thought. Had she found her courage?

The hesitation was palpable.

"At your girlfriend's?"

She looked toward Peter and caressed his face. No more, she thought. It's my life. But she did not answer the question.

"You take Tray to the boat show. I'll pick him up later. Is that okay?"

"Of course, dear." There was another long hesitation, an awkward moment. "Are you all right?"

"I'm fine." She felt Peter's breath on her hair. "Wonderful, in fact."

"You sound strange."

"Strange or different?" she said playfully.

Actually, she wanted Molly to know and was bursting to tell her. Molly surely would understand. Not Charlie. Suddenly, a dark cloud seemed to roll over her thoughts. She felt a tug of guilt.

"Here's Tray, dear," Molly said. She heard fumbling with the phone, then Tray's high-pitched voice.

"Grampa painted the wagon. Daddy's wagon."

She felt the gloom deepen.

"It's really pretty. All red and shiny. And guess what we named it?"

"I give up."

"*Three Charlies*. Me, Daddy, and Grampa. That's us. Three Charlies."

"That's terrific," she said without conviction.

"And next year, Grampa promised we're going to get a boat, a sailboat, like he got for Daddy. And you know what we're going to name it?" He didn't wait for her answer this time. "*Three Charlies*."

"Well, you have a good time today. Mommy will pick you up tonight."

"Wanna speak to Gramma?"

"That's all right. I'll see you tonight." She hung up. Her stomach felt knotted, and she closed her eyes as if in pain.

"What is it?" Peter asked.

"Nothing. Just kid stuff."

"More than that," he said.

"I suppose you can't blame him," she sighed.

"Blame who?"

"Charlie. My father-in-law. Chuck was a junior. And he insisted on naming our son Charles, the third. That's why we call him Tray."

"Tray?"

"*Uno, dos, tres.* Spanish. It was Charlie's idea. He had a Hispanic marine buddy who was also a third. He was killed."

"Certainly less confusing than three generations with the same name."

"I wasn't too happy with the idea. But then I had no real choice."

"You were the child's mother."

"But this was a son, you see. Charlie's grandson. If it had been a daughter, that would have been another story."

The memory of her acquiescence confounded her. She had wanted to name the child Sam, after her own father. "Let's do it for Dad," Chuck insisted. "He's big on continuity." She had never been able to fathom the relationship between men, especially between fathers and sons. In particular between Charlie and Chuck. She felt compelled to explain, to bring it up to date.

"Charlie's love for Chuck was, well—fierce. I always felt inadequate to it. It was as if Chuck was always living under this weight of his father's love. Now it seems to be happening again— Tray." She shook her head.

"It must be tough on a father to lose a son."

"And on a son to lose a father," she said, surprised at the sudden belligerence of her tone. "It's all very mysterious."

"What is?" He kissed the back of her neck and stroked her hair.

"The male animal," she said.

"Not at all," he said. "We're rather obvious."

When she turned round and saw him, she caught his meaning. Of course, she thought. But there was a lot more to it than just that.

It was dark when she pulled up to her in-laws' house in Dundalk. They were in the den watching television. Tray was sitting on Charlie's lap.

"It's kind of late," Charlie said, looking at his watch. "We were really worried, weren't we, Tray?"

"It does her good to get out, Charlie." Molly said, peering over her half-glasses. "She's over twenty-one." She was sitting at the table, the inevitable pile of her students' papers in front of her, pencil poised over some fifth-grade composition.

"Doesn't mean you stop worrying," Charlie said. He winked at Frances. "And this little guy is bushed."

"I am not, Grampa," Tray said, frowning. His forehead wrinkled over heavy eyelids.

"Want toothpicks to keep them up?" Charlie laughed. He smiled at Frances. "We had one heck of a wonderful day. Saw the most fantastic boats."

"Grampa is going to get me my own sailboat someday. Like he did for Daddy."

"He'll have to earn it, though," Charlie said. Tray's eyes closed, and he laid his head on his grandfather's shoulder. "We did have a great day," Charlie whispered. He looked at the boy, as if to be sure he was dozing, then raised his eyes to Frances. She felt she was being inspected.

"How's Sally?" Charlie asked. She caught a tiny note of suspicion.

"Sally?" It had been a reflexive blunder, and before she could recover, Charlie reacted.

"You were out with Sally?"

"Yes, we had a wonderful time." It was too late, of course. The lie, she was certain, was loose in the room. Molly took off her glasses and looked at her curiously. Frances focused on the piece of crepe that Charlie wore pinned to his shirt. It only added to her sudden gloom.

"Where were you, Frances?" Charlie asked. She felt a sudden rush of guilt feelings.

"Now, Charlie, that is none of your business," Molly chided gently.

"I'd like to meet this Sally," Charlie said, watching Frances with hurt eyes. He had the haggard look of the inconsolable. His usually neat pepper-gray hair, once so well groomed, was shaggy and his long face seemed longer, the lines that framed his mouth deeper, the circles under his eyes darker.

"One day you will, I'm sure," Frances murmured, the effort to sustain the lie, she knew, a hollow sham. She detested herself for trying to perpetuate it.

"Of course we will," Molly said, with little conviction.

"Where does she live?" Charlie asked. Yet his probe seemed halfhearted, as if he hated the idea of knowing more.

"Oh, not far." Her pores had opened and perspiration began to slide down her back. She moved toward Tray and tapped his head. "Come on, little man, it's time to go." Tray opened his eyes briefly and closed them again.

Charlie embraced the boy and seemed to tighten his grip.

"Really, Charlie," Molly interjected.

"I was just curious." He seemed embarrassed by his own interrogation.

"I really should take Tray home," Frances said.

"It's not that I'm prying."

"But you are," Molly said.

"A recently widowed woman stays out the whole night—"

"Charlie, please," Molly snapped. "We have no right to question her. She slept at Sally's. Didn't you, Frances?"

Frances offered a nod, knowing it was meaningless. She was simply not made for lies.

"I didn't want to hurt you," Frances said. She had difficulty getting the words out.

Charlie turned toward Molly.

"You said I was thinking the worst. Chuck's not even cold, Molly." Frances heard the whine of pain.

"She has every right—" Molly began.

"A little respect. That's all one could ask. A little respect."

"I know how you feel," Frances said.

"Bet there isn't even a Sally." His dark eyes had moistened.

"I made that up," Frances said bravely. "I'm sorry. Believe me, I understand."

"I just felt"— he paused to gather control, still clutching Tray —"that you owed my son his honor. At least his honor. Instead of shacking up— "

"Charlie!" Molly snapped. Tray opened his eyes listlessly.

"I don't feel too good about this, is all." With some effort, he put Tray off his lap. Still sleeping, he leaned against his mother. Charlie stood up.

"You just couldn't wait," he said, choking on a sob.

"There's nothing to wait for, Charlie," Molly said. "Chuck's gone. She has her life."

"I hadn't intended to hurt you. Either of you. It just—well— came about," Frances said. She wanted to convey the beauty and wonder of it, but they could never understand.

"It's a lousy thing to do," Charlie said.

"I'm sorry, Charlie," she whispered as he left the room. She took Tray's hand. Molly followed her out to her car.

"He doesn't understand, Frances," Molly said.

She was beginning to resent her defensiveness, her guilt feelings, her dishonesty.

"I don't know what he means. I did not dishonor Chuck. Chuck is dead."

"It's just his own idea of right and wrong. Just bear with it, Frances. Please."

"But he made me feel so dirty."

"He's just hurt. He can't focus on anything but Chuck." She patted Tray's head.

She got into the car and strapped Tray in beside her. Nodding good-bye to Molly, she drove away. Tears of rage and anger gave the streetlights halos. "It *is* my life," she cried. Tray stirred, and she patted him back to sleep.

After she put Tray to bed, she sat in the tiny living room of her shabby one-bedroom apartment. She had tried to keep it neat and cheerful, but the curtains had faded, and Tray's boyish roughhousing had partially torn the curtain rods from the walls. The material on the couch and chairs was frayed, the rugs were stained. Paint was peeling off the ceiling. A picture of a sunset that Chuck had bought on their packaged honeymoon trip to the Poconos was awry. A fouled nest, she thought, grown cold and dreary with neglect. She felt helpless and inert in this environment.

Molly and Charlie had wanted her to come and live with them after Chuck had died. How could they know that the offer had become the most potent element of her anxiety? Once more, she would have to surrender her life. And Tray's. But her refusal had been tentative, given in the guise of a postponement. "We'll see," she had told them, deflecting their gentle arguments and the temptations of security, especially for Tray. She would not tell them that she had impossible dreams of making it on her own, of being, at long last, responsible for herself and her child.

Flights of fancy, she thought, scraps of tissue in the wind. Was she merely an easy mark for flattery and attention? She rebuked herself for the question. Peter had been totally sincere, offering a generous heart, devotion, sincerity, and sexual compatibility, an irresistible combination. A blurred picture of Chuck's corpse, his flesh still warm in his casket beneath the ground, animated by her betrayal, forcing his arms against the closed lid, made her leap out of her chair. With her heart pounding, she paced the room, peered out the windows, double-checked the lock, looked in on Tray sleeping on the cot next to her empty double bed.

Maybe Charlie was right and this punishment of fear was the reward of her whorish act? She shook her head, hoping the movement would chase the terrible thought from her mind. I must resist, she begged herself. Help me, Peter, she whispered, remembering her ecstatic response, the sheer surprise at her body's awakening as he led her into what had been, until then, uncharted territory. Nature's way of telling me that I am a woman, she assured herself, grateful for his attention, his enveloping warmth, his sweet tenderness and consideration. And Charlie had thrown mud in the face of her joy, glorifying Chuck, who had given her none.

She reached for the phone, looked at the dial, then realized that she did not have Peter's home number. But as she looked it up in the directory she had second thoughts. If she called, he would see how terribly vulnerable she really was, would understand the full extent of her need. Men were mysteries, she told herself. But he said he was crazy about her, hadn't he? Or was that only an empty phrase, part of the way men concocted seductions? Had she sent him the signal of willingness to surrender herself, to give herself away to the first comer?

And worst of all, would he lose interest in her by morning? She closed the telephone book and tossed it aside.

Miraculously, he didn't lose interest. In fact, he was more pressing and attentive than was proper for appearances at work.

"I'll never be the same again," he said. He was forever finding ways to pass her desk and excuses to chat, and she felt his eyes following her everywhere. When she went to the ladies' room, he was on her trail.

"Not in here," she had laughed.

"I don't want to let you out of my sight."

"There's only one door."

"Then I'll wait."

To her surprise, he did wait and accompanied her back to her desk.

"People will talk."

"I hope so."

At lunch, she was tempted to tell him about what Charlie had said, but she deliberately left it alone. No point in wallowing in that, she told herself, although the gloomy thoughts of last night had left their impression.

"Did you think of me?" he asked, holding her hand under the cafeteria table like a high school kid.

"Of course." She returned his hand's squeeze.

"Last weekend was the most important event of my life," he said. "I tried to analyze it, but I gave up. Something to do with the attraction of molecules."

"Don't try."

"You think you could pencil me in for next weekend?" he asked.

Charlie's words rushed back at her. Damn him, she thought. And what about Tray?

"I'll try."

"Just that?"

"There's Tray." She felt the pull of motherly responsibility.

"Bring him, too."

She looked at him, wondering if he was sincere.

"He's five and very active."

"He's yours, isn't he?"

"Of course." She wondered if she sounded indignant. And Chuck's, she wanted to say, but didn't.

"Well, then," he said, looking at her anxiously. "Bring him."

"Maybe I can get my in-laws to take him?" No maybes about it, she thought. They would insist and there was sure to be more trouble with Charlie.

"Whatever is best for you, Frances."

"It wouldn't be like last weekend. A small boy wants attention."

"Then we'll give it to him."

"Easier said than done."

She watched his face go through patterns of confusion. He grew hesitant, his eyes searching hers.

"The question is, do you want to be with me this weekend?"

It was, she decided, very difficult to explain. And it hurt to see Tray as an obstacle.

"I'm a widow with a young child—" she began, knowing as she heard her words that it was the wrong way to explain it.

"I know that," he said with sudden authority. The love-struck adolescent had popped back into his turtle shell. "I know he comes with the territory, Frances. I'm prepared for that. I don't understand the problem. He's yours. What's yours is important to me.

So we'll give him our attention." He hesitated and swallowed. "Like a family. I'm not stupid, Frances. If I don't make it with him, I don't make it with you."

She felt a sob begin deep in her chest and turned away to hide her emotions, lifting a cup of tepid coffee to her lips. Her hands shook, betraying her, and he helped her put down the cup. Then he kissed her hands.

"You don't understand, darling. I'm in this all the way."

"You're almost too good to be true, Peter," she whispered.

"I have my bad side," he said gently. "And I am frightened."

"Of what?"

"Of losing another round," he said quickly. Deliberately, she did not convey her own fear in that regard.

"I think we've both got to forget the past," she said simply. She began to feel better.

"You said it, Frances. I declare last weekend to be the first moment of our lives. Okay?" She let the question hang.

He kissed her hands again, then made a warming gesture with his own.

"So you're booked for the weekend? You and the little guy?"

"Just give me a little more time." She made it sound cute and not standoffish.

"You got it," he winked. "Before the day is over?"

"I promise."

"I couldn't bear to go home alone without knowing."

"Oh, you're overdramatizing, Peter," she said good-naturedly. "It's just that—well, I don't want to spoil it for you."

"Aha, a martyr type."

"Or for me."

She smiled shyly.

"And that boy of yours, he does sleep," he said.

"Soundly." She felt the heat in her face.

But when Molly called later in the day to apologize for Charlie, her stomach began to churn.

"You know your father-in-law. More bark than bite. I can tell you, he's very contrite today. He really doesn't want to spoil anything for you, Frances. You know what he's like. And he doesn't want you to get so mad at him that it will hurt his relationship with Tray. So let's let bygones be bygones."

"I don't need any aggravation myself, Molly."

"So just file it away."

"Consider it filed."

"Next weekend we'll have a barbecue. Maybe have some of Tray's friends over from kindergarten. Make it a party."

"I don't—" Somehow, she could not find the will to respond in full.

"You'll see, Charlie won't bat an eye. Ever again."

Fat chance, she thought bitterly.

After she hung up, she tried to concentrate on her work, but it was futile. She felt weighed down, stuffed with indignation and frustration. How dare they do this to me? she cried within herself. Without realizing it, she had brought the heel of her fist down on her desk. It was not a particularly attention-getting gesture, but Peter was watching. Sensing his gaze, she turned toward his office and managed a smile.

Then she nodded.

He pantomimed the acceptance of her message by clapping his hands soundlessly.

"I love you," his lips said.

"I need you," she responded in kind.

Chapter 2

THE WEEKEND was an exercise in thwarted expectations. Tray was moody and disoriented by the abrupt change in his routine. He kept asking, "When are we going to Grampa and Gramma's?" Frances offered evasive answers. Peter tried valiantly to deflect the child's interest and gain his attention. He brought toys and games and went through a complete repertoire of performances to gain the boy's confidence. Nothing worked. To make matters worse, it rained and they stayed indoors.

"I'm sorry about this," Frances said after they had tucked Tray into bed in the room across the hall from Peter's. They both kissed and hugged him. His only response was: "Will we go to Gramma and Grampa's in the morning?"

"No apologies," he told her, drawing her into his arms. "I'm very tenacious."

"I hope so."

But resentment and disappointment had a dampening effect and, although they clung together like new lovers throughout the night, her mind wandered and her concentration wavered. She felt inert, suffocated by the influence of her in-laws, a condition that had marked her marriage and now threatened her future.

As she had expected, they had not taken kindly to her announcement that she was spending the weekend with Peter. She had told them the truth—lying always made her anxious. She had deliberately called when she knew that Charlie would still be at the plant.

"Do you think that's wise, dear?" Molly asked in her typically gentle rhetorical manner. It was the way she had dealt with Chuck, always with minimal success.

"I think it's necessary," Frances had responded. "And comforting. The man wants to know my child."

"What should I tell Charlie?"

"The truth," she said boldly.

"He'll be very upset."

"I really can't help that." She was thankful for the safety of the telephone.

"And next weekend?"

"We'll see."

"He did promise to make Tray a tire swing and take him for a ride in the new wagon."

"I know."

Beads of perspiration had popped out under her hair. She felt the tug of some powerful barbed hook, the same sensation, she imagined, that a landed fish felt thrashing impotently to free itself from the line. Now, in Peter's bed, she felt a similar sensation.

"What is it?" he had asked. Her restlessness had awakened him.

"Odd thoughts," she whispered, stroking his arm, placating his concern.

"Like what?"

She hesitated for a long time. At first, he did not intrude on her silence. Why should she inject this discordant note into what seemed like a very promising relationship? Perhaps it was wrong to have brought Tray.

"It would have been better to come alone."

"That would have been a cop-out," he acknowledged, kissing her earlobe. "Sooner or later, we'll have to come to grips with it."

"It could be too soon."

"Am I pressing?"

"In some ways."

She did not elaborate, fearful that further explanations might endanger their still-fragile bond. Instead, she offered a round-about compromise. He had to know, after all, the real reason for her anxiety. Do not misinterpret this, she begged him silently.

"My ex-husband's parents," she said, surprised at the way she now expressed the relationship. "My father-in-law especially. He doesn't think this is proper."

"This not proper?" He kissed her lips and caressed her. There seemed to be an element of defiance in the gesture. "Who is he to say?" he asked firmly.

"He thinks it's too soon after Chuck's death." She took a deep breath. "And bringing Tray here . . ."

"You mean there are supposed to be time limits on human emotions?" he asked irritably.

"In Charlie's mind it's a question of what he views as right and wrong."

"He's got his nerve, Frances. He doesn't own you."

"I know what he's going through."

"It's what you're going through—we're going through—that counts."

"Of course. I know that."

"He has absolutely no right to make you feel this way."

"Of course I know that. But he still makes me feel as if I'm kicking a hurt dog."

"You couldn't do that, darling. Not you."

"And Tray's grown very attached to them, especially to Charlie. My father-in—my ex-husband's father." Inexplicably, she felt embarrassed, and she rolled on her side away from him.

"It's over, Frances," Peter said. She felt his breath on the back of her neck. "I'm here now." Reaching back, she touched him.

"I know," she said. "And I'm afraid of their spoiling it."

"Never. I'll never let them do that to us," he said belligerently, which frightened her. She was beginning to feel the growing strength of her attachment to him. It was enveloping her, changing her, becoming central to her life.

"You wanted to know," she said, turning toward him again.

"I'll always want to know what concerns you, and I'm grateful for your sharing it. Isn't that what a real relationship is all about?"

For the first time in years, she did not feel alone.

Still, there was no sense in not trying to make things right with Molly and Charlie. She did not go out of the way to aggravate the situation. The next weekend, she left Tray with his grandparents and spent the weekend alone with Peter. By then, although she avoided any confrontation with Charlie, Frances found a grudging acceptance on his part through her conversations with Molly.

"He doesn't like it, but he's not ranting and raving," Molly told her.

"That's sensible."

"And weekends with Tray really help."

It also helped to be alone with Peter without the pressure of his trying to make friends with Tray.

"Everything in due time," he assured her.

Soon any caution about discussing the future evaporated. They openly discussed marriage and a life together.

"It will not be easy taking on another man's child."

"He'll be my child. Our child."

She was growing less and less reticent about expressing her secret fears.

"I just worry about his accepting the change."

"Kids thrive in a loving home," he said emphatically. "He'll adapt. I promise you."

"Hopefully, we'll have other kids. He won't be lonely. Neither will I."

"Or I."

Not to be lonely, she thought. Was it possible at last?

She went up to Syracuse to visit Peter's folks and found them kind and, unlike her first experience with potential in-laws, grateful.

"Just love my son and be wonderful," his mother told her. His father, a doctor, nodded happily and, after the weekend, they both embraced her and promised that they would be the best grandparents in the world to Tray and whoever else dropped in. The rapport she felt was beyond her wildest hopes.

Yet the problem of Molly and Charlie nagged at her. She had kept Molly partially abreast of what was happening, and Tray continued to spend weekends with them, which silenced any blatant protest on Charlie's part.

She held back from telling them that she and Peter had set a date and had planned a wedding in Peter's parents' home in October, which was less than three weeks away. There was, they had reasoned, no point in being hypocrites. On weekends they lived as man and wife. Nor did she tell them that Peter had already put a down payment on a big house in Columbia and was planning to adopt Tray. One step at a time, she told herself.

To break the news, Frances persuaded Molly to allow Peter and her to "drop in" on Sunday during one of the weekends that Tray spent with his grandparents.

Peter had mildly protested the subterfuge.

"They're going to have to meet you someday," Frances told him. "Not for approval," she added hastily. "That doesn't really matter. Just for the record."

"Only if it's important to you."

"I just want to eliminate potential problems."

"As long as they don't aggravate you or come between us."

"Never," she said firmly. "Call it biting the bullet."

"Don't worry. I'll be the soul of diplomacy."

"You'll be perfect."

Molly asked them to come in the late afternoon. She told them that she would put up some fried chicken and potato salad and offer a casual dinner, continuing the charade, she added, to make

Charlie think she had just thrown some things together at the spur of the moment.

It was a beautiful fall day, with just enough nip to bring out the roses in Tray's cheeks. He was out in the yard with his grandfather, who was teaching him the intricacies of using a catcher's mitt.

"So this is Peter," Molly said. A tic in her jaw betrayed her nervousness.

"I've heard a lot about you, Mrs. Waters," Peter said awkwardly, as if it was a line he had rehearsed. Molly brought them into the den and offered beer.

"That would be great," Frances replied, accepting for both of them, although Peter detested beer. They had taken seats at either end of the couch. No displays of affection, Frances had warned. Molly went up to the kitchen. They heard her open the door and call out to Charlie and Tray.

"Mommy's here."

Soon Tray, flushed and happy, rushed into the room and into his mother's arms.

"I'm a catcher now," he squealed.

"And say hello to Uncle Peter."

Tray politely allowed himself to be kissed by Peter.

"Grampa says you're not my real uncle."

"He's right about that," Peter said, affecting a patient smile. He looked at Frances, who shook her head. Molly arrived with a tray of filled beer steins and a bowl of peanuts. Gray-faced and under obvious duress, Charlie followed her into the den. Frances noted the scrap of black crepe pinned to his shirt.

"This is Peter Graham, Charlie," Frances said pleasantly.

"Frances's friend," Molly interjected superfluously.

Peter put out his hand, which Charlie took with a less than firm grip. He took a beer and sat down on a chair. Molly had obviously given him some preparation, although he could not hide his awkwardness.

"That's a great collection of guns," Peter said, looking toward the gun cabinet. Out of sheer nervousness, Frances scooped up a handful of peanuts.

"Yeah," Charlie mumbled. "Used to hunt a lot with Chuck."

"He's going to take me someday," Tray said, bounding into his grandfather's lap. "I'm going to shoot the same gun as my Daddy did. Go after the big buck, Nasty Jake."

"Nasty Jake?"

"That's the big one," Charlie said, hugging the boy with his free arm. Tray's proximity seemed to comfort him. "We never did get that one, Chuck and I."

"I'm going to get it," Tray squealed.

"You bet your sweet patooty."

Frances began to relax.

"Ever do much hunting?" Charlie asked.

"I'm afraid not. I don't like killing things."

"We only shoot what we eat," Charlie said, not looking at Peter directly. Frances remembered how Chuck used to echo his words, which had never made sense to her.

"I just go to the supermarket," Peter said lightly.

"They kill those animals, too," Charlie said. "People forget that. Man feasts on other creatures to survive. It's the law of nature."

"It's a sport," Peter said, "It's the killing of things as sport that I object to."

"Different strokes for different folks," Frances interrupted. She wished they would get off that subject.

"I understand you're in computers, Peter," Molly said, her voice obviously strained.

Peter nodded.

"He's an engineer. They're into big stuff for defense. High tech," Frances said. Out of the corner of her eye, she saw Charlie tense and suddenly remembered how he had railed against the "high-tech boys ruining it for the people who built this country."

"I hear you're at Bethlehem, Charlie," Peter said.

"More than thirty years," Molly said.

"Things are still pretty tough over there, I guess," Peter said. There seemed to be no subject between them that was neutral.

She saw Charlie's face grow ashen.

"We just sat back while we gave away the country to the Japs. Hell, I killed Japs in the war. When I think of the guys who died in that one, I get a little sick to my stomach to see how we snatched this defeat from the jaws of victory. Used to be Sparrows Point was pounding out steel on three shifts. Now there's barely enough work for one." His voice rose and his lips seemed to go bloodless. He was becoming agitated.

"The Japanese are tough competition in my field, too," Peter said, looking helplessly at Frances. He hadn't expected Charlie's reaction.

"All those guys out on the street. You can't imagine the pain that's been caused to families out there. You know what it means to get laid off? Lots of guys in their forties and fifties. Too old for retraining. Makes my blood boil the way they've screwed things up." He drifted into a deep gloom.

"I know what you mean," Peter said gamely.

"Do you really?" Charlie shook his head. "You're all set. World's set up for guys like you now. High-tech boys got it made."

"Let's face it, Charlie, high tech is the cutting edge of the future." He looked at Frances. "We've got a lot of things ahead of us, Frances and I. We've made plans. For Tray, too." At the sound of his name, Tray looked up.

"Why don't you go outside and play?" Frances asked pleasantly. She sensed a looming confrontation. Tray bounced off his grandfather's lap.

"You coming, Grampa?"

"In a little while, Tray."

Frances watched Charlie's face. Had a shadow crossed it suddenly? He looked confused and turned toward Molly. Tray ran up the stairs.

"We're getting married in a few weeks," Peter said with a smile after the boy had gone. They hadn't discussed strategy. Perhaps she had hoped that the news would simply materialize. Well, it had.

"Married?"

"In less than three weeks," Peter said. "At my folks' house in Syracuse."

"Of course, you're both invited," Frances said, watching Charlie's stunned face.

"That's—that's wonderful," Molly said, her voice tremulous. She made no move to kiss the intended bride. Frances suddenly had a sinking feeling in her stomach.

"That's only—" Charlie began, passing his fingers through his hair. His eyes grew shiny with moisture. "A few months," he said haltingly. "Four months since . . ."

"It has nothing to do with Chuck, Charlie," Frances said gently.

"You can't wait?" Charlie said with an air of helpless pleading.

"There's no point in that. We're together now anyway. Why not get on with our lives?"

"I think it's disgusting," Charlie hissed, obviously making a great effort to repress an outburst. "My son's barely cold."

"It's best, Charlie," Frances whispered.

"Best for who?" Charlie snapped. "It's an insult to my son's memory. Why can't you see that? Doesn't his life stand for anything?"

"You're being very irrational about this, Waters," Peter said. It was adding fuel to the fire, Frances saw, but there was little that could be done. Not now. Her gaze met Molly's. We have to stop this, her mother-in-law's eyes implored.

"You're humiliating us," Charlie said. "That's what you're doing. He was a good boy, my Chuck. Maybe he wasn't perfect, but nobody is. A good husband. A good provider. A good father."

None of those, Frances thought, but she kept her silence. Peter looked at her and shrugged.

"You're defaming his memory." He looked at Molly. "That's what they're doing, babe. It's selfish and inhuman." Charlie pointed a finger at Frances, but still did not raise his voice. Then he turned again to Frances. "Someday you'll pay for this." His voice broke, and he cleared his throat. "Tray will grow up and he'll want to know why you couldn't wait, why you didn't respect his father's memory." Eyes narrowing, his face seemed to contort as if he were suffering some terrible physical pain. "Didn't my boy mean anything to you? Anything at all?"

"I think this is going too far, Charlie," Molly said, getting up from her chair. "Let's all have dinner and discuss it sanely."

"There's nothing to discuss," Peter said. He looked at Frances. "I don't need or want your stamp of approval. I also don't want to deliberately hurt you. But I really don't think we have to take this."

"Please, Peter," Frances said. "We mustn't make it worse."

"I think we've given them the courtesy of informing them about our plans. We've invited them to the wedding. What more is there to say?"

"You can't be serious about me coming to your wedding?" Charlie muttered.

"No need to make that decision now," Molly said.

"I've made it," Charlie snapped.

"Why don't we just have dinner?" Molly asked.

"I'm really not sure . . ." Peter said, looking at his watch.

"We'd love to," Frances said, throwing Peter a look of rebuke.

"I'm not hungry," Charlie said.

"You'll see the food, you'll get hungry," Molly said. She went up to the kitchen. Charlie slumped deeper into his chair and said nothing. Peter looked around the den. There was an awkward moment of silence.

"Nice room you have here," Peter observed. His comment sounded hollow, designed merely to fill the silence.

"Charlie built it himself," Frances said, desperately trying to find a common ground.

"Boy was good with his hands," Charlie muttered, shaking his head. He seemed to have shrunk in the last few moments. "He was a good husband and a good father. He doesn't deserve this treatment."

"Not again, Charlie. Please," Frances said. It had become a litany, a litany of lies. He knew little about the real facts of her marriage, the loneliness and indifference.

"Well, he was," Charlie persisted.

"I'm not denying it," Frances said quickly, biting her lip. She did not want Peter to see her agitation.

"Why must you deny it, Frances?" Peter said. "Tell him the truth." He looked pointedly at Charlie. "She had a terrible time."

"She's a liar," Charlie shouted. Molly rushed down the short flight of stairs wiping her hands on her apron.

"I think you're going a bit far, Waters," Peter said. His tone was calm, placating.

"Not far enough," Charlie mumbled.

"I can only apologize for him, Peter," Molly said. "He's still very distraught."

"Damned straight I am," Charlie fumed. "And when I see this—you and her—with him hardly gone four months—what am I supposed to think?" He turned toward Molly. "And stop apologizing for me. Chuck was your son, too."

"You're way out of line, Waters," Peter said. Frances had already observed that instead of becoming openly angry, Peter became deliberate, calculating.

"Maybe I am. The thing is that without respect, there can be no decency, and respect for the dead is sacred. Didn't my son stand for anything? Or are we supposed to throw away his memory, too, like some piece of trash, as if he never existed? I mean, what's it all about? I have a right to be angry, a right to be disgusted—" He seemed too overcome to continue.

Frances felt Peter's intense gaze, but she was too upset to react.

"Before you say something you're going to regret—" Peter began calmly.

"I'll regret nothing. You people don't understand the meaning of honor. In the Marine Corps we knew about honor. We understood a man's dignity. Take away a man's honor, dead or alive, and you destroy his—well—manhood. I think this woman has committed an unpardonable sin. She has shown disrespect for my dead boy. She has dishonored him—"

"This woman?" Molly said. "Now really, Charlie—"

"It's all right," Peter said, his voice raised, commanding authority. "You're creating a myth. She has not dishonored anyone. Certainly not your son. In fact, you dishonor her by questioning her motives." He looked directly at Charlie. "But none of that is relevant to us. What is important is that we're getting married."

Charlie's pallor grew ashen. He stood up, breathing hard, almost gasping with anger.

"You never loved him. You drove him away," he said to Frances. Then he turned to Peter. "She'll do the same to you. History repeats."

Frances reached out for Peter's hand. It was too awful, too humiliating. She began to shake all over. She felt Peter return the pressure on her hand, then bend over and kiss her forehead.

"Easy, baby," he whispered. He was calm, deliberate, and although Charlie stood menacingly over him, he looked up at him with steady eyes. "I suppose I can't really understand your pain. I'm sorry about your son, your grief. I'm sure it hurts. But that doesn't mean you have to strike out at others who are innocent of any wrongdoing whatsoever. Your sense of time is purely arbitrary. I'm sorry about that. The world is for the living. Always was. Frances has accepted my offer in good faith. We care a great deal about each other. She is entitled to get on with her life. Both of us are. Frankly, I don't care what you think about it. Nor does it matter if we ever see you again."

The sense of menace disappeared. Charlie seemed shattered, defeated. Tears of frustration filled his eyes. He turned and walked slowly up the stairs.

"He'll get over it," Molly said when he had left.

"That's his problem," Peter said, standing up. Frances felt herself gently lifted.

"What can I say?" Molly began, swallowing to hold down the

emotion in her voice. "You know how he was about Chuck. You can understand that. Can't you, Frances?"

"I understand that. Unfortunately, we can't stop living because Chuck is gone."

"You'll see. He'll get over it," Molly said, her tone pleading.

"I'm trying to do it the best way I can, Molly," Frances said. "I have no desire to hurt you. Either of you."

"I know that, dear."

"I have to think of what's best for Tray and Peter and myself."

"Of course you do." Molly paused. "He's really the salt of the earth, you know," she said.

Frances didn't answer. Whatever Charlie's intrinsic goodness, he had never been her ally, but always a thorn in her side. She let it pass.

"We'd better get going," Peter said.

"But dinner is warming—"

"We'll get something later. Please. I don't mean to be rude, but it's better that we be off."

Frances nodded, resisting the urge to embrace Molly. She went up the stairs and called Tray in from the yard.

"We're going to eat out," Frances said.

"But I thought—" Tray began.

"Plans changed," Frances said firmly, taking the boy by the hand. Molly embraced the boy and kissed his head.

"Where's Grampa?" Tray asked.

"Grampa's tired," Frances assured him. After a while, Molly released the boy, and Frances, followed by Peter, led him out the door.

They stopped at McDonald's, ate rubbery hamburgers, and drove back to her apartment in Dundalk.

"I don't think it's going to work," Peter said after they had put Tray to bed.

"Us?" She felt a sudden sense of panic.

"Us? Not a chance. We'll work. It's them. Him. Who needs that pressure? The man is totally beyond logic, caught in an emotional grid-lock. He will never accept us as a couple. And there's so much resentment. He can only make us miserable. And that can't be good for Tray." He stroked Frances's arm. "I'm just not going to let him do it to us. I know what outside circumstances can do to a marriage."

"Time will heal everything, I'm sure," Frances said.

"And in the meantime? Why should we have to compromise our own lives for his grief? I'd say it's his problem, not ours."

His words sounded cruel, but there was a lot of truth in his assumptions, she agreed. Why couldn't Charlie understand? It occurred to her suddenly as she realized that she was concerned with Charlie and Molly's feelings more than her own and Peter's. What, after all, did she owe them? Charlie had never given up one iota of his influence over his beloved prince. Frances had been a mere appendage, her needs always secondary to Chuck's. And Charlie's. The memory of her powerlessness over events in her early life triggered her even deeper resentment. I am free of them now, she assured herself.

"How dare he," she said with a flash of anger. But it quickly dissipated. "I wish it were otherwise."

"But it's not. We have to accept life in the real world."

She nodded, well on the road to conviction.

"The man will only make trouble. Tray will be pushed and pulled and confused." He sighed and shook his head. "He won't ever give it up. He'll never accept me. Never. Molly's okay, but she's committed to him. She says she understands. But what can she do about it? It's sad."

"Maybe in time . . ."

"Maybe. But who needs the aggravation? We're just starting out, Frances. We need the running room, free from that kind of pressure." His eyes wandered around the room as if he was visiting it for the first time. Actually, he had been there twice before.

"So this is what he gave you?"

"Awful, isn't it?" Yet she could remember when she had thought it was lovely, a feeling that might have lasted all of two months. She felt ashamed to have settled for so little.

"You'll never have to go back to this again, darling. That I promise." He took her in his arms and kissed her.

"I don't want anything to come between us, Peter. To spoil our happiness."

"Nothing will."

He held her at arm's length and looked into her eyes. "I'm afraid we're just going to have to erase them from our lives. At least for now."

"I wish there were another way." A brief tug of uncertainty

nagged at her. She knew what it meant to lose people you love. "But I'm afraid it will be a problem."

"Which could tear us apart. I've been through it, and I don't ever want it to happen again." He held her close, and she felt a tremor pass through him.

"Tray will just have to adjust," she said firmly, after he had relaxed.

"Kids are adaptable."

"I don't want anything to come between us," Frances said emphatically.

"Listen, I'm going to be the greatest daddy in the world. And my parents will be the most wonderful grandparents in the world. It's time we started to think about us."

Again he kissed her, for a long moment.

"We're entitled to start fresh. The hell with the past," he said, and she felt his hand stroke her hair. "It wasn't so hot anyhow."

"No, it wasn't," she agreed, beginning to feel better, more confident.

"And we have our lives to live. I promise it will be the best, the very best. And I'll love that child in there with as much feeling and devotion as I love his mother. I know it's the right thing to do, Frances."

"I agree, darling," she said.

She felt suddenly as if a great weight had been lifted from her shoulders. She wanted to cry, but she held back her tears.

Chapter 3

WOOD everywhere, Charlie thought, as his gaze circled like a floodlight around the reception room: polished oak with indented panels not unlike those on the walls of the sprawling old Eastern shore mansions that dotted the points around Crisfield. He'd seen them only because as a boy he had been Big Ed's helper on his chimney sweep rounds back before the war.

Reminders like that plagued him now, not because they didn't comfort him in his daydreams, but because they inevitably ended in the present. He shuddered and lit a cigarette. Beside him, Molly looked up from *House and Garden* to offer a snappish look of disapproval. He had taken up smoking again eighteen months ago, six months after Tray had gone. "No more need to set examples," he had told her then, lighting up an old-fashioned Camel, unfiltered, the real thing, then inhaling all the way down and exhaling through the nose like in his marine days.

He might have said "Mind if I smoke?" if the receptionist had been less disdainful. She was young and pretty and sat discreetly behind an antique desk, ignoring them as she answered the phone with cloying ingratiation. "Banks, Pepper and Forte." It was Forte they had come to see.

"Smells like money," he whispered to Molly, waving the smoke away as he bent toward her.

"It won't be cheap," Molly said, watching him over her half-glasses, her blue eyes still cobalt, like Chuck's, but more watery now than they had been. There were more wrinkles when she smiled, but her figure hadn't gone to seed. "Fifty-eight and still my girl. You and me, babe." It was a thought Charlie often voiced, especially in those harsh, fearsome moments in the dead of night when his rabid and unsleeping mind dwelt on the dead Chuck and the missing Tray and the cruel Frances. Thankfully, they had slept like spoons since the beginning of their marriage, which somehow always managed to bring him through the darkness.

"Nothing cheap wins the day," he murmured, satisfied that these lawyers were used to winning.

"They get paid either way," Molly said, breaking the whispering pattern. It was just like Molly to offer the balanced view, he thought, wishing for more bias on her part.

"We should have never let it happen in the first place," Charlie said. The admonition had become the opening of a nasty game between them. She sighed her usual defense.

"Did we let it happen?" Molly wondered aloud. "How could we have foreseen that it would go on this long? Two years." She shook her head and pursed her lips. Like him, she was still puzzled and confused.

"We were suckers. We could have nipped it in the bud."

"We had no choice. None at all," Molly said, removing her half-glasses and closing the magazine, offering the words by rote.

"You said she would come around in time." He took a deep drag of smoke, then turned away to expel it, with the words, "Two damned years," a bit louder than he would have liked. The receptionist smiled thinly. He stared at her without acknowledgment. A tough one to read, he thought. It was hard enough understanding the old ones. The young ones were impossible.

"Problem is, we haven't got all that much time."

"I hoped she would change her mind," Molly said gently. After all, it was her defeat as well. He took her hand and patted it. "It seemed so logical. They needed time to adjust. All right. We gave them that. Not this. Not forever. Not for all time."

"I know, babe." They were in this together, weren't they?

Seeking legal means just to see their own grandchild, their own flesh and blood. The idea of it was gross; it went against nature. Easy, Charlie, he told himself, trying to stave off a full head of steam. He punched out his cigarette in the ashtray and stood up. Molly's gaze followed him. He looked at his watch again, which stimulated the old demon, his sense of inferior position. Once again, he must wait, always waiting his turn, never important enough to be seen on time. He hated that feeling. Now it was complicated by a retrospective on a failed life. It wasn't long ago when he felt things were pretty good. He had a decent job. Paid-up house. Loving wife, a schoolteacher. A helluva son, Chuck, a helluva son. And little Tray, Charles III. He was beautiful, the image of Chuck. A sob bubbled deep in his chest. He masked it with a cough.

"Sit down, Charlie," Molly said.

"I'm sure Mr. Forte won't be much longer," the receptionist said, softening somewhat as if she sensed their anguish.

"Not as easy as I thought."

"It'll only get worse," Molly said. It was her oblique way of joking.

"Can't understand her attitude," Charlie muttered. When he thought of Frances his midsection tightened up. "Both of them. It makes me so damned angry."

"That won't do us much good."

"It's what I feel."

It annoyed him to see Molly always poised at a lesser degree of indignation.

"I know how you feel. I'm only saying that getting all riled up seems like the wrong strategy."

"Next thing you'll be telling me the bit about catching more flies with honey."

"Might be a good idea for a change."

"In the end you still have to answer to yourself."

"Pretty lonely stuff—answering just to yourself."

"I have to say what I mean. Be what I am."

"That first part's the problem, Charlie."

"Guess I do shoot from the hip," Charlie mumbled.

"You can't blame yourself all the time, Charlie. There's more to it than that. Nothing's black and white. Let's see what the lawyer has to say."

"Seems crazy, doesn't it? All we want to do is see our grandson. Wouldn't think you'd need a lawyer for that."

They had seen a brief story in the papers about a case in New York state that dealt with grandparents' visitation rights. Robert Forte had been quoted. "Yes, there is a statute in the state of Maryland which gives grandparents the right to petition for visitation rights under certain conditions." It had taken ten minutes to make the call and a lifetime for the call to be returned. He had offered Forte a fractured outline, unable to sustain a simple, smoothly told narrative. Forte had been patient but probing and had offered an initial interview without promises. They might as well, Molly had agreed. They had nothing to lose.

Charlie felt himself growing sullen and patted her hand again. She put her other hand on top of his. He shrugged, looking at what he and Tray had called a hand sandwich. Instead of a grin, he felt morbid, drained of even the possibility of joy. Tears had come on without warning lately, as well as lips that moved, offering silent curses, which Molly had the good grace to pretend not to see.

"At least we'll get her attention," Molly said.

"I don't want her damned attention. I want Tray."

She smoothed the shoulder of his jacket, patting away as if there were dust or dandruff there. Mostly it was, he knew, a gesture to soothe his agitation. He felt another lecture coming on.

"If you show too much emotion, it turns people off. Especially anger. It just won't do any good to show anger. Do you understand what I mean?" Her tone changed suddenly. "I don't want to sound like a schoolteacher, Charlie. I just want us to make the best presentation possible."

"You think I'll blow it?"

"Of course not."

She concentrated on his tie now, tightening the knot, then moving her hand to his still-full head of hair, another gesture of concern. Surprisingly, he was not embarrassed by her ministrations, which usually were done only in private. For a while he had toyed with the idea of pinning the patch of black crepe to his lapel again, but it didn't seem right after all this time, although the ache in his heart was still as strong as ever.

He shot her a wink and a smile. He had always been proud of her. She was a good teacher and all her kids adored her. Not that he had done too badly himself, for a fellow with merely a high school diploma. The war had taken his college years, and Bethlehem Steel had taken the rest. He had been a damned good inspector, and rarely had he ever felt that what he did was beneath what she did. So he hadn't worn a jacket and tie to do his work. But not a piece of pipe had gone out of that plant that didn't meet its specs to a T. He took pride in what he had done and had been paid well for the effort, and it annoyed him even to raise the matter in his mind.

"Who'll do the talking?" he asked. He knew that emotion would get in the way of his words, but it was impossible to stand aside and let Molly's sweet reasonableness prevail. What they had to tell the lawyer needed bite, sharpness, outrage. What he feared was that her words would not excite the needed commitment on the lawyer's part.

"He'll need to hear from both of us," she said sensibly.

"Let me start, then."

"Just be calm."

"Steady as she goes." He stretched out his hand to prove the absence of tremors. It was not a very wisely chosen illustration.

The receptionist punched a lighted button on the board and murmured into the tiny microphone she wore on a wire, one tributary of which led to her ear. High tech, he thought contemptuously, thinking suddenly of the plant and all the lives displaced because of high tech. People had become like watermelon seeds, discarded and ground up in the disposal. He felt the cutting edge of depression surface again and then recede as the receptionist's voice rang out, a clarion of hope.

"Mr. Forte will see you now," she chirped, as if she was glad for them. Something she had observed about them must have blunted her disdain. Now he resented her compassion, thinking he and Molly must be transparent in their pain. He hated showing such things to strangers. "Make a left turn and follow the corridor to the last office." Her instructions immediately went out of his mind and he nearly turned right. Molly gently guided him leftward.

"Now just be calm," she warned again.

"Hey, babe, I got it the first time," he said. His heart was beating a tattoo against his rib cage, and perspiration had begun to crawl down his back. He noted a slight chattering of his teeth and bit down on his lower lip to still it. Molly led the way to an open door beside which on the wall was a gold nameplate engraved with the lawyer's name, Robert Forte. He stood up as they entered.

Charlie saw a full head of black curls, some tipped with premature gray; large, dark brown eyes, thick-lashed and heavy lidded; olive-tinted skin that set off white teeth in a boyish smile. A navy blue blazer hung over the back of his large leather chair. The collar of his striped shirt was high, made higher by a gold pin over which crawled the tight knot of a yellow tie. His waist was small, and he wore a gold bracelet just below the buttoned cuff on his left hand. On his desk was a picture of a pretty blonde woman and another of Forte and two small boys on the deck of a sailboat. On the wall were diplomas. Charlie's weight shifted from foot to foot, and his eyes wavered from the lawyer's firm gaze.

"I'm glad you could see us, Mr. Forte," Molly said, jumping into Charlie's gap of silence after the handshakes and polite preliminaries. The lawyer's hand felt cool, while his own was clammy, a constant cause of embarrassment. He hadn't remembered to wipe his palm on his pants.

"As I told Mr. Waters on the phone, I thought the case worth discussing. The grandparents' angle is beginning to make its way into domestic law as more and more senior citizens' groups lobby the legislatures."

On the phone Forte had seemed older, more sympathetic than he appeared now. A pretty boy, Charlie thought. Too many curls.

"Can I get you some coffee?" he said.

"That would be nice," Molly answered. Charlie shrugged a grudging consent. He'd already had four cups that morning. What else was there to do?

He felt an antagonistic first impression growing in his mind. Was he going to spill his guts to this overeducated smoothie half his age? His roving gaze picked up the word *Harvard* on one of the diplomas.

Pressing a button, Forte gave the coffee order into the intercom, smiling as he caught Charlie studying the picture of the two boys on the sailboat.

"Columbia Thirty-two," Forte said, leaning back in his chair.

"I had a Rhodes Meridian," Charlie heard himself say. "Not too wide in the beam, but a good cruiser." He swallowed, remembering Chuck hanging out on a low heel, scaring them white and climbing the mast like a squirrel.

"When the kids get bigger, we'll trade up. Something to be said for growing your own crew."

"Sold mine a couple of years ago. Was beginning to look around for another for when my grandson got older. . . ." He checked himself, looked swiftly at Molly, who turned away.

The coffee came in china cups on a silver tray carried by a tall secretary who set it down and left the room. Molly lifted hers daintily and sipped. Charlie held back, his hands pressed under his thighs, fearful that they would shake.

Forte talked some more about sailboats in general, and Charlie waited for the inevitable cliché, which came on schedule.

"The happiest two days of a boating man's life are the day he buys his first boat and the day he sells it."

Charlie forced a smile, a little less intimidated now that he had heard Forte's broad Baltimore *O*. Boat was "boot," which brought him down a peg or two from his Harvard diploma and the oak panels in the reception room and the Columbia 32 and the gold bracelet.

Forte leaned back in his chair, playing with a black pen. Behind him, Charlie could see the Baltimore harbor in all its resurrected glory.

"You say your daughter-in-law refuses to allow you to see your grandchild," Forte said, his eyes roaming to take in both their faces.

Charlie nodded. Saying it so bluntly was like blowing on live ashes.

"That, more or less, is the problem," Charlie said, unable to keep the sarcasm out of his voice. He looked toward Molly, who nodded approval, perhaps of his calm, which encouraged him to go further. "The question is, can she do that to us?"

"Depends," Forte said. "There are now new ways of looking at the situation."

"That's what the story talked about," Charlie said. "And why we're here."

"How long has it been since you've seen your grandson?"

"Two years," Charlie said, swallowing a ball of phlegm that had jumped into his throat. "Not since she got married again and moved to Columbia. Guess we're not good enough for them anymore." Molly snapped him a look of disapproval. "My wife thought she would come around."

"You've talked to her about this?" Forte asked.

"You might call it that." Charlie shrugged toward Molly, who acknowledged that fact with a nod and a pursing of her lips. Forte looked toward her, provoking an explanation.

"I've had two—no, three conversations with her," Molly said. For some reason, Charlie held back mentioning his own confrontation on that last day and the later one at school. Nor how awful they had felt on the last two Christmases. On the first one, Frances had actually sent back their gifts to Tray. On the second one, they had not exposed themselves to the humiliation. He wasn't ready to relive that, not yet.

"Counting when she left," Charlie interrupted. That was the crucial conversation, he thought, after which Molly had said that Frances would come around, that it was only a condition of the moment to impress her new husband, to make him more secure by ignoring the past.

"Left?"

"When she married her new husband and took Tray."

"What reasons did she give?" Forte asked, turning to Molly. Somehow Charlie felt that he hadn't quite finished, that it was too early to throw Molly the ball. At first she looked at him, perhaps to show him her reluctance. It did not prevent her from answering.

"She said that she wanted to get on with her life, that the most important consideration was Tray and Peter, and Peter wanted to start fresh. No ties to the past." Molly swallowed and cleared her throat. "She said she hadn't been too happy with our Chuck." Her eyes glazed over for a moment, moistened, then cleared after a deep breath. "She also said that she knew we were being hurt, but that we had to bear that for Tray's sake. She just wanted to start all over, and we were part of the past."

"Just being damned selfish," Charlie muttered, feeling the inevitable tightening in his gut. "Maybe she's afraid she's gonna blow this new marriage like she blew the one with Chuck. If she had been a good wife, maybe he wouldn't have gone away." His remarks, he knew, qualified as an outburst, and he shot Molly a sheepish grin, embellished with a shrug.

"Gone away?"

"He worked on oil rigs in the North Sea and the Persian Gulf. Good money, but dangerous."

"And he died when?"

"Less than two and a half years ago," Charlie croaked hoarsely, trying to hide the old ache. "Fell off a rig in a storm. Probably took some damn fool chances—just like him. Anyway, she was in the sack with Peter in no more than ninety days; married less than six months after the funeral—couldn't stand to wait a proper time, insulted his memory, his honor—which gives you some idea of the kind of woman she is."

"You haven't tried to see the child?" Forte studied both their faces, deliberately skirting a response. Charlie cast a frightened look at Molly. As always, he thought, he had probably gone too far.

"Did you or didn't you?" Forte asked firmly.

"I did," Charlie said.

"Did what?"

"Tried to see him." Charlie shook his head. "I did see him. It turned out badly. She accused me of harassment and threatened to call the cops."

"I'm sorry," Forte said, but he didn't press for any further explanation.

"Can she do that?" Charlie asked, unable to hide his bitterness.

Forte sat back in his chair and made a cathedral with his fingers.

"Did the new husband adopt the child?" Both the question and the pose seemed ominous. Charlie looked at Molly, puzzled.

"Yes," he answered hesitantly.

"I was afraid of that."

"What difference does that make?"

Forte shrugged.

"The law. I could read it to you. In a terminated marriage the grandparents have rights. But in the case of adoption and re-marriage"— he waved his graceful fingers as if he were blowing away the words —"the new father and his parents have all paternal rights. In other words, in the eyes of the law, you no longer exist as grandparents."

Charlie felt as if he had been kicked in the midsection. He could see his own condition mirrored in Molly's face, which had gone white.

"You could have contested the adoption," Forte said gently.

"That"— Charlie cleared his throat —"didn't seem our busi-ness. How are we supposed to know about the law?" Frances had told Molly about the adoption, but how could they know that it would forfeit their rights? Who was there to tell them about such things? No, they hadn't liked the idea, but what could they have done about it?

"But we are in fact his grandparents," Molly said emphatically. "Law or no law. That's the truth. That child is our blood."

Charlie nodded vigorously.

"The law is the law," Forte said. "And there has never been a Maryland case on that point."

"So she can do it?" Charlie asked.

"I'm afraid so. Legally, that is. She can always claim it is in the best interests of the child. That's the ball game."

"Which means we're dead in the water," Charlie muttered.

"It means that you have a weak legal case under the present law."

"Which stinks," Charlie said, discovering suddenly that he had clawed his nails into his palms. "I don't understand any of it."

He hated to flaunt his ignorance on any matter. But this confounded him. He and Molly loved this child. And he was sure that Tray loved them. What more had to be decided than that?

"I hope this won't sound insulting," the lawyer said, getting up from his chair. He looked out toward the harbor, shimmering in the midwinter sun, then turned around and faced them. Charlie wondered how he really felt about all this, whether there was any compassion or involvement. He wasn't sure. "But she must feel that somehow your association with the child would be a detriment to his well-being—"

"That's a crock," Charlie snapped, his voice rising, his fist slapping the arm of the leather chair.

"Charlie, please," Molly said, reaching out to touch his forearm.

"But it is a crock. We love the boy. I've been more than a grandfather. When Chuck died . . ."

"Not now, Charlie," Molly pleaded, watching him.

"But I was both father and grandfather to that child. And you, Molly. He was as much ours as . . ." He felt the sputtering of overwhelming rage.

"We know that, Charlie. That's not the point of this conversation. Mr. Forte is informing us of the problems because of the adoption. All right, we didn't know what to do. Maybe they didn't realize, either—"

"Bull. That Peter knew what he was doing."

"Really, Charlie . . ."

"It's wrong. It's unjust. It's against nature." Without quite realizing it, he was now banging both fists against the arms of the chair.

Forte walked to the open door and shut it, an act that made its point. Charlie settled down.

"Tantrums don't help, Mr. Waters," Forte said. "I've seen enough of them to know."

"You haven't seen anything like this. Not like this."

"You'll have to excuse him, Mr. Forte. He's taking it rather badly."

"She's pretty cold-blooded herself," Charlie mumbled.

"He thinks I feel it less than he does," Molly sighed.

"She was the one who said it would all pass."

"Not that again, Charlie."

"You did, though."

"All right, I was wrong."

"Maybe we could have stopped it then, nipped it in the bud, instead of crawling here to these fancy lawyers."

Forte leaned against the wall, hands folded.

"He wasn't always this cynical about things, Mr. Forte," Molly said.

"You could have fooled me."

Charlie reached for the coffee cup. The tremors in his fingers made it clatter against the saucer. Control, he begged himself. He was silent as he sipped his coffee.

"It just gets me so damned mad," he said when he had regained control. "Putting a little kid through that."

"Through what, Mr. Waters?"

The Italian face seemed to expand in the room, filling the space like a giant balloon. The brown eyes grew larger, more luminous, their gaze inescapable. He felt as if he were being turned inside out, and he didn't like that at all. It was like a child's nightmare, where imagined shame and guilt were futilely defended against a punishing and inevitable force.

"Being deprived of his grandparents' love," Molly interjected. "In today's world a child needs all he can get." Charlie felt the strength of her alliance and the image of the monster receded. "And for us as well. We need it, too." Her hand reached out and grabbed his, which returned the squeeze. "Some might call it selfish. But it's a two-way street."

"Except that as a legal entity you don't exist," the lawyer said calmly.

"Then what are we doing here?" Charlie said. "You could have told us all this on the phone."

"Sometimes it still pays to talk," Forte said.

"Pays you, you mean," Charlie blurted. Molly shot him a rebuking glance. "I'm sorry, Mr. Forte. I'm just so damned disappointed."

"I know," the lawyer said, studying them. "But this doesn't mean that there isn't some form of action to be taken."

"Like what?"

"There are always steps before litigation," Forte said slowly. "We could petition for visitation rights, show determination, and hope that your former daughter-in-law and her new husband, rather than go through the hassle of hiring a lawyer and contesting the petition, might"— he shrugged and looked up at the ceiling —"come around."

"And if they don't?" Molly asked.

"It might be worth a shot," the lawyer said tentatively.

"But you said—" Molly began.

"I know what I said and I know what I would do if I were a judge. But who knows, we might draw a judge who makes a decision counter to prevailing law, which means that they could take it and appeal to a higher court, where it is likely to be reversed."

"So why do it?" Molly asked.

"To wear 'em down," Forte said. "It depends on your commitment."

"Our commitment?" Charlie said, his voice rising again. "All the way, that's our commitment. Whatever it costs."

"That's another side to the coin, Mr. Waters. You'll have to come up with a five thousand dollar retainer against my hourly rate, which is two hundred dollars an hour. This could cost up to ten thousand, and double that if we go to appeal."

The costs shocked Charlie, and he felt he was not hiding it very well. Again, he looked helplessly at Molly, who said it for him.

"That's a lot of money."

"How serious are you?"

"It's our lives," Molly said.

"It could be a total disappointment."

"No more than it is now."

"And very painful."

"You've got grandparents, Mr. Forte?" Charlie asked.

"The extended family is a cultural phenomenon among the Italians." Forte said, a little pompously, but offering a broad smile. "If you must know, I get a kick out of my grandparents. They give me a chance to practice my Italian. *Se niente va bene, chiama nonno e nonna.*"

Charlie looked at him blankly.

"It means," Forte said, " 'If nothing else is going well, call your grandfather and grandmother.' "

"I like that," Charlie said, brightening. "Let's hear it again."

"*Se niente va bene, chiama nonno e nonna.*"

Charlie repeated it with a bad accent, but he felt better now, more favorably disposed to the younger man. Molly smiled, and her cobalt eyes twinkled their approval.

"It changes nothing," Forte said, sitting down at his desk again and making another cathedral out of his long delicate fingers ridged with fine black hair. "Are you really ready for this? I kid you not, Mr. and Mrs. Waters, if we carry this forward, it will curdle your guts. I want you to understand that. The deck is stacked against you. And even if, by some remote chance, you win, you might actually cause more damage to the child than by leaving him alone. Only time will tell on that, though. The mother could continue to be hostile and resentful even if the judge grants you visitation rights, and this is bound to reflect on the child and his mental health—"

"I'm a teacher, Mr. Waters," Molly interjected with passion. "I have never seen a sincere expression of love and support hurt a child."

Forte tapped his fingers together lightly.

"And you're convinced that all avenues of reconciliation have been exhausted?"

"That's why we're here," Charlie said. "Maybe if she sees we mean business, she won't want to hassle it."

"What are their economic circumstances?" the lawyer asked.

"Good. He's a computer engineer with a good job. And she's still got twenty thousand dollars from Chuck's insurance, which is proof of how much he cared for her and Tray." It was a tenuous argument, he knew, but he persisted in it just the same.

"It may only make them more stubborn in their resistance. I have seen families literally ruin themselves in litigation."

"So we'll fight harder," Charlie said. He looked at Forte's face for a long time in silence. "How can anyone think that our seeing Tray is going to hurt him?"

The lawyer raised his eyebrows, his lips forming what seemed to Charlie to be a knowing smirk. He was beginning not to like the fellow again.

"If they contest, they will do so on the ground that your physical presence will be harmful to your grandson's interests."

"They'll be laughed out of court," Charlie said with rising bravado.

"Even in today's world the mother is rarely laughed out of court, Mr. Waters."

"Not after we get through with her," Charlie said.

"I don't understand, Mr. Waters. What is your contention? Is she an incompetent mother?"

He felt a growing discomfort again and avoided looking at

Molly. Sweat had broken out again under his shirt. His mouth had gone suddenly dry. He's playing with me, Charlie thought. Testing.

"No. I wouldn't say that," Charlie answered after a long pause.

"A good mother, then?"

"Generally speaking." He was determined not to be tricked.

"Is she a drunkard, a dope addict, physically unable to take care of the boy?"

"None of those," he answered, offering Molly a thin but confident smile.

"The boy's home environment is wholesome? The adoptive father: Is he loving and devoted?"

"I wouldn't know. I don't live there."

"When she lived with your son, was there any reason to question the way she ran her home and cared for the boy?"

A nerve began to palpitate in his jaw. His confidence ebbed.

"You never really know what goes on behind closed doors."

"What does that mean?"

"If she was a good and faithful wife, maybe Chuck would have stayed closer to home."

"Are you saying she was unfaithful?" Forte paused, nailing Charlie with his eyes. Charlie looked at his hands, which suddenly felt clumsy and uncoordinated. He deliberately did not look at Molly. Why was the lawyer sparing her, he wondered?

"Depends on how you define that," Charlie mumbled.

"Come on, Charlie," Molly said. "She wasn't that at all."

"Jumping in the sack a couple of months after Chuck's death—what do you call that?"

"She had no obligation to a dead man. She was not being unfaithful." Molly addressed herself to the lawyer. "She was a good and loyal wife."

"There you go, defending her again," Charlie said with rising fury. "The fact is that he felt better being away from her."

"There are men like that. Chuck was like that," Molly said softly.

"He was a damned good husband and father."

"I don't think that argument will hold in court, Mr. Waters," Forte interjected. "Was he away for very long stretches of time?"

"Sometimes for six, seven months at a time," Molly said. "Then he'd stay two weeks and be off again."

"When you talk to my wife, you have to be very careful," Charlie said, knowing in advance that he would catch hell for what he was about to say. "On some things the women stick together."

"I'm only trying to tell him the truth," Molly said, a flush rising on her cheeks.

"The truth!"

"That's exactly the point, Mr. Waters, the truth is often obscured by a mishmash of emotions."

"How can we win if she goes on like that?"

"This is not a custody battle, Mr. Waters. Tearing down the character of Tray's mother will not further your case. The issue here, aside from the very obvious one of your having no rights as grandparents, which may preclude our ever getting into court in the first place, is, unfortunately, your character—yours and your wife's. If we get a hearing, and they contest, their ploy will be to paint you, and her previous marriage, in the worst possible light. At least that's what I would do. The only way you can win is by proving that you and your wife will enhance the child's well-being." He put his hands flat on the yellow pad. "What I'm saying is that any way you cut it, this will not be easy. I'm trying to give you something of a preview of what you both can expect."

"You trying to talk us out of this?" Charlie asked, trying to maintain his composure despite his growing agitation. He felt he had made a botch of it.

"In a way," Forte shrugged. "I don't want you to have any illusions that if you go through with this it is going to be a joyride. It's going to hurt, hurt everybody it touches."

Not you, Charlie thought. He had stopped sweating and now felt a chill.

"You don't think we have a chance in hell, do you?" Charlie asked with a glance toward Molly.

"He didn't say that, Charlie," she said. "He's only saying that it's not going to be easy on us."

"Well, dammit, it's not easy on us now."

"Would you like me to leave the room while you talk it over between you?"

"No need for that," Charlie snapped. Was it condescension he detected? Hell, the wounds were all open and bleeding—what was there to hide?

"And there's the expense to be considered," Forte said.

"Who can forget that? At Bethlehem my last rate was eighteen bucks an hour."

"There are no bargains in this business, Mr. Waters," Forte said lightly.

"I know. You get what you pay for."

"And no guarantees," Forte added. It was as if he was deliberately turning the knife.

Charlie turned helplessly to Molly, who reached over and patted his thigh.

"There's only the two of us, Mr. Forte. We've got money put aside. And I'm still teaching. We're committed to this."

What good was all the money they had put away over the years, Charlie thought, the careful planning, the scrupulous accounting? It wasn't as if they'd had more than one child. Wasn't in the cards, Charlie thought, although they both had wanted more. Having Chuck had been a big risk to Molly as it was. No, he decided, in the face of losing Tray forever, money had little value.

"It's not the money," Charlie muttered. It annoyed him to feel the taste of defeat before the battle.

"It would be wrong to take this case without presenting the emotional and financial risks. Legal recourse is always a last resort, and a favorable decision doesn't necessarily mean you've won anything," Forte said with a touch of contrition in his tone. "I know I've been rough, but the reality is that the going will be much rougher than what I've given you. What I want is for you to be sure, absolutely certain in your mind that this is the way for both of you to go. It would be wrong to pursue this if you have the slightest doubt in your mind."

"We're not dumb, Mr. Forte." He was instantly sorry for the inadvertent flash of anger. "What I mean is that you've made it quite clear."

"Now would you like me to leave the room?" the lawyer said gently.

Charlie looked at Molly. Anger had seeped away. What was left was a kind of void, a circumscribed place with hurt around the edges.

"No need for that, Mr. Forte," Molly said, reaching for Charlie's hand, clasping his fingers. "There's no other way for us. At our stage in life you don't get over things. It *is* wrong for her to keep us from seeing our grandson, isn't it?"

"I don't want anything I say to color your decision," the lawyer said.

Charlie felt Molly's eyes exploring him. He deliberately did not look at her. It can't be only for me, he thought. It has to be for both of us.

"Do you think you can handle it, Charlie?" Molly asked gently.

He really wasn't sure, nor was it a question he wanted to confront. In a way it was like death, he realized. It had to be faced. The alternative was to be eaten up alive by longing and frustration, to fester in bitterness and regret. He'd lost a son through no fault of his own. Was he prepared to lose a grandson? He had walked into this office with a commitment in his heart and gut. He tried to prepare his mind for an answer that would be scrupulously honest. No sense fooling himself. Was the cause worth the pain? He felt himself nodding, but that wasn't the whole truth.

"I'll try my damnedest, babe. I just know in my bones it's right."

"So do I," Molly said firmly.

"No second thoughts?" Forte asked.

"None," Charlie said. He took a deep breath, feeling better. Like in his memories of combat. Once you hit the beach, the fear congealed somewhere in the back of your mind.

"All right then," the lawyer said, his own relief apparent as well. He opened a leather folder in which was a clean yellow legal pad. "Let's get down to business."

Molly reached over suddenly and put her palm over the pad.

"First the answer to my question," she said.

The lawyer looked up startled.

"Which?"

"It *is* wrong, isn't it? What she's doing? To Tray and to us?"

The lawyer swiveled back in his chair and rubbed his chin, his eyes darting from face to face. It was Charlie's question as well, spoken for both of them.

"It's very hard for a lawyer to do his best for a client in whose cause he does not believe."

Molly lifted her palm.

"That's good," she said nodding her head. "That's very good. Don't you think so, Charlie?"

He squeezed her hand in response.

Chapter 4

RANCES guided the Datsun to a spot at the curb which gave her a clear view of the school's side door. Then she flicked the ignition and the car shuddered into silence. Taking a tissue from the box beside her, she wiped the baby's spit-up from his chin and nuzzled his cheek. The baby purred contentedly and smiled. He liked rides, liked to play with his little toy steering wheel. Mostly, he curled over and bit into it. He was eight months old and teething.

She looked at her watch. It was ten minutes to four. She liked to be earlier. Better to be prudent than to worry the child. In five minutes he'd be running out the door, jacket unbuttoned, arms akimbo, flushed with the fever of excitement, the inevitable drawing flapping in the breeze. He would be doubly excited today, the first day of rehearsal for the school play. He had been cast as a raindrop. The girls were snowflakes. She grinned, a trill of laughter bubbling in her chest. A raindrop?

Maybe she had a snowflake growing inside of her? She giggled out loud at the illogic of the image.

"Would you like a sister, Baby Mark?"

She kneaded her knuckle into the baby's belly, which was partially protected by his diaper. Ticklish, he smiled and squirmed. He was a happy baby. Why not? She was happy. Peter was happy. She couldn't wait to tell him the news that she was pregnant. Six weeks and counting, the doctor had said. So much for the rhythm method. She hadn't wanted to start the pill while nursing, and they had discussed a two-year wait before trying for—another joke between them—the caboose. One more try for the girl, he had agreed. She laughed out loud and gently flicked the baby's chin with her thumb. "Shows to go ya," she whispered. "Ah never knowed what love can do," she hummed.

Then she saw Tray, skipping out ahead of the others, not pausing to button his jacket, taller by a head than the others in the second grade. He was big and handsome like his father. She brushed aside the memory, leaned over, and opened the door on the passenger side.

"It's chilly, Tray," she cried when he hopped in. Reaching over the baby, she kissed his forehead and buttoned him up. "How many times must I tell you?" He showed her the drawing.

"Very good, Tray." She held it up and turned it upside down. "What is it?"

"A sailboat in the woods."

"No water?"

"It's in the water, only you can't see it. It's a creek."

She let it pass. At first she had been sensitive about reminders of Charlie. Now she took them in stride. After all, he could have come up with a sailboat image from anywhere. She started the motor and eased the car into the street.

"I did good as a raindrop," Tray said. "The snowflakes were gross." He made a face.

"You don't like girls, eh?"

"Yuck."

You'll get over that, she thought, smiling at the images that danced in her head. Peter had given her a whole new point of view about that part of marriage. A flush warmed her cheeks suddenly as she realized that in their lives, sex was as good and sweet and natural as breathing air. Not like it had been with Chuck. There was a huge chasm between acquiescence and desire. She deliberately chased away the intrusive thought. Such comparisons were odious, she told herself firmly.

She eased the car through the Columbia traffic. Wide curving streets and a rational stoplight system made daytime driving easy for those with the occupational specialty of full-time mother. She looked at her burgeoning brood beside her and grinned. The title she had acquired had a certain cachet.

"And what do you do, Frances?" It was a question without novelty in her new circle, mostly the couples from Peter's high-tech company shop.

"I'm a full-time mother." She would pause and look them straight in the eye.

"How wonderful."

The object was to head off the inevitable "And what did you do before?" No response could adequately describe the truth of what she had done before, since much of it had been done to escape the four walls of loneliness while Chuck was off on adventures far from home. Temp work wasn't exactly a career, although she could have said she had been an executive secretary. Receptionist would have been closer to the truth.

But not quite the whole truth. Her most active occupation had been working behind the counter of her Uncle Walter's bakery in northwest Baltimore. A chop for a chop, he had told her, which meant that his largesse of room and board had to be paid for with hard labor. How she had hated that sense of powerlessness and obligation. Not that Uncle Walter, her late father's brother, was a cruel man. In his mind, he was doing the right thing by his orphaned niece. How could he know the anguish and loneliness an adolescent girl had to endure?

Both her mother and father had been late babies, and her grandparents were long gone when she was born. So there was only Uncle Walter on whose doorstep she had stumbled, a secondary victim of the Vietnam war. Just the idea of that was enough to cripple her with self-pity for a time, until she realized that she was doomed to spend her life in Uncle Walter's bakery unless she acted in her own behalf, which she did. Chuck had arrived with his promise of what seemed like a normal life; but soon she was back to square one, powerless and, once again, lonely.

She had done light office work until Tray arrived. That first year with Chuck was almost bearable. But when Tray came, it seemed to be the signal for Chuck to leave.

As she drove, Frances felt her mind drifting too deeply and precariously into the past. Actually, such rehashing of her earlier life had become less and less of a bother until Charlie had shown up that day in school and foolishly tried to tamper with the new environment she had created for Tray and herself. Because of that, she had lost ground, and now there were these occasional bouts of painful memories that tended to float in and out of her thoughts at the oddest moments.

She turned into her street and made a hard right into the driveway. The sight of their four-bedroom colonial provided instant relief and put her back in her original happy mood. They had chosen the model with an old brick facade and big bay windows in the dining room and kitchen and an extravagant fieldstone fireplace that covered one wall of the den. It was spacious and cozy at the same time, and she had decorated it in her favorite colors, beige and fawn for backgrounds and olives and reds for accents. People said she had a flair for decorating, and she was entertaining ideas of studying the art when the kids became semi-independent. Besides, it gave her an excellent answer when the social queries shifted to the future.

"I have a yen for professional decorating," she would say, pausing. "When motherhood moves from full to part time."

Tray bounded out of the car and made faces at Goldy, the Labrador that now stood on its hind legs barking a greeting behind the kitchen bay window. Tray stuck fingers inside his puffed cheeks and crossed his eyes. The dog responded with louder barking, leaving mist marks on the panes.

Frances lifted the baby out of the car seat, opened the door, stepped over the pile of mail on the hall floor, and deftly avoided Goldy's surge toward the front lawn bushes. The tall clock in the hall struck five, which meant she was running slightly behind a self-imposed schedule that culminated in cocktails at seven with Peter and dinner at seven-thirty. Tonight, she decided, was a dining room night. The announcement of her news required a bit of human engineering.

She gathered up the mail, put it on a kitchen countertop without looking at it, changed the baby, put him in the playpen, prepared the children's dinner, and put two baking potatoes in the oven for her and Peter. Then she made a salad, put out the steaks, and set the dining room table with the good crystal and silver and cloth napkins on the lace tablecloth. She was conscious of purring along at a high energy level, which augured well for a good pregnancy. Her two earlier births had gone off with peasant-woman routine, even with Peter in the room during labor and delivery of Baby Mark. It was all she could do to stop him from taking pictures. Again, the past intruded. When Tray was born, Chuck had been out hunting with his father and she had had to interrupt Molly at a PTA meeting to get her to drive her to the hospital.

Maybe I could send my daughter off by herself to be born, she thought, as she uncorked a good Beaujolais to let it breathe, as Peter had taught her.

"I've come a long way from Dundalk, baby," she said often to Peter.

"It's only thirty miles."

"And a thousand light-years."

"You exaggerate."

"But I have narrowed the gap, haven't I?"

"There wasn't any. It was all in your head."

Computers, which made them a good living, were only one side of Peter Graham. He not only liked fine wine, lovely paintings, good books, and classical music, he took the time and exercised the patience to make Frances understand why it was important to make a place for these things in her life. Above all, he was tolerant of her lack of education, and she never felt put down.

She ascribed finding Peter to pure luck, which she superstitiously refused to analyze. There was such a thing as accepting a good thing with grace and not repeatedly counting her blessings as if she were afraid they would go away. But she let him go on about his own good fortune in finding her. Although she wouldn't dare admit it to him, she always loved hearing him say it—especially in the afterglow of their lovemaking.

"What I always wanted was a family," he told her from the beginning. "Wife, kids, house, dog, love, security, friendship, devotion, absolute honesty, kindness." He paused. "All of it. Satisfactions of body, spirit, and emotions."

"I wish I could put things that way," she said in response.

"They're just words," he said. "It's in the doing. And in that regard, you're more eloquent than I am."

It was little touches like that which made Peter so endearing.

So she had happily converted what were essentially her most potent skills, motherhood and wifehood. As it turned out, she offered much more in good household management than he had any reason to expect. On her part, she asked him, acutely conscious of her naiveté, to "teach her things," a request that he had eagerly begun to fulfill by unraveling for her the mysteries of the home computer on which she assiduously kept all the household information. He also joined her in a daily helping of *The New York Times* on the ground that it would give them both a world view, stressing that it would also force him out of the narrow tunnel vision of most scientists and engineers. It was, indeed, an accurate measure of their security that she wasn't the only one confessing her shortcomings.

All this came under the heading of truly balancing the equations that had eluded their first marriages, including the part of it they called, with stifled giggles, "bedhood." That element of the equation seemed in perfect balance. Maybe too balanced. She wondered if her upcoming little revelation would require some adjustments on one or another side of the equal sign.

After the children's dinner, she let Tray watch television and settled down to the mail with the baby at her breast. She was still making good milk, and the marvel of watching and feeling the process of his acquiring nourishment in this way always filled her with the sweet warmth of indescribably joyous feelings.

She opened the mail, junk mail first, then bills, then what seemed to require slightly more concentration. One letter in an impressive envelope caught her eye and she assumed it was for Peter. It was only after she had gone through the pile that she noted it was addressed to her. She was puzzled at the return address, Banks, Pepper and Forte, and turned it over a few times before opening the envelope with the tip of her nail.

It took only the first line of the letter to spark her rage. She felt the blood rush to her head. Her breath grew short and gasping as she shifted her weight in the chair. The abrupt movement made Baby Mark lose the nipple although his little lips continued to suck. Frustrated, his frown deepened and his face grew scarlet, but before he could let loose with a scream, she had the nipple in place again. With that brief movement, the letter had floated to the floor, requiring her to detach the baby, pick up the letter, and begin the nursing process again.

"I have been retained by Mr. and Mrs. Charles Waters to seek legal means to secure visitation rights with their grandson, Charles Everett Waters III."

The words, she knew, would be indelible in her memory.

"Rights!" she cried. Again her body twisted in anger and again Baby Mark lost the nipple. This time she returned it before he realized it was gone, smoothing his head with gentle caresses and kissing his little hands. She resented this terrible imposition, this intrusion, this breaking of the sacred rhythm between a nursing mother and her child. How dare they? She tried to calm herself, to concentrate on the baby's need for contentment, to tamp down her outrage.

"How dare they?" she whispered, trying desperately to cap her indignation. Hadn't they agreed to let her and Tray alone? Self-ishness. Pure selfishness, she decided. Hadn't she made it clear to Charlie when he precipitated that ridiculous incident at Tray's school by lying to the school authorities and interrupting his class on the pretext of giving him that silly wagon? It was confusing to the child, perhaps damaging. He had a new father, a father more authentic than the original, and new grandparents. Peter's parents, although they lived in upstate New York, were as solicitous and loving as any grandparents could be.

Besides, she had made peace with the idea, for which she took equal responsibility despite the fact that it had been Peter's suggestion in the first place. It wasn't that Peter was cruel or jealous. He hadn't a mean streak in him. He was thinking of their new life, and he had every right to begin without the problems of yesteryear. Hadn't he spent years in purgatory because of a terrible first marriage? And hadn't she done the same? Of course, it had hurt to make the break, knowing Charlie's and Molly's attachment to Tray. But it had to be done. There was simply no sense complicating Tray's life, confusing him. Not now. Perhaps someday. She granted that possibility. But not now. Not yet.

Logic temporarily assuaged emotion. Surely she and Peter could not consciously have dismissed the possibility that Molly and Charlie would react in some way. They simply had not prepared themselves to deal with it. Well, they'd have to now. Deal with it they would, she thought pugnaciously. After all, Tray and their little immediate family were the number one priority. Not Molly and Charlie, however one might understand—even sympathize with—their point of view.

It was hard enough for the child to bear another man's name. Nor was it easy for Peter, either. But she had drawn that line herself. There was no way to erase Tray's father. She did not have that right. Right? The word from the lawyer's letter jumped into her mind. Well, she also had rights over the life of her child.

Her mind was so far away from her present task that at first she did not see that Baby Mark had fallen asleep, his lips losing their hold on her breast. She eased him upward over her shoulder and patted him gently until he let loose a contented burp. She held him for a moment more, savoring his warmth, as she squeezed him gently. Why can't people get their priorities straight? she thought. Certainly a mother knows what's best for her own child.

She carried the baby upstairs and put him in his crib, then came down and briefly stood behind Tray while he watched *Sesame Street* with intense concentration. Frances got down on her knees behind him and enveloped him in her arms. Her chest heaved in a stifled sob. Her eyes misted, and she sniffled and brushed away an errant tear. Tray, oblivious to his mother's anguish, continued to be absorbed in the program.

"Never," Frances said, releasing Tray and standing up.

"What, Mommy?"

"I said never."

He looked up, confused, then turned again toward the television set. Frances rose and went back to the kitchen. By then rage had turned to resolve, and she picked up the letter and read it through.

"I have been retained by Mr. and Mrs. Charles Waters to secure by legal means visitation rights with their grandson, Charles Everett Waters III." She paused and allowed herself a deep breath. She read on:

"Forty-nine states, including Maryland, now recognize the right of grandparents to petition the courts to seek legal access to the natural offspring of their progeny whether divorced or deceased when it has been denied. Before we petition the court for a hearing on this matter . . ."

Something seemed awry. A red flag rose in her mind. He is trying to be cunning, she decided, telescoping what might be coming next. She was right.

". . . my clients believe that this matter can be settled amicably through reasonable negotiation of the parties, and given a cool appraisal, it may not be necessary to pursue protracted and costly litigation. My clients have urged me to make this view known to you and to implore your cooperation.

"With this in mind, they have asked that no action be taken by this office for two weeks from the above date so that you may have sufficient time to consider this proposal." At this point, she expected the homily and was right again. "Domestic relationships are often complex and entangled with emotion which can sometimes translate good intentions into inadvertent and preventable destructive patterns. In this case, it would seem that loving grandparents, who have already suffered the devastating trauma of a child's loss, should not have to bear the additional burden of losing the comfort of their natural grandchild.

"Surely, the loving interest that can be provided by sincere grandparents cannot possibly be interpreted as being adverse to the child's interest. Indeed, most psychologists would agree that the grandparent relationship greatly enhances the child's mental environment and should not be withheld. My clients are hopeful that, in the light of what has been presented and your own compassion and awareness of what is truly in the best interest of your child, you will reconsider your position and agree to an arrangement whereby my clients can visit their grandchild on a regular basis.

"Sincerely Yours, Robert Forte, Esq."

On second reading, her agitation accelerated. She felt put upon, victimized. They were setting the big guns in place behind a smokescreen of reason, elaborately laced with guilt-provoking subtleties. Behind the smokescreen was the very real threat of expensive litigation, emotional trauma, a whole gamut of hurtful and time-consuming events.

She fingered the expensive stationery, in itself an implied threat, noting that the address, in the complex overlooking the rejuvenated Baltimore port area, was a further persuader that this was not a law firm to be taken lightly. So they had generously given her two weeks to mull things over, she thought bitterly, folding the letter and slipping it back in the envelope. Time enough for that, she decided, bravely slapping her thighs as she stood up. Dizzy suddenly from rising too fast, she braced herself for a moment against the table, remembering her pregnancy and the hopefulness with which she had looked forward to dinner tonight.

"They're ruining everything," she whispered, as she brought the wooden bowl filled with salad to the dining room table. It was annoying to be forced to deal with this new aggravation, she thought, a notion that only increased her anger. Before leaving the dining room, she poured herself a glass of Beaujolais from the opened bottle and gulped it down like medicine.

Peter, who was compulsively punctual, arrived at seven. Tray popped up from his seat on the leather hassock in the den and rushed to embrace him, his eyes searching for the "tingies" that Peter frequently brought. Tingies were toys and computer games and athletic equipment that, by now, had filled all the chests and shelves in Tray's room. If there was an element of bribery in it, Frances let it pass without comment, pleased that Peter balanced his largesse with ample helpings of discipline, dispensed fairly and nonviolently. He never raised his voice to the boy in anger or lifted a hand to inflict punishment. Indeed, it was he who advised leniency when she chose a harsher mode of discipline.

Peter and Tray went through a ritual of guessing before the new tingie was presented.

"You'll spoil him," Frances rebuked, a gesture that was also part of the ritual. They both watched Tray tear off the wrapping.

"Chess," Tray squealed, unveiling the computer game currently being pushed on television.

"Isn't he a bit young for that?" Frances asked. She, too, had appeared for their mutual homecoming embrace, which meant more tonight than ever, and she stayed tucked in Peter's free arm.

"Mozart wrote his first symphony at the age of three," he countered. "Let him get an early start. It builds confidence and mental agility. Right, Tray? And it's a lot better than Pac Man."

"Right, Daddy," Tray said, going off to his room to try out the game on his Atari.

While Peter went off to the bathroom, Frances put the steaks on and checked the baked potatoes. She had, she realized, forgotten to freshen her makeup, a new habit she had acquired in this marriage. With Chuck, her appearance had almost become a matter of indifference, and his absences had accentuated her tendency to forget what she looked like. Her private prenuptial resolution was to keep her physical assets well tuned and polished, more as a gift to Peter than an expression of insecurity.

"You're beautiful," he told her often.

"You're not so bad yourself," she would shoot back.

The fact was that he was very well made. It irritated her to make clandestine comparisons between Peter and Chuck, but she simply could not help it. After all, she had known only two men in her life. Where Chuck had been heavily muscled from a strenuous outdoor life, Peter was thin, more delicate, and shorter, with a flat belly and fine hair on his arms and legs. Peter's hair was jet black, his eyes dark; Chuck had had hair the color of spun gold and eyes cobalt blue like his mother's, both genetic gifts handed down to Tray.

Some physical comparisons were, well, embarrassing, almost odious. Chuck had begun to develop a hard, pooching gut and his body had bulk and heaviness, which emphasized his rather bovine indifference in their infrequent lovemaking. Peter was wiry, less to hold, but far more agile and original, as well as considerate, in his approach to her. Chuck took. Peter shared. To put it another way, when she gave, Chuck accepted it as if it were his rightful tribute. Peter accepted with gratitude and warmth.

There were times, she confessed to herself, when the physicality of the two of them became a bit jumbled in her mind and the differences blurred, but those were becoming less and less frequent. Intellectual comparisons were simpler.

It was in the emotional area that she had felt the largest discrepancy. With Chuck she had never felt needed and, except for a brief period after they got married, certainly not desired. He had never been consciously cruel, and it had actually been a shock for him to learn that she bitterly resented his absences. Even in the early days of their marriage, she had assumed that men like Chuck were supposed to go on extended male-only hunting and fishing trips, drink beer with the boys, and generally pursue a whole range of womanless, and therefore wifeless, activities. Hadn't his father done that, and hadn't Molly accepted such activities as a fact of life with that type of man?

Well, Frances hadn't. She had merely endured. If she faulted herself, it was not for the blind acceptance of such loneliness, but for her lack of courage in not communicating her feelings to Chuck. Not that it would have changed anything. But at least it would have been more honest than pining quietly and letting bitterness grow like mold on their marriage. With Peter, she had promised herself to always say what she felt and meant and let the chips fall where they may.

When he came back to the den, she had already mixed the martinis and popped in the olives. Actually the amount of alcohol was of less importance than the ritual, and the most they ever drank was one.

"Interesting meeting," Peter said, lifting his feet to the hassock that Tray had just vacated. "For once Evans was not the best salesman in the room. Sanders aced him out in ten minutes. . . ."

His small talk washed over her without comprehension, although she tried to remember the words. Another prenuptial resolution of hers was not to be indifferent to his business life, to listen and react. Where else could he deflect the tension, lay off his fears and apprehensions, share the little victories, and work off the pain of the defeats? She expected him to do the same for her.

But this evening she was not being true to her resolve, and apparently it showed.

"You're not listening?" he asked gently, squinting with exaggerated scrutiny.

The first sip of her martini had brought on a slight nausea, reminding her that ingesting alcohol held some risk for the fetus. She put the glass down on the end table beside the couch where she hung back with more room between them than usual.

"I'm afraid not, darling."

What the debate had come down to was what to give him first, the good news or the bad. Shrugging, she decided to convey the thought. Earlier, the coming baby had been definitely good news to her.

"I've got some good news and some bad news," she said. Her stomach tightened, and she forgot her nausea.

"Is the baby okay?"

"He's fine," she said, adding quickly, "nothing like that."

The frown of concern on his forehead quickly disappeared. He sipped his martini and continued to hold the glass, his fingers steady, a mischievous smile on his lips.

"Well then, what's the catastrophe?"

She knew he wasn't being patronizing. Home and hearth, his principal priorities beyond his work, seemed to be in good shape.

"We're going to have a snowflake," she blurted.

"A snowflake?"

He seemed genuinely confused.

"Well, that's the part they give the girls in Tray's play."

She watched comprehension dawn. He drew his glass to his lips and upended it.

"You're kidding."

She wondered if he was offering her the real face of panic or simply joking. If he took this as the bad news, she wondered how he would characterize the other news.

"I never kid about conception," she said lightly.

He slapped his forehead.

"All I have to do is hang my pants on the bedpost."

"A bit more than that, darling."

His face lit up with a broad smile.

"You're sure?"

"The doctor will be happy to make book on it."

He reached for her and moved closer on the couch, embracing her, kissing her deeply on the mouth, caressing her hair. She returned his affection in kind.

"And he's sure it's a—a snowflake?"

"One or the other." She paused. "The snowflake is my idea."

"I'll take whatever comes."

He got up and poured the remainder of the martini from the mixer, noting that she had barely touched hers. Seeing this, she picked up the glass and touched his, but didn't drink. She was relieved, but too concerned about her other news to be ecstatic.

"To Snowflake," he said, tipping his glass, pausing in midair, before raising it to his lips. "Sixteen months apart. It'll be like twins."

"Twins are easier. Only once to the well."

"I'll be right there. Like with Mark." He pecked her on the cheek. "If it were biologically possible, I'd have it for you."

"If it were biologically possible, I'd let you."

He was in such a good mood, she did not wish to spoil it, and let him have his dinner first. She had lit candles, and the flicker had the romantic effect she had planned. But romance was the farthest thing from her mind. Tray came down, sat with them awhile with his nightly cookie and milk, then, after the usual protestations, kissed them both and went off to bed.

She brought the letter in with the coffee, blew out the candles, and put on the light.

"And now the bad news," she said, placing the letter beside him as she poured.

She watched as he slipped the letter from the envelope. He read the words slowly, and she knew that he was deliberately withholding his reaction, mulling over in his scientific mind the best option, the one that would be easiest on her.

"Rough stuff," she said impatiently when his reaction was longer in coming than she expected. He shrugged and lifted his eyes. Unlike her, anger made him more controlled and deliberate.

"It's only a typical lawyer's letter," he said. "No cause for panic."

"I don't like the timing," she pouted.

"It's an act of desperation. Very transparent. I'm not a lawyer, but I'd say they haven't got a leg to stand on." He shook his head. "Damned shame."

"You really think they'd take us into court?"

"Anybody could do that. The question is, on what grounds."

"So they could be bluffing?"

"They have nothing to lose. You'd think that if they had Tray's real interest at heart, they would leave it alone. It's been two years. By now one would think they would have adjusted to the situation."

"I can understand their being upset. But this—I think it's very selfish of them," she said, watching him tentatively. "They're just trying to aggravate us. It's an intrusion, that's what it is."

He looked thoughtfully into his coffee cup. After a while he lifted it to his lips, watching her over the cup's rim.

"It's sad, Frances. But it doesn't make it right."

"In time, I'm sure we would have come to some agreement."

"But on our terms, not theirs. They're trying to force something that we're not ready for."

"It's so unlike them. I can't remember their ever dealing with lawyers."

"I especially don't like ultimatums," Peter said. "They're offensive."

"Two weeks," she said.

"We could do without the pressure," Peter said with typical understatement. "Especially now." He reached out and took her hand. "We could always capitulate." His eyes studied her, and she was the first to turn away.

"No," she said, although the negative shake of her head came before the words. "I don't think we're ready for that. I don't want any disruptions, Peter. Not now. Not for Tray either. He's survived marvelously well for two years without them. He's happy as a clam. And your folks have been wonderful."

"I don't want to come out as Attila the Hun on this," Peter said, caressing her cheek with the back of his other hand.

"See what they're doing. Now you're guilty."

"It's not very pleasant knowing that you're the cause of other people's unhappiness and desperation." He paused and looked at his hands. "It's a matter of priorities. We'll just have to keep biting the bullet. If they sue, they sue."

"As you can see, they've laid on the hearts and flowers in thick gobs." She paused and tapped her forefinger on the edge of her cup. "As if I were some sort of unfeeling monster with neither compassion nor pity. Most of all, I resent that. Imagine going to a lawyer."

"The bottom line is Tray," he said. "As far as I can see, he's doing exceptionally well."

"He certainly is," she said with rising indignation. "I'm his mother and I know what's best for my child," she said, conscious of a slight mistiness clouding her vision.

"Our child," he corrected. She took the hand that was caressing her cheek and kissed it.

"Why can't they just let us get on with our lives? Tray is happy, happier than he has ever been. He loves you, Peter."

"I know that." He cleared his throat. "And I love him."

"That day when Charlie accosted him in school, I saw the child.

He was confused, harassed. I have no idea what Charlie told the boy, I got there too late. Maybe just in the nick of time. It was humiliating for Charlie. And it troubled Tray. Why can't they just leave him alone?" Her voice had risen, and she felt a tightness in her chest, but it did not stop the flow of words. "I don't hate them. I know they care about Tray. They just don't understand. They're only thinking of themselves, as if being with Tray would be some kind of therapy. Well, I don't owe them that. I didn't marry them. I married their son." She felt a sense of rising hysteria. "And it was awful. Just awful—"

"You mustn't upset yourself," Peter said, leaning across the table to kiss her cheek. "Not now."

"Why can't they understand?"

"Because they're not thinking of anybody but themselves."

"They have no right to interfere in our lives. Chuck detested the idea of fatherhood, as if it were one more intrusion on his freedom. In the last couple of years, he barely even saw the child."

"You don't have to convince me, Frances," Peter said gently.

"I'm sure they made it sound to the lawyer that somehow I was acting out of spite, taking it out on them for a bad marriage to their son. I was a good and faithful wife." She shrugged. "Maybe not so good in their terms. But certainly faithful. I tried, Peter."

"You're going off on a tangent, darling," Peter said gently. "The issue hasn't changed. Now who's whipping herself with guilt? The issue is Tray. Not your marriage to Chuck. Not his parent's feelings. The issue is Tray. That's it. That's the bottom line."

"And you, Peter," she said. "They have no right to rain on your parade. I wish they would just go away."

He picked up the envelope, slipped the letter out, read it again, and replaced it. Then he flipped it casually so that it slid to the other end of the table. His attitude calmed her, and she grew more confident.

"Believe me," she said, "I understand what they must be feeling. They never did have a good grasp on what was real. Especially my father-in-law, who couldn't believe it was possible that his wonderful son could make anybody unhappy. Molly's okay, but, like me, she was an outsider in that father-son club. Well, I certainly don't want a repetition of that. Not for my son." She looked up and rapped the table with her knuckles. "No. I know what's best for my child."

"Our child," he whispered.

"Our child."

Her resolve quieted her, as she touched something tough and strong within herself, a determination to be assertive, as she had been when she had decided to leave Uncle Walter's protection. Maybe at the beginning what she had done regarding Charlie and Molly had seemed an aberration. Now it seemed natural, even necessary. Peter and she had every right to make decisions for their child. How dare they threaten to put that decision in the hands of a judge, a total stranger? The old life was gone, and good riddance.

"We're going to call their bluff, Peter," she said.

"No question about that."

"And if they take us to court, we're going to fight them."

"I agree," he said, reaching out again for her hand, which he gripped tightly. "But you must take it in stride. You mustn't allow yourself to get upset. That's the one thing we have to guard against. You've got enough to worry about."

She understood his words, but her racing mind disregarded them.

"And any expenses are to come out of Chuck's insurance money," she said emphatically. Her original idea had been to use that money to acquire a college education for herself. But when Peter came along, she had put it in the bank for Tray's education.

"That's not—" he began.

"Yes," she said firmly. "It's what I want."

He said nothing, obviously turning it over in his mind. Inside herself, she felt a sudden drain of energy, like air seeping from a tire. No matter what, she knew, no amount of strength or bravado could truly stop the impending pain. As if in response, a tiny spasm knotted the lower part of her abdomen. She said nothing, and it soon passed.

Chapter 5

THROUGH the kitchen window, Molly could see Charlie puttering in the yard. She stood at the sink, rinsing the breakfast dishes before putting them into the dishwasher. It was an overcast morning, chilly for early October, and Charlie was puffing vapor as he bent and rose in the process of flinging dead branches into the wheelbarrow. Early fall was clean-up time. Charlie would fuss with the remains of his vegetable garden, preparing the beds for next year's crop of the inevitable tomatoes, cucumbers, squash, and lettuce that would make up the bulk of their summer salads. He would also prune back the recently harvested apple and pear trees. Putting the fruits up in jars had become an annual ritual.

Goaded by Charlie's use of the latest fertilizers and insecticides, the garden and trees yielded more each year. In years past, some of it had always been earmarked for Chuck and Frances. Tray had especially loved the way Molly did the pears. Frances's polite note after she had married and taken Tray abruptly halted all that. Now that Charlie had officially retired, there wouldn't be jars going to his coworkers. And there were limits to how many she could give away to the neighbors and the other teachers and students at the school. By now everybody was so well stocked that even a polite acceptance seemed forced and hollow.

It wasn't only that, of course. The whole idea of people and social contacts had taken on a new dimension. In their age group, people talked about their children and grandchildren, of incidents, births, marriages, holidays together. Even worse, they showed pictures. It was simply impossible to hide one's feelings, to assuage the pain. Molly had all she could do to keep Charlie from seeing her own agony, for it only exacerbated his. It was better, and safer, to keep to themselves these days.

They had lived in their house in Dundalk for more than thirty years. The plot of land backed onto a stand of trees on the edge of a flood plain that had mercifully escaped the ravages of the overflowing creeks and marshland that bordered the industrial edge of the Chesapeake Bay shore. Built of brick, the house, which had gone through a series of periodic remodelings, was a cut above those in the neighborhood, a big fish in a small pond.

They had often joked about the eclectic architecture of the area, where the facades ranged from clapboard to aluminum to false stone. But they had always taken a feisty pride in the individual nature of Dundalk's inhabitants and enjoyed the good-natured jokes about its lack of, to say the least, cachet. Many of the people who had been there when they first moved into the neighborhood had gone, and younger people were coming in with a lot more in common with each other than with an over-the-hill couple like themselves.

When the subject of selling the place came up, they had always concluded that they just weren't "movers." As proof, they could point to generations of their forebears who had rooted in the comparatively small Maryland towns of Frederick and Crisfield, and they reasoned that they had already expended the energy of their blood by taking the radical step of moving to the metropolis of Baltimore.

Something in the way Charlie worked arrested Molly's attention. She couldn't quite articulate it in her mind, like a missing word in a familiar lyric that required humming the tune again to catch the omission. She stood transfixed, studying this man with whom she had shared—how did the lawyers say it?—bed and board for thirty-seven years. He wore his familiar yard uniform, a tattered orange-background mackinaw, Budweiser peak cap, old wide winter khakis, and work boots that had replaced the original marine issue combat boots he had managed, by care and persistence, to keep usable for nearly twenty years after the war.

Then it occurred to her that she wasn't just casting a watchful eye over him as she had done for years from that very same spot. She was seeing the memories of the past. There was Chuck, dancing around him, first as pup, then as helper, then as equal. Gripping the sink, she looked away and saw her knuckles go white as she strained to make that old image go away. It was still too raw for conscious recapture. It was more than enough to bear to see them, like old movies, in her dreams. Often the running reel was interrupted by tremors of sobbing hysteria, and she would wake up and need the succor of Charlie's reassuring presence and caress. At times, the tables would turn and it was she that would have to provide passage through a nightmare.

Finally she chased away the old memories and began to inspect Charlie, analyzing, studying, trying to determine just what it was that was awry. In the nearly two weeks since they had seen the lawyer, she had seen his mood change. As the deadline for Frances's response grew closer, he had gone from determined optimism to sullen discouragement. She wondered if it had been a good idea to consult the lawyer. Not that she was having second thoughts. But both of them expected a more concrete reaction. The uncertainty took its toll. Silences between them lengthened. At breakfast that morning, Charlie had done little more than issue perfunctory grumbles while he pretended to read the Sunday *Sun*.

As she continued to watch him, her eyes misted and she felt the food she had just eaten congeal in her stomach. He seemed to be slowing down, showing his age. Always when she looked at him in a reflective way, she could see the outlines of the younger man, her sweet golden prince, as she had first seen him in his dress blues. Now the lines were blurring, and the ravages of time and disappointment were showing signs of their inevitable victory. He seemed to be hesitating after each movement, deliberately stringing out the activity, squandering time as if it hardly mattered anymore.

It was strange to observe, since he had always rushed through time, treating it like a precious commodity to be allocated carefully for his many hobbies. He loved to putter and fix things around the house and yard. In the branches of the unleafing oak, she could see the tree house he had built for Chuck, half-rehabilitated when Tray had been around, now rotting with the seasons. Even the tire replaced as a swing for Tray looked shriveled and lifeless as it dangled in the light breeze. During that brief time of their having him, Tray had, like Chuck, become Charlie's pup, and Charlie had responded with a flurry of energy, putting the old pull wagon and sandbox in shape in a single weekend. For him, the activity went a long way to assuage the grief of Chuck's death.

He had even been planning to buy another sailboat. She tried to laugh out loud at the memory of the first one, but only a brief squawk came, more like a sob. Originally dubbed *Molly's Thing*, it had soon become apparent that the name was all wrong, and she had insisted it be changed to *Two Charlies*. She had gone along most of the time at the beginning but finally succumbed to the brutal fact that while Dramamine prevented the nausea of seasickness, it also made her too drowsy to be any fun. By the time Chuck was ten, he and his father were off alone on weekend cruises.

He had stenciled the words "Three Charlies" on Tray's reconditioned wagon, a true harbinger of the sailboat to come. For some reason she found herself mesmerized by the bitter-sweetness of the memories, and she did not turn away from Charlie performing his now joyless chores among the dead and dying symbols strewn about. There was the hoop of the basket attached to the garage wall, now rusted, the basket shredded, where Charlie had taught Chuck to "dump the b-ball"; the weathered warren cubbies where Charlie and Chuck had raised rabbits until the population had become impossible to control; the grass rise that they had flattened to make a well-drained place for Chuck's tent for summer sleep-outs with his friends.

Suddenly, sensing her inspection, Charlie stopped, turned quickly, and shot her a puzzled look. He was not smiling, nor did he wave, as if, having read her mind, he disapproved of her watching him. Out of respect, she turned away and moved back, out of sight.

She poured herself another cup of coffee and went into the den, where she planned to mark a briefcase full of papers. How many nights and weekends had she spent on papers? She wondered if she had used time wisely when Chuck was growing up, a thought that had begun to gnaw at her since Frances and Tray had gone, as if she had missed doing something that might have prevented what had happened. Perhaps Chuck might still be alive? She shrugged away the question with a silent rebuke.

Sitting opposite the gun cabinet that hung on the paneled wall, she found that somehow its just being there was deflecting her concentration, nagging her to confront it. She had hardly noticed it for years, although it was a routine feature of her life to see Charlie polishing the stocks and cleaning the barrels regularly, even though they hadn't been used since one of the last times Chuck had come home to visit.

Hunting, boating, fishing, going to ball games. They were the expected rituals of manliness. She had never questioned them. Indeed, such things were traditional among the men in her family before she married. They were to be accepted, the loneliness never resented.

"Builds self-reliance," Charlie had assured her repeatedly, perhaps reacting to his own uneasiness about leaving her alone on those occasions. Actually, in keeping with her own early memories, she had welcomed the display of companionship, the bonding of the male generations. It fulfilled the expectations of her conditioning. In that environment girls giggled and sewed and cooked, and those, like her, who wore glasses were excused their bookishness. Her mother had lived her life ordering the men around, and they usually obeyed. But she would never, never interfere or, even inadvertently, spoil their special pleasure in manly pursuits.

Of course, the guns always frightened her to death, and no amount of reassurance on Charlie's part ever chased away her fear when he and Chuck went off during the season. They would bring back venison and rabbit already skinned and butchered for cooking, which Charlie duly piled in the freezer with solemn mystical allusions to the meaning of the hunt.

"One must kill only to eat," he would intone, which was enormously hypocritical, since they could buy all the meat they needed at the supermarket. She shivered, remembering how that had set off that crucial argument with Peter. Then she pushed it out of her thoughts.

Once she had come into the den to see him showing Tray how the guns worked. He had stood behind the boy, holding the gun and showing him how to sight. Tray squinted behind the stock and pulled the trigger.

"Got 'em," Charlie had squealed, smiling at her. It was, she realized now, the very first time he had smiled since Chuck had been reported dead. The memory confused her, superimposed on a more ominous image of a dejected Charlie on the day after his sixtieth birthday, before he had told her what actually happened on that day. He was sitting in the den with Chuck's old hunting gun across his knees. He hadn't heard her come in, although she had made no effort to muffle her entrance. It was the way he held the gun that frightened her, one hand on the stock, the other around the trigger guard, one finger unmistakably through the loop. She had seen no cleaning things in sight, and she had scanned the room, looking for a shell box.

"What are you doing, Charlie?" she had asked, bending to get a better look at his eyes, which seemed fixed on an internal apparition. She had to shake his shoulder for him to raise his head.

"Just getting ready to clean this," he had responded, shaking his head as if that might dissipate what was obviously a most unhappy daydream.

"Didn't you just clean that gun a couple of weeks ago?" She hadn't been sure, and she did not want him to ignore her concern.

"Never can clean these damned things enough," he had responded.

Looking at the gun case now brought back not only the memory but her uneasiness. She would tell herself later that it was merely caused by her active imagination.

Nevertheless, it made her put up defenses against succumbing to her own depression. She owed it to Charlie to keep her own spirits up. Therefore, she promised herself, she would assume the role of cheerleader. There was not much choice in the decision, since he was obviously not presently fit for that role. Also, she had her work. In an odd way, one might say, she had her children, had always had her children. To her, they were eternally fifth graders, still perched on the better edge of innocence and, therefore, still available for love, complete with hugs and kisses.

Not that her grief did not gnaw at her. But for her it wasn't just grief, it was the old wounds of infertility that could bring her down, the terrible inadequacy that had come from her difficulty in conceiving Chuck, a fact that had lent an awful tension to at least ten years of their marriage. In that period, Charlie was the cheerleader, as sweet and understanding a liar and hypocrite as ever there was. She had, she knew, ruined his expectations for a larger family. Her own as well. She alone was the defective—the humiliating tests of his potency always revealed a sperm count that could father a nation.

To see him unhappy now, this wonderful, good, and loving man, had made her angry and impatient with Frances and Peter for taking this cruel tack at exactly that point when he—and she, too—needed the comfort of Tray most. Thankfully, she was able to put it all aside for at least part of the day. Not like Charlie, in whom it simmered at every moment of every hour.

She hadn't told him all of that last serious conversation with Frances, only of her assurance that the condition was temporary. She had, of course, mentioned the adoption, but in the context of the entire traumatic event, that had seemed merely a secondary priority. How could they know that it would come back to haunt them?

"Peter is taking Tray on—as a father," Frances had said. "He's adopting him." To her credit, it was not something casually mentioned on the telephone. Frances had come over to the house in the late afternoon while Charlie was at work. She had been in the yard playing ball with Tray when Molly came home from school. A week had gone by since the scene between Peter and Charlie. It had not been a happy week. Charlie had been moody and depressed, still not able to accept the reality of the impending marriage. For her part, Molly had her own worries about the new term and a new, very young principal.

The weather was still warm enough for cold lemonade, which she had made and brought to the patio. Sensory memories always made the recollection seem more real. Even now she could savor the tangy taste, which, as the conversation proceeded, grew bitter and metallic.

"I owe Tray this chance."

Frances's lips trembled, and her voice was shaky.

"Are you all right, dear?" Molly had said.

"No, I'm not." She had paused. "This hurts."

"What does?" Molly had been genuinely confused. It did concern her that Charlie had not exactly given his blessing to the marriage so soon after Chuck's death, but then again, he hadn't been happy about Chuck's marrying Frances in the first place. He'd get over this as he had gotten over the other, Molly thought. Or had he?

"You and Charlie won't be coming to the wedding," Frances had said bluntly.

Molly had thought that over for a moment. They had received invitations. But the statement and the flat way in which it was delivered startled her. Had it been a question or a command?

"There is always the possibility that Charlie might change his mind. You know how he is. Of course, out of respect for his views I wouldn't go without him. He's just still depressed over Chuck."

"It wouldn't matter in any event, Molly. Peter and I both think it's best." She had paused and lowered her eyes. "I'm sorry."

"I suppose it is understandable," Molly had said without conviction. "What with Peter's family and all. Considering the circumstances, it's probably more appropriate to leave us out." She'd tell that to Charlie, leaving him with one less problem to grapple with.

"And after we're married, we'll need lots of space, Molly."

Frances seemed to have gained courage, and the lip tremors had stopped. Briefly, Molly had been taken aback, as if she were speaking to a person other than the one she had known for the past six years. The other Frances had kept more to herself, an internal type, rarely confiding and certainly not as assertive as she now appeared. Peter's influence had already wrought changes in her.

"I've never been that kind of a mother-in-law. You know that, Frances."

"What I mean is"— Frances stammered —"is that we really want you and Charlie not to visit."

"You know Charlie and his pride. He'd never go where he wasn't invited."

Molly had noted that Frances had averted her eyes. Her shyness had always made eye contact difficult. Now she was deliberately avoiding any attempt at it. Although the sun shone brightly and Tray played contentedly with the ball, the atmosphere had suddenly become ominous.

"Then you do understand what I'm saying?" She grimaced as if she were in pain.

"I understand what you're saying. I'm not sure what you mean," Molly had said haltingly. "You know that Charlie and I will do nothing that will interfere with your happiness." She paused, trying to gather her wits, not daring to contemplate what was coming next. "I hope you won't be too hard on Charlie. He really wasn't very nice to you and Peter the other day. I hope you're not holding it against him. He just can't hold things in. Doesn't seem to do much good to tell him, either. But he's a good man." She said the last emphatically, almost as if it were a sales pitch. She wanted to keep talking, but she couldn't think of much else to say.

"This is very hard for me," Frances said. "And I don't want to cry."

"Of course not, dear." She was having difficulty holding back tears herself.

"I owe this to Peter. He's been simply wonderful about Tray. And me. I know it's the right thing for us."

"I want only what's best for you and Tray," Molly managed to say. "We'll be happy to stay away for a while. Of course, you need time to adjust to each other without us hanging around and bothering things."

"I was afraid of that. I don't think you completely understand, Molly," Frances said, her voice barely a whisper. "What I mean is—" She paused, began again, swallowed the words, cleared her throat, and said, "I mean for you both to stay away completely."

"I told you we'll do it, Frances," Molly said with rising irritation. "Depend on it."

"Until we say otherwise, Molly. Now do you understand?"

It was like a club to the head. Was she getting the point?

"I'm a bit confused." Molly had responded with the same tone that she often used with her students.

"From Tray as well," Frances said, almost swallowing the words.

Molly felt suddenly groggy, slightly dizzy. She was having difficulty understanding.

"You mean never see our grandson? You mean that?"

"Not never, Molly. Just for now."

"No visits?"

"Not for now."

"No telephone calls? No letters?"

"Just until Tray adjusts. For the time being."

"You're saying that we're to have no contact with our grandson." She felt foolish in the repetition.

"It makes sense for Tray."

There had been a long pause as Molly coped with a sudden shortness of breath.

"I know you'll think we're heartless and cruel. I would like you to understand. But if you don't, I'll have to accept that." She began to race along now. "I want this to be a completely fresh start for Peter and me. Tray, too. For the three of us. We'll see how it goes." For a moment Molly felt the uncommon inspection of Frances's eyes. "I'm not saying it's forever," she added quickly.

"Is this your idea?" She had felt helpless by then, ready to grasp any lifeline.

"Mine and Peter's."

"But why? We love Tray. How can it possibly hurt to see him?"

"It's not that, Molly. The boy's been through enough. Let him accept his new life. Think of his well-being first." She shook her head and clicked her tongue. "I know you think I'm being cruel and heartless."

"Misguided, maybe. But no, not cruel and heartless." I will not give her that satisfaction, Molly thought bitterly. I will not make it easy for her.

"I feel awful about it, Molly. But I think it's the right thing.

He'll have Peter's folks. We just think it would be too complicated.
We don't need any outside pressures just now. Let's all adjust to
the situation first."

"We're his grandparents. Not the enemy."

"That's not the issue, Molly. It's just—just that we want to make
a fresh start." She was repeating herself now, as if she had mem-
orized a speech. "There's Peter to think about. He had a very bad
first marriage, and he worries about anything that might hurt
ours. Besides, why should he have to cope with resentments that
have nothing to do with him—with another man's parents to remind him that he wasn't the first?"

"He said that?"

"Not in so many words, but I imagine he could be thinking it."

"He'll have Tray to remind him of that."

"But he'll be Tray's father. Legally and otherwise."

"Not otherwise. Just legally," Molly had snapped, instantly
regretting her sudden outburst.

"There. You see? I don't fault you for it. It's an attitude. None
of us should have to contend with that for now."

"I don't know what to say." She felt drained.

"Maybe someday we'll think differently, but for now, I pray
that you won't be too unhappy."

A numbness had begun to set in and, in her mind, she managed
a subtle shift of focus to Charlie.

"It's going to be rough on Charlie. You know how much he
adores Tray."

"I know."

Molly had half expected her to bring up a point about Tray's
being a kind of surrogate son for Charlie, but wisely Frances left
that alone. There is something more here than meets the eye,
Molly had decided, something unspoken. She wondered if, keeping her wits about her, she could bring it to the surface. Anything,
she thought. Anything but this.

"Don't you think that this step is, well, to say the least, a little
drastic?"

"Yes, it is. But it can't avoided."

"You think we'll be a bad influence on Tray?"

"Certainly not bad. But confusing. Let's just try it, Molly. Nothing is forever."

"Not childhood either. Nor our lives." She had been trying

desperately to keep her composure, but soon her eyes were misting and she could not disguise a sterling effort to hold back a tearful collapse.

"This is not easy for me either, Molly," Frances had said, her voice catching.

"You don't know the half of it." She managed to hold back her tears while her mind tried to conceive of strategies that might get Frances to change her mind. "It somehow doesn't seem right. Charlie and I are blood kin to Tray, unselfishly devoted and loving."

"Please, Molly. I don't question that."

It was impossible to think and grieve at the same time. All mental and emotional strength seemed to have run out of her. There was only room for a desperate probe.

"It's not because of Chuck, is it?"

They had rarely discussed that issue. Now she regretted her deliberate avoidance of the subject.

"Now that you ask, it was awful, Molly. Being alone so much. It wasn't a marriage. Maybe at first. No. It wasn't very good. Not for me. It was lonely and—why am I going on like this? Let's just say that it wasn't like yours and Charlie's. Not like most loving married couples. Chuck didn't want to be married, Molly. He didn't want the responsibility. He just wasn't satisfied with me—or Tray. He didn't want Tray, you know."

Molly felt a flash of anger.

"Now that's not true, Frances." In her heart, of course, she knew otherwise.

"Maybe not Tray, specifically. Rather the whole idea of being tied down, of fatherhood. Of answering to one woman." She had grown nervous again, and the lip tremors resumed.

"Really, Frances—"

"He was away for six months or more at a time. I admit I've been naive, but I'm not a fool. There are men like that. They like the freedom and danger of that kind of life. A wife and children don't fit into it."

"You should have demanded he stay home."

"I tried. You know I tried," she said, her voice again lowering to a whisper. But her answer was tentative, and Molly saw her sense of shame and failure.

"Maybe you weren't assertive enough," Molly said, knowing

there was a barb in it. She felt a stab of guilt. When it came to Chuck, maybe none of them had been assertive enough, including herself.

"Well then," Frances replied. "I don't want to make the same mistake again. I'm not afraid anymore. I have my priorities and I don't intend ever to be silent again."

Priorities, Molly thought. She could not remember Frances ever using that term. It seemed scientific—sounded like Peter's word. She was Peter's spokesman, Molly decided.

Her anger was rising now, and she knew that soon she would reach the point of no return, when words could be weapons of total destruction. There was no point in citing Frances's lack of assertion or any other imagined faults, no point in implying that they were the cause of Chuck's death. Not now. Too many people were already blaming themselves. But this business of priorities had an ominous air about it. Worse, she understood exactly what it meant. Molly, too, at this point in time, had her priorities. And they were in direct conflict with Frances's.

Molly, too, had consciously reordered her priorities at one point in her life, perhaps not with as much revolutionary fervor as Frances, but to the men around her it had seemed radical at the time. She chose to take up her teaching job again when Chuck was barely out of diapers, a decision that had shaken the rafters of her own marriage. No, there could be no retreat from a woman's reordered priorities. The game was lost, she knew.

The conversation had finally dwindled. There was nothing more to say, nothing left to do but hug Tray and hide her tears.

"You're squeezing too hard, Gramma," Tray had said. Sniffling, she disguised her anguish by tickling his ribs. Tray had squealed with laughter, a sound that had since replayed itself at odd moments of quietude on sunny afternoons in the backyard, along with the remembered sound of Chuck's boyhood voice.

Finally she had kissed Tray's head, his soft blond hair like Chuck's, and held him at arm's length.

"Now you remember the proverb Grandma taught you." She had embroidered it in petit point, and it had hung, suitably framed, on all her classroom walls.

She watched Tray's eyes, so like hers and Chuck's, sparkling in a flash of sunlight.

"Do unto others as you would have"— he kicked his toe into

the patio's edge, then looked up again —"as you would have others do unto you."

"And what do they call that?"

"The Golden Rule, Gramma."

She had pulled herself up to her full height, which was a few inches taller than Frances. Then why are we bending it? she had thought to herself. She embraced her daughter-in-law, willing herself to go beyond tears, as Frances was doing, knowing that they were both deliberately resisting the womanly cliché of disintegrating into inconsolable guilt-drenched tears. We'll both cry later, she thought.

"Do I have to go now, Mommy?" Tray asked. "Can't I stay here with Gramma and play?"

"I'm afraid not," Frances replied.

"Only for a little while. Pleeeez."

"Not now," Molly said, turning so he wouldn't see her tears. She wished she could say more, but it was impossible to go on.

"But why?"

"Because," Frances said. After all, what more was there to say?

Before he was out of sight, Molly had turned again, watching the child disappear in the mist of her anguish. She saw him wave and could barely muster the strength to wave back. Then she had collapsed on her knees on the patio.

But confronting Charlie was, hands down, the most painful part of the episode. Frances must have known it would be, must have chosen the moment precisely, the day before she, Tray, and Peter were to leave for Syracuse to prepare for the wedding. Until then Charlie had been threatening wildly not to attend "out of respect for Chuck." Molly had been cautioning him on going too far, fearful of alienating Peter, who could punish them through Tray. Her reasoning galled her, and the irony was, even now, as painful to remember as to confront.

Charlie's reaction was explosive. There had been no way to break the news gently. It had, of course, confirmed her husband's most potently paranoid fear, the loss of his grandson. Of their grandson, she corrected in her mind.

"You can't be serious." She had expected disbelief, then denial, which came predictably. "I don't believe it. No. It can't be true."

"It's a temporary thing," she had said, words that would be flung back at her ad infinitum. "Understandable from her point of view." Was it to calm him with reason or feed his anger?

"I won't stand for it." Actually, she remembered, he had sat down, looking suddenly shriveled like a sail without wind. "She can't do that."

"She can and will," Molly had said with firmness, offering him a kind of statement of finality. "It's an emotional time for her. She's frightened. She doesn't want any upsetting ripples. Not now."

"We're the child's grandparents, for crying out loud. You don't just cut off grandparents. It's not human." The sudden weakness caused by the initial shock had worn off swiftly, and he had bounced out of the chair and begun to pace the room, directing all his anger and frustration in Molly's direction. She had expected nothing less. "I always knew she was a mean bitch. All quiet and sweet on the surface. Now I can see why Chuck couldn't stand to be with her. He would still be here today, if he hadn't married that woman. You see?" He had waved a finger in front of Molly's nose, but she had chosen to stand her ground, to take the assault. "I was right and you were wrong. Why do you think he went away to risk his life? He ran from her. Couldn't stand being near her. That's why. Well, I have no intention of letting her get away with it. Not with my boy's son. Not with Tray. I swear I won't let her get away with it. Never."

"You have no say in this, Charlie," she said quietly, knowing it would focus his anger more directly on herself. He had begun to pace the room like a caged animal, suddenly stopping in front of her, his face distorted with rage. There was nothing to do but let him rant. It was a futile gesture, especially for an essentially good and gentle man. But at that point any sign of pity on her part would only have made things worse. He shook a threatening finger at her face.

"I blame you most of all for being so accepting of Chuck's decision to marry her. She hated her uncle. All she wanted was to get the hell out of that situation. I was right. She was one lousy wife, too. Now she's getting married while Chuck's body is still warm. There's the proof that she never did love him. She couldn't have loved him. How could she have loved him and jumped into another man's bed so soon after—? You could have stopped it. A woman knows about other women. Men are stupid about things like that." His voice had broken. "Now Chuck's dead because of it, and she's going to take Tray away from me as well."

"From us," she had corrected softly. He hadn't paid the slightest attention.

"Well, I'm not going to let her get away with it." He was smoldering now like red hot ashes.

"It's not forever, Charlie," she said, forcing herself to remain calm. "We have to give it time."

"That's what you say." She could see the flames erupting again. He turned away and paced the room, muttering to himself. Soon he was running a full head of macho steam, strutting and posturing. He punched his chest. "I'm not going to let her get away with it. No way. I've had it with her."

"It's not only her," she said protectively.

"No way," he said, listening only to his harsh inner voices. It was sad and futile, like someone spitting into the wind.

But when he had stormed out of the house, she became alarmed and ran after him to the garage. He had gotten into the car and had slammed and locked the door, gunning the motor, its sound echoing his fury. She tried to open the door, then beat on the window with her fists. Later she had wondered why she had not simply stood in front of the car, blocking it with her body. Was she afraid that he would run her over? No, she was dead certain he would not do that. He would never have gone against his own instincts. Then why had she not done it? Because she had wanted him to go, because she had wanted him to make this last-ditch effort to save Tray for them.

But she had dashed to the telephone to warn Frances, only to be rebuffed by a recording that Frances's telephone had been disconnected. She had even toyed with the idea of calling the police, but it revolted her. She had always looked down her nose at families who needed police action to intervene in domestic quarrels. It was demeaning, unworthy of mature people. It was a ten-minute drive to Frances's apartment. She had felt totally helpless, unable to think or function logically. She could have called for a taxi. But she didn't. The waiting became agony. In her memory, it was the hour of her greatest terror.

It was Peter who had finally called her.

"He came in like a lion and went out like a lamb," Peter had said. "I knew you'd be worried. I guess he'll ride around a bit. Maybe stop at a bar."

"Charlie's not much of a drinker. It's not his way." She had resented the implication.

"At first, I thought he might be violent. Thankfully, Tray was at a neighbor's."

"He didn't even see Tray?"

"Frances got him from the neighbors.

"At least Charlie got to see him. Did it tear him up?"

"It wasn't a very happy moment for him. I can tell you Tray was also shaken up."

"It could have been avoided, Peter."

"I don't think so, Molly. It's a lot more complex than meets the eye. And really, you must understand it has nothing to do with you or Charlie."

"Nothing? Tray is our grandchild."

"I understand that," he said sympathetically. "But there is a question of priorities." There was that word again, she thought.

"I think your decision is wrong," she said. Thinking of Charlie's anguish, the fight had gone out of her.

"Maybe so. But we must have this chance. And we're not saying it will be forever."

"Yes. I heard all that this afternoon."

There was a long pause. She listened attentively for any regretful sigh, but none came.

"I'm just calling to say that Charlie is all right, as well as can be expected, and that I'm sorry. With a little patience, things might work out for all of us. The main thing is Tray."

Peter had hung up and she remembered that she had held the phone for a long time, until she heard the car purring back into the garage. She did not go out to greet him. He had cut the motor but did not appear for a long time. Molly had waited, seated in the living room. Then he came in. He was definitely not the same man who had left less than an hour before. Ashen, he was the picture of defeat, more broken than he had been at the news of Chuck's death. Be strong, she begged herself, although her own hurt was, she was sure, equal to his.

He dropped onto a chair in the kitchen like a puppet that had been cast aside, no longer needed for the show.

"I couldn't stand it," he whispered. "Saying good-bye. I broke down." He looked as if he might be getting ready to do that again. His nose was runny, and his eyes were red from crying. He swallowed hard. "He asked me why I was crying." He was falling apart. She came toward him and laid his head against her breast.

"It will be all right, Charlie. A little patience. It will be. You'll see," she whispered, forcing her stability. While he was in this state, she knew, she needed to appear strong. He desperately needed her to lean on.

"And—" He started to talk, stopped; then, forcing a brief sense of control, he continued. " 'Grampa,' he asked me, 'where does it hurt?' He asked me that. Where does it hurt?" He trembled and sobbed for a moment, then managed to speak again. "I told him . . . 'Tray,' I said. 'It hurts everywhere.' Everywhere. . . ." Then he broke down again.

That night they had clung to each other in bed not merely like two spoons, but like one. How else were they expected to get through that dreadful night?

Sitting in the den now, having difficulty concentrating on her papers, she concluded that remembering was both painful and necessary. You couldn't hide from life. Ultimately, everything had to be faced squarely. There was still life ahead, she assured herself, looking at the papers. At least she had her work and the opportunity to see hope on the faces of her fifth-grade children. There was renewal in that, she decided, thankfully. Unfortunately, Charlie did not have that opportunity, she thought sadly, and that made it doubly necessary for her to husband her courage and gather the shreds of optimism.

Poor Charlie. She had tried to buck him up as he confronted the looming horror of early retirement. At first it had been an option, then a necessity. All his choices had narrowed, then closed.

"I fought for this country," he had said, a theme he had taken up often, as if his present state was because of some national betrayal.

"You can't blame it on the country," she had countered sensibly.

"Then what?"

It was a question that defied any soothing answer.

She heard him stamping his boots on the mat outside, then his footsteps moving into the house. He seemed to have chucked the yard chores earlier than usual. But then Sundays were not special for him anymore. She listened, unable to focus on the papers. He was making coffee in the coffee maker. He was always dosing himself with caffeine.

Soon he was sitting opposite her in the den, and she put aside her papers to give him her undivided attention. On Sundays, certainly, he was entitled to that.

"Might as well face it, Molly," he said, a cigarette dangling from his lips, both hands cupping the mug for warmth. She felt encouraged by the talk. He was right: They had better face facts. "They have no damned intention of answering."

"That's the way it looks, doesn't it?"

"Lawyers," he said, removing his cigarette. Some of the paper stuck to his lips. "Pack of liars. Doesn't matter to them."

"That's not fair, Charlie. He laid it out for us."

"Leaves us hanging."

When he did not speak for a long time, she feared that he was falling back into silence.

"We could always cut and run." She knew it would shock him into alertness.

"You want that?"

"No, I don't," she said firmly. "I want Tray."

"Damned right," he agreed. "We're in it for the whole nine yards."

"There's no sense brooding about it," she said. "That's not the way a boxer prepares himself." She smiled. "Do unto others before they do unto you." He chuckled. That saying always got a rise out of him.

He sipped his coffee, then punched out his cigarette and lit another. It was not a time for admonishment. "It'll start really costing now." He became silent again, took deep drags on his cigarette. "Bet he's grown four, five inches." He shook his head. "Sundays are the pits." She knew what he meant. Sunday had been Chuck's big day. And Tray's. "We used to have lots of fun on Sundays."

"That's being broody, Charlie," she rebuked.

"They can't take away memories."

"Nobody can touch those."

"If we get to court, she's going to have to tell it different than it was," Charlie said. "Make us out like we were a couple of rats." He reached out and touched her hand. "We weren't, were we?"

"Don't be silly."

"I mean it's what she has to say to win. Like the lawyer said."

"Well, then we'll have to refute all charges."

"How can anyone call us rats?"

"It wouldn't be honest—just a ploy anyway."

"We were damned good parents and grandparents. Weren't we?"

"By any standard. Especially love."

"It was her that was the bad one. Chuck made one big mistake." He shook his head. "Besides, they were too young. Now we gotta pay the piper. It's not fair."

"What *is* fair?"

"We were good, Molly. We were always good. Weren't we?"

"You musn't question that. Of course we were."

"Are you sure?"

"Sure I'm sure. Whatever has gotten into you?" It was a kind of mock rebuke, mostly to deflect his being too hard on himself.

"Something I might have done to Chuck. As a father. You know what I mean. Something I didn't know I was doing. I really thought he was a fine young man, that we had done one helluva job. I mean he was out there working for his wife and kid."

"You've got to stop that, Charlie."

"I'm just trying to analyze the situation. It's important."

"I don't mean that. I mean taking it all on yourself, as if I wasn't there."

"I didn't mean that, Molly."

"All this me, my, I. Remember, I was there, too."

He shook his head and frowned.

"I guess I'm not myself."

"There it is again. I. My."

He got up from the table and paced around the den, stopping in front of the gun cabinet.

"I really miss that kid," he said. She wondered whom he meant, Chuck or Tray. He had used the singular. She refused to probe, sure he meant both, as she did in her mind. In a way, it would be the weakest part of their case, although they had not yet fully explored the issue. Was Tray merely the surrogate for their lost son? That would underline their selfishness, in legal terms. She was sure of it.

"You think Forte will advise that we wait a few more days?" Charlie asked, turning suddenly.

"I doubt it."

"Then he should hop right on it first thing in the morning. File papers or something."

"I guess that's what he intends to do."

"And you're ready? Come what may?"

"What else have I got to do?" she said. Deliberately, she pushed the papers aside, softening the sarcasm, sorry the words had popped out in that way.

"I want to go all the way. No matter how weak he says the case is. To the end." She could see a flush begin along the sides of his neck and it alarmed her. He slipped into silence again.

"Doesn't look too good, does it, babe? Them not even answering."

"Pessimism won't help," she said.

"It's these damned Sundays," he muttered.

"Tomorrow's Monday."

"That's something," he said, throwing his cigarette butt into the coffee dregs. "Maybe I need a good fight. I was always good in the clutch."

Was it really a flicker of the old courage? Or an illusion? It was not the fight itself she feared. It was a question of how many times he could rise from the floor.

Chapter 6

CHARLIE had, he assured himself, deliberately cut short clearing the fall debris in the yard so that he would have something to do on Monday. He knew it was an illusion, but it was better than waking up to no expectations whatsoever. The idea was to rake out the dead brush and break up the fallen tree branches for the winter's fireplace tinder.

On Monday it rained, but not before the tension of the uncertain weather had already destroyed any hopefulness the day might bring.

Since the two weeks given for Frances's response were now officially over, he did expect the lawyer's call, which was a purposeful excuse to hang around the house. After the yard work, he had planned to make a few phone calls, feelers for jobs. With winter coming on, he had a compelling need to fill his time. In fact, the need had little to do with the seasons. Now, of course, he'd have to postpone his calls, since he did not want to tie up the line.

After Molly left for school and he had assured himself that the rain would continue, he toyed with the urge to go back to bed. But he was afraid he wouldn't be able, or lucky enough, to sleep. As if to underline the assumption, he had a fourth cup of coffee while he tried to interest himself in the gothic theatrics of Baltimore politics described luridly in the second section of the *Baltimore Sun*. The articles quickly became incomprehensible, and he turned to the obituaries, where the deaths reported were people he had never heard of. He checked their ages. Most were in their seventies and eighties, which ordinarily might have been reassuring. Now it merely emphasized how much time still had to be filled. Not much comfort in that, he decided, refolding the paper.

In bathrobe and backless slippers, he roamed the house trying to focus on something that would thwart his aimlessness. Thirty-five years he and Molly had lived here. The rooms and objects in this house had once defined their lives. Now they were taking on the aspect of a prison. And yet, all of it was paid for, which was supposed to signify freedom.

"From what?" he heard himself ask aloud. He pictured in his mind a checklist, possibly from years of occupational habit. A quality control inspector was a living checklist. From economic worry? The Depression scars that had marked his parents' lives had long since faded. In Crisfield, and later when he and Molly were first married, being worried about money was a way of life. It wasn't the specter of starvation that caused the fear, but rather the terror of losing one's self-respect and social dignity.

Retirement had, indeed, freed him from economic worry for the rest of his life. Counting what he and Molly had put away, and with the retirement checks rolling in month after month, and with Molly's salary and impending retirement pension, they were financially secure forever. In all the working years of his life, his focus had been on financial security, something that had always eluded his own parents. Not that he hadn't bitched about his job. The worst part had always been brown-nosing incompetent superiors. But then, he had been brown-nosed by those under his authority. He was damned competent, and that fact had been underscored by raises and promotions.

Yet, in truth, he had fantasized about retirement. The yoke would at last be lifted from the ox. Time would be his alone. He would be free from rigid schedules, deadlines, and brown-nosing. He'd done his time. The moment had come to reap the rewards. As he passed the hall mirror, his reflection sailed past him, unshaven, hair mussed, coffee stains on his robe. Free at last. Free at last, he muttered. God, did he miss that job. The clatter and noise of steel, rolling, sliced, welded, always moving; the voices of men shouting above the din; the smells and dust and confusion and aggravations, the great joy of doing, of work itself.

The humiliating rationalization was wearing thin. As for taking early retirement in the first place, they hadn't given him a choice. But in the rigid terms of the checklist, he was, indeed, free of economic insecurity.

Which brought him to the next question. Was he free from worrying about his family? What family? he sighed. It was no coincidence that he had come to Chuck's room, although he could not find the courage today to turn the doorknob. Unfortunately, the room's layout was indelible in his mind, the solid maple furniture that he had carted himself in a rented trailer from the furniture store; the striped bedspreads that Molly had made; the rock star posters and team banners tacked to the wall, now curling at the edges; the drawers full of clothes and souvenirs of a boy's life—a boy who, in that room, had moved from cradle to manhood. Actually only the furniture was still there, the rest banished on the scrap heap of material history. Charlie stood before the door, then turned and leaned his head against it as if the immutable wood might reincarnate as the flesh of the lost boy.

The lost boy!

In fact, the boy was not lost. He was still in Charlie's living memory, each moment of intimacy and passage engraved indelibly in his mind by constant replay.

He could remember Molly in her hospital bed unwrapping the swaddling clothes and undiapering the pink-fleshed doll to reveal every living millimeter of what they had created.

"Look how perfect, Charlie," she had said. "Not a flaw." He had stuck his rough forefinger into the child's hand, which had closed around it automatically.

"Strong, too," he had said, feeling that first flush of a father's pride, the great baggage of hopes and aspirations that filled his heart with joy and delight. "Mine," he had whispered.

"Ours," she had corrected, her eyes feasting on the tiny human replica that had come out of her womb. Then she had smiled and offered a sly wink. "A perfect specimen. Just like his old man."

He remembered blushing, although it was a matter of masculine pride that the boy was well made there as well.

"Thank you, God," Molly had said, while their hands smoothed and inspected their creation. Little wells of tears spilled onto her cheeks, tears of joy and thanks. And of relief. The little tyke had been ten years in the making.

"It's been a rough haul, babe."

"That's why I want him to have your name, Charlie."

"Charlie?"

"No. Charles, Jr. But we won't call him junior."

"Chuck. In the marines they called me Chuck." He wasn't sure how he had lost the name. Molly always called him Charlie, which had become his monicker at the plant as well.

"It'll be the beginning of a long line of Charlies," Molly had whispered as he had bent down to kiss her lips. It was the caboose for them, and they both knew it. The doctor had warned that there was no sense in taking chances anymore and had tied her tubes.

"Looks like he's pretty well-equipped for production," Charlie had joked.

"We'll make it up in grandchildren." She kissed the baby's chest. "Won't we, Chuckie?"

"Better believe," Charlie said, jiggling the baby's hand with his finger.

"I'm so happy he's a boy," Molly had said.

"A girl like you wouldn't have been so bad either." He had meant it, of course. But he had been certain it would be a boy.

It was a dream a long time coming, he had thought. Out there in the mosquito swamps of Guadalcanal, he had lived with the idea that he was making the world safe for his unborn children. With death all around, it was not an uncommon prayer in the dank and lonely foxholes. What was the killing all about if not for that? So the fathering of Chuck had taken on a mystical quality long before the baby had arrived. The fact that he was a replication of himself, a man, merely confirmed the symbolism. The boy had taken his time about it because he had had to fight his way into life, and now that he was here he had to be carefully nurtured and initiated into the exclusive mysteries of manliness.

"We've got great hopes for you, fella," Molly had said, kissing the baby's forehead.

"Better believe."

The memory strangled on its own pain.

Back in Crisfield, the tiny town that hugged the eastern shore of the Chesapeake Bay and was home to the Waterses for a hundred years, fathers passed the essence of manhood from one generation to the next in the same time-honored ways. Even though Charlie's own father had chosen not to seek his living from harvesting the bay, it did not mean that he was absolved from instructing his son in the outdoor arts—fishing, hunting, and sailing—and the ways in which indigenous foods such as crabs were prepared. That, too, along with bull roasts and barbecues, was man's work.

Charlie's old man had been a traveling salesman in ladies' ready-to-wear, albeit a lousy one; but when he was home, he was a good dad, and sitting with him in a duck blind shivering in the icy dawn was as near to paradise as Charlie ever thought he might get. And when his dad was on the road, there were grandfathers on both sides who shared the chores of manly instruction. Not that his mother and grandmothers were to be ignored, nor all the aunts and uncles and others that weren't blood kin, but who seemed so. In those days a man's role and obligation to his male child were clearly defined, a path to be followed generation after generation.

Charlie had taken Chuck down to Crisfield when his dad was still alive, and it was good to fish with three generations off the sailing boats of wood that were traditional to the area. A man had to know his roots. Well, he had shown Chuck his. Each generation, of course, refines the tradition, and Charlie was no exception. Having survived the big one, WWII, he was able to cast himself in the role of hero. Nothing like having a genuine war hero for a dad.

That meant telling Chuck what it was like being a marine, about Iwo Jima and Guadalcanal and Kwajalein, and how men lived and died in comradeship and courage, and how the greatest virtue was to be brave and the greatest goal was glory. Nor did he paint the pain out of the stories, although he sometimes did eliminate the sense of fear and he may have romanticized danger a bit; but those who lived through these events were certainly entitled to a little editorial license, especially when passing them along to their sons. He had seen more death and dying before he was twenty than many men had seen in their lifetimes. Had he been a touch too graphic in his portrayal, he wondered, making Chuck feel somehow deprived so that he went out to seek danger himself? Well, he had one-upped old Charlie there. When death put out its hand, the boy had reached out and grabbed for it.

Bits and pieces of flashing imagery cascaded in memory as if the wood of the door to Chuck's room was a mysterious transmitting device. Chuck laughing, his body nearly supine against the air as the sailboat heeled at the maximum angle. Chuck up on that top branch of the big tulip oak in the yard, long since gone.

"Get down from there this minute," Molly had screamed, dashing from the kitchen, shielding her eyes from the sun.

"Leave him," Charlie had commanded. "He'll be all right."

"He'll fall."

"Only if he becomes afraid."

Charlie had believed that with all his heart. Not being afraid was important in the rites of passage. Fear was an acquired emotion, Charlie taught his son. Fear was nothing to be ashamed of, something to be conquered. Hadn't he conquered it himself on those crazy-named Pacific islands?

Winters they hunted in the Maryland hills, stalking deer in the delicious cold. What he taught Chuck then was the value of patience, of aiming only when you were sure the bullet would bring death to the animal in the most painless way. When Chuck was twelve, he bagged his first big-horned stag with a single shot, a direct hit into the animal's heart.

They had crept close to the dead animal, awestruck at its size, Chuck shouting with excitement and shedding tears of joy at the sight.

"That's one head to be stuffed," Charlie had promised. For years it had hung in the den, until Chuck's death had made it unbearable to view and it had been squirreled away in the attic. It was not the act of killing that made it painful to remember, but the aftermath.

They had slept in one bed in the little cabin in the mountains that had been rented for the weekend, and Chuck had rolled over toward him that night just as Charlie crept in beside him.

"I did good, Dad, didn't I?"

"Great."

"I'm something, eh, Dad."

"The best."

"I love you, Dad."

The boy had kissed his father's cheek with fervor, and Charlie had returned the offer in kind. It was the last time they would kiss in that way. It would no longer be the manly thing between father and son.

As he was growing up, Chuck was beautiful to watch with his golden hair and his burgeoning physique. Girls were quick to discover his beauty.

"Love 'em and leave 'em, kid," was the way he tried to take the seriousness out of it.

"You wouldn't say that if you had a daughter," Molly had rebuked.

"But I don't."

"You'll make him a heartbreaker."

"Same as me."

For some reason, Chuck had lost interest in school by the tenth grade, and no amount of tutoring could make the information

sink in. Not that he was stupid. He just wasn't interested. Sports
and girls mattered, not school. Charlie had tried his best to persuade the boy otherwise.

"You won't go to college, son."

"You didn't, and you did okay."

"The war took that away."

"You didn't have to tell him that." Molly had overheard. She
had tried her best before handing over the problem to him.

"What was I supposed to tell him? That I got married and had
to support a wife?"

"You didn't have to support me. There was the GI Bill. I was
working."

"I didn't want you to work, remember? It wasn't exactly the
thing to do."

"And I didn't care if you liked it or not." ·

But Charlie had gotten himself a damned good job at Bethlehem. Everything was booming then, and there was money to be
made. There was no point in college.

"We've got one degree in the family. That's a pretty good
batting average. Five hundred," he had told her then.

Of course, he could have his regrets now, savor the stink of
recrimination. Blame was something you could hold onto, whip
yourself with. An independent observer might say that he had
made Chuck too self-reliant, too courageous, too freedom-loving.
But, hell, there had been no independent observer around when
he was growing up. Maybe if there had been, Charlie thought, he
might have prodded me to make the kid more of a scholar and
kick his butt into college, which might have stopped him from
getting married at twenty and going off to die at twenty-five.

"You're too damned young," he had railed when Chuck had
brought home the news. "If she's pregnant, there are ways you
can take care of it."

"She's not pregnant."

"You just started a new job." Chuck had just joined a firm that
checked for structural defects in radio towers. Molly had argued
against it as too dangerous, but Charlie had defended it.

"A little danger makes a person more cautious," he had argued.
The remark, of course, had come back to haunt him. But hadn't
he tried to get Chuck on at the plant? By then, the recession and
Japanese competition were really biting, and all hiring had stopped.

"I love her, Dad."

"She's eighteen. You're twenty. What do either of you know about love?"

"Mom says Romeo and Juliet were fourteen."

"Look what happened to them."

"I'm going to do it, permission or not."

"Why can't you wait until you've got some money in the bank?"

"Well, now I'll have something to save for."

"Marriage is forever, son. And forever is a long time."

In retrospect it was an odd observation. But divorce was not a regular occurrence in his perspective. In his experience, marriage was forever. Didn't the vows say "till death do us part"?

"I only know that I love her. And she loves me," Chuck persisted.

"Big deal."

"It is to me."

The harangue had seemed to go on endlessly that summer night. It had to be summer, since the fireflies were lighting up the night and they were sitting on the back patio. Molly had been to a PTA meeting and had come home late to find her two men still locked in combat.

"Why can't you just have fun for a few years? Play around. There's a million fish in the sea."

"He's going to do it anyway, Charlie. You might as well throw in the sponge."

"You got it, Mom."

"But it's dumb. Establish yourself a little first. Get a financial head start. If this is the girl you want, what's wrong with a long engagement? But make sure it's what you want."

"I am sure. And we've known each other three months."

"A lifetime, right? Next thing you know, you'll have a kid. With that will come more financial pressure."

"And grandchildren," Molly interjected.

"I'm too young for that," Charlie had answered.

They had haggled for another hour until it became apparent that nothing was going to change Chuck's mind.

"You're doing your thinking with your crotch."

Molly had finally interposed.

"That's not the issue in today's world, Charlie. Let's face it, Chuck has every right to make this decision. It's not like he's completing an education. He has a job. Marriage might give him a focus, stability. Certainly security."

"The voice of cool reason," he had commented, but by then he had surrendered. Fresh young love was too powerful to be stopped. So he'd sit on the sidelines and watch it grow stale, see who got the last laugh. Could it be that he was arguing with himself, dredging up the old worry that what he and Molly had would one day grow stale? Odd, he thought suddenly, that he had never outgrown that fear.

Leaving Chuck's door, he flapped around upstairs for a while, then came back down to the kitchen and made himself another cup of instant coffee. He stood by the sink as he sipped it, watching the sodden gloom that the rain had cast over the yard. He glanced at the clock. It was ten. Forte probably wouldn't get to the office until about now, he assured himself. Then he made a conscious effort to catalogue the chores he would do in the yard once the rain stopped, which did not look likely.

But it did postpone confronting another point on his checklist, the crucial point: freedom from Tray, from imagining Tray, worrying about Tray, from missing Tray.

Chuck's death had thrown a lifeline between them. Before that, he had been your ordinary run-of-the-mill doting Grampa, and Molly had been Gramma. But there was still the sense for all of them that Chuck was merely "away" and not gone forever. They baby-sat on the evenings when Frances took courses, and had her over with the boy on weekends. Charlie had taken Tray to the local carnivals and to fish on the banks of the nearby creeks. Molly, of course, was more interested in improving his mind and had read to him from the many children's books she had taken from the school library. He was still too young for the real give-and-take of manly communication. But Charlie had looked forward to the day when that moment would arrive.

Of course, by that time he had had to be more than just Grampa. He had to be the lost Dad as well, and that had gone a long way to simmer down the gnawing grief over Chuck's death. He had thought, at first, that Frances had fully accepted this new role for him, encouraging the relationship by letting Tray spend more and more time with Molly and him. After all, they were the only set of grandparents the boy had. Later, in retrospect, he decided that she welcomed the idea of Tray spending so much time with them because it gave her more time to quickly scout out a replacement for Chuck. More than anything, that memory brought back the terrible pain of what she had done to Tray and to them. It had been a deliberate act of betrayal. Pure and simple. Underneath it all, she was hard-hearted and selfish, interested only in herself. As for that Peter, he was beneath contempt.

Some things they had done were, he was convinced, beyond the pale of decent human behavior. Like that first Christmas when he and Molly had sent Tray his Christmas gifts. They were, of course, handicapped by not being able to find out from Tray what he wanted. The truth was, they had been afraid to call for fear Frances would forbid it absolutely. So they had shopped the stores, piling up gifts, mostly toys and games, since Molly was no longer sure of Tray's clothes sizes. They had had the stores send out the gifts, along with the usual handwritten cards, especially poignant because of the conditions imposed on them as absentee grandparents. The cards had not been easy to write, he remembered.

Foolishly, he had set up his own tree in the living room as he had done every year since Chuck was born. As usual, they had loaded the base of the tree with gifts from each other. It wasn't much fun dressing and lighting the tree, but they seemed to carry it out by habit, and Charlie had done everything he could to hide his tears and force his smiles. Molly, of course, did the same.

They had gotten it into their heads that Christmas, being a time of family gatherings and reconciliations, might be the moment when Frances and Peter would relent, realize the stupidity and selfishness of their actions, and pull things together again.

"Don't put too much trust in it, Charlie," Molly had warned.

"Where's that old Christmas spirit?"

"You tell me."

When the packages arrived from the store, they were certain that their dreams had come true. That is, until they opened the note attached to one of the packages.

"Dear Molly and Charlie," the note began. "There is no easy way to do this." Charlie had tossed the letter away without reading further. But Molly had picked it up and read aloud, with her clear teacher's reading voice, making a superhuman effort to hide the emotion with sarcasm. "We know your heart is in the right place. But, at least for this Christmas, while Tray adjusts to his new conditions, we thought it best that we return your gifts. We're not being Scrooge, but if only you could both leave Tray be for awhile until he gets his sea legs in his new situation, we think everyone would be the better for it. We hope this finds you both in good health. And, of course, Merry Christmas. Frances and Peter."

They had both looked dumbly at the packages. Then Charlie picked them up and took them out to the yard, where he dumped them in the big metal can in which he burned the trash, doused them with kerosene, and set them ablaze. Later, he dismantled the tree, chain-sawed it into manageable chunks, and tossed them into the fire.

They spent that Christmas Eve hiding their tears in the darkness. Christmas Day was worse. On the following Christmas, they spared themselves the pain, treating the holiday as just another day. It was not a very pleasant way to live.

Anger stirred him, and he went to the phone and called the lawyer. By the second ring, he got cold feet and quickly put the phone down. Hadn't Molly warned him to be cool? All temporary, she had assured him. He cursed under his breath and in the mirror's reflection discovered that his lips were moving silently. Story of his life, he decided, the silent curse. In his mind, he tore the checklist from the pad, crumpled it up in his hand, and flung it into the garbage. He wasn't a damned inspector anymore.

That had been another unexpected blow, robbing him of whatever hope his sixtieth birthday might have promised, which wasn't very much in the first place. But he had never expected it to be the worst day of his life.

Not that it had started badly. It was a Thursday, December 6, twenty-four hours short of the official Pearl Harbor Day. How did he know he was about to have his own day of infamy?

Molly had awakened him in a special, loving way. Recent events hadn't exactly done wonders for his libido, but Molly's sweet patience had done the trick, and he had been grateful for both the effort and her own response.

"Not bad for an old duffer of sixty."

Actually, years of activity had kept him in fair shape, although his gut wasn't as flat as it might have been.

"The Waterses wear well," he had said, embracing her still-tight haunches. "So do their women."

"I can't believe it. Where did all the years go?"

"Down the tube."

"Just you and me, guy."

"Me and you, babe."

They had just pulled each other through months of loss and despair, and this event in their bed had struck Charlie as perhaps the beginning of yet another chapter in their marriage. They had always been close in ways that they had never articulated to each other. There had, of course, been ups and downs, periods of doubts and reassurances, but the bond itself, the commitment, had never been in danger. It had, of course, occurred to him to be unfaithful, more as a test of manly power than anything more romantic, but he had never taken the plunge. He was dead certain she hadn't. The bottom line in marriage was trust. One might say that their marriage had evolved into a true and loving friendship. By this time, it had even transcended habit.

"You're everything to me, Molly," he had confided solemnly. It was something he could do only in the extreme intimacy of a loving embrace in their bed.

"And you to me."

"At least we did one thing right."

She had dressed quickly and made him a big breakfast.

"Orange juice tastes funny," he had said.

"It's the champagne."

"Pulling out all the stops, eh babe?"

"We're marking the end of the sixth decade. That deserves some attention."

"Real class." He had smacked his lips. He had always been proud of her refinements. "Think you'll ever get me to cross over the border from redneck land?" It was not really a big bone of contention between them. They knew who they were and where they had come from.

"Tonight we're going to the Chesapeake for dinner," she had promised. It was one of Baltimore's most popular restaurants.

"I'll go on one condition."

"What's that?"

"That you don't have those idiot waiters and waitresses sing me happy birthday. And no candles."

"You think I want people to know I live with an old duffer?"

"You're right behind me, wise guy." She was only two years younger.

He had kissed her good-bye deeply and sweetly, actually feeling good for the first time in months.

The guys in the plant also remembered, which had really touched him. He had found a card pasted on the door of his locker signed by all the other inspectors, and Barney Harris, his coworker of many years, told him he had invited some of the boys to join them at the Friendly Tavern to down a few brews and pay their respects to an older man. It was something to look forward to. He remembered almost feeling on the cusp of some kind of a renewal.

At least that was the way he had felt all morning. People slapped him on the back, wished him happy birthday, made a joke or two about his age, and offered good wishes. It was nice to feel noticed. He hadn't really made any enemies in the thirty-five years he had worked at the plant. Hell, he wasn't really what you would call a good ol' boy, but he hadn't been standoffish either, like some. Not until lately. And that was by Charlie and Molly's own choice. Maybe someday, if the hurt ever subsided and the reminders faded, they might be able to pick up where they had left off. That is, if anyone was left by then. Many of their friends were retiring and heading south. In any event, it was nice having the boys remember.

He had lunch in the cafeteria, and the guys stuck a candle in a chocolate cupcake and did the one thing he had banned from his impending night out with Molly—sang happy birthday. They hammed it up, of course, embarrassed to have shown any kind of mushy sentiment. It was funny as hell. But from that moment on, it was downhill all the way.

After lunch Harry Evans, the top supervisor of his section, called him into his office. They had known each other for years, and it had rankled Charlie to see the man jump across the worker-management line. But they had maintained a good working relationship, and it wasn't unreasonable to expect Evans to offer a greeting on his birthday. There was a lot of feel-good stuff going on at the plant these days. The recession had actually brought the remaining senior workers closer together. They weren't really competing with each other anymore. The objective was to stay on the job.

"Sixty years. You old son-of-a-gun," Evans had said to him after first asking him to sit down. That was the first sign of anything really unusual. Evans was a bulky, jolly man with thick shaggy eyebrows, deep-set, rheumy eyes, and a well-earned drinker's nose.

"Just another day," Charlie shrugged.

"I'll say this, Charlie. You don't look it."

"My wife told me that this morning," he said, blushing.

"And I bet that's not all." Evans broke up in laughter. Charlie, slightly resentful of the intruding personal image, smiled thinly.

"Well, I got you a birthday present, hoss," Evans had said.

Charlie was beyond promotion and wages were fixed. He was genuinely puzzled and had no idea what response was required.

"New company policy. You hit sixty, you get a bonus. Early retirement. No penalty. The full deal."

It had been a company policy for months, an optional choice. He had already decided not to take it.

"I'm not ready for that, Harry," he had replied, slightly relieved. He was not looking for any changes in his life. He'd had more than enough of those in the last few months.

"I'd say you're right about that, Charlie. You're not ready to pack it in completely, and I know you won't. It's only the plant that you'll be leaving."

"Leaving?"

His heart had begun to thump wildly against his rib cage.

"Mandatory. First of the year for all people in your category sixty or over. You lucky son-of-a-gun. The full deal. No penalty."

"But I don't want it, Harry."

"Are you crazy, Charlie?"

"What the hell would I do?"

"You gotta be kiddin' me. You're home free, Charlie. Think of it as a kiss, not a kiss-off."

"Why?"

"To make way for the younger guys, the ones with the growing families. They don't want old gray-heads around. Hell, in two more years I'm taking the boat. With joy, Charlie. With joy."

"My work was never better—" Charlie stammered. "I mean, it takes years to train a good quality-control inspector. Not a piece of pipe goes out of here out of spec. I'm one of the best in the business."

"What the hell has that got to do with it?"

"I'm good at it, that's what. And not easy to replace." He felt belligerence begin and a flush rise to his cheeks.

Evans pulled his chair closer to his desk and leaned over it. His breath smelled of sour booze. Lifting a fat finger, he jabbed it in Charlie's direction.

"Let me tell you about your so-called work. It ain't personal, Charlie. But half the workers in this plant, more than half, are as obsolete as the Model T. You included. The Japs can do the work of our entire department with one newfangled robot. You're yesterday, Charlie. Not you. But the work you do. Same goes for me and the others. A little chip no bigger than the head of a pin can do your job. You're dead, man. Prehistoric." He had gotten beet red in his face. "Take the money and run, Charlie. You got no choice."

"No appeal procedures?"

"It's all agreed. Frozen in." He shook his head. "You should be jumping up and down and dancing for joy. The way I'll be doing. What the devil you think you been working for all these years? For the piece of paper, man. The discharge. Get out and see the world. Hell, you still got the stuff to pull down a paycheck in a whole new job. Learn computers, Charlie. That's where it's at. Otherwise you're obsolete. Like the P-47. Remember the P-47?"

No point in sitting there listening to all that talk about his present usefulness. He got up.

"It's still hush-hush, Charlie," Evans told him. "Don't say nothing to anyone. It's going to be announced just before Christmas. I just thought that seeing how long we know each other, it would be nice to have given you this tidbit on your birthday." He shook his head. "I swear I never expected this reaction. Never."

"Yeah," Charlie had said, rising, perfunctorily taking Evans's sweaty fat hand.

"Congratulations."

"Yeah."

Charlie turned, felt a weakness in his knees, but managed to limp out of Evans's office.

"Happy birthday," Evans called to him, just before he shut the door.

He hadn't gone back to the floor. He couldn't even remember getting to his locker, where he changed into his heavy jacket and just walked out the door, an act of irresponsibility he had never committed in his life. It was as if a volcano had erupted inside him and the molten lava covered everything, body and mind, and there was just no way that the outrage, the explosive anger, the indignity and insult and humiliation could get outside of himself.

Even as he drove, he was conscious that he had little control over his actions. He was like a guided missile, carefully set and programmed, speeding toward an irreversible destination. It was not simply the idea of obsolescence. He had known that for years.

Nor was it the aftermath of Chuck's death. He had begun to
weather the storm. Perhaps he had even gotten used to Tray's
absence. It was, in fact, beyond analysis, then or now. He had
simply lost his insight, as if he had died and didn't know it, had
disappeared and, since he was a nonperson and obsolete, he was
also unseen, invisible even to himself. What, then, was left to lose?

Yet there was a certain cunning in living through it. He drove
by rote and soon he was pulling into his own garage and ran-
sacking the shed in the yard. Without any conscious mental effort,
he removed the little pull wagon that had been Chuck's and then
Tray's and wiped it off with a rag until the name he had stenciled
on the rear was clearly visible. *Three Charlies*, it read. Have to
repaint it again, he thought, as he carried it to his car and slid it
into the back seat.

He drove the thirty miles to Columbia as if he had driven it
every day. A few weeks after Tray had left, he and Molly had
gone there. Curiosity, they told themselves. It made them feel like
fugitive aliens in a hostile land, crossing into forbidden territories
with no hope of acceptance. They had driven the car slowly past
the neat, large, two-story colonial where Frances and Tray now
lived with her new husband. More than words, the house told
them how terribly deep the chasm between their lives had become.
One glimpse and they hurried away. Inexplicably, Charlie had
felt ashamed, failed, but he did not convey his feelings to Molly.

He parked the car in front of the school nearest to the house.
He did not question his judgment, nor was he certain that this
was the school Tray attended. He was not operating with any
logic. All he knew was that it was school time and that Tray should
be in school and that this school was closest and therefore the
logical choice. He removed the wagon from the back seat and
carried it through the main entrance.

Because of Molly's long career as a teacher and his many visits,
the atmosphere of schools was not new to him and he quickly
found his way to the door marked Office of the Principal. He felt
no anxiety, no second thoughts, not the slightest doubt of the
correctness of his actions. An administrative secretary worked in
the outer office, a gray-haired lady who squinted through rimless
glasses and looked at him with curiosity as he entered.

"I'm Charles Wat—" he began, momentarily swallowing his
words. "Graham." He had paused, just to make sure he was fully
composed and calm and that the woman would be assured that

he posed no threat to her. Even the use of Peter's last name was meant to put the woman at her ease, just in case she knew what had happened in the family. Since he had not consciously planned what he was doing, it surprised him to hear his own voice. "I'm Charles Everett Waters's grandfather. He's in the second grade, I think. Nothing serious. No trouble. I'm leaving town, you see, and I promised to say good-bye." The woman's eyes were observing the wagon and he looked down at it. "And give him this. A gift." He put the wagon on the office floor, holding the pull rope.

"It is rather unusual," she had said, carefully inspecting him. Despite the instinctive way in which he was operating, it did occur to him that he looked, in his factory work clothes, much different from most aging males in this exclusively white-collar neighborhood. What you see is what you get, he told himself, oddly proud of the difference. I yam what I yam, an inner voice chirped. In his mind, he heard a distant giggle.

"I know," he responded softly. "My wife teaches over at Dundalk."

"Oh," the woman said, smiling, perhaps reassured by the camaraderie of employment.

"It'll only take a minute," Charlie insisted.

The woman hesitated, looked down at the wagon, then shrugged.

"He'll get a kick out of it," Charlie pressed.

"It's very irregular."

"I'm his old grampa," Charlie said, offering a shy smile. "It'll mean a lot to him."

She stood up and grinned, then shook her head and moved into the corridor. He followed her, pulling the wagon. The squeaky wheel caused the woman to turn and look back at him.

"Needs oil," he said, still smiling. It did not occur to him that he was outlandish then, an older man pulling a child's wagon in a school corridor. The woman stopped in front of a classroom door, looked back and put a finger over her lips, and stepped inside. He waited, leaning against the wall. Reaching for a cigarette, he put it in his mouth, then, remembering that it was forbidden, took it out again.

"He'll be right out," the woman said, popping her head out the classroom door.

He nodded. But he felt his inner calm eroding. The gray-haired lady emerged holding the boy by the hand. It wasn't the same Tray he had imagined. Two years had taken the edge off babyhood. He had grown, and he seemed aloof, a stranger. He had expected the boy to run into his arms. Instead, he hung back, confused.

"They're doing reading," the gray-haired lady said.

"I was next," Tray exclaimed with an air of disappointment. "I practiced, too."

"Your grandfather just wanted to say good-bye," the lady said, winking at Charlie. "And to give you this." She pointed to the wagon. The boy looked at it, continuing to be perplexed. "You really shouldn't be too long." If she was surprised that the boy still stood his distance, she said nothing. "I'll leave you two alone." She raised a finger in mock rebuke. "And remember. Not long." Charlie lingered, afraid to confront the boy. Watching her as she walked back to her office, he realized he had begun to sweat. When he turned finally, Tray was watching him with curiosity.

"That's a baby wagon," he said.

"I didn't know you got so big, kiddo."

"I'm the third biggest."

"Just like your old man."

The boy shrugged, not answering. He kicked his heel into the floor.

"I'm Grampa," Charlie said.

"I know that," Tray said.

How long had it been? Charlie thought. Less than two years. Sweat began to ooze down from his hairline.

"Thought I'd come by to say hello," Charlie shrugged. "And to give you that." He pointed to the wagon. "After all, it's yours, Tray. Remember when I painted it? Used to be your father's."

"I remember."

"There's lots of other things, too. Your old basketball." Suddenly he couldn't remember. "Lots of things." His mouth was going dry.

"The lady said you came to say good-bye."

"I told her that just in case she wouldn't let me see you."

The boy hesitated and frowned.

"Mommy said you went away. You and Gramma."

"She said that?"

Tray nodded.

"She said you would be away for a long time."

He felt as if his insides were filling up with some corrosive acid.

"We—we didn't go away," Charlie said haltingly. "We still live in the same house. Do you remember that house?"

"I remember."

"And your daddy?"

"My daddy?"

"My son Chuck. Your daddy."

The boy shifted his weight from foot to foot. The frown deepened on his brow, and he rubbed his nose with the back of his hand.

"You mean the daddy that went away?"

"Your mommy said that, too?"

"Yes."

"Do you miss your daddy?

"The one that went away?"

"My God, yes."

He felt the rising hysteria, the beginning of panic.

The gray-haired woman poked her head out of her office and watched them for a few moments.

"You must let him go back to his class," she said.

"In a minute," he snapped from over his shoulder.

"Now really, Mr.—er—was it Graham?"

"No, not Graham. Waters. Like his." He did not take his eyes off the boy.

He heard her voice closer behind him.

"I resent that attitude, and I'm afraid I'm going to have to ask you to leave."

"As soon as I've said good-bye."

He moved toward the boy and knelt in front of him. Tray looked at him with growing confusion.

"Your grampa loves you," he whispered. Tray said nothing.

"We didn't go away. We live in the same house. Do you remember all the good times we used to have?" He gripped the boy's shoulder. "Do you remember?"

The boy seemed too confused to answer and, without realizing it, Charlie began to shake him.

"You remember the good times we used to have? The fishing? And we were going to get a new sailboat, and we played ball and told jokes and laughed a lot—"

"This has gone far enough," the gray-haired lady said, running back to her office. When she came out again, it was with another, slightly younger woman.

"I've called the child's mother. And this is the principal."

Charlie ignored them both.

"I want to come and visit you, Tray. Would you like to visit me?"

The boy continued to inspect him, then nodded tentatively.

"Can you ask your mommy if you can come and visit us at our house?"

"Can Daddy come, too?"

"Daddy?"

"My daddy, the one that didn't go away. He got me a computer."

"Wouldn't you like to come all by yourself? So it will be just you and me and sometimes Gramma. We really miss you, Tray."

He had the boy in a tight clutch now. At first Tray tried to squirm away, but then gave up.

"It's obvious that the child wants to go back to class. Don't you, Charles?"

"Yes, Miss Flagler," the boy said in the rhythmic way that children address authority.

"Tell your grandfather to let you go, so that you can get back to your class."

He turned and looked at Charlie.

"I don't want to miss my turn, Grampa. You should hear how good I read."

"I'm sure you're terrific. Gramma's got lots of books. When you come over to visit, she'll show them to you. Maybe read some."

He embraced the boy and drew him close to his chest, caressing his head. The boy seemed to be struggling to avoid smelling his breath.

"We miss you, son. We miss you very much. You just don't know how much."

The boy continued to squirm.

"You're squeezing too hard, Grampa."

He heard a woman's clicking footsteps behind him, but he did not turn to see who it was.

"Mommy," the boy screamed.

"I miss you, son. I miss you with all my heart and soul."

"I've tried to get him to go, Mrs. Graham," the principal said.

"It's my fault," the gray-haired lady said apologetically.

He felt a firm hand on his shoulder.

"I want you to release that child this minute," Frances said, her voice rising. "I will not have this."

"I wasn't speaking to you," Charlie said, still not turning to face her. He felt a grip on his arm.

"Please, Charlie. This is no way to behave."

"If you don't mind, I want to visit with my grandson."

"As you can see, your grandson wants to go back to his class," the principal said.

Charlie tried to ignore the cacophony around him, to concentrate on the boy. He loosened his embrace but continued to hold the boy by his upper arms.

"I just wanted to see if you miss your old Gramps," Charlie said. The boy, half-smiling, looked over his shoulder at his mother.

"I—I miss you, Grampa."

"I don't know what to do, Mrs. Graham," the principal said.

By then, another woman, obviously Tray's teacher, opened the door of the classroom, surprised at the drama going on outside.

"The class is waiting, Charles," she said.

"I better get going, Grampa," Tray whispered.

"You must let him go," Frances said, gentler now.

"You'll tell your mom that you want to visit with us, won't you, Tray? Maybe we'll get that sailboat for the summer, a real beauty. What do you say?"

"You may force me to call the authorities," the principal warned.

"It's all right," Frances sighed.

"I'm going to have a lot more time now, Tray," Charlie said. He was drenched with perspiration. "Now, Gramma and I are expecting you, right?"

The boy looked at his mother. Charlie embraced him again, then released his arms and stood up as the gray-haired woman took him by the hand and led him to his teacher. She patted him on the head and quickly closed the door behind him. Suddenly, he remembered the wagon and started after him, pulling it. The gray-haired woman barred his way.

"You can't—"

"He forgot the wagon."

"I'll see that he gets it, Charlie," Frances said. Finally, he turned to look at her. Her face recalled reality, and he felt suddenly exhausted and empty.

"I'm sorry for this," the principal said. "We handled it badly."

"There was nothing you could do," Frances said.

Charlie looked toward the classroom. He felt trapped and helpless, a fool. For a moment he felt disoriented.

"Will you be all right?" the principal asked Frances, who nodded. Charlie felt her eyes burning into him. He turned his own away in embarrassment. He tried to say something, but his throat seemed to have closed on him.

When they were alone in the corridor, Frances shook her head.

"There was no need for this, Charlie," she said. "You disturbed the child. It wasn't fair to him."

"I just wanted to . . ." When he could not go on, she nodded. "I understand that. Truly I do."

"No you don't," he stammered.

"You're just hurting yourself. Don't you see, it's best for him. He's confused by the intrusion. I don't want that. He's been happy. Adjusted. He doesn't need this. Can you understand that?"

"He's my grandson. I just wanted to see him."

"I don't want him to have to contend with this. He's doing beautifully. He has a good life. His father—Peter—loves him. Leave him alone. Perhaps someday the time will come. But it isn't now."

Reality in full force had come hurtling back by then. The turmoil inside had been replaced by a dull ache. The stupid, blind hopefulness that had driven him here was disintegrating.

"I miss him, Frances," he said, coughing into his fist.

"I'm sure you do. But think of him, his welfare."

"You don't understand."

"I do. I really do."

He felt the walls closing in, trapping him. He had to get out. Turning, he felt his knees unlock as he began to move away.

"I won't let this happen again, Charlie. I'll do anything to stop it." She caught up with him and spun him around, forcing him to look at her. "I swear it. Even if it means the police. I want my child left alone. Do you understand that?"

He could not find words to answer, hurrying away, gaining speed as he moved toward the door. Opening it, he looked back suddenly and saw only the little wagon. But he did not break down in tears until he reached the main highway back to Baltimore.

Happy birthday, he muttered to himself. As always, that memory seared him, bringing back the anger and the pain. But by then he had explained it to himself, although the disappointment lingered and festered. Of course the child would not have been enthusiastic, given the fact that he was certain Frances had tried to erase Tray's memory of him and of his natural father. Wasn't that part of what this fight was all about?

The rain, instead of abating, was getting worse. He rinsed out his coffee cup, then looked at the clock. The morning was disappearing rapidly and there was still no call from the lawyer. Again, he picked up the phone.

"I'll see if he's in," the receptionist said.

Another match to dry tinder, Charlie thought. Why can't they tell the truth? Of course he's in. His finger tapped against the kitchen wall. Time ticked away like dripping molasses.

"Yes, Mr. Waters." Forte's voice was smoothly officious.

"I was expecting your call," Charlie stammered.

"You were?" The lawyer sounded surprised.

"The two weeks are up. They were up yesterday."

There was a long silence.

"Oh yes. Apparently there was no response."

"Not to me," Charlie said with growing hostility.

"Then I guess we have no choice but to file."

"Whatever it is, I think it should be done quickly. She mustn't be allowed to get away with this."

"It won't happen overnight," the lawyer said. "And it's sure to get messy."

"I don't care," Charlie said.

"In that case, I'll file the petition."

"As fast as you can."

"They could still throw it out on a technicality. I told you our case is weak."

"No it's not," he blurted, noting the long silence that followed.

"I just want you to be prepared," the lawyer said calmly. "I wouldn't want to mislead you. The laws of adoption are quite tight—"

"You said all that. He's my grandson, and one way or another, I'm not going to lose him."

"I understand, Mr. Waters. I'll file today."

"I'm not kidding around."

"I'm very aware of that."

His mouth had a metallic taste, and he noted that his heartbeat had accelerated. Deep in his gut he felt an overwhelming sense of anticipation and danger. The reactions seemed familiar, and he searched his mind for some thread of memory. Combat. That was it. The moment before the moment of truth. But he did not tell this to the lawyer.

Chapter 7

FRANCES AND PETER sat in the lawyer's conference room on one side of the long, blond wood table waiting for Henry Peck to arrive. If there was anything to be thankful for in this absurd situation, Frances decided, it was that the lawyer's office was in Columbia, only ten minutes from her house. From the beginning, she had had a nagging fear that they would have to go to downtown Baltimore, which would have meant more time away from Mark. Being involved in these proceedings was not exactly the most profitable way for a pregnant nursing mother with household obligations to spend her time.

She looked at her watch and expelled a noisy sigh of frustration.

"I haven't got the time for this," she said. "No matter what, I intend to be back for the baby's twelve-thirty feeding."

"But you left a bottle with the baby-sitter," Peter said.

"He still likes mine better."

Peter shrugged and tapped his fingers on the table.

"It's not exactly convenient for me either."

"I know, darling." She patted his other hand, relenting. "It's the nausea making me irritable."

"Maybe it's too much for you. I can always handle it alone."

"I'm afraid it's really more my problem than yours."

"Now that's not fair," he said.

"What's fair?" she asked, offering a smile to chase the sudden seriousness.

"I just don't want you aggravated," he said, picking up her hand and kissing it.

"No one said it would be easy," she sighed, slipping a dry cracker from her purse, nibbling it, and washing it down with coffee from the cone-shaped cup in front of her.

Henry Peck rushed in, full of apologies, taking his place at the head of the table. He was a big man with a pink face that continued its color over his bald pate. A huge paunch bulged under his vest, impressively hung with a double looping chain attached to a gold watch that he clicked open, shaking his head.

"I originally came here to work less, not harder," he said,

opening the file he had brought with him, quickly reviewing the material. Reading, he rubbed his nose with the back of his hand. He kept his hair longish along the rim of his pate, which would have been eccentric enough without the string tie and round, steel-rimmed glasses. "As I said on the phone, we'll have to answer the petition. We can't ignore it."

"But have they got a case?" Peter asked.

"Not in my opinion. The adoption laws of Maryland are quite strong."

"Then why are they suing?" Frances asked.

"Anyone can sue anyone."

"Even if the law is against it?" Frances pressed.

"Even then. Which is why I'm going to ask for a technical hearing. We might just get it thrown out of court right away."

"That would be great," Peter said.

"And if we don't?" Frances persisted.

"We go to court."

"And then?"

"They present their case. We refute. In my opinion the law is with us. But it is not unusual for a judge to be swayed by emotion or a powerful presentation. Which only means that we have to appeal. In this case, I can't believe we could lose on appeal."

"But if their case is so weak, why are they suing?" Peter asked.

Peck shrugged.

"Desperation. Harassment. Who knows what people's motives are? The fact is that there are now forty-nine states that have laws saying that grandparents have a right to be heard. Grey clout. That's what it is. Organizations of older people showing their muscle. Seventy-five percent of all older Americans are grandparents. And most legislatures are made up of older people, too. Not to mention judges."

"That sounds ominous," Peter said.

"It's reality. But the law is still the law. Did they try to protest the adoption?"

"No."

"That was their first mistake."

"But the judge can still decide in their favor, force these visits?"

"I'm not saying it can't happen. There are examples in other states—New York, for example. They have a law now that deals with cases like yours, where adoption has taken place."

"But this is Maryland," Frances said.

"That doesn't mean they can't cite situations in other states. I'll protest, of course, but the judge is the judge."

Frances had a sudden sinking feeling that only intensified her nausea.

"I can't believe this is happening," Frances said. It had been a repetitious comment on her part, but it exasperated her to know that such things could occur.

"Believe it, Mrs. Graham."

Because he was large, Peck also seemed overbearing and blunt. Peter had told her that he had researched the various lawyers who dealt with domestic matters and Peck was considered an excellent choice, and that it was no coincidence that he was in Columbia. The upwardly mobile, middle-class planned community had the perfect demographics for domestic difficulties. Peck was no fool, Peter assured her.

"I want only what's best for my son," Frances said, addressing the lawyer with what she hoped was the appearance of uncompromising resolution.

"Our son," Peter corrected.

"That's still the rule of law, folks. The best interest of the child is always the major consideration in a matter of equity dealing with such issues. It's on that point that we go to work."

"They're being selfish," Frances said. "They're not thinking at all about my—our—child's welfare."

The big lawyer sucked in his breath.

"You're right on the money. That's the issue. Will the visits of the grandparents be good or bad for"—he looked at the petition—"for Charles Everett Waters the third." He scratched his bald pate.

"I see you didn't change the boy's name."

"He did know his father," Peter said. "We certainly didn't want to take that away from him. Did we, Frances?"

Frances shook her head.

"Do you think it will have a bearing on the case?" Peter asked.

"You can't tell. But I doubt it. Actually, I think we can show that you did not want to obliterate the boy's past completely, weakening the grandparent's contention that their visits will enhance the child's interests. Our job will be to show that these visits will have a deleterious effect on the boy."

"How will you do that?" Peter asked.

"That's what I get paid for," the lawyer said, smiling.

"What about the effect on the grandparents?" Frances asked.

They could, she knew, portray themselves as worthy of compassion. Indeed, they could appear very sympathetic. At times, she felt that sympathy for them, and it hurt and made her feel guilty. But she was certain that her decision was in Tray's best interest. No, she had no doubts about that. Otherwise, why would she be here?

"That's a good question, Mrs. Graham. But the courts are still deciding in favor of the child's ultimate welfare. And there is still the powerful argument that a mother"— he turned pointedly to Peter —"and a father know what's best for their child."

"Thank God for that," Peter said.

"But it doesn't mean we can let down our guard. Judges are always setting new precedents. At the moment there is no case at issue on this point in our state. But there could be. It could happen in this case. I mention it not to alarm you, but to give you all aspects of the downside. I'm just saying that it's creeping into decisions in other states, and it's possible that the judge could look in that direction." He rubbed his nose. "So far, it has never happened in Maryland. The welfare of the child is still the paramount consideration." It seemed to her that he had unwittingly ventured too far out into muddy water and was now backtracking.

"So the judge is everything," Frances said.

"I'm afraid so."

"How can a judge know what is best for my child?"

"That is one contention, Mrs. Graham, that you must never, ever allow, even in your most secret thoughts. Think of the judge as God. It will help you understand why we are here and what we must do. Our job is to convince God that we are on the side of the angels and that your dead husband's parents are on the side of the devil."

Frances shivered at the image, but she said nothing.

The lawyer looked at her through his round steel frames, his eyes glowing like hot coals.

"Why then, Mrs. Graham, will you not let your deceased husband's parents visit their natural grandchild?"

She hadn't expected the question, nor the lawyer's deadpan expression. She frowned and took a deep breath.

"You mean why would their visits be bad for my child?"

"I'm afraid that you would not have the luxury to rephrase the question in a court of law," the lawyer said pedantically, his expression rigid.

She looked at Peter.

"I see," Frances began haltingly, understanding the mock drama that the lawyer had initiated. "Because they would confuse the child," she said, clearing her throat in preparation for assuming the role of witness. "He has a father now, and his father's parents are loving grandparents. I do not believe it would be in his interests to consider himself different in any way from the other children. Also, before my marriage to Mr. Graham, they had begun to treat him as if he were their dead son. I did not think that healthy. Nor do I believe that the ideas they used to bring up Chuck—my first husband—would be beneficial to my child in his present environment. Especially my ex-father-in-law, who is possessive and very compulsive."

"So you say their influence would be detrimental?" the lawyer asked, with exaggerated aggressiveness.

"Yes," she said, assuming an air of satisfied finality.

"Do they drink? Have they been physically abusive? Sexually loose? Irresponsible in any way? Have they been unstable? Mentally incompetent? Do they fight often? What are their character flaws? Are there any witnesses to their meanness? Have they been demonstrably unkind?"

Her head whirled with the staccato speed of his questions. They seemed crude and outlandish.

"I couldn't be specific," she stammered. "No. I—I can't say—"

"So they are essentially decent people?" the lawyer shot back before she could finish. She realized suddenly that she was responding too swiftly and forced herself to become more deliberative.

"It depends on the way you define that," she said.

"All right, how about well-meaning?" the lawyer pressed.

"Well-meaning?" She tossed it around her mind. "Maybe from their point of view."

"So they mean well?"

"I suppose you might say that. . . ." she answered grudgingly.

"I'm saying it. Are they or are they not well-meaning, Mrs. Graham?"

"I think this is going too far." Peter interrupted.

"No. Please, Peter. It's important." She looked directly into the lawyer's eyes. "Yes. They are well-meaning."

"Then why don't you want them to visit your son?"

"Whose side are you on, counselor?" Peter asked. Peck ignored Peter's protest.

But before she could conceive another answer, the lawyer was at her again.

"On the phone your husband told me that the child's paternal grandfather paid a visit to the boy at school."

"He was extremely disruptive," Frances answered quickly. She was beginning to feel slightly dizzy, and the nausea was returning.

"Oh?" the lawyer said, shamming his surprise. "What was the boy's reaction?"

"He was very upset."

"How so? Did he become withdrawn, hyperactive, disobedient, emotionally difficult, sleepless, physically ill?"

"I can't be specific. He was"— she paused, searching for the right word —"disturbed." She felt Peter step protectively beside her, and she squeezed his hand to quiet him. It was important to play this game, to hold herself together, to prepare herself. In a courtroom, she realized, it would be far worse.

"What were the symptoms of this disturbance?"

She looked toward Peter, who frowned.

"Confused then. Maybe inside he felt a sense of divided loyalties. I'm not sure. I only sense that it didn't do him any good."

"That is not a very wise answer," the lawyer said, gentler now. Perhaps he had observed her growing tension. Had the blood drained from her face? Had her voice weakened? Her head was spinning. "I think that a much stronger manifestation of disturbance must be stated."

"Like what?" Frances asked.

"Something like"— Peck hesitated —"like some difficulty that the child experienced immediately after the visit. Something tangible. Like bed-wetting or profoundly disturbing nightmares, loss of appetite, lack of concentration at school, listlessness. Aberrant behavior, temper tantrums, visible depression."

"There was nothing like that. Perhaps I should have been more observant," Frances whispered. She felt like gagging.

"He was extremely withdrawn as far as I was concerned, as though he was wary of me, frightened. I saw a definite change in our relationship," Peter interjected. His comment surprised her. She hadn't noticed such specifics. "A father knows his son."

"Good. That's good, Mr. Graham."

Peter nodded, pleased with himself, then turned to Frances and smiled. Frances wasn't sure what it all meant, but the lawyer did make it sound encouraging.

"I hadn't realized it would be so, well, complicated," she said.

"Worse than that," the lawyer said. "It's a kind of war. And in this war, lots of the participants come away dead or wounded."

"As long as it isn't Tray," Frances said.

"I just wanted to give you a preview, Mrs. Graham. These will be some of the issues. Their lawyer will be far more aggressive, I can assure you. He's tough, and he'll go for the jugular. If you want to avoid the lumps, then you might as well let the grandparents visit," Peck said, pausing to observe her pointedly. "And stop wasting your money."

She felt a growing powerlessness under the lawyer's inspective gaze, which only fortified her will to resist. But the effort was increasing her bodily indisposition. She was beginning to see spotted floating images as her nausea increased.

"They're the ones who started this," Frances said. "And I'm not going to surrender. Not under any circumstances."

"They must also know what they're up against," Peter said. "Maybe they've decided that since they're miserable, why not try to make us miserable."

"I'm sure they've been well advised." Peck shrugged. "They probably feel that they have nothing to lose but money." He rubbed his nose. "And speaking of money, this is not going to be cheap."

"I'm prepared to pay," Frances said.

"In emotional terms as well?" the lawyer asked.

"Whatever it takes."

She had already begun to pay, she thought. She felt terrible. A layer of cold perspiration had formed on her face. She reached into her pocketbook and pulled out a handkerchief.

"Is there anything wrong?" Peck asked.

"My God, she's pale as a ghost," Peter cried.

"Just a little water," Frances managed to say. She felt on the verge of a fainting spell. The lawyer punched a button and ordered a secretary to hurry in with a glass of water.

Frances drew out another cracker from her pocketbook, but before she bit into it, she gagged. The secretary came in with a paper cone of water. Peter took it and lifted it to her lips. She drank a few quick swallows and felt slightly better.

"I'm sorry," she said weakly.

"She's pregnant," Peter said. "It's so damned unfair to make her go through this, especially now."

"Pregnant?" The lawyer's reaction was a sudden concentration, a honed alertness. "How many months?"

"Two, we think," Peter said, attending to his wife. He took Frances's handkerchief, dipped it in the remaining water, and pressed it to her temples.

Peck rubbed his nose in contemplation.

"It certainly raises the question of whether or not she would be up for a trial. This little exercise is nothing compared to the emotional trauma that can be generated by a trial. It's a factor to be weighed carefully."

Frances gulped a few fresh breaths of air and felt more stable, no longer afraid of fainting.

"I'll be fine," Frances said weakly.

"Are you sure?" Peter asked, resoaking the handkerchief. "We have to think of you—and the other children."

His reaction brought her up short. Was he thinking more of his two natural children than of Tray? She felt the thought an unworthy one.

"It's something to consider," the lawyer said. He seemed to be probing, looking for weak spots.

"I'm sure," she whispered. Was she really? She wondered if she was overreacting to her past, seeking a punishment far too severe for the crime. What crime? She became confused, disoriented.

"I don't want to go ahead and then find that you are not up to pursuing it. I want to be honest, scrupulously honest. This case will drain you, Mrs. Graham. You really should give it some deep thought."

"But I have," Frances mumbled.

"That's enough strain for one day, Mrs. Graham," the lawyer said. "I'm sorry if I put you through an ordeal."

"No sense pulling punches," she shrugged. The lawyer stood up and shook their hands in turn.

Frances rose, still a bit dizzy, her heart pounding. She felt Peter's firm arm buttressing her.

"Think it over, both of you," Peck said, as his eyes studied them through the round lenses. What was he looking for? she wondered. Peter started to lead her out of the conference room. The lawyer's voice made them pause.

"Of course, a nursing mother who was also obviously pregnant would have a profound effect on the judge," he said. "As they say, all's fair in love and war."

In the ladies' room, she dry heaved, then dabbed away the perspiration and washed her face in cold water. Then she had another cracker and washed it down with scoops of water from the tap. Soon, she felt somewhat better, although through her discomfort she did feel some vague stirrings of anger and resentment. Mostly they were directed against her former in-laws, but there were others not entirely blameless. Herself included. She wondered, too, what effect all this emotional trauma would have on the baby growing inside her. Hadn't she read somewhere that emotional upsets during pregnancy could have profound effects on the fetus?

Cupping her breasts, she also wondered what effect all this might have on her milk, which had flowed steadily and copiously and on which Mark was thriving. Each proliferating danger only fueled more animosity. First Chuck, now this, she thought bitterly, glancing suddenly at herself in the mirror, not certain if she truly liked what she saw.

Silently they drove home. Before she moved to get out, Peter kissed her softly on the lips.

"It's worth thinking about," he said. "You're my first priority."

"I don't understand."

"I mean if we can't get their petition thrown out. I don't think I'd want you to be put through that. It really is something to consider."

She turned to look at his face. He was troubled, his brow furrowed, and his hazel eyes moist with tension and concern.

"I have considered it," she said firmly.

"I'd never forgive myself if something should go wrong."

"You mean the baby."

"I mean everything. I—I love my family. I love you. I want things to be right, that's all. It's not too much to ask."

"But I thought it was you who wanted a fresh start, to bury the past."

"Not if it means—well—pain. I never expected it to come to this."

"And what about Tray?"

"Maybe it won't matter as much as we think."

"They're taking us to court, for crying out loud. That's a very drastic step. And haven't we been happy? Peter, it's been wonderful, wonderful for Tray, for us, for Mark, and soon for the new baby. Your folks have been fabulous. Why can't they leave well enough alone? You don't fix things that aren't broken."

"I'm just worried about you."

"There's more to it than just me." She felt a brief twinge of anger.

"I mean us. All of us."

"I'm not going to let other people decide things for me, especially as they concern my child."

"Our child," he corrected gently.

"I don't want him treated differently from the others."

"Of course not."

"I don't ever want him to feel that he's less loved than the others. Ever." She felt herself going too far, but she couldn't stop herself. Memories of old longings and loneliness danced in her mind. An image of her own lost father surfaced vaguely, his arms around her, his beard scratchy, his deep, soft voice soothing her, kissing away some brief flash of pain. Then bitterness intruded as she remembered the long empty nights of Chuck's absences, wandering in the black void of rejection and despair. They never let me have him, she thought.

"That's not fair." She heard Peter's voice, but it seemed distant. "You know how I feel about that child."

"I know what you say you feel about him." Instantly, she regretted the outburst. She moved closer to him, and they embraced. "Forgive me, darling."

He kissed away the moistness on her cheeks.

"Why couldn't they just leave us alone?" he whispered.

"They just don't understand. They never really did. Not about Chuck or me. Or anything."

"You can't blame me for worrying."

"I'll be fine, Peter. Really I will. It's just our baby letting us know how she feels."

He put his hand on her belly and rubbed.

"Well, she had better behave herself."

They kissed, and she slid out of the car, conscious that he had lingered and was watching her walk into the house. Despite the affection, she felt a certain tentativeness in his commitment to the cause, and it troubled her.

The comfort of Mark nursing beside her soon chased away her anxiety. There was nothing more tranquilizing than this experience of delicious dependency, of selfless giving of one's substance to one's own creation. She caressed the child's face, kissing his eyes. Nothing she had ever done in her life was so profoundly hers, so fulfilling, so joyously satisfying as motherhood. Who but a mother could know what was best for her child?

Finally satiated, the baby drowsed. She burped him and let him remain beside her on the bed, drawing his little fingers to her lips, kissing them gently. What defined a woman more than motherhood? she asked herself. How could fatherhood compare?

Another time intruded, dredged up from the swamp of memory, perhaps tossed out in the recent inner storm. She caught a flashing image of the little airless bedroom two flights above the bakery, permeated by the ubiquitous odor of baking bread, which had become as oppressive as the dawn-to-sundown days working in Uncle Walter's bakery where the maddening staccato of her uncle's orders became fearsome, simply by repetition. He was kindly, never raised his voice, but his unceasing demands clearly delineated the extent of her debt. And she had waited for the moment of escape.

Her freedom had come in the form of Chuck, her golden knight errant. There he was, climbing the metal steps of the tower, a brave and graceful figure, alone and unafraid, ascending into the morning mist. He wore a plaid shirt, yellow with blue squares, that matched his cobalt blue eyes and the yellow-gold of his hair. He was tall, made even taller by the high heels of his muddy, scuffed cowboy boots into which he had stuffed the leg ends of his jeans. Slim-hipped and tight-butted, he did not seem vain about his beauty, or so it appeared to her. She was flattered by his obvious interest in her. She wasn't a beauty by a long shot, but she did have a decent figure and, people told her, lovely chestnut hair and good skin. Some said she was cute, although she never could be sure.

Caught on the razor's edge between wariness of, and desperation for, any kind of returned affection, she was transported easily from flirtation to a heavier commitment in a very short time. In less than a month from the moment Chuck had walked into her life, they had become inseparable. Even in retrospect, she could not deny to herself the power of the attraction between them. Whatever it was, it wasn't love, not the kind of devoted, unselfish, and dedicated passionate contract that was between her and Peter.

Chuck was lovely and gentle and quiet during those first months, and her memories were untainted by her later bitterness. She had shrugged off her disappointment in the physical side of their relationship, attributing its failure to some fault of her own. In retrospect, she faulted herself for encouraging him into an early marriage. Perhaps she did it simply because his father had been opposed to it? And there was always the pressure of her potential liberation from Uncle Walter's yoke, even though her new job made it possible to trade servitude in the bakery for cash. In those days she'd had neither the confidence nor the experience to analyze motives or events.

As near as she could figure, she got pregnant on her honeymoon in the Poconos. Even in those days, she had eschewed the then current birth control methods, trusting to luck and the calendar. Unfortunately, her regular cycle had given her not the slightest margin for error—as her present condition attested. The trip had been a gift from her in-laws. She considered it a peace offering, something tendered more out of guilt than sincerity. So, even in the beginning she had been suspicious, as if they were both standing by, especially her father-in-law, waiting for their golden boy's love for her to burn out.

To be fair, Chuck and she had promised each other that they would not start a family for a few years. She still had her job at the radio station, and Chuck was determined to save some money. They rented an inexpensive one-bedroom apartment in Dundalk and began to buy furniture on time. It seemed a sensible way for a young couple to start out. Chuck's father helped him buy a small secondhand Toyota. She hadn't liked the idea, but it wasn't easy to live without a car and she hadn't protested. In fact, in those days she never really protested anything. Where the wind blew, she went.

In those early days the only time that Chuck and she were apart was when his father took him on their male-only hunting and fishing trips. Molly told her it was something she had better get used to. Unfortunately, she never had. It was after one of those hunting trips that Chuck had made the suggestion that she abort the baby. That had certainly turned out to be a reliable clue to the future. By then, of course, she was trapped.

"Isn't it a little ahead of schedule?" he had said. "I was hoping we might be a little better set before we had a kid." He had a point, of course. He was not yet twenty-one. And she had just turned eighteen. "Maybe we should fix it."

"Fix it?"

"You know."

The idea had frightened her.

"It'll bring us luck," she had said. "You'll see."

"We're too damned young."

"It's not like I did it by myself."

"But you promised."

"So did you."

"The timing is no good, baby. That's all I'm saying. Hell, we're still kids ourselves. We hardly make enough to pay for everything now."

"I'll be working right up until I deliver."

"You could have at least been more careful."

"I don't think I should take all the blame."

"I suppose not," he had muttered.

"It will be great, Chuck, you'll see. I promise."

"I was just trying to be practical."

"Practical? You're asking that we do away with our baby." She paused and inspected him. "Are you sure this is your own idea?"

"Whose, then?"

"Like your father's."

"His! Hell, he's the one who warned me in the first place. He'd be the last person I'd tell."

"I don't care whose suggestion it is," she said firmly. "I will not give up my baby. Never. And you should be ashamed of yourself for suggesting it."

"Maybe I'm just not ready for responsibilities. Maybe that's it."

"We have no choice, Chuck."

"Actually, we do. It's a simple deal—doesn't hurt, they tell me."

"They? Who is they?"

"I mean I read about it, heard talk."

He hadn't yet looked her in the eye, and she spent the conversation angling herself to confront him.

"You're talking about our baby. We're married. It's not like I'm in trouble or something."

"I mean, there's got to be plenty more where that one came from."

All her life people had accused Frances of being too stubborn. She never could see their point. It wasn't even a question of principles. She just couldn't bring herself to do things she didn't believe in. Not that she didn't do things against her will. She had hated living with Uncle Walter and working in the store, but that seemed more of a debt to him for being nice to her mother and her when her father had been killed. Some things she had to do for different reasons.

"You can't mean what you're saying."

"Then let's just forget it."

"I'm going to have this baby, no matter what."

"Let's just drop it."

"The thought that you even mentioned it is terrible. Can't you understand that this is not just my baby? It's yours, too."

She wondered if he ever truly understood that.

"I'm really sorry," he said finally, ending the discussion. It never came up again between them. Of course, she had never really accepted the apology. Nor had she forgotten the conversation.

Then one day, Chuck came home to tell her had landed a job working the oil rigs offshore in the North Sea off Scotland. He hadn't told her that he had even applied for the job.

"Are you serious?" she had asked, dumbfounded.

"The pay is fabulous," he had countered. "And with the baby coming, we sure could use it."

"But I'll be alone."

"Just for a few months at a time. No big deal."

"I don't think that's fair."

"It's not a question of fair, baby. It's necessary. You can quit your job and really rest until the kid comes. And when he's born, you won't have to work. In fact, I don't want you to work. The old man thinks it's a damned good idea."

"He knows?"

"Sure he knows. He's my father."

"And I'm your wife."

"What's that got to do with it?"

She had wanted to say that if he truly loved her he wouldn't be doing this, but she had held back. She had become afraid—afraid for herself, afraid for her baby.

"I don't know what to do," she confessed to Molly. She had met her in the coffee shop across from the school, the day after

Chuck had broken the news. Molly, of course, had already been informed by Charlie.

"You mustn't let him go," Molly said firmly. "You're his wife. You've got to be firm about it."

"You're his mother."

"Unfortunately, that hasn't counted for much."

"You let Charlie influence him too much."

"That's an old story. He is very attached to Chuck."

"With a heavy chain."

"Fathers and sons. They baffle me."

"He says it's because of the baby, and that his father thinks it's a good idea." She remembered that she had tried to hide her animosity.

"He's thinking of the money. Men think like that, like hunter providers."

"I'm thinking of my marriage. Of lonely nights and a baby coming."

"Then put your foot down," Molly said. "Can't you say something?"

"I have."

"Try harder."

"He wouldn't do this if he really loved me."

Molly had hesitated, and Frances could see that she was trying to frame a careful response.

"I'm sure it's not that, Frances. But who knows about a man's psyche? Maybe he feels inadequate to the responsibility. Maybe by proving himself, earning big money, facing danger . . ."

"Danger?"

"I don't want to be an alarmist. He is my only child, dear. There have been accidents on those offshore platforms."

It surprised Frances to see what Molly's priorities really were. For her part, she was less worried about the danger. She had seen the grace and caution of his climb. Molly must have also understood the different ways they looked at things, and she tried to quickly bridge the gap.

"I don't really understand it, Frances. Sometimes I think that the gulf that separates men and women is too mammoth to understand." She had reached out and taken Frances's hand in hers. "I would not like to be a young pregnant bride waiting for her baby alone. I mean, you know that Charlie and I will stand by you. If you need anything, you know we'll be there. I want you also to know that I think it's wrong for Chuck to do this and I feel awful about it. But I haven't been able to stop it, I'm afraid."

"And Charlie won't."

"It's not that he won't. He thinks it's self-sacrificing and courageous for Chuck to do this. They just don't see it our way. Look, we were married just before Charlie went overseas, and I didn't see him again for three years. Three long years."

"But there was a war."

"Maybe that's the problem with young men like Chuck. There's no war for them. They need the adventure. Something like that. I don't understand it. There are lots of things I don't understand about men."

"I won't ever forgive him."

Molly seemed alarmed. Perhaps, she thought, she had gone too far in her confidence.

"I don't think you should overreact. Just try your best to get him to stay."

"I don't mean Chuck."

"Not Chuck?"

"Charlie. I won't ever forgive Charlie."

They had parted that day with hugs and embraces. But no amount of persuasion, tears, or vehement protest by either her or Molly could stop Chuck from leaving.

In a last ditch effort, she had made an attempt to get Charlie to intervene. She had gone over to speak to him. It galled her now to remember how humbled she had felt, unable to hide her desperation.

"I don't care about the money. I just want my husband near me."

She knew he felt awkward and uncomfortable. And in his own mind, she was sure he was being sympathetic and understanding, even compassionate.

"I know it's hard, Frances, and I really feel for you. I hope you believe me about that. But I really think you're exaggerating my influence. I've always taught him to be his own man."

"But you agree with his decision," she had protested. "He listens to you."

"Where did you get that idea? I wasn't exactly thrilled about your getting married so young. He didn't listen to me then. You can't blame me for your getting pregnant and putting this kind of pressure on the boy. Can you, Frances? Listen, I'm all for both you kids. I want to see you happy and secure. Like any other father. But you've got to look at it from his point of view, too."

"And the baby's."

"Sure, the baby. You don't know what it costs to raise a baby nowadays. And there'll be more. At least, I hope so. You'll be making up for those we never had. I'm with you, Frances. As long as we're around, you don't have to worry about a thing. But Chuck's got to do what he's got to do. You don't understand that about men. He'll draw big money and that will be great for his confidence. And he'll be learning a helluva skill. Better than being caught in these construction slumps."

"But I'll be alone. And he might not even be here when the baby is born."

"We'll be there. Molly and I will be there. You can bet on that."

"I want Chuck to be there. He's the father."

At that point, she couldn't hold back and began to cry. He had taken her in his arms and patted her back.

"You must understand. A man's got to do what he's got to do. Chuck is only thinking about you and the baby. I can vouch for that. You think it's going to be easy for him to be away from the people he loves? I was away for three years, facing hell itself, never knowing if I was ever going to get back. At least nobody will be shooting at Chuck. He'll make enough to tide you over, then maybe stay home."

"It's wrong."

"You'll get over it, Frances. I know you will. You're not going to stay blubbery and depressed. You've got to think of the baby. He's not going to want to come into this world into the arms of an unhappy mother. You'll be fine. I know you will. Him, too."

"But it will hurt so much to be alone," she had said, humbled and despairing.

"I don't think Chuck would like to hear that," Charlie had said, gripping her shoulders and holding her at arm's length, looking into her eyes. "That certainly won't make it easy for him. Why don't you try telling him that it's a great idea? Hell, he's doing it for you and the baby. It won't be a bed of roses, you know. It's stormy as hell and he'll be living mostly with a bunch of tough older guys. He's got his own problems ahead of him."

The futility of her pleading had finally dawned on her. They were simply talking different languages.

Still, she had not given up and made her last appeal directly to Chuck. They had gone to Haussners, a German restaurant noted for its floor-to-ceiling art. It was Chuck's idea, a farewell dinner. For them, it was enormously expensive.

"It's gonna be nice to have a few bucks for a change," Chuck had said, ordering a bottle of white wine.

"I don't care about the money," she had muttered. It had become her principal refrain by then.

"You're not going to ruin things on my last night, are you, Frances?"

"Don't go, Chuck," she pleaded. "There's still time."

"I've signed the papers. You can't expect me to go back on my word."

"I don't care about that."

"Well, I do. A man's word is everything. Besides, I know it's best, you'll see."

"I love you, Chuck. I can't bear to think about being alone. We've only been married four months. Doesn't it bother you to leave me?"

"Of course it does. You just don't understand." She saw him shift inwardly, saw his mood change. She had remembered his father's words.

"A man's got to do what he's got to do," she mimicked.

"Now you've got it." He had failed to see the sarcasm. "I need to do this."

"Would you have done it if I had gotten rid of the baby?"

"That's bad talk, Frances," he said with growing impatience. "It's all set. You just handle it. I'll be back before you can blink your eyes."

The memory disintegrated. She had been prescient, had seen a glimpse of the future. Even then she had known that he had left her forever. His death had merely been the signature on the writ of separation. But the old anger returned. He had deserted her. He hadn't been there when Tray was born. And his contribution to his son's welfare had been an occasional toy. As for the big money that foreign employment had promised, she had seen precious little of that, as well.

"What do you do with it?" she had asked him once on his infrequent and indifferent returns.

"Living is expensive in those places," he had explained. She suspected how most of it was spent.

"Are you all right?"

It was Peter's voice. She had put the baby back in his crib and fallen asleep, and was surprised at suddenly seeing Peter's face loom in front of her. She felt the breeze of his breath.

"I couldn't concentrate. So I decided to knock off for the rest of the day." He lay down beside her, and they embraced. "You are first in my life, darling. Anything that troubles you troubles me. I just want to be sure."

"About what?"

"That we're doing the right thing for you. For us."

She knew exactly what he meant.

"We decided that from the beginning, didn't we, Peter?"

"I hadn't realized . . ." He kissed her hair and reached over her to touch the sleeping baby. "I wanted to draw a circle around us, to protect us." She felt his breath flutter against her cheeks.

"Well, you have. And it's worked."

"That it has."

He caressed the baby's bare arms, then moved lower and laid his head against her belly. She gathered his head in her arms and pressed him to her.

"You've been fabulous, Peter. I've never been happier. And I don't want anything to spoil it."

She held him against her, her heart full of gratitude and contentment. Anything, any force, that endangered this bond was the enemy, she thought. And her ex-in-laws could be a destructive force. Not with evil intent, she told herself quickly. But intent didn't matter. Their presence was simply not required. Not by Tray and not by her.

"They're not necessary, Peter," Frances whispered. "Not to us. We have to stand up to them. It's our choice, not theirs."

"Of course I agree. I just want to be sure you're up to it."

She sensed her rising militancy. Drawing Peter up, she looked at his face, then kissed him deeply.

"As long as you're beside me, I'm up to anything," she whispered.

His hands moved over her body, and she reached out to return his caresses in kind.

"Especially now," she said.

Chapter 8

CHARLIE hadn't told Molly that he intended to spend the day in Crisfield. She would have been curious, of course, and might have suggested that he wait for the weekend so that they both could go. He did not want her to go with him. This was something he had to do by himself. Nor did he care to worry her any more than she already was about his state of mind.

But suddenly he had gotten it into his head that it was important for him to go back to the little town on the bay where he had been born and raised. He supposed it was not uncommon for a man to go back to his roots when life in the outside world got too rough to handle. Once, he couldn't wait to get away from Crisfield, the tight little world of familiar faces and predictable happenings. Had it been a wrong turn in the road? Was there something he had left there that he needed now? He wasn't sure. In fact, he wasn't sure about anything.

Standing now on the municipal dock in the diamond-bright November sun, which bounced spears of blinding light off the choppy gray bay waters, he was sorry he had come. Where once he had worn the comforting label of being one of the Waters boys, the little one, now he was just another expatriate who had come back to mourn for the sweet old times, savor youthful memories, and bathe in sentiment and nostalgia.

It was not exactly the idea he had had in mind. He had expected to be replenished, spiritually rejuvenated, as he had been that day years ago when Chuck and he had roamed the town and he had pointed out the physical landmarks of his youth. In recalling the experience that morning, he had decided that it was one of the most delicious moments of his life, to be ranked with the time that Molly had confessed that their love was mutual, and with that first day when he had come home from the war.

What he had been doing for the past few weeks was to collect these good moments, hoping that happy memories might chase away the gloom and depression that had taken hold of him and, according to Molly, were damaging his judgment and behavior.

"Stop dwelling on all the hurts, Charlie," she had pleaded with him. "You'll ruin any chance we have of winning our case. And Tray."

It had become the central theme of her campaign to shake him out of his depression. And she did not have to expand very much on the threat. He had already made an ass of himself with his lawyer, with Frances, and with Tray.

"Maybe we should dump the idea?"

"Give up all hope of seeing Tray?"

She seemed to have gained the steadiness that he had lost.

"Maybe if we stop pressing her, she'll come around."

"That's what I thought, remember?" She had paused thoughtfully. "I don't think so now."

"What changed your mind?" he asked, with a deliberate touch of sarcasm.

"The facts. It's been two years, now. She's moving farther and farther away from us. Tray, too. Another year or so and he might forget what we look like. Instead of getting used to it, Charlie, it's beginning to hurt more."

"I'll agree with you there. But suppose we lose? That's it. We might as well face that fact. Tray will be lost to us forever."

"And suppose we win?"

"But suppose we lose because of me, because of something stupid that I do?"

"Well then, don't do anything stupid."

"I'll try."

He *was* trying. Visiting Crisfield was part of trying. Everything was part of trying. It absorbed his life now. He had made a couple of stabs at looking for a job, but as soon as an interview was arranged, he invariably got cold feet and canceled the appointment with one excuse or another. Odd, he thought, he did have the sense of anticipation, all the symptoms and signs of the will to fight, but little of the spirit. During the war, he might have thought himself a coward. Where was that old marine sense of "go"? he wondered. It went, he told himself, although he tried to hide it from Molly.

"You'll never find a job that way," Molly had rebuked him gently. When she appeared to be invoking undue pressure, she usually backed off, which only exacerbated Charlie's condition. It told him that she was really afraid that she might nag him just enough to push him over the brink. It was an idea that had taken hold, and it frightened him.

"Where have they all gone?"

Standing on the municipal dock like some invisible alien, he heard the harsh sound of his voice float into the crisp air. He looked around, wondering if anyone had heard. But the dock was deserted, the boats in the inlet rocking emptily in the choppy waters. A few steps off was a telephone booth. A thin telephone book hung from a rusted chain beside it. Putting on his glasses, he thumbed through the Crisfield names, some of which seemed vaguely familiar. He was sure that with a little effort he might find some old school chum; someone still alive who had affected him, perhaps profoundly, in his youth; someone who could offer him that special solace that was his present need.

There were still other Waterses around, blood kin. His maiden Aunt Meg, whom he hadn't seen in five or six years, still lived someplace in the town, and there were certain to be second and third cousins, featureless images that danced weakly in his mind. Absence made strangers of everybody. The idea brought back the memory of Tray's face in the school corridor, tentative and unsure, as the boy confronted the reality of his grandfather's fading identity.

Fading identities were what plagued Charlie at this very moment, as he tried to conjure up the emotion of the old life and all the complicated ties of blood relationships. There had been a time when everyone who had ever lived and mattered was alive, his grandparents on both sides, his father and mother, his brother, Ned, aunts, uncles, cousins; even relatives who were beyond the circumscribed world of Crisfield, who sent messages via the mail and called occasionally from wherever they had settled.

Once, this extended family and their activities had been his entire world and, such was his childish concept of time, he had taken for granted that it would continue on into infinity. It had lasted with all the longevity of the blink of an eye. An eye? From the swirl of memory came an odd feeling of panic, as this concrete image burst into his reverie.

He had been playing at the bay's edge, throwing pebbles into the water with other children, and one had been misthrown into his eye. The pain had exploded in his head and he had run, panicked and screaming, back to his house, which was empty. Mother was probably at the market; his father, surely on the road; his brother, Ned, at school. He had felt momentarily forlorn and deserted in his agony, a feeling replicated in present time with all the original passion and intensity. Inside of him, he now felt the same futility and despair as he had in that long-ago moment. When no solace had been available at his house, he had run as fast as his feet could carry him around the corner to Grampa and Granny Harper's house, only to find that empty as well. The horror of this awesome desertion escalated, and he ran screaming for still another block to the home of Grampa and Granny Waters. Even now, the familiar banging of the kitchen screen door often set his teeth ajar with the frantic memory of that ancient hurt. Thank the Lord, Granny had been in the kitchen, her soft, all-encompassing, ample figure wrapped in its perpetual pink apron, her arms ready, reaching out to gather him into the billowy cloud of her soothing presence. The pain, most of it psychic by then, receded under her careful ministrations. He was safe at last, engulfed and forever protected by her warm and wonderful aura.

Granny Waters, where are you now? he cried within himself. I need you. Nor did the cry in his heart apply specifically to Granny Waters. Any one of the others would do equally well. The backup system of familial protection was an infallible part of his Crisfield childhood and early youth. In those days, no hurt went untended. Arms and chests and soft lips were available in abundance to diminish pain and panic and grief and anguish. Remembering this, he knew what folly it was to come back to this place so late. There was no solace available from inanimate old landmarks and strangers.

Once, it had seemed to him that those he had left behind were the dregs caught at the bottom of the cup after the best of the beverage had been drunk. Over the years the gulf had widened. To them, he had become city folk, a city slicker. Even as his immediate family aged and died, his sense of loss had its roots in another time, as if the town and everything in it had remained forever frozen in the first two decades of his life.

When Charlie had first felt this difference, it had troubled him. He had no right to feel superior to the people with whom he had grown up, the people who loved him. He had wondered if he truly loved them as much as they loved him, and it had made him feel guilty to discover that distance and time might have diluted such emotions.

His grandparents seemed to have been swept away by some

terrible plague during the first ten years of his life. His mother had died a few years after the war. But his father had hung on to the middle seventies. In later years it became something of a chore to visit the old man. He spent most of his time sitting on the porch of their old clapboard house, in good weather and bad, watching the waters of the bay through rheumy, bloodshot eyes. By then he had become merely the symbol of the person who was once Charlie's father, like a painted balloon in which the air had slowly escaped.

But he hadn't stopped taking Chuck on his regular visits, which had become a monthly ritual. Chuck was little then, but somewhat fascinated by the old drummer with his toothless mouth and his penchant for repeating stories of Depression days. Odd, how people who lived through that bad time always remembered it with pride and intensity.

"Couldn't stand still in troubled times," the old man would tell them. "Go out and make it. There's adventure in it, too, for a man. I had them, I can tell you."

"Like what, Grampa?" Chuck would ask.

"You're too young to know about them, sonny." The old man would croak out a wet toothless laugh and slap his thigh. Charlie's attention would invariably drift off. He had, of course, heard the old stories time and time again. But to Chuck they were still fresh and strange enough to hold his interest. How dearly and deeply he had loved that restless man who had been the first to break the mold of the long string of Waterses who had made their living from the bay.

"Got to get away from this place, son," he had once told Charlie. "It's the only way I can really love it when I get home." He was, of course, the first to applaud his sons' leaving town, first Ned, then Charlie. His mother had been less forthcoming.

"Just like your Dad. Too good for little Crisfield. That's why families break up and disappear." She was right, of course, and he had known it then. But they went anyway.

"I'm not sure it was the right thing to do," he had told his father one day much later, sitting on the porch in the dead of summer, sipping soda pop. Chuck sat quietly beside them, listening. "I mean there's dough in it. We have all the material comforts. There's lots going on. On the surface it's damned good, Pop. Damned good."

"Sounds good to me," his father had replied, his eyes roaming the bay waters, his shrunken body gently rocking in the rickety cushioned rocker that had worn a recess in the plank porch floor.

"It was good growing up here, Pop. The best."

"For growing up and dyin', son," his father had said. "It's the in-between part that needs correctin'." He seemed slightly bemused by the weight of his thoughts. "A man should find it near the place in which he's born 'stead of searching all to hell and gone. What the devil are we all lookin' for, Charlie? Whatever it was, I never found it."

"Well, I'm still looking," Charlie had replied cheerfully.

And so he was.

Only, so far that morning in Crisfield, it was nowhere to be found. Not a hint of it. He wondered if he should go by the old house and if that rocker was still there. He would sit in it and look at things with his own eyes and review what his own life amounted to. Maybe that was what Chuck was looking for when he found the hard bottom of an offshore rig. Maybe the reason it couldn't be found was because it didn't exist. He shivered at the thought, since it meant that hope and optimism were also dead in the water.

Once he had had those two commodities in great abundance. Were they also fixed in time, somewhere back before the war? Were they in Crisfield? It suddenly occurred to him that he had been looking for whatever it was for a long, long time.

Years ago, after his father had died, Charlie had taken Chuck on a tour of the landmarks of his past. He had gone down to settle things after his father had died and had felt the urge to pass along the heritage of memory. That was part of the meaning of fatherhood, wasn't it? He took the boy past the old schoolhouse, to the spot on the shore where they skinny-dipped as kids in June before the first nettles came, to one more stop at the old clapboard family house, unpainted and groaning with time, where Aunt Meg still lived. Because she had taken care of his father in his later years, the old man had willed her the house, which she had sold years later.

The old sandlot where he had played first base was a Safeway by then, and the so-called lover's lane a couple of miles from town, near the shore where, before the war, the kids went in their jalopies to neck, had become rows of fancy waterfront homes. They had had a good manly laugh about the necking, which was barely comprehensible to Chuck at that time.

"We didn't know much about sex then," he had told Chuck,

blushing to his roots, less from the explanation than because of the memory. Sexual prowess in those days was measured by a hand cupped around a breast on the outside of the brassiere. "For the real thing you went down the road to Maggie's." Chuck had nodded as if he had understood. It was in the telling that Charlie had found the real joy, the recounting that stimulated recall. It gave him the feeling that he was imparting secret knowledge to his son, his seed, passing coded information from one generation to the next.

They had driven past where Maggie's had been, along a road that was once a narrow two-laner and had become a four-lane highway. He knew the spot, almost by instinct. To his surprise, it had become a McDonald's. Father and son got a kick out of that and had a Big Mac and a giggle to mark the occasion. On that day, he had also taken Chuck to all the best places where they had fished and hunted and played; and he had pointed out where his grandfather, who was a crab fisherman, had first taught him to sail a tiny skiff and where his father and he went clamming when his father got home from his traveling salesman chores.

"How come you left, Dad?" Chuck had asked as they sat in the car, its hood pointed into the sunset of the bay. He had wondered if he had painted too idyllic a picture, one that he truly felt in retrospect, but which did not quite jibe with the reality of the time.

"No place to make a decent living," he told the boy. "A man must have the courage to move on. It's his duty."

His brother Ned, whom he hadn't seen in years, and with whom he talked usually only on Christmas Day, had gone all the way to Kansas City to find a new life with his wife's family, who had put Ned in the hardware business. She was a Catholic, and he had converted. The result was an army of kids working their way down into the third generation. Ned's life was elsewhere and had been for a long time.

But it was not only economic conditions that were responsible for Charlie's leaving. The Depression had been a plague on the young people of Crisfield, but it had been the war that showed them that there was more to the world than this sleepy bay town. At least, that was what they thought. Coming back, especially that time he had come back with Chuck for the obligatory grand tour of his roots, the place had seemed like a paradise.

"Great place to be a boy," he told Chuck.

"I wish you'd never left, Dad."

Hearing that took him by surprise, and he wondered if he had given the boy a brief taste of the same joy that he had known. Or was it that he was looking through the rosy prism of time, painting foolish pictures to impress his son?

And then his grandson.

He had taken Tray down to Crisfield a few months after Chuck had died. Just the two of them. It was a gorgeous spring day in late May and the blossoms had all sprung into bloom. To him, middle spring was always the best time for the bay. It had also seemed to signal the moment to put aside grief, to put Chuck's loss in perspective, which meant accepting his death irrevocably.

They had walked down Main Street to the municipal dock, and Charlie showed him the house where he had grown up. It had been miraculously reconditioned and painted, and there was a tricycle in the front yard and a playpen on the porch, with a baby chewing the railing and gurgling. A young woman came out of the house and waved, and they walked up the path to the porch to greet her.

"My grandpa used to live in this house," Tray told her.

"Really? How lucky." She turned toward Charlie and smiled. "We love it here. My husband works for the bank. It's a great place to raise children. We were both brought up in big cities. This living beats it by a mile."

"Can't argue with that," Charlie had said. "I'm just showing my grandchild around the old place."

"Would you like to go in?"

"That would be very troublesome to you," Charlie said, but it was obvious to the woman that it was what they wanted.

"Not at all."

They followed her into the house, which had been rehabilitated and remodeled completely. Charlie could not restrain a quivering lump in his throat and had all he could do to keep himself from crying.

"That's where your old gramp slept with his brother Ned," he told Tray when they had walked upstairs. One of the walls had been broken through to make a bigger master bedroom suite for the new owner and his wife. He gave Tray a running commentary as they moved from room to room. Coming down, he hesitated on the staircase.

"Third step used to creak. You could never sneak upstairs because of it."

"Oh, we had a whole new staircase built in."

"You did a wonderful job. We had a lot of happy times here."

They went into the kitchen, where memories of his mother flooded back. He was not conscious of squeezing Tray's hand.

"Ouch, Grampa."

He had taken the boy's hand and kissed it.

"Better now, Tray?"

The boy nodded.

Later, he showed him Grampa and Granny Harper's house and Grampa and Granny Waters's house, and the other landmarks of the guided tour. Except, of course, where Maggie's had been, although he did show him the spooning spot beside the bay. Then he had rented a day sailer, and they had spun around the inlet. He had let Tray hold the tiller.

"Would you like to live here someday, Tray?"

"Can we, Grampa?"

"I was thinking about it. Someday when I retire. About eight years from now. Me and Gramma both. We'll get a place down here and you'll stay with us summers and we'll go boating and fishing and clamming."

"What's clamming?"

He explained it as best he could, enjoying the boy's rapt attention.

"Would you like that, Tray?"

"Oh yes, Grampa." He jumped on him and hugged him around the neck, and Charlie hugged and kissed the boy on both cheeks and held him for a long time.

"God, I love you, boy," he said, holding back his tears.

"And I love you, Grampa."

In a few years, he knew, manly reticence would interfere. It was a moment to be savored and cherished and held onto as long as possible. The day would come when the boy would be a man and Charlie would be just another old man with a scratchy beard and sour breath.

"Are you my best friend, Grampa?" the boy asked.

"For ever always."

"And Gramma, too?"

"Of course."

Charlie had hesitated for a moment.

"And Daddy, too. You musn't ever forget your Daddy. He was your best friend, too."

"Even in heaven?"

"Daddies never stop loving their little boys."

"And Mommies?"

"Not Mommies either. Never, never."

Charlie remembered that day and how he had cursed time for not just stopping for a millennium or two, letting them be just as they were, a little boy and his grandfather sitting on the rim of the eternal bay as if it were the remote edge of the planet, basking in the great biological mystery of blood kinship and creation.

In a strange way, that day had blunted his grief for his lost son, and he believed in his heart that God had offered him this child to rear and love in place of Chuck.

Instead of anger, the memories only added greater weight to his already heavy heart. He was no longer the heroic figure of his youth and middle age—the adventurer, soldier, husband-lover, teacher-father, rugged hunter, fisherman, sailor—that could sustain him in the face of what he now knew was the real truth. Hadn't he led a rather pedestrian life, an ordinary man in an ordinary job with an ordinary house and a run of lousy luck? In the end, everything had turned out to be a disappointment— Chuck, Tray, Frances. Now Crisfield. Maybe even Molly.

No!

In his thoughts, he heard Molly's voice berating him for his self-pity and, worse, his self-abasement. He was not ordinary. No man is ordinary. Every man is like his own fingerprint, individual, a miracle, wonderful. It had been a very bad idea to come back to Crisfield with its rich memories of loving families and adolescent hopes and dreams. Life was simply chronologically unfair, he assured himself. An old man who allows himself to view things through the rosy filter of his lost youth plays a fool's game. There was nothing to be found in the physical place of Crisfield that wasn't better in the mind's eye, where you didn't get the intrusion of passing time. He shook himself alert like an old dog and, as the old cowboys used to say, hightailed it out of town.

But by the time he got back to Baltimore, the realization that he had not found in Crisfield what he truly needed had come rushing back to afflict him, providing another disappointment to add to the list. With his luck, he thought bitterly, he might live as long as his father. Except his house didn't have a porch. Nor did he have a son to visit him, if only to pass the time and validate that he had done his God-given duty of replicating the race in his own image. Christ, he thought, what am I going to do with the rest of my life?

Or even the rest of the day?

He had roamed through the house. In the kitchen he made himself a cup of coffee and lit a cigarette, then walked into the den. He sat down on the chair and tried to devise mental strategies to fill up the vast emptiness that stretched out before him. He felt hollowed out, eaten away, corroded.

Not like the shiny hunting rifles proudly exhibited in his gun-case. He had lavished loving care on those, had killed only as a real man kills. For food. And in war, only his enemies.

Feeling for the key above the cabinet, he found it and unlocked the case, removing the shotgun he had bought for Chuck when he was seventeen. The boy had been ecstatic, he remembered, and they had gone up to the beautiful low ranges of West Virginia to hunt deer.

They had rented a cabin tucked away in the midst of a pine stand and slept in sleeping bags laid over plank bunks. Wood smoke had parched the walls and crept into the nap of the woolen clothing in which they slept and hunted, and even the sweetly chilled fall air of predawn morning could not dispel the smell of it. They would roam the winding trails through the woods, eyes alert for tracks or droppings, signaling to each other with shrugs or looks or low grunts as they moved like phantoms to outwit and kill their unsuspecting prey.

He had told Chuck, as his father had told him, and as his grandfather had told his father, that the joy was not in the kill but in the hunter's ingenuity in the pursuit. The animal was to be respected and killed cleanly, to be mourned as a fellow creature who shared the earth, and blessed for providing the human species with food. In these hills Charlie and Chuck shared the common experience of manhood, a kind of secret soldiering that suggested intimacy and courage and the joyful freedom of cutting loose from domestication and women, of being free from the taming constraints of civilization and participating in something primal and profound.

That year they had decided to go for buck only, the biggest they could find, inventing a horned giant with enough fire in his belly to attack even if provoked by nothing more than the human presence. Nasty Jake, they had dubbed him, deciding that they would settle for nothing less. They had come across less—does and mares, all over the place. But when they had the creatures in their sights they had moved their barrels out of range, firing to chase and not to kill. They had even found themselves a buck, but it was not one of sufficient size, and letting him escape to grow more menacing in the years to come had given them continuity and a future to believe in.

Coming back to the cabin, bone-weary but exhilarated, they lit the wood fire of the old-fashioned wrought-iron range and threw steaks on a hot fry pan and slivers of peeled potatoes into boiling oil. They ate the steaks and french fries smothered in ketchup while the coffee perked happily on the range and the room was all aglow from the log fire crackling in the stone fireplace. Charlie was surprised at the remarkable accuracy of his recall, or so it seemed. He could see the orange flicker of the wood flame on Chuck's smooth, boyish face, the ridge of black on his nail tips, the roughened chap on his own hands. He could taste the chewy meatiness of the steaks and the crisp hardness of the potatoes, the hot pungency of the strong coffee. He could feel the dried texture of the old table, the porcupine sprout of his own beard.

The voice that floated with pristine accuracy in his mind's ear was Chuck's. Somehow in the magic chronology of memory the table had been cleared, the cracked plates washed and dried. The fire spit fierce sparks over the rim of the metal grate on which their boots rested. They had spread their sleeping bags on the floor in front of the fire and crossed their arms behind their heads, eyes raised to the exposed, smoke-soaked low rafters of the old cabin.

"I hope we never get him, Dad." It was still a boy's voice, although the body was a man's.

"Who?" It wasn't that his mind had wandered, just that in memory the response was necessary since he was also remembering himself.

"Nasty Jake," the boy said. "I want to see him, get close enough for a good shot, but I want him to get away. Next year, too. And the year after that and the year after that."

"With that attitude, we'll never get him. You've got to want to get him."

"I'm not saying we shouldn't stalk him and nail him in our sights. I want him to know we can get him. I just want him to keep going."

Never mind that Nasty Jake existed only in imagination. He had become as real as he had to be.

"Kind of defeats the purpose of the hunt, doesn't it?"

"The thing is—" The boy seemed to stumble over his words. "If we keep him alive and free, then he'll be around to keep us challenged. And we'll always have him."

"That's one way of looking at it. But suppose another hunter gets him."

"Not him, Dad. Not Nasty Jake. He's ours. Yours and mine."

"I see what you mean."

"He's ours," the boy repeated.

"Damn right."

And so he's still out there somewhere, Charlie thought, spun back into present time by the unbearable burden of loss. Chuck's share of Nasty Jake was to have been handed over to Tray. It was against the natural flow of events to prevent such things. It was wrong, repellent, selfish, insensitive. He had felt himself exploding with anger, hardly aware that he had risen from the chair and walked over to the gun cabinet where, in a drawer below the case, he kept his shells. Also without realizing it, he had broken the stock and loaded two shells in the chambers, then returned to the chair, the rifle resting across his knees, safety off, finger on the trigger.

He had wondered if the time had finally come to kill Nasty Jake.

Chapter 9

I DON'T SEE what that has to do with it," Charlie said for about the fourth or fifth time.

Robert Forte looked toward Molly, then up at the ceiling. Actually, Molly thought, he was being patient. Charlie had been difficult all morning, even before they had arrived at the lawyer's office. They had stopped first at the bank, where the manager told them there would be a penalty for cashing in their money market certificate thirty days earlier than it was due.

"That's not very fair," Charlie told the neat, crisply dressed young woman behind the desk. They were everywhere now, Molly thought, like *The Invasion of the Body Snatchers*. Well-groomed, confident younger women. Where did they learn to use makeup so well, and to talk with such command and assurance? She glanced at the woman's hands, smooth and creamy as alabaster, and hid her own liver-spotted ones under her pocketbook. The woman was devoting most of her conversational attention to Charlie, who did not take to her kindly.

"I'm sorry," the woman said to Charlie. "If you wait thirty more days, there will be no penalty." Officiously, she pointed out the rules on the back of the certificate.

"I can read," Charlie said. "I still think it stinks."

Molly might have intervened at that point, but she held her silence. Forte had asked for a five-thousand-dollar retainer and, bitch though he might, Charlie was determined to deliver as scheduled. A matter of pride, he had told her at breakfast. A deal is a deal.

"I've been working with this bank for thirty years," Charlie said as he signed the certificate and passed it along for Molly's countersignature. "Now they're always looking for the edge. Wasn't that way before, was it, Molly?"

Molly nodded, as if with high conviction. Actually, she had always found the bank personnel patronizing and officious. This young woman had made them appear even more so.

"Would you like a certified check?" the woman asked.

"Absolutely not," Charlie had replied.

He had filled out a deposit slip that lay on the desk before her. A certified check might have made it appear that they were trying too hard to convince the lawyer that they really did have the money to finance the case. He had already written the check and put it in an envelope, which was in the inside pocket of his jacket.

"We are grateful for your business, Mr. Waters," the young woman said, flashing one of those synthetic television commercial smiles.

"We do it all for you," Molly hummed, handing her the certificate. The woman looked at it closely in what seemed to be a deliberate gesture of uncertainty, turned it over, then got up and walked with sleek arrogance to the far side of the teller's counter.

"They own the world now," Charlie said, following her with his eyes. Had he meant the young, or women? There were times when she challenged his view. Not today. She nodded in grudging agreement, reminding herself that they had also invaded the school system.

"Like Frances—young, unfeeling, and indifferent," he muttered. "I'd rather have given that money to Tray." He shook his head. "What a waste."

It was, of course, a hint of what was to come. Driving downtown, he was sullen, and she noted that his lips moved soundlessly. Was he starting to talk to himself again? she wondered, suddenly alarmed.

"Stop that, Charlie."

"Stop what?"

"Cussing under your breath."

The brief rebuke had stopped his lips from moving, but he remained uncommunicative all the way to the office. His first act was to hand the lawyer the envelope, which remained on the desk all morning. Forte had called in a stenographer, who had brought one of those machines that they used in court.

At first, the lawyer had only asked for facts, a kind of personal history—dates of birth, where they had been raised, what schools they had attended, occupational statistics for both of them, his marine record, their church affiliation. Nothing controversial. Forte got up from his desk and walked to the window, looking out at the harbor. Turning, he began to pace the room, straightening a picture, lifting his coffee cup.

"Thank you, Miss Farber," he said, after nearly an hour of

questioning. The stenographer gathered up her equipment and left the room. Then he sat down again at his desk, a ball-point pen poised over his yellow pad, and turned to Molly.

"How would you characterize your son's marriage, Mrs. Waters?"

She glanced at Charlie, then recrossed her legs in the opposite direction. For some reason, Molly found the question had taken her by surprise, although she had known it was coming. In fact, she had gone over it in her mind dozens of times.

"He was away a lot," she said. It was not exactly the answer she had prepared.

"Supporting his family," Charlie interjected.

"He asked me the question, Charlie," she rebuked, shooting him an angry glance. "You promised."

"I'm cool," he said, showing both palms. "I won't butt in."

"But when he did come home, he seemed happy at first but then became moody and morose. Before you knew it, he was off again."

"Because she didn't make him happy . . ." Charlie interrupted. Molly looked at him sternly. "Sorry," he said to the lawyer.

"She hated the idea of his going. She tried everything to stop him. Until finally I guess she just became resigned. I felt sorry for her and tried to fill in the gaps. We had her over every Sunday. Sometimes for the whole weekend. And I would call her three or four times a week." From the corner of her eye, she could see Charlie and sense his attempt at self-control. They had been discussing this topic for years, and their perceptions were still miles apart. Yet, even now, she could not bring herself to reveal what she had chosen to keep buried.

Even while she answered the lawyer's questions with what she hoped were precision and clarity, she sensed that it could never be the whole truth. Beneath the surface of her careful answers, other thoughts were running on a parallel track. Not thoughts, really. A memory that could be reproduced only in perfect fidelity, too painful to be exposed to a stranger's interpretation.

Chuck had come by himself to Molly's house. The timing had surprised her. She had just come from school. Charlie would not be home for another two hours. What had occurred to her then was that rarely, perhaps never since he was twelve or thirteen, had she and Chuck ever been exclusively together. Not in quite this way, where he had actually sought her out. She had made him a mug of coffee, and they had sat at the kitchen table.

He was twenty-five by then, filled out, his skin weathered and tanned, giving his beauty a harder edge than she remembered. His hands were rough and callused, and sun wrinkles had begun to be visible along the temples, beside his cobalt eyes. Her eyes. Nonetheless, she could still see the baby in the man, and if he had allowed it, she could easily have curled him in her arms and laid his head against her breast. His macho standoffishness had only secretly increased her yearning for demonstrative affection.

He had been home for nearly two weeks and was to leave in a few more days, and she could sense clearly the restlessness in his taut body.

"Is the baby okay?"

"Fine."

"Frances?"

"Fine."

They went through the amenities with unusual awkwardness, and after a while he pushed the coffee mug away, stood up, walked to the refrigerator, and took out a beer. He was silent for a long time.

"What is it, Chuck?"

She eschewed the usual clichés about a mother knowing. She had known for years, not quite certain what she knew, except that somehow her child was not what he seemed.

"I've been trying to figure it out, Mom," he had said. Not responding, she let the silence draw him out. "I don't like coming home. I'm not sure why."

"I don't need a ton of bricks to fall on my head to see that."

"It's not Frances," he added hastily. "It's me. When I'm away, I like the memory of her and Tray. I really have a sense of feeling about them. But when I'm home, it's gone. I don't know why. I mean I really feel for them when I'm away." He upended the beer can. His Adam's apple worked up and down his neck.

"Us, too?"

"In a way, yes."

She had shrugged.

"That's the kind of thing you wouldn't reveal unless it was the absolute truth," she had told him.

"I've talked about this to the other guys. Some of them feel the same way. I couldn't tell this to Dad. I don't know why. Maybe

I'd be ashamed. But I'm happy out there working those rigs."
Pausing, he snapped his fingers. "The beat of it, the whole rhythm
of it. The hard physical work, the danger, the freedom."

In the ensuing silence, she had questioned herself and Charlie.
How had they made him like this? Their little family had always
seemed loving, was still loving. Would she now have to spend a
lifetime retracing her life whenever she thought about Chuck?
Was it the "manliness" that Charlie had instilled, the initiation
rites in some secret society from which females were forever barred?

"There are a lot of men like me, Mom. I'm not as different as
you think. In our hearts, maybe, we're family men. But not in
action." He got up and took another beer. "God, I hate to tell you
this. When we work, we work hard. And we play hard." He took
a deep swig of the beer and wiped his mouth with the back of his
hand. The gesture seemed to illustrate his revelation. He was,
indeed, an undomesticated man.

"You don't have to say this, Chuck."

"I've been to Hong Kong and Sydney three times this year.
It's part of it. The playing. I'm not out there for the money, Mom.
Hell, I blow a lot of it." He had offered a shy, crinkly smile. "On
women. I don't think I can ever settle down again. This life isn't
for me, Mom. I've tried to explain this to Frances."

"About the women?"

"Never that. About the way I feel."

"And her reaction?"

"It makes her unhappy."

"Can you blame her?"

"She says she loves me. I guess in a way I love her. But from
a distance. That's the worst part. When I'm with her, I feel nothing."

"Poor thing. Has she asked for a divorce?"

"No. Maybe she thinks it will all go away."

"And you? What will you do about it?"

For a long time, he didn't respond, finishing his beer.

"What is there to do? I live my life the way I want. Maybe I
stick with it so I can have a place to come home to from time to
time. Who knows?"

"What about Tray?"

"He's one helluva kid."

"And you're his father."

"I know, Mom." He had looked out the window into the yard.
His eyes seemed to turn inward, glaze over. "Who would think I

would turn out like this? I feel bad about what it might be doing to others, but I really don't feel like a bad person. You know what I mean?"

She had watched him carefully as he talked, trying to see what was beyond the words, the hidden man. Then she realized that he was hiding nothing, that what he was giving her was the most accurate picture of himself that he could articulate. What you see is what you get, he seemed to be telling her. It troubled her to learn how far he was from her own image of him. So that business of a mother truly knowing her child was just another myth, she thought.

"Dad would probably think I'm a bum."

"No—he wouldn't," she had protested. "Definitely not." She wasn't sure. Charlie might actually be envious of Chuck's freedom, but Charlie had never shirked responsibility.

"So let's keep it between ourselves, Mom."

Molly nodded her consent.

She had been true to her promise. Would Charlie be jealous? Was Chuck saying something that men only told men? She had not wished to find the answer to that and therefore continued to say nothing. But that did not preclude her from offering an interpretation based on what she knew.

She had answered all the lawyer's questions from that perspective, regardless of how Charlie fumed beside her. The inescapable conclusion by any independent observer was that her son's marriage had not been a happy one.

"Did they fight?" the lawyer asked.

"I never heard them."

"Was she unfaithful?"

"No. I doubt it."

"I wouldn't be so sure," Charlie muttered.

"That's not fair, Charlie," Molly interjected. "She was a good girl in that respect. It's wrong to make such an accusation."

"Considering what I know now, I wouldn't put anything past her," Charlie persisted.

But when he was questioned by the lawyer, he did not refute Molly's assessment of Frances's unhappiness.

"Maybe she was unhappy. I'm not saying no. A happy man doesn't stray from the nest, either. If she was that unhappy, she should have asked him for a divorce. In marriage there are always problems." He looked sheepishly toward Molly. Their marriage wasn't perfect, but it was better than most. Come on, Charlie, she begged him silently. We're as good as you can get. They were friends and still lovers and he was being a damned macho liar. But still, she wouldn't tell him that.

After more questions, the lawyer inspected their faces, his large brown eyes as intense as spotlights.

"The picture I get is of a marriage barely held together. About the only real common denominator is the child. Any judge will see that. So why deny it? That fact is that, whatever the marriage was like, it's still not totally relevant. Your relationship with her was a good one, wasn't it?"

"As good as any," Molly said. "We never really had arguments. Maybe mild disagreements. And we spent time with her and Tray on weekends."

"She just didn't like being alone," Charlie said.

"No woman likes that," Molly snapped. "You men out there playing with your toys. Your special games." She caught herself up short. No, she never did like that.

"And the child? Always a good relationship with the boy?"

"Not just good," Molly said, as if to make up for her previous outburst. "Wonderful." There was more to it than just being with the boy, filling time, even in a loving way. Wasn't he also getting the benefit of their experience in life, the gift of wisdom that only a gray head and an unselfish loving heart could convey? Surely there was a benefit to the boy in being exposed to living ties with the past? Quality time was what they gave, Molly thought, reviewing the ways in which they had spent it with Tray. It was a loss for the child as well.

"And being deprived of that relationship has been traumatic?"

It came as a kind of general question, but it instantly confirmed her suspicion that the benefits of grandparenting on the child would be difficult, if not impossible, to prove, no less defend. The lawyer looked pointedly at Charlie.

"You've been very depressed about this separation, especially since it comes at a time of comparative idleness. Haven't you?"

"I don't know what you mean by that," Charlie said helplessly.

"I mean it's had a devastating effect on both of you, especially you, Mr. Waters."

"We were pretty close," Charlie mumbled defensively. He hated to show any signs of weakness. "I don't see what that has to do with it."

The lawyer was leading him now.

"What I want to establish is not only the effect on the child, but on you as well. The deprivation of the loving relationship with your grandchild has also had a profound and debilitating effect on you." Charlie squirmed in his seat. He looked at Molly and seemed uncertain about a response. "Well, has it, or hasn't it?" Forte pressed him. "Why would you be here otherwise?"

"I guess you have a point."

"Have you had trouble sleeping? Have you been irritable, nervous, or depressed? Has it interfered with your well-being, your physical health, your mental capacity?"

"I don't see what that has to do with it." Again, Charlie glanced helplessly toward Molly. "What about Tray?" he snarled. "How has it hurt Tray to be away from us? I saw him. He definitely wasn't the same boy I said good-bye to two years ago."

Molly could see that the lawyer had taken this unsubtle shifting of the spotlight to Tray as a kind of affirmative answer to his questions. She could see immediately the problems that they would have to face in court. How could the benefit derived by Tray from his grandparents' company be adequately explained through lawyers, with their trick questions and procedures?

"Like what?" the lawyer asked, accepting the shift.

"Like he wasn't himself."

"In his attitude toward you?"

"Like he was frightened."

"As if you had been painted to be someone unsavory? A bad influence?"

"No. Not like that."

"As if he didn't know you?"

"Not that either. It was as if—as if he saw me as a stranger." Charlie nodded vigorously. "That's it. Like I was a stranger."

Molly felt uncomfortable with that analysis, but she held her peace.

"I was already feeling lousy. And on top of that they threatened to call the cops if I came around again. It was pretty terrible."

"Who threatened?"

"Frances did." He grimaced and shook his head. "I think she got a little frightened. I must have been in a state."

"He had a very bad reaction to the experience," Molly said, also remembering how she had found him on that day he had visited Crisfield.

She had worked late, and when she came home, he was sitting in the dark in the living room, his coat still on. She had put on the light and he had tried to hide it with his arms, but in the brief flash she had seen him and, in his face, the etched pain, the eyes puffy with tears, helpless in his despair.

She looked at Charlie to see how far she should go. He had turned pale, and she could see the protest in his eyes.

It would humiliate him to hear it said aloud, she knew, the way she found him in the den, with the loaded gun on his lap.

The fabric of his manhood had been unceremoniously unraveled, and he was momentarily disoriented, his identity challenged. He had lost most of the things that defined him as a man, his work, his son, his grandson. His collapse had seemed total, and it panicked her momentarily, since his stability and manhood were also the bedrock of her own life. She had had little choice but to go back with him to helpless babyhood and play the mother as he sobbed away the substance of his life.

He had clung to her like a helpless infant, sputtering out his confessions of despair, the failure of his aspirations, the overwhelming wave of events that had brought him down. She had held him in her arms for days, it seemed, until finally she had entered the cage with him and slowly led him out. Now her fear was that he might become suspicious that this revelation of his weakness and vulnerability had actually diminished him in her eyes. More than ever, lately, she had made an effort to stroke his sense of manhood, wondering if her ministrations were transparent. Above all, she did not want him to feel dependent on her strength, or challenged by it.

"I don't see what that has to do with it," he had said a few moments ago. She clearly understood the coded message to her.

"It would have a bad effect on anybody," said Molly.

"It was one lousy birthday, I can tell you," Charlie said, somewhat relieved. The lawyer did not pursue the issue further, choosing instead to break for lunch.

They went up the elevator to a dining club on the penthouse floor, with high windows that offered a spectacular view of the harbor and surrounding skyline. It was obviously a place of privilege, Molly observed, an enclave for the power elite that ran the city. It was both impressive and awesome, and she felt out of place and intimidated, feelings mirrored by Charlie, who looked forlorn and uncomfortable. The opulence of the room and the apparent arrogance and self-confidence of the diners only made his personal sense of failure more acute.

"Drink?" Forte asked after they were seated at one of the better tables alongside the window.

"A beer," Charlie said.

"Make it two." She looked toward Charlie and winked. Mostly to comfort him. In this place, they were as good as aliens.

"Campari and soda for me," Forte told the gray-haired, black waiter.

"Nice place," Charlie said after a long, awkward silence while all three studied the menu.

"Not bad," Forte said. "And you can't beat the crab cakes."

The drinks came, and they placed their order, but they had barely had their first sips when a large man with a floppy bow tie and round steel-rimmed glasses came by and shook Forte's hand.

"Looks like we got another one, Bob," the big man said.

"Looks like it." He looked nervously at Molly and Charlie.

"Always a pleasure to lock horns with you downtown hotshots."

"You guys in the suburbs are the ones with the horns," he smiled thinly. "By the way, I'd like you to meet—"

"You playing Saturday?"

Forte nodded.

"He's a scratch golfer. We're a perfect pair. I've got a ten handicap."

Ignoring the banter, Forte cleared his throat.

"This is Charles and Molly Waters. Meet Henry Peck, a worthy opponent."

The name meant nothing to Molly, who shook the man's hand when her turn came.

"He's representing your daughter-in-law and her husband," Forte said. If he was discomfited, it didn't show. But Molly felt strange.

Peck was polite, made no references to the case, and went away with nods and smiles. When their silence became awkward, Forte broke the ice.

"He's one shrewd bastard, that one."

"But you're friendly," Charlie said, his response predictable. Molly had held herself back from offering the same comment.

"We're just professionals," Forte said patiently. "One thing has nothing to do with the other."

Charlie drank a gulp of beer.

"Doesn't seem right somehow," he said. "I mean, you're opponents."

"So are boxers. Many of them are friends or acquaintances. In the ring, they're out to kill each other. Same with us."

Molly knew what Charlie was thinking. They hadn't, after all, had much experience with lawyers. The situation came as a shock, to her as well, to see how impersonal and unemotional it was for them. How can they possibly be touched by our sense of outrage? she thought.

"Do you ever discuss cases between yourselves? I mean on the golf course?" she asked, glancing at Charlie.

"Not usually," Forte answered. "When we play golf, we want to get away from business."

"That's a hard one to swallow," Charlie said. He was clearly becoming agitated.

"Legal ethics prohibits our discussing cases where we are on opposing sides."

"But you get yours, win or lose," Charlie said.

"Do I detect a note of apprehension?" Forte replied, frowning.

"I don't understand it, is all," Charlie mumbled, looking into the beer, which had flattened. "I'm from a different side of the tracks. When we take sides, we take sides."

"It does sound odd, I know. But we're nothing more than paid advocates."

"I know that, all right," Charlie said. "Hell, you could both get together and stall this thing and stretch the payments out to the next century."

"The entire system depends on trust, Mr. Waters." The lawyer looked toward Molly for alliance. Finding none, he shrugged and lapsed into silence.

"I never did trust lawyers," Charlie said, upending his glass. Thankfully, the waiter brought their orders, and they began to eat in studied silence. "I just think it smells," Charlie said abruptly, after swallowing a bite of crab cake and washing it down with water. The lawyer put down his knife and fork.

"What smells, Mr. Waters?" Forte began pointedly. Molly held her breath, her heart pounding. "Is it the botched-up relationships that families get themselves into? The fact is that a court of law is not the place to sort out personal relationships. It is a last resort, a recognition of the failure of human beings to work out their own problems. You hired me because you and your daughter-in-law and her husband cannot work out the most simple and basic impulses of human understanding. You don't blame the messenger for the bad news, Mr. Waters. Peck and I sell time and legal expertise. We both know our jobs. Mine is to get a legal order that permits you to visit your grandchild. Peck's is to prevent that. We're both going to do our damnedest to win because the business we get is based on how well we do for our clients. A doctor who persistently kills off his patients by negligence, stupidity, or ethical lapses soon finds his waiting room empty."

It could only be classified as an outburst, although the words came out as if they had been heated on a pure blue flame. Charlie was obviously cowed. His eyes seemed like loose marbles rolling around in their whites. Molly knew she had to somehow fill the breach.

"That's what we're paying for, counselor," she said. "You convinced me."

Charlie looked down at his food, picking at it with his knife and fork. The lawyer glanced at her and nodded understanding. He had, she realized, just fallen short of telling them both what to do with their case. She tried some small talk about the view and the weather, soliciting Charlie to join in, but he appeared too busy nursing a bruised ego, a daily occurrence these days. Forte's lecture, she could tell, had unnerved him. When he started to play with his food, rearranging it without eating, she became concerned.

"Want another beer, Mr. Waters?" the lawyer asked with a stealthy glance at Molly that did not conceal his anxiety. Charlie shook his head, then put down his knife and fork and stood up.

"Back in a minute," he mumbled, ambling off.

They watched his receding back.

"He's beginning to really worry me," the lawyer said with obvious concern. "I hadn't intended to be so tough."

"He'll get over it," Molly replied, unconvincingly. She was, indeed, worried.

"If they see his weakness under pressure, they'll exploit it."

"It's been a couple of rough years."

"Why doesn't he get a job?"

"I thought he would. Maybe after the case is over."

"That's not very wise. They could stall this for months. It's not that he'll be doing any real work on it. I'm afraid this is not a day-to-day job."

She knew he was right, of course. The loss of his work had been a crushing blow. Perhaps almost fatal. Quickly, she erased the terrible image from her mind.

"At least I have my work and my fifth grade kids. I understand what he's going through. That's why I went along with the case. He needed the hope, you see." She paused to compose herself. "So did I."

"You seem to be taking it better than he, Mrs. Waters."

"I don't miss Tray any less, Mr. Forte." She sensed a touch of indignation in her tone. "But Charlie's the one that's down, a lot farther than I am. I have to appear strong for his sake." She was strong, she told herself, hating the idea that she was stronger than Charlie. He had been through the toughening process of war, for God's sake.

In a brief flash of memory, she saw him as he was then, her courageous young warrior, ready to laugh down fate, a twinkle in his eyes and a smile on his lips. Hadn't she always deferred to his courage and good sense, his strong, wise, manly ways? No, she protested, he'll come back. Hadn't he protected and encouraged her through their years together, through the dark times of her miscarriages, her intimate failures? Hadn't he shored up her defenses, poured devotion and trust and love into the cracks of her own failed dreams of a large, loving family? It was her turn now, her turn to backstop him.

"I'm thinking of the case. Mostly the courtroom confrontations. If they mash away at him and he blows, they'll make their case for his instability. If we don't appear calm and kindly in that courtroom, we'll be up the creek without a paddle."

"You mean you get judged on appearaces," she said sarcastically, searching the room for any sign of Charlie, missing him.

"On perceptions. At least in a jury trial you've got twelve chances. In a domestic case, you've got only one."

"I think if I explained it carefully, he would get himself under control," she said with mock conviction.

"Look, Mrs. Waters. Their strategy will be to crucify you both,

to exaggerate your every flaw and to hide behind the tight re-
strictions of adoption law. That's bad enough to face, and even if
you clear that hurdle, they'll be defaming your character, selling
you both to the judge as bad influences on your grandson. Our
only comeback will be a strong, aggressive defense of your character, your past, your parenting and grandparenting, your general
all-around goodness and decency. That's our case. A long shot at
best. We may not even get that far. Not if your husband blows
his cork. It will turn off the judge and give their side an opening
you can put an army through."

"He wasn't always like that," she said thoughtfully. "Used to
be a reasonably contented man." She glanced up at the lawyer.
"We've had our troubles, Mr. Forte."

"Now that's the attitude we need, Mrs. Waters. Be a victim.
Show that. Not an angry victim. Anger makes people seem ugly.
If he doesn't get himself under control, you'll be wasting your
money. Not to mention the emotional agony of it."

"He can't hide things, I guess."

"He has no choice."

"Poor Charlie." The words came out before she could stop
them. She had been a true and loyal wife, an ally and a friend.
At the beginning they had planned a large family. Charlie would
have been perfect in the role of wise father for a large brood
instead of investing so much in one child. It was her fault. She
had let him down. Suddenly she pulled herself up short. What
am I doing? she rebuked herself.

"Here he comes," the lawyer said.

"Look, Mr. Forte," she said hurriedly, "I'll handle it. He'll be
fine."

"He has to be, Mrs. Waters. I kid you not."

Charlie strode across the dining room, trying to put some
confidence in his step. See, he will be fine, she told herself. But
it was without conviction.

"I guarantee it," she said, forcing her bravado, her mind
searching for another course of action. If they didn't win this case,
Charlie might never recover from the loss. Never!

I'll have to confront Frances one more time, she told herself.
I'll beg her to save my Charlie.

Chapter 10

For the third time that morning, Frances found herself instructing Maria, their three-day-a-week cleaning woman, on the care and feeding of Baby Mark. It was the language barrier that made her anxious, even though Maria had birthed eight children in Peru and there was not the slightest doubt of her reliability and competence.

"No worry, Meeses," Maria said, patting Frances's arm. Baby Mark slept peacefully, bundled in his carriage on the patio, clearly visible through the breakfast nook bay window.

"Bottle in the refrigerator," Frances said. She looked at the kitchen clock. "I come back two, three hours."

"No worry, Meeses," Maria smiled, glancing at the carriage in its pool of bright winter sun.

Her anxiety and discomfort were not totally attributable to Baby Mark. Her decision to meet with Molly seemed to fly in the face of her best instincts, and she felt now as if she were disobeying the inner voice of reason. To make matters worse, she had not told Peter about the meeting although she had mentioned Molly's previous calls, both of which she had cut short with a curt, "It's out of my hands now."

"What else could you do?" Peter had responded. "To talk to her would only exacerbate the situation."

Exacerbate! The word had lingered in her mind from another time.

"Wouldn't it be wise to send them back?" he had asked then. "They'll only exacerbate the situation." At first she had been stunned by the question. Send back Molly and Charlie's Christmas presents for Tray? They had been married a little over two months, and Tray seemed to have been slowly weaned away from the idea of Chuck's parents as central to his life. But it was the word Peter used, *exacerbate*, that placed an additional note of confusion on the issue, and she rushed to the dictionary to get its meaning. "To exasperate, make angry."

He hadn't meant to flaunt a superior education. The word had come naturally. Yet it seemed so much more threatening and ominous than the word *angry.*

"He's always had gifts from them at Christmas," Frances had argued, although "exacerbate" had considerably weakened her protest. She certainly did not want to have their new happy little family threatened by exacerbation. "He must be expecting them."

"A Christmas gift demands some form of reciprocation. Are you planning to give them a gift?"

"Well, no," she said hesitantly, having already determined that such sentiment would open the door to premature communication.

"And Tray?"

"He mentions it in passing, of course. I sort of turn away the idea by ignoring it. Anyway, kids are more interested in themselves at Christmas. It's their holiday."

"At this point I think we should just be concerned with reminders. No matter how you rationalize, their gifts would come with fishing lines. Before you know it, they would be reeling them in. Do you want to start the cycle of resentment all over again?"

"Of course not. But this seems so harsh."

"And I suppose I seem like Ebenezer Scrooge for suggesting it."

"In a way you do," she said. "But it probably makes sense for the moment. He does still ask questions about them."

"Do you think Tray will be upset?" Peter asked.

"It's hard to tell. He's adjusted so well. It depends on the way we handle it."

"He could do without the pressure," Peter pointed out, not with any burning advocacy, but in his patient, logical manner. "Give him a little breathing room. Let's not push over the apple cart in a moment of sentimental weakness."

It was, of course, compelling logic. He had begun to call Peter "Daddy," and the two were growing closer by the day, with Peter making a special effort to win Tray's trust and, of course, affection.

"It just seems so cruel."

"Not cruel. Realistic and consistent. We've either committed to it or we haven't."

"But it's Christmas. A special time."

"Exactly the point," he said gently. "It's a time of vulnerability. The question we have to ask ourselves is, are we ready to accept the burden, the resentment, the sarcasm and bitterness. There's a pecking order of priorities here. Leave the door ajar, and soon we'll have the fox back in the chicken coop."

She didn't like the idea, although she did agree with the concept. Even as they discussed it, she began to resent her ex-in-laws' intrusion in her family's otherwise tranquil and happy new lives. Actually, since her marriage, they seemed to intrude less and less, and their influence was diminishing. No more guilt. No more self-recrimination. No more gut-wrenching second thoughts about her conduct.

Molly and Charlie's presents were spread out in boxes on the floor of the foyer. She looked at them and shook her head.

"It looks like they bought out the store."

"You can't blame them. They want to pound the point home."

"It was hard enough telling them. I try not to think about how they're taking it." She crossed her arms over her stomach. She had just learned that she was pregnant. The gesture seemed to trigger his emphasis.

"You mustn't. We have other concerns. We're putting together a new life. There's the house. All the work that goes into getting it in shape. And the baby. Not to mention Tray and his problems. His new school, a new father. And your getting used to me. I'm sure that's not too easy either." He was fishing for a little solace now, she knew. Like her, he hated deliberately hurting other people. Despite his arguments, she knew he was just as distressed as she was.

"You've been wonderful, Peter. I have no complaints in that department." She moved toward him, and he embraced her.

"You don't think I'm a little stodgy? Engineers have that reputation."

"But I know what's beneath the surface, you see." She lifted her face, and he kissed her deeply.

"It comes down to the old question. What's best for us? Let Tray get used to the new nest. Why remind him of the old one? At least, not yet."

"I still feel funny about it."

"So do I."

She looked at the presents.

"It's so much. It seems like . . ."

"A bribe."

"That's one way of looking at it."

Peter's parents had already sent their gifts. They were, of course, more than generous. But not nearly as abundant as those sent by Molly and Charlie. No, she decided, she would leave that alone. Her new in-laws were coming for Christmas, the first with their son's new family.

"But I'll go with whatever decision you make," Peter said.

"No you won't. This will have to be a joint decision."

He looked at her intensely, waiting. She remembered that she had stood in the foyer among the gifts, facing him.

"I'll just leave one of the cards," she said finally.

"That's probably the best compromise."

Later, it surprised her how little she brooded over it, even knowing that it was an act of cruelty on her part. Odd, how the mind rationalizes, she had thought, and makes itself well again. Besides, as a genuinely loving and devoted mother and wife, living a busy, happy life, she could not conceive of herself as intrinsically cruel. It was like reading a newpaper story of some hideous act, far away. It touched her for the moment, then passed.

Not quite. On Christmas morning, Tray went through his gifts with the usual gurgles of surprise and satisfaction, with Peter's parents greatly enjoying the spectacle. It was truly wonderful to see how they had taken Tray into their hearts. Tray had responded in kind, and the whole scene was one of warm, familial affection. Then, suddenly, Tray had asked, "Didn't Grampa and Gramma Waters send me anything?"

"They sent this lovely card, Tray," Frances said, as her heart jumped to her throat. Tray looked at it with some confusion, started to say something, then frowned. Seeing his reaction, Peter jumped between them with a loud exclamation.

"Bet I can get to the castle first." He was referring to the computer game he had just unwrapped, a game of knights and dragons. Tray hesitated, obviously still wrestling with the idea of the missing gifts. Peter reached out and tickled his ribs. The boy giggled.

"Bet I can," Peter pressed as Tray squirmed.

"Bet you can't."

Frances was relieved. A critical moment had passed. Or had it? Had it been the right thing to do? she wondered, taking some comfort from seeing her son and his new father eagerly at play, full of smiles. She took the card and quietly replaced it under the tree, amid the cluttered jungle of unopened gifts.

Nevertheless, Frances had agreed to see Molly, whose call yesterday bore an ominous note of desperation that somehow triggered her conscience.

"It's strictly between us, Frances," Molly had said. "Woman to woman."

"But it won't change anything, Molly."

"There's no harm in talking."

"It's an unnecessary aggravation. I have my kids to worry about. And Peter."

"We've never been enemies, Frances."

"But we are involved in a very delicate controversy."

"I'm not asking for anything more than talk," Molly pleaded. "Just talk."

"Can't we do it on the telephone, then?" It had been her first mistake. Fight off the guilt, she had begged herself. As she begged herself now.

"Face to face, Frances. Please."

"Peter would never approve." She was immediately regretful. Approval was not the proper word. Agree, she thought. He would never agree. Approval made her appear subservient. Nevertheless, she let it pass.

"Just between us," Molly pressed.

"But look at the terrible position you put me in. I have no intention of changing my mind."

"So then where's the harm?"

"There is harm in it, Molly."

"I promise I will not bother you again. I promise." Her tone was urgent, pressured.

"Does that mean you will drop the suit?" She felt oddly encouraged. Perhaps such an idea was germinating in Molly's mind. "You realize, of course, that it is a terrible disruption for Peter and myself."

"For us, too." There was a long pause. "Maybe," Molly said hesitantly.

"You mean maybe you will drop the suit?"

"There are endless possibilities if human beings will just sit down and talk."

"That doesn't answer my question," Frances had countered.

They had gone round and round in that vein, but since the

possiblity of ending the suit had been broached, she had finally agreed. Very quickly it had seemed more like capitulation on her part.

For their meeting, they had picked a Burger King on Route 40, about a half hour from Columbia. It was Molly's suggestion that they get there by ten-thirty, just after breakfast and before the lunch-hour crowds would arrive. There was, she knew, a great deal of unspoken subtlety involved even in that decision. Somehow it seemed like neutral ground, a spot where they could appear anonymous, a midway point between their present worlds.

This sense of intrigue annoyed Frances, as well. She had never lied to Peter. Not that she had lied about meeting with Molly, but to her mind, the failure to mention it was as good as a lie. She knew it was an exaggeration, but she could not shake the suggestion of betrayal. Childishly, she wondered what form her punishment would take, whether it would strike her or her children. It was awful to contemplate and, before she reached the door to leave, she was overwhelmed by the desire to call the whole thing off.

Rushing to the phone in the den, she misdialed Molly's number, discovering that it had disappeared from her memory. Information provided it, but she got no answer. Then she tried Molly's school. One of the clerks in the principal's office told her that Molly had complained of feeling ill and had taken off for the day. She knew, of course, what that meant. Still, she did not leave the house. With growing anxiety, she paced the living room. Molly was, she was certain, on her way to their meeting place. She looked at the tall clock in the hall. If she left now, she would already be fifteen minutes late. Perhaps she should wait until ten-thirty, call Burger King, and tell Molly she had had second thoughts.

She wondered if she should call Peter, confess her foolishness, and ask his advice. Actually, she knew in advance what his advice would be: Don't go. She pictured Molly sitting there in the restaurant, stomach churning with apprehension and anxiety, watching the entering patrons, searching their faces, waiting for the moment that would not come. Suddenly she felt a strange tightness in what she was sure was her uterus where her new baby was growing. It passed quickly, but it left her with worrisome thoughts. Would all this angst have any effect on her daughter?

With a great effort of will, Frances put aside her increasing anxiety.

"There's no harm in it," Molly had promised.

"There had better not be," she told herself.

She was nearly forty minutes late. Road construction and traffic had held her up even more than her initial hesitation.

"I'm sorry," she told Molly, who looked up, ashen-faced, from what was obviously tepid coffee.

The lunchtime crowds were arriving in droves. The lines were long and the atmosphere noisy. She slid in across the booth from Molly.

"I hope they don't throw us out for loitering," Molly said. She looked toward the busy counters. "Do you want something?"

"I'm fine," Frances said. Molly looked tired, much older than she had appeared when Frances had last seen her.

"I'm afraid he doesn't have much of a light touch," Molly shrugged.

"Who?"

"Father Time." Molly's eyes inspected her. "But you're looking wonderful, Frances. Radiant."

"I'm happy." She had resolved not to tell her about the new baby.

"And Tray?"

"He's doing fine. The baby, too."

"Peter?"

"Everybody is wonderful, Molly. Really wonderful. I have a good life now." She wished she hadn't said "now."

"So it's all behind you? Us? Chuck?"

The irony of the face-to-face confrontation, Frances thought, was that it put Molly at a distinct disadvantage. The knowledge calmed her.

"I'm afraid so." She hesitated. "Except for that lawsuit. It's something we all could have done without."

"I'm really sorry about that. But there didn't seem to be another way. Sometimes you get into a situation that cannot be resolved except by an outside source."

"If only you would both realize—" Frances began.

"Still the hard-nose, eh, Frances?" Molly said, shaking her head. Her attitude had a sharper, more confrontational edge than Frances had seen in her before.

"What I'm trying to say is that pressing the issue only makes it worse. I've told you that you've got to give us all time."

Frances watched Molly's eyes narrow. Her nostrils quivered. "Your concept of time and ours is vastly different. For God's sake, Frances, it's been two years. Are you saying that if we let things alone, give up the suit, you'll give us some future date when you'll let us see Tray? Is that what you mean?"

"I suppose I do," Frances said.

"But it's now that it counts the most."

"For whom?"

"For Tray, of course."

"I think that's where we differ, Molly," she said gently. "It's now that Tray needs the stability of what he presently has. Perhaps later, when he gets into his teens, the situation won't be as disruptive."

"Like what? Like thirteen? Fourteen? Seventeen?"

"I'm not sure."

"At eighteen he can choose for himself whether to see us or not. By then he'll have forgotten what we look like or who we are." She was obviously holding back her anger, although her voice was still soft. Around them the noise level was rising as more customers poured into the place.

"That's eleven years from now. We'll have missed the best part of his life."

"That's just the point, Molly. It's him I have to think about first," she sighed. "I guess I can't make you see it."

"There's nothing to see," Molly said bitterly.

"That's because you won't look. Peter is Tray's father now. That is an inescapable fact of Tray's life. He is a real, living, caring father. Not a substitute. A true father. And Tray loves him. The boy is happy. He has a brother." Frances hesitated, then continued. "You and Charlie are part of another life. How many times must I say it? It's not said out of cruelty or spite or anger. The boy doesn't need you. I know it sounds awful. But it's true. I mean, I've kept the boy's name. I haven't totally erased Chuck's memory. But it's my and Peter's responsibility to decide what's best for him."

"What about us?"

"Don't you understand? I can't look at it that way."

"Were we so mean and terrible to you?" Molly asked pointedly.

"Not really." She had hesitated, just enough to convey the real truth of her earlier unhappiness. "It has nothing to do with that."

"But you do see us as a kind of enemy?"

Frances looked around her uncomfortably. Guard against this, she told herself.

"That's ridiculous," she said. "You people see everything from the wrong end of the telescope."

"Afraid that somehow we'll corrupt our own grandchild?"

"Now you're going too far, Molly."

"I can't help it. I just don't understand. Are you really afraid that we'll hurt Tray? Is it Peter you're worried about? Or maybe—" Frances sensed that something truly awful was coming, something totally out of character for Molly. She said nothing and waited.

"We've seen your house, Frances. And you. Your clothes. Even the way you talk. It's like the rough edges have been smoothed out."

"I really don't know what you're talking about."

"Dundalk is a long way from Columbia."

"Not as far as you think."

"It's like you moved up a notch or two and don't want to be reminded—"

"I'm not going to sit here and listen to that, Molly," Frances said, her agitation rising. Molly was pressing sensitive buttons, as if she knew exactly what would get the most telling reactions. Frances started to slide out of the booth. Molly put a hand on her arm.

"It's not that, Frances," Molly said, her lips trembling. "Not that at all." Her eyes glazed over as if she were focusing on something deep inside of her. "It's killing Charlie." Her neck muscles knotted with the effort to keep herself under control. Clearing her throat, she tried to continue, then coughed into her fist.

"I'm sorry, Molly. Really I am."

"You can't understand what has happened to him. Chuck, Tray, his job, everything that meant anything in his life has simply disappeared. It seems like such a little thing, a simple regular visit with the only grandchild he has"— she coughed again —"we have."

Molly's gaze seemed to sweep through her like a cold wind. She felt stripped of flesh, transparent.

"You must think I'm a terrible woman, Molly," Frances said.

"No." She shook her head a number of times. "Just misdirected."

"I'm not directed, Molly. It's a joint decision," Frances said indignantly. "I have to get on with my life as best I can. Do what's going to be right for Tray." She paused, and her hands tightened into fists. "I didn't exactly have things easy. Life with Chuck wasn't a bed of roses." She had not intended the reference and could see in Molly's face the confusion it raised.

"Is that the real issue then?" Molly asked. "Not just Tray." She obviously wanted to say more, but held off. No, she thought. Not just Tray.

Frances felt the beginnings of a great retch growing in her stomach. This is madness, she thought. Why am I subjecting myself to this? Time to go. "So you will not drop the suit?" she asked.

"We will if you let us visit Tray. The solution seems quite simple."

"Not to me. Not to Peter and certainly not to Tray."

"Frances, dammit," Molly's voice rose above the din. People turned around to look at her. To Frances, the flare-up seemed totally out of character, and it frightened her. Seeing that she had made a stir, Molly lowered her voice and spoke through her teeth. "I think Charlie is thinking about committing suicide."

Am I a punching bag? Frances asked herself. Letting myself in for this? It had been a mistake. Her first instincts had been correct.

"I don't understand," she said after a long pause.

"I've never lied to you, Frances. I've always tried to be forthright and above board. I'm sorry. To me this is a matter of life or death. I have reason to believe that Charlie has suicide on his mind." She averted her eyes, perhaps embarrassed by the revelation.

"You can't be serious."

"Can't I? Did you ever see a man sit with a loaded gun on his lap in the middle of the afternoon?"

"But you can't be sure—"

"I can't take that chance."

"Over not seeing Tray? Is that what you're implying?"

"Over everything."

"And you're saying that if he doesn't get to see Tray and he then takes his life, somehow it will be because of that."

"I had no intention of putting it in those terms, Frances. Really I didn't."

"I think it's awful to even suggest it."

Molly averted her eyes and played with her fingers. "I have my life, too." With an obvious effort of will, she withheld her tears. "And Charlie is my life. I'm here—I've begged you to come here so that I can beg you to let—well, at least Charlie—come and see Tray. Let them visit on any terms acceptable to you. I'm willing to stand aside if it will help. I'm not a martyr type, Frances. You know that. And I love Tray. I don't know if this makes any sense. But Charlie needs this. He needs it desperately. Why can't you reconsider? Persuade Peter to reconsider. Frances, we've lost our only son. Can you know what that means? I know you're a good girl, a decent girl, a caring person. You've got to give Charlie this chance. . . ."

It was no longer possible for Molly to hold it in, and she let go, but not completely. She had balled a napkin in one of her hands. She now flattened its wrinkles and lifted it to wipe her tears. Frances watched her, angry, stupefied, and shocked. She was also moved, but in a strange way it only solidified her resolve to keep them from seeing Tray, to keep him from being exposed to the terror of such thoughts. "My God, Molly. Why must everything rest on this? Why don't you find some other way to fill your lives? I mean, in a way you're free, totally without demands and responsibilities. You can travel. You can do anything you want."

"I still have my job," Molly whispered, sniffling.

"It just seems that you're both getting morbid about all this." She had never seen Molly in such a state of helplessness. There had always been an air of self-contentment and reserve about her. Even Chuck's characterization of his mother as the family's defensive back seemed to be diminished by her pleading. It shocked Frances to see Molly's eroding strength.

"It's not very pleasant to see your husband disintegrate," Molly said, the pointed sarcasm somehow steadying her. Frances resolved to leave as soon as she could. Molly had trapped her, she decided. She was working on her guilt. Feeling panicked within herself, she cried silently for Peter.

The restaurant was getting extremely crowded, and patrons carrying full trays as they passed looked at them with beady-eyed resentment. Yet she did not want to make the first move for fear that it would plunge Molly into even deeper despair.

"I never expected things to get as bad as this," Frances said.

"And you have it in your power to put it all in reverse."

The intensity of Molly's sudden inspection burned into her. The tears had dried. The inner hysteria seemed to have dissipated, leaving Frances even more suspicious of Molly's motives. She could not seem to move out of the glare of the older woman's pressuring gaze. "I'll do anything you ask, Frances. Once a month is all Charlie needs. That's not much to ask, is it?"

"That's not the point."

"Then every two months if that's the way you want it."

"Why are you doing this to yourself, Molly?"

"It doesn't have to be long, either. Maybe an afternoon. Just one lousy afternoon. If you want, they can stay in the neighborhood—"

"It has nothing to do with how long or how many times. It has nothing to do with that."

"Then what?"

She saw the man she presumed was the manager eyeing them from behind the counter. He disappeared, then emerged from a side door across from their table. Molly, facing Frances, did not see him.

"You're just upsetting yourself with that kind of reasoning," Frances sighed, knowing it was not reasoning at all, but the hysterical voice of the woman's heart. I can't really help the way she feels, she told herself. I must not be manipulated. I must do what is best for Tray. For Peter. For my family.

"It's wrong, Frances. Charlie says it's against nature."

She saw the man approach and swallowed her response, which, in any event, would have seemed belligerent. Tray does not exist to provide Charlie with psychiatric therapy, was what she had in mind, borrowing from Peter's more scientific reasoning.

"I'm sorry, ladies," the man said. "But you can't hold that table for an unreasonable amount of time." He waved his hand around the room. "We're loaded."

"We'll be ready very shortly," Molly shot back.

"Really it's not fair," the man said.

"What's fair?" Molly countered.

"I think he has a point," Frances said.

"Thank you, lady,"

"In a minute, then." Molly squinted up at him with unmistakable contempt, startling the man with her vehemence, but with enough authority to get him to leave. The gesture had the effect of making Frances step back even further from the abyss of pity.

"I really have to go, Molly." To emphasize the point, she looked at her watch. "The woman I've got taking care of the baby can't speak English."

"So there's nothing I can say or do?" Molly asked.

"I'm sorry."

"That's not much help."

Frances lifted her eyes, and Molly met her glance directly. For a long moment, they held this stare across the table.

"I guess we have different priorities," Frances said quietly. "I know you think I'm an unfeeling bitch, but I can't help that."

"Charlie does. I'm not sure. I like to think that you're just obeying Peter's wishes. That doesn't help us, but in a funny way it does take the onus off our grandchild's mother."

Frances stood up. It was useless to continue the conversation. Besides, she was getting another cramped feeling in her uterus and had begun to get anxious about the baby.

"So I'll see you in court," Molly said, rising. Her dress was creased and a strained look gave her an air of desperation and confusion. So different from their first meeting when Chuck had brought Frances to his home. Molly had seemed so formidable then, crisp, self-assured, wise and knowing. It was not that old Molly that she saw now, and their confrontation had only widened the distance between them. It's over, she told herself. Yesterday is dead.

"It's a free country," Frances said, with a haughtiness she had not intended.

They moved through the crowds to the street. Frances walked ahead. But once outside, she stopped and waited for Molly to catch up. No sense leaving this meeting with spitefulness, she thought, reaching out her hand. Molly looked at it, hesitating, then took it and shook it vigorously.

"You can't imagine how terrible it will be in court," Molly said ominously. "For both of us."

She pulled her hand out of Molly's grasp. "It wasn't my idea."

Molly did not respond. Frances stood awkwardly facing her for a moment, disoriented.

"I hope Charlie is okay," she said. At that moment a cloud passed over the sun, and it grew suddenly cold. She shivered. "It has gotten much colder."

"Yes, it has," Molly replied. She looked at Frances, a slightly bemused expression on her face. "You're right about one thing. I don't understand any of it."

"I know," Frances said as she turned away and began to stride toward the car. As she walked, a cramp gripped her, and she stopped. A flutter of pain continued for a few moments, then subsided. Peripherally, she saw Molly puzzling over her action. But when the pain had gone, she walked purposefully to the car.

By the time she arrived home, she was genuinely concerned over the periodic cramping she was experiencing, filling her with anxious thoughts and fears for the child she was nurturing. Had the confrontation shocked her yet unformed baby? If so, she knew she could never forgive herself for exposing it to such danger. What did she expect? Through her growing panic, she was certain that she had handled her ex-mother-in-law with skill and determination. Unfortunately, it appeared that she would be paying a heavy price for her supposed strength. But such logic soon disintegrated into an ugly and illogical suspicion that perhaps Molly had brought her there to abort her baby with psychic pain.

The offensive thought lingered, along with anxieties about Baby Mark, who turned out to be just fine. She found him dozing off in Maria's arms. An empty bottle stood on the table beside her.

"He hungry *niño*," Maria said.

As Frances went upstairs, the painful flutter began again with what seemed like more intensity. In the bathroom, she checked to see if she was staining. Relieved that she was not, she called the doctor, who instructed her to get into bed and stay there. It wasn't, she knew, quite that simple. She had to arrange for Tray to be picked up, for Baby Mark's next feeding, for dinner, for Maria to stay on. It's all falling apart, she thought bitterly. All because I didn't follow my instincts, because I did not put my immediate family first.

Thankfully, she got one of her neighbors to pick up Tray and did persuade Maria to stay later than usual to feed the baby and prepare dinner, which would consist of a frozen meat-loaf dish thrown into the microwave oven, the intricacies of which she had to painstakingly describe to Maria.

She deliberately did not call Peter at the office to inform him of her condition. No sense worrying him, she thought, dreading what she had to tell him. She tried to nap, but painful thoughts and Molly's morbid pleas kept interfering.

Peter arrived at his usual time. She heard Maria answering his questions in pidgin English, then his panicked two-at-a-time steps as he bounded up the stairs.

"What is it?" he said coming into the room. He hadn't taken off his coat.

"Just a little pain. Nothing serious. The doctor said I should stay in bed."

Bending over, he kissed her on the forehead.

"Are you sure?"

"I feel better already," she said tentatively, although the painful flutters continued to plague her. "I'll be fine," she said bravely. "The doctor said it happens sometimes."

"It didn't happen before," he looked down at her and rubbed his chin. "Did it happen with Tray?"

She shook her head.

"I hope it's not too much for you, darling. It's not easy having them one after another. Damn." He turned away, hiding his anger with himself.

"Don't be silly, Peter," she said, reaching out and touching his sleeve. "It's just as much my fault. I just overdid things today."

"Well, you've got to stop that." He turned to face her, offering a smile and smoothing her forehead with his hand. She grabbed his wrist and brought it down to her lips. "What the devil did you do today, Frances?"

Gripping his wrist, she applied some inadvertent pressure. Her guilty secret was not sitting well at all. In fact, it was bubbling inside of her, aching to be revealed.

"I saw Molly today."

"You what?"

She restrained him by putting her hand over his lips and looking him straight in the eye and quickly explaining what she had done in the most succinct way she could, watching his expression run the gamut from annoyance to anger to indignation.

"I know," she said finally. "I was a fool."

"And look at the state it got you into."

"I was wrong. I'm sorry. I feel terrible about it. I should not have done it, although I felt I did handle it very well."

"She had no right to put you in that position," Peter snapped. Then he lowered his voice. "You should have told me, darling."

"I know." She felt like a rebuked child.

"We could have checked with the lawyer. Who knows how

much it has compromised the case? Besides putting you in this state."

"I was very foolish. I admit it. Worse, I didn't tell you what I was going to do. Somehow I got it into my head that she was going to tell me that she was prepared to drop the case."

"People can be very mean when they want something badly enough, Frances. You should have shared it with me."

"It's spilt milk, Peter."

Peter stood up and circled the room. Then he came back to the bed.

"Bet she laid a guilt trip on you."

"That she did. But I coped with it very well."

"Except for this." He gestured toward the bed with an open palm.

"I don't think you can blame this on her. It might have happened anyway."

"I doubt it. She created needless stress."

"Still—"

"If you hadn't gone, it might not have happened."

"Well, we'll never know," she said testily.

"I wonder if her lawyer put her up to it," he mused.

"I doubt it."

"Why would you doubt it?"

"I'm not sure." She felt a brief flutter and a sense of rising tension. Something more had to be said, she decided. "She said that Charlie was contemplating suicide, that she found him sitting in the den with a loaded gun on his lap."

"Damn," Peter muttered. "How rotten of her." She could see his face flush with white-hot anger, a rare occurrence. "How could she have done such a terrible thing? And I suppose she told you that the only thing she could think of to shake him out of this was for us to make a deal on Tray?"

"Something like that."

"How cunning."

"I think you're being too hard on her, Peter. I understand her concern. I really do. She was desperate. Charlie is probably very depressed. I didn't quite expect it to go that way."

"Well then, what did you expect?"

His aggressive manner shocked her, and she frowned.

"I'm sorry," he said quickly. "I'm just so aggravated. Seeing you like this." He paused and looked at her for a moment, trying to gather some control. "Did you tell her you were pregnant?" She shook her head vehemently.

"Of course not."

"Well, thank God for that. It would have blown Peck's strategy."

"I'm not that stupid, Peter." She felt a sudden surge of resentment. Peter turned away, still fighting his anger. When he showed her his face again, he was calmer.

"It was just something you shouldn't have done," he muttered.

"I know that now," Frances said.

"We could have avoided this. She threw this at you deliberately. That's what she did. She would love to see you in this state."

"What state? I'm not in any state. I told you the doctor just said to stay in bed."

"If that woman causes you to miscarry . . ."

"I'll be fine." Even to her, the words sounded far away, like the bleat of a lost lamb.

He sat down on the bed and took her in his arms.

"Why are they doing this to us? Why can't they leave us alone? Tray is fine and happy. Everything was going beautifully."

Frances burrowed her nose into his neck.

He held her and said nothing for a long time. It was comforting to be in his protective arms. He had saved her, she thought, given her a new life. He was her rock.

"I'm so sorry, Peter," she whispered.

"It's not your fault, darling. Not your fault at all. You wanted to do the right thing, that's all. It just wasn't right in the final analysis."

The words were reassuring, but they did not eliminate her anxiety.

She stayed in bed for a week. During that time, Peter took off from work, performed the household chores and the driving, supervised Maria, fed the dog, and generally pampered her. Because of the language barrier, he expressed fear of leaving Maria in charge despite Frances's protestations.

"She is perfectly capable," Frances told him. She was definitely not comfortable with his sacrifice, although she knew it was sincere.

"You and the kids are my number one priority."

"But this could go on for months."

"So be it."

Thankfully, it didn't. The pain receded, then disappeared completely, and the doctor allowed her to get out of bed and test the water.

"I'm fine now," she assured Peter, who, nevertheless, put in a couple of half-days at the office until she insisted that it was not necessary.

"Now you've got to promise. No more capers on your own."

"I promise." She crossed her heart and pecked him on the lips.

Soon she was back at her regular pace. The rest, she discovered, had done her good. Her doctor agreed. He examined her and found her sound.

"It was just one of those things," he said. "Everything's perfectly normal as far as I can see."

"Maybe it was my imagination."

"It pays to be cautious, anyhow. Don't overdo."

"It's not like it's the first one, doctor," she said with mock indignation.

"Sometimes when one pregnancy follows hard on the heels of another, these little blips occur."

"Well, they're scary just the same."

The reassurance sparked her optimism, and she tucked her anxieties away in the back of her mind.

There were reminders, of course. Despite the two-year separation, Tray would sometimes wonder aloud about Grampa and Gramma Waters.

"You think Grampa will still get me the sailboat?" It was a question he asked, not often, but enough to be noticed. Usually it was when Peter was not within earshot.

"Of course he will," she would answer casually, quickly changing the subject, wondering what else was going through the child's mind. Somehow she felt her answers to that question and others never really satisfied him. He had asked numerous other questions when she had said good night to him after the confrontation with Charlie at the school.

"He just wanted to stop by and say hello," Frances told him, hoping that her noncommittal answers would deflect his attention.

"But it was right in the middle of school. The teacher was angry."

"I suppose he saw that old wagon and wanted to give it to you. That's all."

"Why couldn't he just bring it here?"

"It's not that important."

She saw him frown and sensed his inner agitation. Why couldn't he just leave well enough alone? she thought bitterly. Then she had hugged him and changed the subject once again, knowing that it had not yet settled in his mind.

But the suit, of course, would not go away, and Peter's frequent whispered phone conversations with the lawyer attested to the fact that it was very active indeed. Whenever she referred to it, he deflected her interest, waving the subject away as if it were a mild disturbance, not worth her concern. She was perfectly willing to ignore it, knowing that, however long the pause, the inevitable would come crashing through the window of her illusions.

It came nearly three months after her episode with Molly. She was into the fat and happy period of her pregnancy. The baby was kicking up a storm, and it was sometimes the object of family wonder and amusement as they, children included, would touch, listen, and watch the undulating antics of the growing mound of life in her belly.

The expectation blunted her surprise when Peter had announced one day that there was no avoiding the inevitable any longer. Peck had insisted that they meet in his office. There were decisions to make, and a trial was imminent. In a way, she was relieved.

"Above all, I want you to remain calm," Peter warned as they were ushered into the conference room.

"I know my priorities," she replied, patting her belly and offering an amused grin.

Henry Peck carried his bulk into the office. He brought with him a fat accordion folder, which he untied with thick fingers, then slid out files and a yellow legal pad. Then he rubbed his nose with the back of his hand and peered at Frances through his steel-rimmed glasses. She noted that his gaze dropped to take in her condition, not clearly visible over the conference table.

"Lot of water over the dam since we last met," he said with an ironic chuckle and a pull on his polka dot bow tie.

"As you know, I haven't really been filling her in, Henry," Peter said, clearing his throat, slightly uncomfortable with the

explanation. The first-name intimacy seemed strange, and she felt
some annoyance in observing it, as if they had formed a private
little alliance that excluded her.

"I realize that, Peter," Peck said, turning his attention to Frances.
Again, he rubbed his nose. "There comes a time," he sighed.
Frances looked toward Peter, who raised his eyes toward the ceil-
ing and shrugged.

"That's why I'm here," Frances said, with some determination.

"We've gone the route of petitioning the judge on a technical
ruling, citing the adoptive laws and the fact that there is no point
of law in this type of case and, therefore, that your former in-
laws do not have a bona fide case." Again he rubbed his nose.
"He wasn't buying. Not because we weren't right. But Forte cited
all those cases in other states, and I think the judge, being a
grandparent himself, felt more comfortable with the matter being
aired at a full hearing."

Frances looked at Peter.

"That doesn't sound too good."

"Not as bad as you think," Peter said.

"But it means we have to have a trial."

"That's correct," the lawyer said. He had taken off his glasses
and was cleaning them with a tissue, looking at her with pale,
myopic eyes. "I never did expect to win the technical issue, especially with that judge."

"Isn't it the same judge that will hear our case?"

"Usually," the lawyer said, replacing his glasses and showing
her a thin cryptic smile. "And I seriously considered a postponement, more stalling. Then we got lucky."

"We did!" Frances exclaimed.

"No judge really likes these domestic equity cases. They alternate assignments every six months. This time, the old duffer got
out of it, by tossing it to the newest member of the bench."

"And that's good?" Frances asked.

"I think so," Peck said. "In fact, I'm sure of it." Shamming a
smug expression, he studied each face in turn. "We've drawn
ourselves Judge Anne Stokes, an interim appointee. Annie Stokes
is pretty sharp. And this is her first domestic relations case. She's
in her mid-forties, with two teenage kids. Lost her husband several
years ago. Knows the territory, so to speak. Above all, she's not a
grandparent. And since she's new at the game, and up for her
first election, she'll be in no mood to stretch the law and chance

getting it reversed on appeal. It wouldn't look good for her around election time. The thing is, Forte was a bit cocky when the technical ruling came down. Now he's got to eat crow."

"But can't he stall, ask for a postponement?" Frances asked.

"She'll sit on this bench for six months. A postponement won't look good for him. After all, he's the petitioner. And since his clients live within the city limits it won't be easy for him to ask to be heard in the county. No, I think he's got to take his chances with Annie."

"When is the trial?" Frances asked.

"In six weeks," Peck said flatly, looking at her. "That will put you in the eighth month—exactly."

Frances looked quickly at Peter.

"I've discussed it with the doctor, Frances," Peter said. "He wouldn't recommend it, but he doesn't see it as a major threat. Just as long as you're reasonably protected from undue aggravation."

"Which may be impossible," Peck said.

Frances frowned.

"I don't like it myself. But hear him out," Peter said.

She turned toward the lawyer, waiting. The baby moved suddenly, and she started, smiling. It gave a false impression of her inner feelings.

Encouraged, Peck began.

"As I explained earlier, the judge decides. What's best for the child is the main criterion for judgment. Also the stability of the family unit is paramount." He leaned back in his chair and folded his hands across his ample stomach. "Who can dispute that you are a happy, well-adjusted, loving, caring family with Charles the third as much a part of it as your natural child and the one soon to arrive?" His tongue flicked out and moistened his lips. "Now. What we must do is show the judge that Mr. and Mrs. Waters will inject a dark force into this otherwise happy situation, create tensions inimical to the family and, by obvious inference, to your son."

"I understand that," Frances said impatiently.

"I know you do, Mrs. Graham," Peck said gently. "But we are in the business of manipulating the emotions. Granted, we have a fertile subject in this widowed lady judge. But we must strike hard and deep into the heart of the judge's psyche. Everything counts—the obvious, the subtle, and the unconsciously perceived.

In terms of the obvious we have Mr. Waters's instability, his compulsive behavior, and"—his gaze shot toward Peter—"his suicidal tendencies—"

Frances felt an inner lurch, a thudding echo in her head.

"I didn't—" she interrupted.

"Of course I told him, Frances," Peter said. "Also about your meeting with Molly and your near miscarriage. It's all relevant. It can't be helped."

"Your husband is right," Peck continued. "It happens to be a good break for us."

"Some break," Frances said indignantly, confused by her defensiveness.

"It was an episode that required medical advice," Peck said.

"No question about that," Peter agreed. "And it did upset the family. I had to take off from work." He reached out and patted Frances's hand. "It's a factor."

"Undoubtedly," Peck said, waiting patiently for further comment. When none came, he continued. "It's a big plus for us. As for the subtle, we have your condition as exhibit A, Mrs. Graham." She had half expected him to call her Frances and was prepared to resent the intimacy. Instead, she merely resented the idea. Peck was apparently quick to understand. "It's part of the game. We're in the business of transmitting messages. And this is one that will not be lost on the judge. Or on our opponents."

"We have to use every arrow in the quiver, baby," Peter said.

"The fact is that we may actually have a better case than it seemed originally. A child should not be used as therapy for the aged. Unless, of course, the child benefits as well. This fellow, Waters, from what Peter tells me, is easily provoked. Am I right?"

Although the question was addressed to Frances, it was Peter who answered.

"I told him how Charlie acted on the night we left town. After Frances broke the news about Tray. He was like a crazy man, irrational. For a minute there, I thought he was going to attack both of us."

"He was very upset," Frances said.

"And at the school?"

"He was definitely not himself."

Peck shook his head.

"Not that way," he said. "On the stand, you can't say that. You will have to imply that he *was* himself, showing his real persona. That is critical. But I'll be briefing you on that."

She nodded. No, she told herself, it would not be pleasant. And weren't Charlie and Molly the ones who were pressing the suit? She was simply defending her position. Think of Tray, she urged herself.

"I understand," she said, feeling an inner stiffening of resolve. "It won't be a piece of cake."

"Can I ask a question?" Peter asked suddenly. It was the way he said it that seemed somehow pedantic, as if he already knew the answer. Peck looked at him and nodded, as if they had rehearsed the scene.

"Is it possible to postpone the trial until the baby comes?"

"Maybe. But it would be throwing away a good card."

"But can we win without it?"

"Who can say?" Peck said. "In this business we deal in probabilities. That doesn't mean my reasoning is not all wet."

"Sooner or later we'll have to face it," Peter said. "Unless they withdraw the suit, which doesn't seem likely."

"I'm afraid you're right. They have absolutely nothing to lose except time and money."

"It's a tough call," Peter said. He looked at Frances. "You're damned if you do, damned if you don't."

"An axiom of domestic relations," Peck said.

"I don't want anything to hurt her," Peter mused. She could tell he was on the razor's edge of indecision. She felt certain now that he and the lawyer had had this discussion before and were replaying it for her benefit.

"I'll do whatever Mr. Peck thinks," Frances said, to relieve Peter of the pressure. "I'm sure I'm strong enough. In fact, I'm in excellent shape and not afraid." Peter's hand reached for hers under the table and they entwined fingers. "We might as well get on with it. Get it behind us."

"You're my only worry. And the kids. All of them," Peter said, and she knew he meant it. She could see that Henry Peck was pleased. It was obvious that Peter had agonized over the question with the lawyer. "If anything happens to her because of this, I'll never forgive myself."

"I won't feel too good about it either," Frances said lightly. "And I like the idea of a woman judge." Although she didn't much like Henry Peck, she knew he was right. A widowed woman in the process of raising children would surely understand.

"So it's go?" Peck asked.

"I'll be as big as a house," Frances said.

"The bigger the better."

Chapter 11

MOLLY sat in the empty classroom marking the math tests of her fifth grade children. It was a gray day, and the rain swept against the windowpanes. She was not happy with the test results. Nearly half the test papers had shown a failing grade. She placed the blame for this poor showing directly on her own head. Pure and simple, she was losing her effectiveness as a teacher.

Putting down her pencil, she removed her glasses and massaged the upper part of her nose. Then she leaned back in her chair and looked about the room, at the rows of empty desks, the American flag, the blackboard with that day's examples, the pictures of animals, and framed proverbs: DO UNTO OTHERS AS YOU WOULD HAVE OTHERS DO UNTO YOU, A STITCH IN TIME SAVES NINE, and her favorite, TODAY IS THE DAY YOU WORRIED ABOUT YESTERDAY AND ALL IS WELL. Only all wasn't well.

Charlie was draining her energies with worry and anxiety. She had managed, by constant cajoling, to get him out of the house to look for a job. He had gotten one as a clerk in a tire store, but that hadn't panned out. Then he had landed one as a gas jockey in a filling station, which she had had to talk him out of, and now he was working in a plant nursery from which, as far as she could see, he derived some satisfaction. He had always liked growing things. At least she hadn't come home to find him with a loaded rifle across his knees. She shivered at the memory.

Like a creeping mass of volcanic lava, the worrisome aspects of her life were slowly approaching, and she was already beginning to feel their deadly powers of destruction. These papers, she thought, putting her hand on the top of the pile, were proof positive that she was losing her touch.

For years, her teaching job, her role as purveyor of knowledge, had sustained her. Through Chuck's death and Tray's departure, it had given her a sense of proud purpose. Each day, as she entered the world of her classroom and looked into the eager faces of her children, she was able to throw off the shackles of disappointments and tragedy that had marred the last few years and pursue a noble purpose. What she did in the classroom truly mattered. But the oasis seemed to be disintegrating. The well was running dry.

And here was the evidence, she told herself, putting on her glasses again and picking up her marking pencil. Her condition was not something you could hide, especially from the children. They were always the first to notice. Nor had it escaped the eagle eye of Miss Parsons, the new principal. Molly had never worried about new brooms. Her popularity and competence had always commanded the respect of her superiors, her students, and their parents.

At their conference that morning, Miss Parsons had been all kindness and concern. She was trying so hard to be liked. Since her arrival, she had treated the staff with deference, which was, Molly knew, the modus operandi of all new brooms. Gain everyone's confidence first, then watch for flaws and take quick action. Union protection might save a teacher's job, but to be judged mediocre did little for the psyche.

"You have an outstanding record, Molly," Miss Parsons had said. She had thin lips and the tiniest hint of a lisp. Her auburn hair was frosted blonde, and she favored beiges and browns and white blouses with large bows. Her eyes crinkled around the edges when she smiled. Actually, hers was a big, luminous smile that involved her entire face and, Molly decided, was the secret of her swift rise in the school system.

"I appreciate that, Miss Parsons," Molly had responded, wary of praise, since she knew she was not living up to her reputation.

"The spirit of excellence is in the air these days, Molly. The board demands that we raise the overall level of our test results. I have no doubt that you will give us your best."

"I always have."

"For more than thirty years."

"Thirty-four in September."

"If only the younger teachers had your motivation, Molly," Miss Parsons said.

Molly wondered if all this dwelling on age was an ominous sign. What came next convinced her.

"It's so important for you to be an example." Miss Parsons had folded her immaculate white hands primly on her desk. "That's why I want us to have a special relationship." She turned on her brightest smile. "I'm asking for your confidence and, of course, your frankness. If there is anything, anything ever on your mind,

I want you to know that you will have a receptive ear in this office. Even now."

There was no escaping the fact that Molly had taken more leave and sick days in the last few months than for a like period in her entire career. But a lawyer's time was precious and had to be programmed more for his convenience than hers. Not that she didn't resent the implication that a teacher's time was less valuable than a lawyer's. The fact that she was taking another half-day off tomorrow was undoubtedly what had prompted Miss Parsons to summon her to a conference. Her absences were certainly an inconvenience to the other teachers and an imposition on the students at a critical time in the term. With the trial coming up in less than three weeks, she would shortly have to ask for additional time off. She felt the surveillance of Miss Parsons's eyes, probing and relentless, despite the smile crinkles. Does she mean now? Molly speculated.

"I do have this personal business," Molly began tentatively, testing the waters. Miss Parsons's silence told Molly that there was no going back, that the issue was the real purpose of their meeting. "A legal matter that, unfortunately, requires time. It's coming to a head in a few weeks, and I hope, one way or another, that will be the end of it."

"I'm very relieved to hear that, Mrs. Waters. These matters do debilitate one's energy and concentration."

Miss Parsons's words had stuck in her mind, and their truth was never more apparent than at that moment with the evidence of the awful results of this test clearly documented. Again she took off her glasses. She had hung on to her teaching job through thick and thin. Many of the friends with whom she had started had long since retired. Some had gone off to the South and West seeking warmer climes. Others had found second careers.

There was no avoiding the fact that a dramatic change was coming to her life as well. If the case was lost, there would be no point in staying in Baltimore. Tray's proximity and unavailability would just be too much for her and Charlie to bear. Nor could she sustain any enthusiasm for her job if her effectiveness was eroded by outside pressures. What would I do with myself? she thought gloomily.

Her life had started out with such promise. Charlie Waters, her handsome young marine, the warrior prince of her secret imaginings, had come up to Frederick to the weekly dance when she was a junior at Hood College. In his dress blues, sporting a medal for marksmanship on his chest, and with the confidence of just having finished boot camp at Quantico, he was fully convinced that he had reached the pinnacle of manhood and that it was his right and obligation to offer himself up for female worship. He had never quite gotten it out of his mind that it was he who had made the choice. Molly knew better. One look at him and her lifelong goose was cooked. His, too.

Nothing had ever been sweeter than this discovery of mutual love, the delicious confession of feeling. In those days young girls from good families scrupulously preserved their virginity for the marriage bed, and that, too, had its own delicate sweetness, although couples allowed some imagination and sexual resourcefulness into the physical process of courtship. There were simple joys in withholding and waiting, and she did both for three years while he fought America's last good war. How wonderful it had been to be loyal and true and brave, as if any violation of these virtues would have had the direst consequences for him on the battlefield.

"It was your love that brought me through it," he had written, then told her at last in person. Nothing could ever surpass the miraculous joy of reunion. It was the most vivid and heart-stirring remembrance of her life.

In their three years of being apart, they had written often. She wrote daily, pouring out her dreams for their future. His response was always to agree wholeheartedly. In retrospect, they were simple, innocent, and undemanding dreams. It was the era of the picket fence fantasy—a little house, three beautiful children, a car, a dog, and endless happily ever afters. Although it had not been specified then, it must have surely included the ultimate reward of the earned joy of being grandparents, and of a wise and painless old age.

There was no denying, even now, the goodness and sustaining power of the old dreams. But it was the shock of bitter reality, such as infertility and sudden death, that was the real test of life. It wasn't fair, especially now when one could see no light at the end of the tunnel. Don't talk to me of the hereafter, Molly thought, as she grew more and more contemplative about her life's ending. What about the here and now?

It had never occurred to either of them to violate the caveat of the marriage ceremony that pledged sustained union through better or worse. Well, the time of "worse" was upon her.

She tried to shake herself out of these increasingly repetitive and depressing thoughts, a goal that was growing more and more difficult to attain. After all, they had their health. It seemed so, at least in a shallow physical sense. But a man who sat alone in a darkened room with a loaded rifle poised across his legs wasn't exactly in tip-top mental condition. In a swift, sudden motion she stabbed her pencil into the paper she was marking. The point broke and, in an uncommon gesture of frustration, she threw the useless pencil across the room.

It wasn't only the overwhelming number of wrong answers on the papers that made her testy, but the recognition of so many wrong answers in her own life. I'm flunking, too, she decided. F for wife. F for mother. F for mother-in-law. F for grandmother, and now F for teacher. She giggled hysterically at these conclusions. Never had she held herself in such low esteem.

Gathering up her papers, she put on her raincoat, shut off the lights in the classroom, and let herself out of the near-deserted school. Rain, driven by the wind, wet her face and stockings. It did not help her gloomy attitude.

Driving home had lately been fraught with sinking apprehensions. What would Charlie be like? How low would he be? Would he be brooding and morose? It had come down to what degree of depression she would have to confront. Her reserves of optimistic encouragement were running out. There was nothing sadder than an overage cheerleader doing somersaults before near-empty stands.

She found Charlie sitting in the kitchen, sipping from a mug of hot coffee, smoking a cigarette and looking out into the yard. Lately their evening meal had consisted of salad, a baked potato, and some broiled meat or fish. It was an unspoken rule between them that whoever arrived first was to set the table, make the salad, and put the potatoes in to bake. That none of this had been done was, in itself, an ominous sign.

"What is it now?" she asked, letting her briefcase full of papers fall to the floor with a purposeful thud. The sound startled him into alertness, and he looked at her with some confusion.

"You blew it, right?" She felt her sense of control burst, and she wished she could withdraw the tone of her question.

"Blew what?"

His answer confused her.

"Your job," she pressed, wanting to strike out. "Don't try to kid me, Charlie. You blew your job. Why else would you be home so early?"

"It's raining."

"I am aware of that," she snapped.

"Too hard to work in the mud. Simple as that."

She felt ashamed, humiliated. It seemed now to be the regular condition of her life. Ever since she had met with Frances, she had had to contend with the terror of what she had done. It gnawed at her, colored everything she did and thought. And now she had shown her lack of confidence in Charlie, her lack of faith. Had she also demonstrated that in the manner in which she recounted her meeting with Frances? She had, of course, told both Charlie and Forte about their meeting, offering, with precise editing of the most important facts, the most graphic retelling she could muster, illustrating Frances's total intransigence and willingness to fight to the last to enforce her and Peter's decision. But she had, with great willpower and reluctance, omitted any reference to Charlie and his "suicidal tendencies." In fact, the revelation filled her with revulsion and disgust, and she lived with the hope that, in the courtroom, the information would be respected as confidential, although she was not overly optimistic on that point. It was a self-inflicted agony, she had decided, her cross to bear for the moment, notwithstanding that it was driving her crazy with anxiety. There was no sense alarming either Charlie or the lawyer, especially since hers could have been an overreactive interpretation. Besides, a similar event had not occurred, although she had hidden the shells as a precaution. Not that it mattered. He could always get more if he wanted them.

"Thought we might go out for dinner is all," Charlie said. "You all right?"

The weight of it all was pressing down on her, squeezing her insides. There seemed to be no way to stop it.

"I wish we hadn't started it," she said suddenly, the words beyond her control. She could see the hasty anger tremble through him.

"A little late in the game, Molly."

"Maybe this business about the lady judge . . ." Forte had briefed them and given them a less than optimistic view. From the beginning, he had hoped to be heard before one of the older judges.

Yet, she had actually been encouraged by this new prospect. A woman would understand, she told herself. But then she had never been widowed. She looked at Charlie, and the thought chilled her.

"No turning back now," Charlie shrugged. "Win, lose, or draw."

"It's just"— she made a great effort to soften her words, fearing that she might set off new explosions inside him that were too dangerous to contemplate —"just that nothing's been the same since all this began."

"We didn't start it, Molly. We're the victims."

"Maybe that's what I don't like," she sighed.

"And it began long before we saw a lawyer. The lawyer was a last resort, remember?" He got up from the chair, walked toward the outside door, hesitated, then started toward the den. Then he turned to face her again. It was as if he were acting out their entrapment, the absence of escape. His arm shot out, and he pointed a finger at her.

"It all started with that woman. If it wasn't for her, we would still have our Chuck. And Tray." He waved the finger, unable to get the words out. When they came, they seemed to sputter on his tongue. "It was you who was the soft one, letting it happen. I could have talked him out of her. I know I could. You were the one who let it happen. He had no business marrying that woman, no business at all. I made the one big mistake of my life. I let you lead me, like a damned donkey." His voice started to rise, reaching a pitch that she had never heard before. He seemed to be changing into another person before her eyes, as if all the bitterness inside had erupted and the acid was eating away his protective covering. "You defended her, always defended her, when it was Chuck we should have been looking after. Chuckie." His voice broke, became a gargle, then found its full timbre again. Wrapping her arms around herself, she lowered her eyes. It was excruciating enough just to hear his words without seeing the distortion in his features. "You didn't love him enough. That was it from the beginning, right? You didn't love him enough. Not me either. And not Tray. You were glad to see her come along and break us up. And it was you who said she'd come around one day after she took Tray away. Like a damned dummy, I listened to you." She wished she could shut out the words. "So now you wish you hadn't started it. I say shit to that, woman." She heard banging and, lifting her eyes, saw him swinging his fist against the wall. The sound of his fury boomed through the house. "No. No. No," he cried. In her heart, she knew what his fists were pounding, and she got up and gripped him from behind, hugging him to her.

"You mustn't, Charlie. Please."

He stopped, finally, laying his head against the wall, sobbing quietly.

"If it was me, I'm sorry," she whispered. Against her, his body lurched and shivered with the tremors of his agony.

"I just want my grandson. Is that so much to ask?" he said, after he had quieted.

"No, it is not, my darling." She continued to hold him. "Our grandson," she whispered, tears rolling over her cheeks. After a while, he turned and they stood leaning against the wall, locked in an embrace, holding each other as if to let go would be the end of life itself.

"I am so sorry, babe. So sorry sorry sorry sorry." She felt the breeze of his words against her ear. "How can I blame you? It's terrible. Me blaming you."

"There's only us, kiddo," she whispered after a while.

"I nearly blew that."

"Never, Charlie. Never that."

"I know, babe."

"It's got us crazy."

"I lost control. It scares me. I didn't mean it, Molly. You know that."

"Better to get it out like that than keep it in."

He gathered her closer.

"As long as I have you, I'll be okay."

"Then you'll be okay."

"How does an old bastard like me say I love you?"

"Same way he always did."

"I love you, Molly."

She lifted one hand and stroked the back of his head.

"And I love you." The tears continued to roll over her cheeks, but she did not sob.

"No matter what, we'll still have each other, right, Molly?"

"That was never in doubt," she whispered, feeling the crush of his strong arms, remembering earlier moments. It had been a long time since they had embraced like this. She felt suddenly the old sense of abandon when they were first married and would indulge in spontaneous, uninhibited lovemaking whenever and wherever in the house the spirit seized them. She felt a line of kisses along her wet cheeks reaching her lips. The years fell away. When he hesitated, she helped him, insistently.

"Here in the kitchen?" he asked, sounding and feeling, to her, much like the young, golden warrior of her old dreams.

"It's ours. And we are married, you know."

That night they lay in bed, energized and alert, not wishing to sleep. Molly understood what it meant to both of them, prolonging and savoring this moment of connection. On the night of the day when they had learned that Chuck had died, they had held each other all night long, sobbing and hysterical. Since hope was dead, there seemed little to do except to curse fate and confront their helplessness, like beasts caught in a jungle trap. Somehow it was different now, as if the time had come to rid themselves of remorse and prepare to look the future square in the eye.

"In the end you wind up with only each other," Charlie said, as if it were the conclusion of what he had been saying. He had been going on about his trip to Crisfield and how it had all changed, and she had listened quietly as he described it, knowing that somehow it had been good for him to get it out, to get everything out.

"Not true, Charlie," she said playfully, knuckling his stomach, which, despite everything, was still tight and hard. He was still lean, still her handsome prince. "In the end, it's only you yourself that they lower down into the pit."

"I don't count that."

"Neither do I."

"I count this. Us. Together all these years."

"An old broad and an old goat."

"Still getting it on, as the kids say. For a moment there, I felt like twenty."

"And acted like it."

"A man needs to have that. I have to tell you, babe. It may sound like kid's stuff. But it made me feel like—like a somebody. I haven't been feeling much like a somebody these days."

"That's not prepubescent kid's stuff. It's—well—adolescent." She kissed him on the ear to tell him she was just playing. She couldn't remember when they had last played together like this.

"I'm serious."

"You're too serious."

"And if this thing with Tray doesn't work out, hell, we've still got each other."

"And they'll never be able to take away the piece of us and Chuck that Tray has."

He grew silent, and looking over at him in the darkness, she saw that his eyes were still open. To show him that they were still engaged, she traced his features with her fingers.

"I know she thinks I'm a sonofabitch. Maybe from her point of view she's right. After all, I didn't approve of her marriage with Chuck. I fought it. You can't deny that."

"I won't try."

"He wasn't ready is all. It had nothing to do with her."

She pinched his nose.

"Come on, Charlie. Truth time. You didn't want to share him with anybody. Sometimes, not even with me."

She held her breath and felt her heartbeat accelerate, hoping she would not change his mood.

"Maybe she has a point." Charlie sighed. "I never did warm up to her. Not like you."

"No matter. We're both the enemy now."

"People are damned stupid. Us, too." He paused, and she could hear him sucking air between his teeth. "You really think we should walk away?"

She hesitated. Then he raised himself on one arm and looked into her eyes.

"Tell me true, Molly. Is it worth all the pain and money? I mean it, babe. I'm not a fool. I know what it's doing to me. To us. Is it worth it? Will it amount to a hill of beans if we see the kid or not? Maybe Frances is right. Maybe it will hurt the kid, confuse him, disrupt his growing up. The thing about being a parent, or a grandparent, is that we never know what our effect really is on kids until it's too late. You know what I mean?"

Pressed to answer, she had to assimilate all the thoughts she had had on the subject. First her misgivings, then her consent, then her hesitation and her worries about Charlie. And now herself. It wasn't just for Charlie any longer.

"Like you, Charlie, I can only go by instinct. I won't talk about the pros and cons of our bringing up Chuck. We did the best we could, and not for one moment did he ever doubt we loved him. And that's something damned precious." She felt suddenly militant, and her hand strayed to his bicep, which she gripped. "Lord knows, there isn't that much of it to go around. Maybe there is a little selfishness connected with it. To give love isn't such a bad idea either, and it's as good for the giver as the getter. I'm not going to analyze the mysterious ties of blood and family and possession that make us love and long for Tray. Maybe it's an ego thing. I'm not smart enough to understand what it all means. All I know is that we, you and I, can't hurt that child by giving him our love and interest and understanding, and we surely can't hurt ourselves by it either." She slapped his upper arm. "It may sound confused, Charlie. But what's wrong with letting Tray know that we fought to be with him, that we fought with all our heart and soul? So, if we lose it will hurt like hell. And that's what worries me. I don't want you to go off the deep end if we do. Scares the hell out of me. I think I'm prepared for it, but I'm not sure. Even if we win, there's a lot of lingering bitterness to contend with. But at least our grandchild will know that we fought for him, that we loved him enough to fight for him. At least he'll have that."

She saw him nod and stir in the darkness, and he leaned over and kissed her on the forehead, then on the eyes and the lips.

"Now I see what it means."

"What what means?"

"I wish I could talk like you do when you get wound up." He cleared his throat. "Give me a minute."

"You got it, kiddo," she said, looking up, her hand caressing his face. In the semidarkness, the shadows filled in the wrinkles, and he looked younger, which meant she did as well.

"What I'm trying to say is that I really think I got lucky once and that's in getting you—"

She started to say something, but he gently put his palm over her lips.

"And the need . . . me needing you . . . grows stronger as I grow older. You know what I mean?"

"What an egotist you are, Charlie."

"Me?" He seemed genuinely confused.

"Always looking at things through such a narrow keyhole. Always you and your needs. What about mine?"

"What about yours?"

"Shut up and drink your beer."

She pulled his face down and kissed him deeply. His response was clearly evident.

"Again?" she whispered. "What a man."

Charlie picked her up at the school the next afternoon, and they drove downtown to see the lawyer. He had been gone when she had awakened that morning, and she was concerned that his brief high might dissipate during his idle morning alone. Miraculously, hers hadn't. She had tackled her classroom chores with her old zealousness, including a strong rebuke to students whose attention was wandering. As she walked down the corridor, she had passed Miss Parsons and offered a wide smile and squared shoulders, feeling not the slightest bit of guilt at leaving early. Hadn't she earned her privileges?

He greeted her with a peck on the cheek and twinkling wink and was neatly turned out in his good navy blue suit, red and blue tie, and striped shirt. She also noted that his shoes were shined and he smelled of cologne.

"Smell good?" he asked through a wide smile.

"Not bad."

"It's that old stuff you gave me once for my birthday. I forget which. It had never been opened."

He started to whistle, watching her peripherally.

"You and me, babe," he said, making a clicking sound with his tongue.

"Me and you."

"And Tray if we can do it. Right, kiddo?"

"Right."

But an old echo shook her momentarily. He used to say "the three of us," meaning them and Chuck, back in the old days, a kind of solidarity cheer. The memory rolled back to take the edge off the high. In a car, moving with the freedom of the road, Chuck sitting beside them, first in his car chair, then on the seat itself, Charlie would sing out his happiness in that self-contained world of theirs. "Us three against 'em all." Since their son's ages merged in her mind, Chuck's voice responding "One for all and all for one" spoke for all of them, child, woman, and man. And she had added, "The three mosquiters." Even the old laughter echoed with unbearable clarity.

Then Charlie began to whistle old tunes, saying little. She recognized one from an old movie, a song of lost love and longing. She shrugged off the sad note of memory and touched his thigh, hoping that they weren't just little frightened kids whistling in the cemetery.

He parked the car in the big lot under the building, but before they got out, he turned to her.

"You don't have to worry about me anymore, babe," he said. "I'm cool as a cucumber. No more temper tantrums." His hand reached out and he spread his fingers. "See? Steady as she goes."

"That's good, Charlie," she said, pecking him on the lips. "It'll make a big difference."

"I've got you, babe. That's the difference."

He slid quickly out of the car, and they took the elevator to the lawyer's office.

From the way the lawyer's eyes darted toward her, she was certain that Charlie's outward appearance of confidence was a surprise to him. As always he stood up to greet them and gestured them to sit down in front of his desk after the inevitable offer of coffee, to which they consented. Molly estimated that this was their seventh personal visit with the lawyer. At first she had tried to keep a record of hours spent to check the bills, which kept coming with relentless punctuality. He had estimated the pretrial expenses as eight thousand dollars, and they were swiftly approaching that figure.

"For the best, it costs," she had assured Charlie. The assurance was double-edged, since neither of them had ever paid out that kind of money for lawyers.

"Highway robbery," was Charlie's muttered response every time he saw the bills.

But the bills were paid almost as fast as they were delivered. They were not ones to let bills pile up. Consequences of their class insecurities, she supposed. She wondered if Frances and Peter were paying their bills as promptly.

"Well, the battlefield is cleared for action," Forte said. "Unfortunately, we're stuck with the woman. Sometimes these things work in our favor. She might bend over backward to be more open, to establish herself as an individual independent of personal emotion."

He intertwined his fingers and leaned back in his chair, as if his mind were drifting.

"Depends on the way we play it," he continued. "We have to go in strong and optimistic."

"That's us," Molly said.

The lawyer looked at her archly.

"It will depend more on style than substance," Forte mused. Molly looked at Charlie, who shrugged.

"Picture a woman in her mid-forties, tough, an achiever, two teenagers, widowed early, thrust on her own resources. No one to protect her." He paused and looked at them pointedly. Molly saw it immediately.

"Unlike Frances—Mrs. Graham," she said.

"It didn't come to me until this morning," the lawyer said.

"But that might have been her conscious decision—to make it on her own. Not to be dependent. There's a whole new world out there, they tell me," said Molly.

"No mother in her right mind turns down a breadwinner," Charlie interjected. The lawyer smiled.

"Think it, Mr. Waters. Don't say it," Forte said. "But it's the line I intend to follow."

"I'm confused," Molly said.

"I've got to bring this down to a level that this judge will understand. Security, for instance. The lengths to which people will go for security. Money."

"Money is not the issue here," Charlie said, fully aware of his pose of self-assurance.

"Not directly," Forte said. "Follow my reasoning. We know that our opponents' lawyer is going to try to break down your credibility, cite instability and such. I've told you all that before." Molly stiffened, remembering what she had edited out of her reported conversation with Frances. "It might be wise to put forth a strong argument that a pact was made with the new husband, a trade, if you will, protection, support, that is, money, in exchange for total capitulation on the issue of"— he made quotation marks in the air —" 'the past.' That would make the new husband the villain, the evil influence. I'm not sure, but if we can transfer the enmity, your quarrel, from your daughter-in-law to her new husband, we might be able to come in on her subconscious level. The idea of enslavement and control. It presses the hot buttons of achieving women in today's climate."

"You mean make Peter the evil manipulator?" Molly asked, masking her uneasiness.

"It might be easier than you think," Forte said. "Down deep it might actually be the cause of the problem. But it has its dangers."

"Like what?" Charlie asked calmly, as if the idea already had great appeal to him.

"It could drive a wedge between her and her husband. These things can get out of hand in a courtroom. If we hit her where she is most vulnerable, we could force the first shot between them, stimulate resentment that could undermine their marriage."

"None of my business," Charlie said, continuing to smile. "What happens between them is none of our business. We're out of that, aren't we, Molly?" He turned toward her.

"I wouldn't want them to break up over this," she said hesitantly.

"It's just not our business," Charlie said emphatically, but with complete control. "I'm not interested in their domestic bliss. I just want to have the right to see my grandson."

"I mention it only as a possibility," Forte said, backtracking, noting her concern. "In a way, it depends on what kind of hardball they play. There are lots of ways to view the matter. It all boils down to one thing: God is the Judge and the judge is God."

"I'd like to avoid that, if we can," Molly said suddenly, noting the tentativeness of the lawyer's suggestion.

"I wouldn't," Charlie said with an air of finality.

"How can it help Tray if their marriage goes sour?"

"Now, now. I'm just speculating. What you don't want is to wind up with blame—"

"I don't understand any of this," Charlie said, his cheeks flushing. She did not like the direction in which this was going.

"It's a possibility," Molly replied softly.

"The objective here is to win," Charlie said, his voice a decibel lower. "And whatever we have to do to win is what we have to do. That's what we're paying for. I don't care about these other things. We can't be responsible for what happens to them. That's not fair." It wasn't quite indignation, Molly thought, although the turmoil just beneath the surface was beginning to show.

"We're not talking here about fairness, Mr. Waters. I just feel it's my duty to lay these things before you. Among our options on which way to go in this case, that issue has to be considered. I didn't mean to alarm you. After all, I'm not a psychologist, only a lawyer."

"I think you should remember that," Charlie said with authority, still wearing his mask of control. It was beginning to worry her.

But the lawyer's words had frightened her. She hadn't considered such a possibility. As always, Molly noted, the young lawyer was elegantly cool. He was, however, studying Charlie carefully with his large brown eyes.

"Domestic relations are like ecology," he said slowly, as if the words were being carefully chosen. "You inject a new life-form, and it changes the character of the environment. Relationships are very fragile. They depend on silent compacts, under the table deals, shaky compromises, perceived trust. The courtroom is a battlefield, but the armies ranged against each other are shadows. The real people and motives are sometimes hidden—"

Charlie shot Molly a look of confusion. Forte, she felt, was deliberately talking over his head, and she resented it.

"Of course we understand that, Mr. Forte," she said, nodding toward Charlie. It was all gloss, she decided suddenly. He was patronizing them, showing his contempt. Empathy had been merely a sales pitch. He was a professional simply doing his job for money. It occurred to her that she had never thought otherwise, but it annoyed her just the same.

"Just what is he trying to say?" Charlie asked, scratching his head.

"That when the bomb goes off, the damage is unpredictable," Molly said, oddly proud of the metaphor and Forte's nod of approval.

"What the hell do either of you know about bombs?" Charlie said, his voice rising for the first time that day. Recovering quickly, he changed his tone. "I can tell you about bombs. I've seen enough of them in my time. You always knew that they were coming, and when your sixth sense told you they were on the way, you hugged the ground and prayed. After all, you had no control over them. The object was to do everything you could to protect your own ass." He narrowed his eyes and looked at the lawyer. Then he winked at Molly. "You're the CO, pal. Take the objective. You give the orders, and we do it your way. Don't give us all these warnings and such. I don't give a tinker's damn who gets killed or wounded on the other side. As long as we and Tray come out alive."

"You really don't understand, do you, Mr. Waters?" Forte said with a sigh. Molly could see that Charlie was totally confused by the lawyer's comment, just when he felt he had illustrated a profound philosophical point. She braced herself for what she knew was coming.

"Understand what?"

"If you come over like that, you're dead in the water."

"Like what?" Charlie looked helplessly at Molly.

"Hate, Mr. Waters. It will turn off the judge faster than an ice cold shower."

"Hate?" Charlie's smile dripped with sarcasm. "I love my grandson."

"He doesn't mean that, Charlie," Molly whispered. But it was too late to soften the blow.

Charlie's gaze flitted around the room. He bit his lower lip and rubbed his cheek. She could see his confidence wilt like a water-starved plant.

"If you come over like that in the courtroom, you'll blow our case. The objective is for us to portray you and your wife a victims who are worthy of compassion. We want your sense of victimization to be gut-wrenching for the judge. If you show her that you hate your daughter-in-law and her husband, our case is finished. Don't you understand that, Mr. Waters?"

"Of course he understands that," Molly said. Too late to stop it, she knew she was making matters worse.

"You make it sound like I'm a helluva liability," Charlie said lamely, making an effort to regain his composure.

"Only if you drop the mask."

"The mask?"

"You've got to hide your feelings of antagonism for your daughter-in-law and her husband. No tantrums. No projecting animosity. Anything that detracts from the image of the wise old Gramps is the kiss of death."

She noted that Forte was no longer pulling his punches, no longer patronizing. He was cracking the whip, taking charge. Wasn't that what Charlie had asked for?

"You want me to keep my mouth shut?"

"As much as possible. Answer all questions in monosyllables. You have only one message to deliver. Your love can be an asset to your grandson. No matter what they say or how they say it. No matter what sins they attribute to you and Mrs. Waters. No matter how your character is abused. No matter what parental crimes you and Mrs. Waters are accused of. You are not to react except as innocent victims and good Christians. What you must show that judge—always—no matter how difficult it gets is"— he paused and watched them —"the other cheek." He got up from his chair, his strong, slim figure a picture of contained energy. Coming round his desk, he stood over them. "You must think of yourself as martyrs. Christ on the cross. Do you understand that, Mr. Waters?" He looked at Molly. "Mrs. Waters?"

But both she and the lawyer ended up training their eyes on Charlie, who was obviously squirming.

"I don't know if I can be that good an actor," he whispered hesitantly.

"He's no hater, Mr. Forte. His bark is worse than his bite." Her efforts at placation seemed hollow and insincere. She searched her own heart. Did she hate Frances and Peter for taking Tray from them? No, she decided, she did not hate. Hate was an emotion to which they were both strangers. Charlie couldn't hate. Not even Frances. All he wanted to do was love. Just love. She reached out and touched Charlie's arm, and he patted her hand.

"I just wanted to make it clear," the lawyer said, walking back behind his desk. "I don't like to lose."

"The question is," Molly began, "what do we win if we win?"

"We win the right to see Tray," Charlie said. "That's what we win."

"But what will he see when he sees us?" Molly whispered.

"Good question, Mrs. Waters," the lawyer said. But he made no attempt to give an answer.

Chapter 12

J UDGE ANNIE STOKES frowned as she watched her daughter
Peggy reach for the butter. Peggy must have noticed, and her
reaction was predictable. She sliced a larger sliver from the
stick and spread it thickly over the raisin toast. Then she thrust
the toast belligerently into her mouth and noisily chomped off a
large wedge.

"No lectures, mother," Peggy said through her stuffed mouth.

"I wasn't giving any."

"But you were thinking of it."

"So now you've become a mind reader?" As much as she would
promise herself, she could not resist the sarcasm. It had almost
become second nature between them, a kind of verbal Ping-Pong.
Peggy was sixteen and difficult, growing more difficult by the
minute. In the last year she had put on twenty pounds and her
figure, once merely well-endowed, had run to fat. Like Harold,
Annie thought. It had killed him at thirty-seven.

Unlike her other daughter, nineteen-year-old Laura, a straight-
A sophomore at Harvard, Peggy was having a tough time of it.
A nagging problem, Annie sighed, despite her certainty that the
root was Harold's early death. It did offer a convenient explanation. But, unfortunately, not the cure. As always, when memories of Harold and how he died surfaced in her mind, her stomach
froze, its contents congealed. Did he, beneath it all, have a suicidal
compulsion to eat himself to death? He might have just as well
slit his throat. Always with the memory had come the old blame.
But hadn't she tried her best to help him fight this compulsive
need he had had to gorge himself? Hadn't she tried everything?

A dispassionate observer might have seen his death as comic.
Certainly it was ludicrous. It had occurred at a celebration of sorts.
Peggy was one month old, and this was to be the beginning of yet
another new chapter, a last gasp before Harold turned himself in
to the doctors to shed the fat that was sure to kill him.

"You have a wife and two daughters, Harold. You owe it to
me, and to them."

Finally, she had decided, her one-note perpetual message had
hit home. He had promised, and with his promise had also come

vows of greater frugality. No more bad real estate deals. No more wild investments. No more compulsions, unrealistic hunches, and aspirations.

That night in New York was etched irrevocably in her memory and the recall of it was relentless and inescapable, unbearable in its fidelity. She saw his face, sweat pouring down his cheeks as he shoveled in the ample portions that represented double helpings of Mamma Leone's best culinary effort.

"This may be my last chance," he had told her, his face beet red with the effort. By then, he had bulked to nearly 270 pounds and smoked three packs a day. At least he had called it accurately, which was much more than he had done in life.

It was so ugly, so humiliating to die that way, right there at the table, red pasta sauce sliding down his shirt. In retrospect it seemed like a scene in a black comedy. People at the other tables cast irritated glances at the resuscitation squad that had to be called in, or simply did their best to contemptuously ignore the scene, obviously angered by so gauche a gesture as dying disgustingly in a crowded restaurant where they had come to relax and enjoy themselves.

Her reaction then, which time had not eroded, was indignation and helplessness, and she had vowed never to be helpless again, never to tie her tail to a kite on which she did not hold the anchoring string. Except for Peggy. That string was always slipping, and errant, unforeseen winds buffeted the kite.

He had left her with two small children, no insurance, massive debts, and worst of all, an inheritance of cloying pity. Poor little widow Annie. Sad eyes seemed to follow her everywhere, and she would imagine the soft clucking murmurs of observers. Faced with the stark reality of her situation, she did not crawl quickly back into dependence. She simply became more determined than ever to rise above the debacle. For that she was grateful. It was the best legacy she could have had, although she knew in her heart she could never forgive him for his early and ignominious exit.

When Peggy reached once again for the butter, Annie could not contain herself, swiftly removing the plate to her end of the table.

"Mother," Peggy whined.

"Look in the mirror. You'll get the message. You can lay out a whole deck of cards on your backside."

"Well, it is mine," Peggy pouted.

"It will destroy your self-image. Make you hate yourself." She had tried everything, everything that also had not worked with Harold, from being overly supportive to simply ignoring the problem. It didn't matter. Peggy was relentless. Calling attention to the problem only made it worse. But she couldn't help herself. It was even more difficult to remain silent.

Yet, she was certain she understood the heart of their problem. Peggy was created in Harold's image, a genetic match so precise that it ensured his immortality. Where was that piece of herself? Annie had wondered, even at the moment when she inspected the soft, round little body for the first time, counting its fingers and toes? Had the child known even then?

Based on the presumption that self-knowledge was the beginning of wisdom, she had set about to root out any prejudices within herself that might hurt the child. This took the form of innumerable conversations with an imaginary Peggy.

"You hate me because you hated Daddy."

"I didn't."

"And you were mad at him for dying."

"I resented fate for taking him away so soon."

"Not true. You wanted him gone. And you see him in me."

"I love you."

"How can you if you hated him?"

"That's a lie."

"It's the truth."

Intelligence and logic were things you called upon to solve all problems. The fact was that she had started out not loving the child, not with the same zeal and passion she had for her older daughter, the one that did not remind her of Harold, the one loaded with her own genes. Then, oddly, as Peggy grew more and more like her dead husband and her efforts to resolve the dilemma inside herself grew more frenetic, she began to love her more. And the more she loved the child, the less she could convey the sense of it to her. Worse, Peggy grew more and more certain that she was unloved, more and more convinced that she was only her father's daughter, more distant and alienated.

Yet she continued to try. A time would come when Peggy would have to cope with life on her own, put aside the role of hurt child, and enter the jungle of competing adults. For that, she needed every advantage, every edge. And she was showing increasing signs of lagging, falling badly behind.

She was already getting failing grades, and unless she straightened out, she would never get into college. For Annie that was a vowed goal that had to be fulfilled. For Peggy's sake. Even the girl's social life, which had started out with such promise, had been reduced to a few close friends, all of them of dubious motivation. It was awful watching history play out a repeat performance of what she had gone through with Harold.

Nor had she neglected seeking outside help. Professionals sought out professionals, didn't they? Unfortunately, the two psychiatrists she had seen merely confirmed what she already knew. They also confirmed that it was the child who needed the help, not the mother. But Peggy had refused to see either of them.

"I'm not crazy," she had told Annie with a vehemence that suggested that further discussion was useless.

Peggy reached across the table with her knife and sliced off another heavy gob of butter. Annie watched with resignation.

"I could cry," she said.

"No you couldn't. You don't cry."

"You're my daughter, and I love you."

"It doesn't necessarily follow."

"I can't bear to see how unattractive you're making yourself."

"Then don't look." Peggy stuffed the heavily buttered raisin toast in her mouth. Her cheeks inflated.

"In life, when you fall behind, it's very difficult to catch up," Annie said. It was actually a homily that might have worked well with Laura if she had needed it, which she didn't. It had had just the opposite effect on Peggy. "You are falling behind, you know."

"Don't be such a judge."

"It's second nature now," she said, trying to lighten the mood. The fact was that Peggy hated her being a judge, despised her success. That, too, she felt she understood. It had something to do with the humiliation of her dead father. Always, she took that into account. And in the end, it wrecked any relationship with a man that might have flourished in her long widowhood. That was the silent trade-off with her daughter. At least her staying single had made their life together tolerable, although barely.

But to cope with each other, they had to deal in euphemisms and evasions. For example, Peggy's stated reason for opposing Annie's judgeship was money, or the lack of it. To become a judge,

Annie had chosen to give up a lucrative salary in one of the city's most prestigious law firms. That meant that Peggy couldn't have the car she had been promised, or some other extras that today's teenagers expected. The real reason, of course, was the old one. Again, knowing the reason changed nothing. On the other hand, Laura had been approving, supportive, proud. But then, Laura was a different story. Laura had gotten a scholarship to Harvard.

"It's what I want to do with my life," Annie had explained to both her daughters when her appointment to the bench was being considered. It had always been her first career choice, even when Harold was alive. His sudden death very nearly put an end to that dream. She was in her last year at the University of Baltimore Law School, not the most prestigious school in the country, but convenient for a mother with two children, and, of course, she could take night courses. Harold had been supportive of her ambition. Perhaps he saw what was coming.

After Harold's death, it wasn't moral and emotional support that was needed. It was money. It took some doing to get herself through her last year. She'd had to hold down a full-time job, on top of caring for the kids and going to school. She could have gotten a loan from her parents. Harold's parents, too, although poorer than hers, offered modest help. She refused, less out of logic than instinct. She cast herself in a heroic role, the struggling widow and mother. In fact, her independence gave her good feelings about herself. It taught her that anything was possible.

"It's my life," she told her own parents and in-laws. "And my responsibility."

"What are parents for?" her mother had protested. Harold's parents, on the other hand, might have been relieved by her refusal. Harold's death, she sensed, had made them resentful that she had survived him. She wasn't completely certain that this was true, but it did inhibit her desire to be around them. In fact, she detested being around them. She hated being, for them, a reminder of Harold's short and failed life. Nor could she shake the feeling that they secretly blamed her for the loss of their son.

As for the girls, at first she allowed them frequent visits. They lived in Philadelphia, an hour on the train from Baltimore. They would always come home from these visits laden with gifts, especially of good things to eat that Gramma Stokes had made. She wondered silently if that had been the root of Harold's problem.

"You really should tell them that they're spoiling you both," she told them, not without a note of subtle rebuke. It worried her, too, that the Stokeses were completely nonjudgmental in terms of the girls, perhaps frightened that the children, the only real evidence of Harold's existence, would slowly drift away from them. She understood that, of course, although it did not thwart a nagging worry that somehow the relationship was not completely healthy. She longed for the day when the girls would develop interests that would inevitably rearrange their priorities and slacken their visits. To her relief, it came soon enough.

"Just tell them that I have other plans." First Laura, whose studies became the number one passion of her life. Then Peggy. In Peggy's case she was becoming more and more gregarious, long before her present stage of rebelliousness.

"I'm not going to do your dirty work."

"They'll think I'm encouraging you to stay away," Annie said.

"They'll think that anyway," Peggy told her.

"Then you explain it."

"What should I tell them?"

"The truth."

"You think they'll be hurt?"

"There is no substitute for the truth."

It was all part of Annie's theory that people had to meet their responsibilities head on. Telling the truth was part of that recognition.

Annie's mother, on the other hand, could not understand her ideas on total independence. "It's no sin to accept help from your parents."

"That has nothing to do with sin. I want my girls to be prepared to function without depending on anyone else."

"Sometimes people have to depend on other people."

"You've done your job," she told her mother. "I have no right to live on your dole."

"But why punish the girls?"

"I'm not punishing them. I'm teaching them never to grovel, especially to a man."

"That's a terrible burden to put on female children."

"I'm their mother, and it's my choice. And I'm strong, smart, healthy, independent, and wish to remain so."

"Stubborn, too," her mother said. Her father was at a complete loss about her attitude. "It's all that women's stuff about making it on their own," he told Annie.

"It's not 'stuff.' "

"I think it's stupid—whatever your gender," her father had persisted. "We're your parents, for crying out loud. Call it a loan, then. Don't take any of it yourself. Give it to the kids."

"They're my kids."

"They're our flesh and blood, too, Annie. Never forget that."

"That doesn't entitle you to direct their lives. Until they're twenty-one, they're my responsibility."

How could she explain to them that Harold's death had also taught her that adversity was part of the human experience? The point was to be able to direct your own life, control the decision-making process as much as was humanly possible, concoct strategies to overcome vicissitudes. Lives should have a theme, she had reasoned. And that was hers. Every day brought further proof of the validity of her ideas. Above all, she wanted to be a role model for her children. Hadn't she succeeded with Laura? Why not with Peggy?

It had been exciting being a lawyer in a large firm. There, she had earned her spurs, but she made no secret of the fact that she wanted to be a judge someday. Nothing was more important than to be a judge. A judge made decisions that mattered. A judge helped direct the course of human events. A judge had a chance to make a difference, to be relevant.

"Go for it, Mom," Laura had said. Since both girls were directly affected by her decision, she thought she owed it to them to let them participate in making it—or, at the least, to hear it first from her lips. Besides, she wanted the blessing and approval of her children.

"It just means you'll be busier than ever," Peggy said.

"Doing important work. Not just for money."

"I don't think it's so important."

"Well, I do, and I'll be real proud," Laura said, throwing a rebuking glance at her sister. Laura had always been appreciative and admiring, had understood what it all meant, especially what it meant to be a woman alone.

Even from the early stages of her widowhood, when Annie began to date, Laura had been understanding and Peggy difficult. Indeed, the fact was that Peggy's attitude toward Annie's male friends, despite her own understanding of that attitude, was off-putting. She was intimidating enough to men without Peggy's microscopic observations and nagging interference. The result had been a reticence on her part that created a wall too high for any male to scale.

"But it's your life," the men would remonstrate after her inevitable and sometimes half-baked explanations for her rejection of their more intimate overtures. Over the years she had been to bed with only two of them, and that had been brief and unsatisfactory.

"I just need more time."

Her problem wasn't time at all, she knew. Rather, it was abject fear that any relationship would push Peggy over some emotional cliff, the consequences of which weren't worth the risk.

Finally, she decided to wait until Peggy was off to college before she would encourage a resumption of her so-called romantic life. Besides, meaningful and absorbing work could go a long way in compensating for other comforts. Or so she convinced herself.

But she was flattered when men fussed over her, and she kept herself well groomed and her figure in good shape. There were, she knew, career advantages in being a woman, and sex appeal was still a potent tool of manipulation as far as men were concerned. Besides, there was no way to move ahead without their support. There was nothing cynical or deliberately manipulative in that fact, she assured herself. Such knowledge for a woman was as necessary as nourishment.

"And the interim appointment is for one year," she explained to her daughters, taking particular pains to be especially understanding about Peggy's sullen objections. When it pertained to her work and ambitions, Annie's life and course of action were clearly defined, Peggy's disapproval notwithstanding. Of course Annie wanted her support and approval. But that did not mean that she was going to let herself be terrorized into abandoning her career. "Then I'll have to run for office on my own." It was an idea that she liked. Anything that offered a challenge and a chance to prove herself was attractive to her.

"We'll help in the campaign," Laura said. "Won't we, Peggy?"

"Not me," Peggy had muttered. Part of the pattern, Annie had reasoned. Anything that made her mother happy automatically made Peggy unhappy. Nevertheless, she took pains to explain to Peggy what it would mean, sparing nothing, explaining the long hours and the cut in pay, which meant monetary sacrifices like the car she had promised. She had always carefully explained to Peggy why she had made various choices. She hoped that in this way she might teach her how self-interest governed the decision-making process and how to set priorities and goals. When the current stage of Peggy's discontent passed, Annie was certain that these lessons would prevail.

"Someday you'll have a goal, Peggy, and you will have to make sacrifices to achieve it. Because we're women, we have to work harder, give more. I can't very well turn down an opportunity like this. It's what I want, what I've worked for."

"What about what I want?" Peggy asked. Beneath the mask of teenage arrogance, Annie had seen the fear and vulnerability. Why can't I be her role model, she wondered? She was puzzled. What did Peggy really want? Her father? When would she finally surrender to the reality? When would she accept it?

"Why can't you say 'Good luck, Mommy. I'm happy for you'?"

"Because I'm not," Peggy had replied.

"Maybe when you get older, you'll understand."

"She'll get over it, Mom," Laura said.

"She'll have to," Annie agreed.

"It doesn't matter what I think, anyhow," Peggy had said with a smirk, as if she actually enjoyed the prospect of continuing antagonism and confrontation. "You always think of yourself first."

"You may learn to do that as well someday. Sometimes it's called respecting yourself."

She had already made up her mind about the appointment, anyhow. Nor was she going to let herself be terrorized by a teenager.

The Baltimore city judicial system required its fifteen sitting judges to alternate between types of cases. Annie had spent her first three months in criminal court, hearing felony cases and dispensing sentences to fit the crimes. Already, she had gained some reputation as a no-nonsense judge who played it by the book. With an eye on the future election, she did not want to be known as either a sob sister or a nagging judge.

She had enjoyed criminal court, but her colleague and sponsor, Judge Samuel Compton, a crusty old political war-horse and acknowledged chief of the court, had suggested she get some "domestic squabble" under her belt, an idea that she had considered with much hesitation.

"It's the ass end of the business," he told her. "We all hate it."

"How come?" she had asked. Her own legal specialty had been corporate law.

"Tears you up. Everybody's guilty. Everybody's innocent."

She had only the vaguest idea what he meant. But since she was the most junior of the judges, she was unanimously chosen for the chore. Actually, it was Compton himself who had been scheduled to sit, and there was little room for refusal.

"The best way to handle it is to stick to the precedents. Don't try to revolutionize the law. You'll love it. It's like reading *True Confessions*."

"I don't read *True Confessions*."

"It's not easy to maintain your distance," he had told her.

"It hasn't been difficult so far to maintain professional objectivity."

"We'll see," he said smugly.

As in the case of similar comments made by those whose patronage she needed for career purposes, she withheld further comment. Besides, she imagined that men would be more impatient in the domestic arena. Play the game, she urged herself. Half the world was men, and most of them were totally insensitive to what made a woman tick.

She was, she knew, suffering from a similar communication problem with her teenage daughter. This, too, shall pass, she assured herself as she watched Peggy across the breakfast table. The girl had just ladled five spoons of sugar into the coffee cup.

"I can't seem to reach you," Annie sighed.

"But you *have* reached me."

"For whatever I did, I apologize." She felt herself getting increasingly agitated. It was a condition she did not appreciate when she was on the threshold of a new experience.

"I didn't ask to be born," Peggy said smugly.

"That's quite true. But the gift of life is the best gift of all. Why can't you enjoy it?"

"I don't know," Peggy said with more candor than she had volunteered all morning. Then she shrugged and put another spoonful of sugar in her coffee.

It's getting worse, Annie thought, feeling resentment build inside her. Is it me? she asked herself again. Something I've done? She resisted the temptation to ask the question aloud.

"This aggravation is not very helpful. It's my first day in domestic relations. I don't need this, Peggy."

"That's a laugh."

"What is?" It was, she knew, a mistake to ask. But it was better than no dialogue at all, she told herself, rationalizing.

"Domestic relations. What do you know about domestic relations? You haven't even had a husband for nearly thirteen years."

No thanks to you, she thought, with a flash of bitterness.

"I don't have to sit here and take that, young lady."

"Neither do I," Peggy said, pushing away from the table. Her coffee spilled.

Annie sat there for a long time, staring at the shivering brown puddle on the glass table. There was simply no way to reach her. Peggy had slammed the door to her room. She wondered what was expected of her, how she could accommodate herself to the distortions in Peggy's mind. She had contemplated therapy, had even suggested it again to Peggy, whose indignation had turned into a temper tantrum.

"Now I'm crazy!" her daughter had screamed.

"Troubled," she had explained. "You can't seem to deal with your anger."

"It's you who makes me angry." Her face had flushed beet red, reminding her of Harold on that fateful night.

"Me?"

Remembering that awful scene, she decided to resign herself, at least for now. No sense complicating her day. A judge had to stifle emotion, force neutrality, isolate the intellect, divorce any personal strife from the decision-making process. These were the caveats of her profession, she told herself. Indeed, perhaps they were the very reasons she had chosen such a profession as her ultimate goal. Someone had to sort things out, someone to whom detachment was a working discipline.

But the brief injection of nobility of purpose did little to harness her inner turmoil. She could not dismiss Peggy and her irrational anger from her mind. Yet she must do it or be unfit to do her job. Getting up from the table, she knocked softly on Peggy's door.

"Don't forget school, dear," she said gently. She looked at her watch. She'd hoped to have some time to review the papers her law clerk had stuffed into her briefcase concerning the day's trial. But this business with Peggy had caused a drastic revision in her schedule. When there was no response from Peggy, she tried the door, which was locked.

"Really, Peggy, you have got to stop these tantrums." She listened, but no answer came. So she was now to get the silent treatment, she thought. The last one had gone on for nearly a week.

"Just remember that it's a school day," she said, waiting. Still no answer. Again, she looked at her watch. The material in her briefcase nagged at her. She had deliberately gone to bed early to be fresh for the new court experience.

"I'd like to get this settled before I leave," she called. Still no answer. "You are not being fair to me."

"Go away."

That was something. At least, a response.

"Please, Peggy. Not today."

Again no answer came. Her agitation, she knew, precluded getting any work done. She had responsibilities, priorities. Her lack of preparation was making her anxious.

"I have got to leave!" she cried.

"Then go."

There was no point in standing before her daughter's locked door, she decided, trying valiantly to refocus her attention. She'd have to rush downtown and try to get her head together for the trial.

"It's not very fair of you, Peggy. Especially today."

She waited for a long moment. When no answer came, she went to the bathroom and patted her short hair into place. In the mirror, she noted her pinched look, especially around the eyes. She put a bit of powder on her nose and forehead, but little else, wondering if her appearance would be neutral enough for tackling the events of the day.

Before she left the apartment, she went to Peggy's door again, feeling vaguely guilty.

"Peggy," she called softly. She tapped lightly on the door. There was no answer. "Please, darling. Don't be so hard on yourself."

When no response came, she shook her head and went out the door. Anxiety had turned to anger. Soon, she knew, the anger would become frustration, then guilt again, and her mind would flood with flashbacks that would plumb her psyche to determine the question of how and why her relationship with her younger daughter had gone sour. Then would come the inevitable answers. Inevitably, she would wind up blaming Harold, which was the worst part, since it offered no solutions. And what good was a judge who could offer no solutions?

The traffic on the way to the courthouse was very heavy and she arrived at her office less than a half hour from the time set for the trial. Carter Foley, her law clerk, came in from the outer office. He was a very intense, gangling young man with a prominent Adam's apple and a wisp of moustache over his thin lips.

"Did you go over it?" he asked. "*Waters* versus *Graham*."

"Not with the care I should have," she admitted, without giving a reason. Although he shared much of her courthouse world, she kept her personal life to herself. She looked at her watch. "Brief me."

She knew it was a sloppy way to begin, but she did rely on her ability to grasp things quickly. It angered her to think that Peggy's morning tantrum had interfered with her duties. Being not fully prepared also meant that she would really have to clear her mind and listen intently to the proceedings. Sometimes, when she sat on the bench trying criminal cases, her mind wandered. When this occurred, it filled her with a gnawing sense of inadequacy, as if she was somehow being unfair, fraudulent. It was something she must guard against, she told herself, making a mental note to discuss the condition with some of the other judges.

"This is a grandparents' visitation case," Carter began. There was a touch of pedantry about him, which she liked, although his intellectual arrogance sometimes irritated her. She tolerated that because she was a great believer in smart backup. A judge needed all the competent help she could get. He was extraordinarily energetic and ambitious as well. For old-hand advice, she relied on the wily Sam Compton.

Carter had opened her briefcase and was poking around in the files. "Paternal grandparents have petitioned. Their son, the husband, was killed in an accident. She meets and marries another man who adopts her five-year-old boy. Now seven. The new couple decide to pursue their new life without the burdens or benefits of the old in-laws, the natural grandparents. After two years the grandparents take this action."

"And the case law?"

"Adoption laws are tough in this state. The new father has all the rights of a natural father and, therefore, absolute power over the minor child—with the wife, of course. There are numerous cases attesting this. The grandparents have absolutely no rights in this matter."

"Then why the petition?"

"Grey power," Carter said with a smile, pointing to his hair, his Adam's apple bobbing. He fished in the file for a paper.

"I don't understand."

"We're one of forty-nine states that now have a law granting the right of grandparents to petition for visitation rights. It's a phenomenon of the aging population. The old common law rarely allowed that. So the old folks are feeling their oats, petitioning all over the lot. In this case, they come smack up against the adoption laws. Actually, the first ploy of the defense was to get the case thrown out on a technical plea. Peck, the Grahams' lawyer, cited a number of decisions which explicitly rule out the grandparents' rights after adoption. But Judge Compton didn't allow it."

"Why not? If the adoption statutes were so explicit."

"Maybe he wanted you to have an easy one first time out."

"Easy? Nothing's easy in this business."

"Wrong word," he said. "Should have said safe." He looked at his watch. "I'm really sorry you didn't get to read this," he said, holding up a sheaf of papers.

"We still have a few minutes." Her mind was beginning to hum now. She felt her earlier emotions departing. Like a boxer going into the ring, she thought, welcoming the feeling.

"Here are the parameters," Carter said scanning his notes. "The *Succession of Reiss*, 1894, the beginning of case history on this matter. The courts ruled that parental control is fundamental and accountable to no one, that the obligation of a parent to permit grandparents visitation is not a legal one, that visitation by a grandparent over the protest of a fit parent is unenforceable. Remember we're talking visitation. Not custody. Ironically, if the grandparents were to prove the unfitness of the parents, they would blow their case for visitation. It would become a custody case. Catch-22."

Annie nodded, prodding him to continue.

"There's a lot in between, of course. Our law passed a couple of years ago under pressure of the grey lobby allows the court to determine who shall have visitation rights to a child following the termination of a marriage." He held up what she assumed was the text of the statute. "The kicker is termination of the marriage. Like divorce. Or death of a parent. In this case, the surviving parent has remarried. Hence, no termination. Round one for Graham. But the real heart of it all is this." He read from the paper in his hand. " 'And may grant such visitation if the court believes it to be in the best interests of the child.' In other words, despite the reams of cases, citations, and common law practice, the fundamental measure in every situation involving a minor child is," he read again, " 'the best interests of the child.' "

"So there is latitude."

"Some. In this case, narrow. Too much case law on the rights of adoptive parents. If you rule for the grandparents, you could get it thrown back at you on appeal. Key word, 'could.' Just file it in the back of your mind." He paused. "Then, of course, there are certain political considerations. After all, none of this is done in a vacuum."

"Political?"

"It's something to consider, Judge. You are, after all, political."

"Certainly you're not suggesting that I be political in my decisions?" She deliberately expressed just enough indignation for him to get the point.

"Once again, back to grey power, the clout of our aging population. Did you know that there is a resolution before the Senate of the United States, already passed by the House of Representatives, urging a Model Act on Grandparents' Visitation? They want all states to have a uniform law. It's now before the Senate."

It was already past ten o'clock, but she did not make a move to leave, giving him permission to continue.

"Let me give you the gist." He scanned the paper in his hand. "Here. I quote. 'The relationship between grandparents and grandchildren can provide continuity in a child's life after the stress of divorce, and it is a relationship that can be good for grandparents and grandchildren alike.' Get that. 'Good for grandparents and grandchildren alike.' That's the first time such a thought has been injected into the mix. The courts have never ever considered the welfare of the grandparents in such situations. You know why? Politics. Pure and simple. And it comes in the whereases to this very same resolution. Shall I continue?"

She nodded.

" 'Whereas approximately 75 per centum of all older Americans.' " He paused and looked at her. "Read 'voters.' " He smiled and continued. " 'Whereas grandparents play a vital role in millions of American families.' " He paused again, obviously skipping. " 'And whereas such procedural rights to petition State courts often do not provide grandparents with adequate opportunities to be fully heard with respect to the granting of such visitation privileges.' " Again he paused and looked at his watch. "Then the resolution asks for the states to adopt a uniform law. Get my drift?"

"I do, indeed. But I'm a judge when I hear cases."

"And a politician when you go for the job on a permanent basis."

"I hereby wipe such a thought from my mind." She said it lightly, but she meant it sincerely. She could deal only with existing law. Don't blaze trails, she cautioned herself, remembering the word Carter had used. "Safe."

She felt better now. The aggravation of the morning had been locked in a separate compartment of her mind. She stood up and Carter helped her on with her robe. She looked into the mirror. "Heah come da judge," she told her image. Turning, she swept through the door into the courtroom.

She enjoyed the ritual and etiquette of the courtroom, but it was the deference and respect for her presence that she loved the most. Even though she knew it was accorded to the office and not to her as such, she soaked up the obeisance and was thrilled by the symbols of her rank, the black robe, the vantage of the high bench, the exhibition of power and its ultimate exercise. When she walked into the courtroom, she became totally aware that what she thought, how she saw and heard, and, despite the caveats and admonitions, how she felt, created destiny.

Although the high-ceilinged old courtroom, with its baroque intention barely disguised by repeated attempts at remodeling, was the one she had used to try criminal cases, the atmosphere was decidedly different, the air of tension and anxiety surprisingly more pervasive. At first, it confused her. A potential loss of freedom seemed, on the surface, far more ominous and anxiety-provoking than a domestic dispute. But the faces looking up at her were more charged with desperation than those of most of the robbers and murderers who had come before her bench.

As the younger lawyer rose, she felt the full and intimidating impact of her own power. He wasn't addressing a jury. The twelve seats behind the rail were empty.

"Your honor," the younger lawyer began, his voice steady, its timbre deep and resonant, echoing in the empty chamber. Oddly, there were no spectators, not even the usual strays who haunted courtrooms in search of entertainment or simply to pass the time. She listened as he outlined the complaint, letting the words roll through her as she surveyed the tense faces, each a mirror of his individual motives.

Forcing herself to maintain a rigid expression, she let her eyes roam over the faces of the antagonists and their lawyers. Show nothing but neutrality, she urged herself, hoping she could achieve such a pose throughout the trial. But beneath the mask, her mind reacted. She fixed the names of the participants in her mind. The Waters couple. She looked at her file: Molly and Charles. They were gray-faced, tense, uneasy, very much misplaced in this atmosphere, confronted, obviously, by a confusing conflict of values, caught in the clichés and stereotypes of old-fashioned sentiment. Tragic figures, she decided.

On the other hand, here were the Grahams, carrying the banner of youth and fecundity, hope and success. The woman was, as they say, heavy with child—wearing a white maternity blouse with a big red bow, carefully groomed, cheeks flushed, eyes bright, attentive and calm, soothed by her obviously devoted husband, who held her hand. He was an intense type, with eyes that burned into the young lawyer. She looked at the file to confirm her analysis. Computer engineer. She gave herself a silent pat for insight. Beside them sat their lawyer, whom she knew casually, a big man with a distinct, carefully studied manner and dress. String tie, creased beige suit, a jowly face, his lips pursed and eyes down as he made notes. Shrewd. Cunning.

With the names and the players carefully fixed in her mind, she directed her full attention to the younger lawyer, who was vaguely familiar. Again she looked at her notes. Robert Forte, who bore the dark good looks of the slender Italian, elegantly swathed in European designer clothes, a gold bracelet visible under his rounded, buttoned cuff, which emphasized the vast chasm between him and his clients.

She listened as he cited case after case designed to buttress his arguments. Unfortunately, most of the cases were from other states, although his words were charged with emphatic decisiveness. Beneath the surface of his arguments, she read the subtle messages of sentiment and emotion as he delicately shifted the focus from the child to the grandparents. Clearly, she saw the design, invisibly shaking her head as she scanned the notes that Carter had put into the file. In the best interests of the child. He had highlighted the words with a yellow marker.

". . . and so, your Honor," Forte continued as his tone hinted that he was winding down, "we believe that the bond between grandparent and grandchild is of such special importance to the emotional growth of the child that its deprivation can have consequences not unlike growing cells being deprived of nourishment. Under no circumstances can it be considered in the child's best interests to deliberately withhold the selfless love and affection that has been dispensed by grandparents since time immemorial."

Eloquent, she decided, but strangely unmoving. A brief flash of memory intruded. Her own grandparents had faded from her consciousness. For some reason, her recall was olfactory, musky body odors as she suffered their display of affection. Her mother's people were Poles, immersed in the ethnic world of the old ways and the old language. Her memories of them were laced with good doughy things to eat and long conversations that excluded her. The booming voice of the other lawyer recalled her to the present. He was commanding in his manner, as histrionic as his dress. She forced herself not to smile as he embarked on a predictable path, citing case after case of adoptive laws and decisions.

As was the protocol in such introductions, he did not come to the heart of his strategy until the windup.

"We agree with learned counsel, your Honor, on the question of the bond between grandparents and grandchildren. The child in question, because of his adoption by Mr. Graham, has been provided with devoted, loving, stable grandparents. Note, too, that no attempt has been made to erase his antecedents. The name of his natural father has been retained. But my clients believe that contact with the parents of his deceased father would destabilize the child"— with elephantine deliberation, he turned his head and looked toward the older man —"in the light of certain unstable behavior, manifested particularly by Mr. Waters, which would be inimical to the child's emotional welfare." Peck paused, giving her the needed time to survey the obviously uncomfortable Mr. Waters, whose ashen face described the rigid control he was exercising over his emotions, staring straight ahead, eyes glazed and forlorn.

When the big man had begun, she had half-expected him to dramatize the issue of the woman's widowhood. She had no illusions about the ways in which lawyers factored a judge's personal life into their approach. Any lawyer worth his salt would be remiss if he avoided such considerations. They certainly probed every aspect of a jury candidate's background and personal life, and in this case the judge was also the jury. In fact, she was somewhat amused by the clever way Peck avoided the issue, as if to even mention it would somehow suggest pandering.

Still she did not connect emotionally, which, she told herself, remembering Judge Compton's ominous remark, was a relief. She felt as if she had already passed some sort of special test. For a judge, it was more important to observe pain than to identify with it. It was worth another silent pat on her back. She was perfectly capable of traversing a strictly legal and intellectual line, listening, but not empathizing. With the strategy clearly outlined for both sides, she could sit back, absorb the arguments, listen to the testimony, then make a fair, wise, and dispassionate ruling. Wasn't that what being a judge meant?

Forte called Mrs. Waters first, taking her through the usual questions to establish background. She spoke in a clear voice, obviously in the tone and manner in which she communicated with her young students. Judge Stokes could detect no signs of instability or any trait that might make the woman an unfit grandmother. That was not the real issue, of course, she warned herself, glancing at Carter's highlighted notes. "As grandparents, because of the adoption, the Waterses do not legally exist."

"And what were your relations like with Mrs. Graham," Forte asked, offering the body language of the sympathetic while his voice strained for the noncommittal, "both during her marriage and immediately after your son's death?" Mrs. Waters looked toward her former daughter-in-law who met her gaze for a brief moment, then lowered her eyes.

"I always thought they were fine. She was often at our house and, of course, Tray spent a good deal of his time there, especially after"— she cleared her throat —"Chuck was killed. It came as a shock to both of us to learn that Frances wanted us to stop seeing Tray."

"But you took no action to stop this from happening?"

"What could we have done? I thought it might be just a passing phase, until Tray adjusted to his new situation."

"When did you realize that your inability to see your grandson seemed to be developing into a permanent condition?"

"Nearly two years went by. We heard nothing. Our gifts were returned. As far as we were concerned, Tray had been spirited off to the ends of the earth."

"And you both missed him?"

"Of course we did. And Tray must have missed us. We were very close."

"How do you know he missed you?"

"You don't just take a child away from loving grandparents and expect him to accept it willingly. Not after the relationship we had with him. As for us, it was awful. We missed him so terribly. It just didn't seem natural, not to see him at Christmas, on his birthdays. It just didn't seem natural."

There was a brief catch in the woman's throat. One could not argue with Mrs. Waters's genuine portrayal of her deep hurt.

The younger lawyer looked up from the bench, as if to assess Annie's involvement. She deliberately kept her face frozen, nor did she move her head to acknowledge any response.

"Can you describe how you and your husband spent your time with Tray?"

"Well, we have this house and yard. Charlie and he spent a lot of time together. They made toys, a wagon, a basketball hoop, a tire swing. Things like that. Charlie, my husband, is very good with his hands and he likes the outdoor life. They worked in the garden together. And Charlie taught Tray things. Sports. How to throw and catch a ball. How to use a baseball glove. How to fish. The usual things that an older man imparts to a male child. Tray followed him around like a shadow. They were inseparable. And we all went out together a great deal. To the movies, to amusement parks, to any event that a young boy might be interested in. Cultural things, too. I took him to the plays in my school. And I read to him a great deal. We took long walks, played games together. We had good times, wonderful times. We loved him deeply, you see. And he loved us." She paused and, with scrupulous dignity, took out a handkerchief and blew her nose.

"And all this was done with the approval of the boy's mother?"

"Not only that. She was included as much as possible. She was as much a part of our family as Tray."

"And she manifested no antagonism, no hostility? There were no arguments, no animosity, no ugly scenes?"

"Not at all. I'd say it was a normal relationship for such a situation."

"Situation? Would you explain, please?"

"Well—" The woman looked up at Annie, as if searching for some sisterly connection. "We had just lost our only son. It was a terrible blow." Her voice broke, but she straightened her shoulders, quickly regaining control. "He was all we had, you see. We couldn't have others. And he came a bit late. Anyway, it was a terrible tragedy for all of us. So we all sort of pulled together to soften the blow for everyone. We took solace in each other."

It was, Annie thought, strong and involving testimony, which the woman gave with clarity and dignity. Despite all her own caveats, she could not help but sympathize. The loss of a child had to be the most devastating trauma for a woman to go through. Suddenly, she remembered the pain of giving birth, and seeing her children for the first time. Quickly, she wiped the image from her mind. The man's death was not the issue in this case.

"And Tray? What would you say the impact of his father's death was on him?"

"It's hard to tell," Mrs. Waters said slowly. "I'd say he must have detected the sense of grieving around him. Young children sometimes don't react the way adults expect them to. I'm a teacher, you see—" She seemed to have interrupted herself, to have started off on another track, and then hesitating, came back again. "I'm sure he felt a sense of something missing. We tried to make up the loss. To show him little of the terrible hurt to ourselves."

The younger lawyer led Mrs. Waters through what Annie felt was a clever interrogation, establishing a genuine loving tie between grandparents and grandchild. A good start for their side, she thought. She definitely liked Mrs. Waters. She wasn't cloying or overbearingly sentimental, and Annie noted that her husband's eyes, moist and intense, looked at her with unmistakable admiration.

Of course, when Peck got up to cross-examine, the whole tenor of the interrogation changed, although Annie could see that the big man went out of his way not to appear hostile or overbearing. As expected, he asked benign questions at first, standard procedure to lull witnesses into a false sense of security. From the beginning, she could sense Mrs. Waters's discomfort.

"Did you know, Mrs. Waters, that the marriage between your son and his wife, Frances, was not a happy one?"

The woman had paused to compose herself, although it was obvious that she had been wound up, waiting for the hostility to begin.

"How can anyone know what goes on in a marriage?"

Good answer, Annie observed.

"You were the man's mother, Mrs. Waters," the big man said

gently. "Are you saying that he never confided in you? Or that your daughter-in-law, who was, in fact, an orphan and had no one other than you and your husband to confide in, never mentioned that her marriage was unsatisfactory?"

"Your Honor," Forte said, standing up. "I object to this line of questioning. The condition of Mrs. Graham's first marriage is irrelevant. We are dealing here with the relationship of the grandparents to the child."

"I don't agree, Mr. Forte," Annie said, a bit too quickly. There are roots to be considered here, she thought. The younger lawyer sat down and began to make notes on a yellow pad. Peck, on the other hand, rubbed his nose and waited for Mrs. Waters's answer.

"It was not that he was unhappy . . ." Mrs. Waters began, clearing her throat, looking helplessly at both her lawyer and her husband. "My son did confide in me. Only once. He tried to explain why he preferred to live a life away. . . ." She hesitated again, as if she knew she was getting deeper and deeper into a maze. "He was trying to tell me that he wasn't irresponsible, that he cared about his family very much, but that he liked living as he did."

"And his wife, Frances. Was she happy with the arrangement of having her husband off working in foreign countries most of the time?"

"No, she wasn't."

"She told you that?"

"Yes."

"In fact, it was a terrible marriage, wasn't it, Mrs. Waters?"

"I wouldn't use that strong a word."

"Not a good one, then?"

"Maybe."

"A marriage that a young girl might want to forget?"

"My son was still Tray's father," Mrs. Waters whispered. Then trying to rally, she said, "He loved his son."

"But you couldn't call him an especially good father?"

"When he was home—"

"But he was hardly home. Now, that is not a good father in the traditional sense, is it, Mrs. Waters?"

Mrs. Waters shrugged. For a moment, she seemed to lose her poise and looked toward her former daughter-in-law, who averted her eyes.

"The point is that I was always very supportive of Frances."

She continued to look intensely at the young woman. "Wasn't I, Frances?"

Mrs. Graham looked up suddenly, and their eyes met.

"Just answer the questions, Mrs. Waters," Annie said. Peck continued.

"How did you feel about your daughter-in-law's marriage to Mr. Graham?"

"I was very happy for her."

"Despite the fact that it was so soon after your son's death?"

"I thought it was the best thing for her. She needed someone to take care of her. And Tray needed a father. I had no objection."

"Not to the adoption, either?"

She seemed suddenly to lose her poise. "What could we do?"

"Did you object?"

"No. We didn't consider—"

"You didn't object?"

"No."

"And your husband? What was his attitude toward the marriage with Mr. Graham?"

She hesitated and looked helplessly at her husband. Forte nodded and closed his eyes in a reassuring gesture.

"He wasn't too happy about it. He felt it was, well, not respectful to marry so soon."

"And did he try to prevent it?"

"He couldn't prevent it, could he? He merely expressed his opinion that it was too soon after . . ."

"In point of fact, he reacted very badly, didn't he? Offering insults . . ."

"Okay then, he was not very happy about it. He loved his son very much. I understood his point." She was obviously rattled.

"But you, too, loved your son. And you didn't object."

"I guess maybe that was because I'm a woman—I suppose I understood her needs."

"And you also understood it when Frances came to you and said you were not to see your grandson for the time being so that he could adjust to his new situation?"

"I understood. Yes. But I thought it would be temporary. I never expected it to go on for so long."

"But your husband was completely hostile to the idea and created still another scene."

"He did not like the idea of not seeing his own grandson—for whatever length of time."

"But you understood?"

"I didn't approve."

"And you did consent not to interfere with the decision?"

"Only because, as I told you, I thought it was temporary. I trusted her on that score."

"So what made you suddenly change your mind?"

"It wasn't suddenly. It was two years."

Annie wasn't sure where this was leading, and she wondered if she was letting it go too far. What was Peck trying to establish and why? she wondered. Mrs. Waters seemed to gather the threads of her composure, which had begun to unravel. She sucked in a deep breath.

"We missed our grandson," she whispered.

Peck leaned over and cocked an ear.

"A bit louder, please, Mrs. Waters."

"We missed our grandson," she repeated, only slightly louder. "Is there something wrong with that?"

The big lawyer rubbed his nose, a quirk that Annie thought detracted from the high drama he was trying to create. Suddenly, he looked up at Annie.

"There has never been a decision in this state that considers the welfare, interest, or well-being of grandparents above those of the child. This case cannot be considered on the basis of the needs of grandparents—"

"I'll be the judge of that, counselor," Annie said, foreclosing on the younger lawyer's protest. But Peck had made his point. The woman on the stand looked confused and demoralized.

"Thank you, Mrs. Waters," Peck said, making no attempt to finish his impromptu statement. She watched the woman return to her seat. Her face had paled. As she sat down, her lawyer leaned over and patted her arm. But she did not respond, merely shook her head in a gesture of resignation and defeat.

Peripherally, Annie observed the younger woman, wondering what was going through her mind. Her own widowhood had generated a different reaction in Harold's parents. They did not seem to have this overwhelming need to see her children. Perhaps, in a way, they somehow blamed themselves, their upbringing, as a cause of his death. Or maybe they blamed her. Again she had to abort the drift in her thoughts and recall her concentration to the proceedings before her.

She watched as Mr. Waters walked to the stand, noting the exaggeration with which he carried himself, shoulders squared, head high, in a kind of ramrod military posture. He was a rugged man with a weathered face, obviously trying to appear solemnly respectable and very much in charge of himself. A bit rough-edged. Backbone-of-America type, she thought oddly, wearing his pride like a shield.

Forte quickly brought out the routine questions, establishing the man's relationship and background details. Mr. Waters answered him with clipped efficiency. For some reason, she felt the atmosphere in the courtroom change, the tension rise, the expressions on the faces of Mr. and Mrs. Graham and their lawyer grow more intense.

"How would you describe your relationship with your grandson, Mr. Waters?" Forte asked with a smile.

"We were pals," Mr. Waters said pleasantly. "He's quite a kid."

"You saw a lot of him then?"

"Are you kidding? Every chance I got."

"Both before and after your son was killed?"

"Even more after."

"Why was that?"

"Well . . ." Mr. Waters shrugged. Annie decided that he was a bit embarrassed to be showing vulnerability. "A little kid loses his dad. That's rough. Kind of rough on me, too. He obviously needed me even more than before. Had to be both a Grampa—a grand-father—and a father. We spent lots of time together. Had fun, too. We got a kick out of each other." He was growing expansive, and his lawyer made no move to stop him, letting him meander. "We both looked forward to the weekends. I made him lots of toys. A wagon. It was—" He swallowed deeply, heading into more emotional territory. Forte let him, and soon Waters had to clear his throat and swallow a sob, but not before one had escaped. The point made, the young lawyer jumped in again with a question.

"Did it come as a shock to you to learn that your daughter-in-law had decided to cut you both off from any visits to your grandson?"

"Worse than that."

"You were angry?"

"Damned right."

"And you made it known to your daughter-in-law and her future husband?"

"Yes, I did. It was wrong. Unnatural. He was my flesh and blood." He glanced quickly at his wife. "Our flesh and blood."

"And you made a scene when you found out?"

"I expressed my anger. Yes."

"And then you agreed to go along with it?"

"What choice did I have?"

"And Tray? How do you think he felt about it?"

"He had no choice either. How can anyone have expected him to feel? No sooner did he lose his father than he lost his grandfather and grandmother. I mean, you don't have to be a genius to figure out how that can hurt a little kid." He hissed air between his teeth and shook his head. "Wrong is wrong. There's nothing on earth we wouldn't do for that boy." He stopped suddenly and stared at his former daughter-in-law. "She knows that."

Annie saw Mrs. Waters raise her hand in a gesture that appeared to mean that he stay calm. Peck saw the gesture as well and smiled thinly. Trouble ahead, she thought.

"Based on your observations of your daughter-in-law both during the marriage with your son and after his death, was there any reason to expect such treatment?" Forte asked, apparently choosing his words carefully.

"Definitely not," Mr. Waters said, perhaps too quickly, indicating that he had been carefully rehearsed. She saw the big lawyer hunch over his pad and quickly scribble some notes.

"Did you welcome the idea of your grandson's adoption?"

"I didn't think it would create these kinds of problems."

"So you didn't contest it?"

"I didn't know you could."

"Would you have done so if you knew you could?"

"Considering what I know now, yes."

"Did you object to your daughter-in-law's marriage?"

"Not exactly. I just felt that they should have waited a proper amount of time. That's all. Just a few more months is all. Okay, I was getting over that. No big deal. I was even considering going to the wedding. Letting bygones be bygones. I understood all that. Maybe I was a little too heavy-handed at first." He shook his head and looked down at his hands. "He was my only son, my only child, and he was gone less than six months before—less than six months." He sniffled and lifted his head. "But whatever I did, she had no cause not letting us see Tray. As if we were garbage. I mean, that's dirty pool."

"And did you attempt to see him?"

"Not at first. We wanted him to have time to adjust to his new dad. I didn't like the idea, but I was willing to let time pass if it was to help Tray. I understood what he might be thinking," he said, looking up at Mr. Graham. "That he wanted to be number one for Frances, that he didn't need no reminders. I could see his attitude. I really could. Maybe at first. As I say, I didn't like it—"

Now she could see Mr. Graham cock his head in a way that showed the increasing intensity of his interest.

"But after one year passed and nearly another, it began to eat us up. She wouldn't even let us send him Christmas gifts. That really stuck in my craw. It was wrong to do that. Wrong for Tray, too." She could see that it was becoming more and more painful for him to continue. "So one day I upped and visited Tray at school." He took a deep breath and forced a smile. "I had this old wagon that I had repainted. It was Chuck's, and I just had this irresistible urge to give it to him. So I went."

"And you saw him?"

"Yes, I did." She could see that he wanted to cry, but he laughed instead. It came out as a kind of a strained cackle. "Should've seen him. He must have grown three inches. And I could tell that he was happy to see me. But we both played it cool." He took another deep breath and paused. Forte made no attempt to prod him. "Then suddenly it was a big deal. They called Frances, and when she got there, I was asked to leave the school. Then Frances said that if I ever tried to do that again, she would call the cops. Crazy, right? Call the cops on Tray's grandfather."

"How did you feel about that?"

"Lower than a snake. And a little ashamed. For her. And for Tray."

"You made no attempt to see him again?"

"What was the use?"

"It was then that you realized that the only recourse was the courts?"

He shrugged. "All we want to do is visit our grandson." He

looked up at Annie, misty-eyed, his Adam's apple working up and down his throat. "Is that too much to ask? We mean no harm to Frances and her husband. We just want to get to see Tray."

It was pitiful, Annie thought, engaged despite herself, suddenly realizing why the other judges hated this job. Like reading *True Confessions*, Judge Compton had said. He was giving a man's reaction, being deliberately oblique. What he had meant was that it was just too emotional to bear, that it clouded one's sense of neutral judgment. Worse, she discovered. In her heart, she wanted to cry.

"You don't cry," Peggy had said that morning. Well, Peggy was wrong.

Chapter 13

CHARLIE was magnificent, Molly thought, controlled, sincere, candid, just as their lawyer had urged him to be. She was certain that he had made an impression on the judge, who, at first, had seemed cold, all business. The worst, she knew, was yet to come. But Charlie seemed comfortable and self-assured. She had felt awful on the stand, but it was a relief to discover that they had not chosen to make an issue of her visit to Frances, which indicated to her that Frances had kept their secret.

It all seemed so unreal and unnecessary. And it was bizarre to think that that woman up there had the fate of all their lives in her hands. But at least they had been forewarned by Forte that the odds, the issues, and the law were against them, which didn't leave much room for high expectations. It was something that they had to do, for themselves, for Chuck, for Tray. Just hold it together, Charlie, she urged, closing her eyes and concentrating, hoping that she might telepathically transmit her message to him.

Of course, the message that Frances had transmitted with her pregnancy was a real surprise. Cagey lady, Molly thought. Not telling her when they had had their little get-together. All part of the strategy. It was ominous, she decided, wondering what else they had up their sleeves.

She watched as the big lawyer slowly rose, like a bear moving in for the kill. The odd, random image frightened her. But Charlie seemed to be reacting well, chin thrust out, hands on his knees. Be the old tough gyrene, baby, she urged in her heart. She glanced toward Frances. Their eyes met briefly, then parted.

"Mr. Waters." The voice of the big lawyer boomed in the cavernous courtroom. It was meant to be intimidating. Even the judge, reacting to the sound, raised her head and tilted her chin forward.

"What is your occupation, Mr. Waters?" the lawyer asked. He did not smile. His pose was unmistakably aggressive, and Molly grew frightened.

"I used to be an inspector in the pipe division at Bethlehem. Sparrows Point." She noted the sudden glazed look in his eyes. "Just retired."

"And now?"

"Well, I work in a nursery."

"How long have you been at it?"

"Couple of weeks."

"And before that?"

"I had some other jobs. But I didn't stay."

"Why not?"

"Didn't enjoy them, is all."

"You left them quickly. Each in a day or so."

"More or less."

"And how long do you think you'll keep the nursery job?"

Forte jumped to his feet.

"Objection, your Honor."

"Please rephrase the question, Mr. Peck."

"How long do you expect to keep this job—"

"I object to these questions, your Honor."

"I don't see why. They seem perfectly proper to me," Judge Stokes said.

"I don't see the point," Forte said, sitting down.

Peck turned once again to Charlie.

"Do you like your nursery job?"

"To tell you the truth, it's pretty good. Outdoors. I think I'll hang around awhile." He winked at Molly.

"All right then, I'll put it another way. Are you enjoying your retirement?"

She knew what he was getting at, of course. Trying to make Charlie appear unstable. Well, so far he had been outfoxed on that point.

"I'm not that retired," Charlie said, smiling.

Peck lifted his hands in a studied gesture of futility.

"Why did you choose that particular day to visit your grandson at school?"

"I—I just couldn't stand it anymore. I missed him, is all."

"But why that particular day?"

Charlie looked toward Molly, and she forced a smile and a nod.

"My birthday. It was my birthday."

"How old were you?"

"Sixty."

"A very significant milestone, wouldn't you say?"

Charlie nodded.

"What else did that day mark?"

Charlie cleared his throat.

"My retirement day."

"Voluntary retirement?"

"They have this new program. When you hit sixty, you can retire."

"Isn't that kind of young to retire voluntarily in today's world?"

"I put in my years."

"In fact it was an involuntary retirement. A real blow. Wasn't it?"

Molly's stomach knotted.

"Sort of."

"And you felt—well—lousy."

"You would, too. You don't work for a company more than thirty-five years and feel good about leaving. It's only natural."

"So you needed a bit of comfort?"

"Happens to everybody."

"And you ran immediately to see your grandson?"

"Anything wrong with that?"

"From your point of view? Maybe not. From Tray's? That's another question." He lifted his head and looked up at the judge, who remained impassive. Peck began to pace in front of the chair, then looked up suddenly and shot Charlie a question. "How did your grandson react to the confrontation?"

Charlie squirmed in his seat.

"He seemed glad to see me."

"How glad?"

"Just glad." He forced a laugh. It sounded hollow. "I brought him his wagon."

"Where was he when you arrived?"

"In class."

"And your visit interrupted him?"

"Well, yes. I said it would only take a minute."

"How did he express his—his happiness?"

"He sort of smiled."

"Did he rush into your arms?"

"Well, no. He was probably embarrassed to do that."

"Did he say something like, 'Gosh, I missed you, Grampa'? After all, it had been two years. Or did he show confusion and surprise?"

"I guess he was surprised."

"Not confused?"

"I can't be sure."

"In fact, he was totally confused, Mr. Waters. We have it on good authority from the adults who were present. He was interrupted in his class. He really didn't know what was happening. You simply bullied your way in. You did not use your real name. You said you were about to leave town."

"I wanted to see him," Charlie said, obviously feeling the pressure of harassment.

"Because you needed him on that particular day."

"Is that so terrible?"

"But did he need you, Mr. Waters?"

"I'm his grandfather."

"That was not my question, Mr. Waters." Forte began to rise. Peck saw it and lifted his hands, palms up. "All right then, how did you feel when you saw him?"

"Better. I felt better," Charlie said, rattled, but seizing the opportunity to report this sense of relief. "At first. Then when they kind of eased me out, I felt rotten." He looked toward Frances. "She told me that if it happened again, she would call the police. Tell me, what was my crime?"

"No crime, Mr. Waters. The tragedy here is that you needed Tray for therapeutic reasons, to make *you* feel better about the things that had happened to you that day. But Tray didn't need you. He was doing fine. He is doing fine. He was happy. He is happy, adjusted, productive, a normal boy. As much as I hate to say it, he neither needed nor wanted your visit, did he, Mr. Waters?"

"If they'd let it happen in the normal way—"

"We are dealing here with what is best for the child. That is the only issue in this court, Mr. Waters."

"I'm not saying it isn't."

As the cross-examination continued, Molly felt a sinking sensation in her heart. Forte must have seen how she was taking it, and he patted her hand.

"He's throwing everything he has at Charlie, Mrs. Waters," Forte whispered.

"How do you think he's doing?"

"Surprisingly well."

"You think so?"

It encouraged her, but she wasn't sure. After all those years together, she knew her man. Just beneath the surface, he was at the breaking point. But she was still proud of him, and she nodded and smiled.

Then, suddenly, Peck became ingratiating, leading Charlie through a series of questions that focused on his early life, the things he and Chuck had done together, boating, hunting, fishing, the affection and interests that both men had shared.

"It was a terrible blow to lose your only child, your cherished son?"

"Yes, it was."

"You shared so much."

"We did."

"Everyone understands that."

Now Molly was confused. It seemed odd that he wasn't dealing with Charlie's early objections to Chuck's marriage and the cool relationship he had with Frances.

"It depressed you?"

"Very much."

"Then came the loss of your grandson?"

"Yes."

"And of your job after thirty-five years?"

"What is he getting at?" Molly asked Forte, who waved her to be silent.

"No wonder, then, that you were depressed, that you showed rather odd behavior."

"What?" Charlie was rattled again, worse than before. He looked helplessly at Molly.

"And you have been known occasionally to lose your temper?"

"Sometimes. But I don't—"

"All the pressures of life suddenly coming together can wreak havoc on a man's psyche."

"I don't know what you're talking about," Charlie cried, his voice rising, his body taut. Molly gripped Forte's hand.

"I'm talking about . . ." The big lawyer paused, his intense gaze scanning the room, first the judge, then his clients, then Molly, and finally back to Charlie. "I'm terribly sorry, Mr. Waters. But it has to be faced." Molly felt an invisible hand grab at her insides and squeeze.

"What does?"

"Your suicidal tendency, Mr. Waters."

"My . . ." Charlie rose out of his chair, then fell back, ashen, drained, defeated. Forte jumped to his feet.

"I totally reject this line of questioning," Forte said. "This is disgraceful and unprincipled speculation."

"I'm sorry, your Honor," Peck said, shaking his head, as if the revelation were equally painful to him. He turned and looked toward Molly. "The state of Mr. Waters's mental health, as will be shown, was reported by Mrs. Waters herself in a meeting with Mrs. Graham only a few weeks ago. I can discontinue this line now and pick it up again with Mrs. Graham. But I assure you it cannot be swept under the rug."

The judge looked at Charlie with an expression that seemed like sympathy. She shook her head. Forte looked at Molly, his eyes sad and questioning. His gaze seemed to drill through her. She wished she could disappear and hoped that the heart beating in her chest would suddenly explode. She turned toward Frances.

"How could you?" Molly asked. Frances turned away, saying nothing. Tears suddenly obscured Molly's view, and she opened her handbag to look for a tissue. Finding one, she sniffled and wiped her eyes.

"May I request a short recess, your Honor?" Forte asked.

The judge nodded, raised her gavel, and brought it down. She looked at the clock.

"We're nearing lunch. Back in session at one."

Revealing nothing through her features or posture, she stood up, and the clerk called them to attention as she left the courtroom. For a moment, no one moved. Then Molly rushed forward to her husband.

"I'm sorry, Charlie," she said, embracing him. He looked up at her with moist eyes.

"You really think I would have left you alone, babe?" he asked.

Answers tumbled in her mind, but she couldn't find the composure to speak.

Later, sitting at a booth in a delicatessen near the courthouse, Molly managed to find some words of explanation. Forte listened while Charlie brooded and occasionally shook his head in disbelief.

"I was worried," she said, avoiding Charlie's eyes, forcing herself for Charlie's sake to rise above her misery and remain as casual as she was able. Someday maybe she could explain her actions more forthrightly. Now all she could offer were makeshift explanations, hoping Charlie would understand. Betraying Forte was one thing, but hurting Charlie, that touched her to the core. "Maybe I did read into things more than I should have." She touched Charlie's arm and felt a cold shiver travel up her spine.

"But you were depressed, and that night, seeing you with that damned loaded gun across your lap, what was I to think, Charlie? You weren't yourself. I admit that I shouldn't have even called her. But sometimes you try anything." She turned to the lawyer. "I never expected this."

"Tailor-made," Forte muttered. "And he used it with great skill. Great skill. If he wanted to show instability, he scored a home run."

"He hit me right between the eyes," Charlie said with effort. He looked toward Molly and sighed. "Not your fault, babe. You're right. I was acting strange."

"I've always been scared of those guns, Charlie," she said, seeking more ways to deflect his gloom. She hadn't even mentioned it to him at the time, fearful that by saying it she might somehow cause him to act. In her heart she knew she was right. Those guns could never load themselves. The point was that it was a private matter, and to say it to others, especially Frances, was a violation of their intimacy. She bit her lip to stop it from trembling. "Me and my big mouth," she said.

Charlie lifted his head and looked at her with sad eyes.

"Guess we blew it," he sighed.

Their sandwiches came. Molly looked at hers and nearly retched. Surprisingly, Charlie ate his while Forte took a desultory bite now and again. It was obvious his mind was elsewhere.

"It was a curve you threw me, Mrs. Waters. No question of that."

Maybe that was it, she decided. She had thrown them all curves. Maybe all this trouble came from her own doings. All wrong, she decided, a catalogue of self-accusations rising in her mind.

"Not going to be much fun going back in there," Charlie muttered, turning to the lawyer. "You said from the beginning it was a long shot."

"Didn't expect it to be *this* long." He pushed his sandwich plate away. "I don't feel very good about this, folks. A good trial lawyer anticipates. When she walked in pregnant, I knew we were up against it. I should have asked for interrogatories, made observations. Their family setup is strong and tight, well-illustrated. The opposition seems better served."

"No sense running yourself down, Mr. Forte," Molly said. "I'm the one who wrecked the case."

"A lawyer has to establish the right environment for his clients to open up, an atmosphere of candor." It surprised her to see how hard he was taking it. She looked at Charlie, who seemed equally confused. He had told them he believed in their cause, but this attitude seemed beyond the call of duty. "No. I'm afraid it doesn't look good, folks."

"Are you suggesting that we walk away?" Molly asked.

"I suppose it sounds like that," he said.

"That lady up there didn't let on what she was thinking," Charlie said. He seemed to be trying hard to shake off the gloom of impending defeat.

"We'll just have to put our heads down and go forward," Forte said, pulling his plate forward again and taking a bite of his sandwich. "It's not over yet." His eyes glazed over as if his mind had gone elsewhere.

Turning toward Charlie, Molly put her hand over his. "You were terrific up there, Charlie. No matter what, I was very proud."

"I was dying inside, babe. I tell you true."

"Me, too."

Forte seemed lost in thought, and they ignored him.

"Forgive me?" she asked. She knew she would spend a lifetime asking that question.

"For what?" And he would spend a lifetime answering it in just that way.

"I could kick myself," she said.

"Hell you can." He tried to smile. "That's my job."

"If I were Peck, I'd ask for a dismissal," Forte said suddenly, his fingers tapping the table. "It may be over sooner than we think." But it did not seem as if his words ended the thought. "She might not go for that." He seemed to be talking to himself.

"For what?" Molly asked.

"I don't know," Forte shrugged.

"It sounded like you did," Molly said.

"Just an embryo," Forte muttered. "Too complicated to explain."

Molly sensed that he was being evasive and did not pursue the point. She noted that Forte had finished his sandwich.

When the hearing reconvened, the two lawyers stood in front of the bench talking in whispers, then came back to the table.

"She didn't grant his request for a dismissal," Forte said.

"I suppose that's good," Molly said.

"Neither good nor bad. She simply might have no place to go for the rest of the day." Molly detected a note of sarcasm, although Forte seemed uncommonly vague. He was working things out, she decided. She pointedly avoided looking at Frances and Peter.

Then Frances rose and waddled to the witness stand. Peck followed. Despite her size, she looked more radiant than Molly had ever seen her. Her face had filled out, and her skin, devoid of makeup, glowed with health. Clear-eyed, neat in her crisp maternity blouse with its big red bow, she looked the picture of confidence and contentment. Happy. So you put us all behind you, Molly thought, glancing at Charlie. Yet, notwithstanding the dispute, Molly felt more than just a grudging admiration for her. She had come a long away from Dundalk, from Chuck and his indifference. From them. Perhaps, from Frances's point of view, she and Charlie were pariahs, reminders of sadder days, an unwanted, unnecessary, and negative influence on Tray. Maybe it was time to stop this charade.

Peck led Frances gently through her testimony. Earlier, he had driven home the main point of his arguments. It remained to put the frosting on the cake. The initial questioning had clearly established that the life of the Graham family, Tray included, was a model of loving, caring, respect, and, in fact, unbounded happiness.

"And your first marriage, to Charles Waters, Jr., was, to say the least, unsatisfactory?" Peck asked.

"At first it was reasonably happy. Then Tray came along, and my husband went off to foreign countries."

"Rarely coming home?"

"Rarely."

"And when he did come home?"

"He was distant and indifferent."

"Did you contemplate divorce?"

She lowered her eyes and clasped her hands across the expanse of her pregnant middle.

"It was on my mind. Yes."

"Not true," Charlie whispered.

"You don't know that for sure, Charlie," Molly snapped, and he looked at her queerly.

"With respect to your in-laws, how did they treat you during the marriage to their son?"

"We never had words. They were very devoted to Chuck, and

I, of course, was his wife. Molly was thoughtful and understanding. My father-in-law was more interested in"— she hesitated as if searching for exactly the right word —"manly things. His relationship with my husband was very close. Also with Tray. They were not unkind. I'd never say that. Not once. I was married to their son."

"And before?"

"My father-in-law opposed the marriage. It was no secret."

"For what reason?"

"He said it was because Chuck and I were too young."

"That seems logical. Was there any other reason?"

"I think he would have opposed any woman who wanted to marry his son."

Molly squirmed uncomfortably. There was no denying the truth of it.

"Regarding Tray, did they ever treat him badly?"

"Of course not."

"Are they sincere when they say they love him?"

"I believe so."

"Is it true that after your husband's death, they were supportive, loving to Tray?"

"Yes. They were."

"And when your present husband came along, how did your father-in-law react?"

"He did not approve of our getting married so soon after Chuck's death."

"And he made these views known to your future husband?"

"Emphatically."

"But neither he nor your mother-in-law opposed his plan to adopt Tray?"

"No."

Peck paused. Turning, he looked at Molly and Charlie, telescoping the importance of the message that was about to come forth.

"Would you tell the court, Mrs. Graham, in your own words, exactly why you feel that it would be better for your son if Mr. and Mrs. Waters did not visit him at this time."

Frances sucked in a deep breath. Here comes the painful part, she thought. The judge tilted her head toward the witness, her attention totally focused. Molly reached out and took Charlie's hand. He was sweating.

"Tray is a happy, well-adjusted boy. He has a loving father in every respect. He has a new brother whom he loves and, as you can see, another one on the way. Hopefully, a sister. I know that my former in-laws think us cruel and heartless for taking this action. But we have to make decisions that are best for our son. For Tray. The past for him is only a dim memory. Why should he be disturbed, his life disrupted, in any way? He has loving grandparents in my husband's parents. Why should he be treated differently from the other children? It is not necessary for him to visit with Mr. and Mrs. Waters. In fact, it will undoubtedly be bad for him—"

"What makes you say that?" the lawyer interrupted.

"His reaction to Mr. Waters's visit to the school was upsetting. It was an unnecessary intrusion."

"You were surprised at Mr. Waters's sudden visit?"

"It seemed very odd."

"Irrational?"

"I suppose."

"Did it affect you at all?"

"It upset me, too, yes."

"In the light of what you subsequently heard about Mr. Waters, as we learned earlier, have you any doubts about your decision on visitation?"

"None."

"Now let me ask you this, Mrs. Graham. Sometime after Mr. Waters's visit to the school, you were asked by Mrs. Waters to meet with you."

"That is correct."

"And you went?"

"Yes."

"Why?"

"She sounded very troubled and I truly felt that she might be offering to drop this suit."

"So you went?"

"Yes."

"And she told you how unhappy they were and about Mr. Waters's, well, depressed state and his self-destructive thoughts?"

"Yes."

"And how did this affect you?"

"Badly. I began having pains. I thought perhaps it might be a miscarriage coming on. I had to stay in bed for a week."

"Do you blame that on the aggravation of the meeting?"

"I can only assume it was because of that. It could have been a coincidence."

"But you were aggravated by this meeting?"

"Very much so."

"Did it leave you with any regrets, any second thoughts about your decision?"

"None."

Peck nodded and looked up at the judge.

"No more questions, your Honor."

He doesn't have to go much further, Molly thought. Forte stirred beside her. She looked up at him. His eyes were burning with intensity, his lips were bloodless, his olive skin seemed darker. He moved forward, lean and spare, indicating a singleness of purpose that made her wince with fear. Please, God, she thought, don't let him hurt her. He started abruptly, without introductions or preliminaries.

"If you had not married, Mrs. Graham, would you have allowed your former in-laws to have access to your child by their son?"

"I object to that, your Honor," Peck said, rising. "That question is hypothetical and absurd."

"I have no objections, counselor," the judge said.

"Well then?" Forte prodded.

"I don't think that's a fair question," Frances said, looking up toward the judge.

"I'll put it another way, Mrs. Graham. You did not have any objections to your former in-laws' support—physical, psychological, financial, whatever—during the brief term of your widowhood?"

"I had no choice."

"Did you detest it? Was it so terrible?"

"I did not feel comfortable being dependent on them. No." Frances seemed puzzled by Forte's line of reasoning. Molly, too.

"You didn't think that they were a bad influence on their grandchild then?"

"I wasn't overjoyed by their influence. As I said, what choice had I?"

"Why were you unhappy with their influence?"

Frances hesitated, her eyes searching for her husband.

"They weren't such a hot influence on Chuck."

"Are you blaming them for your admittedly unsuccessful marriage?"

"In a way, I suppose—"

"As if you did not exist as a partner in that marriage."

"I don't know what you're getting at," Frances said.

"Nor do I, your Honor," Peck said rising. The judge waved him down.

"I think you should make your line of questioning clearer, counselor," the judge said. Forte nodded consent, not taking his eyes off Frances.

"But you just said you blamed your in-laws for your bad marriage."

"I didn't mean that. Not entirely."

"What did you mean?"

"You have to understand. Chuck was never really mine. He was always torn. His father—his father just possessed him."

"Exercised undue influence, is that what you mean?"

"Well," she hesitated. "Something like that."

"An influence that you perceived as negative?"

"In some ways, yes."

"In what ways?"

"They were together a lot."

"Meaning you were left out."

"In a way."

"That seems very vague, Mrs. Graham."

Peck stood up again.

"I really object to this, your Honor. He's badgering my client."

"I'm inclined to agree, Mr. Forte."

"I'm just trying to make a point."

"What point?" the judge asked.

"If you let me continue, I'll show you."

"Go on then, counselor," the judge said. "But gently, please. This is not a criminal trial."

Forte turned back to Frances.

"So you felt that your father-in-law was a bad influence on your husband and would be a bad influence on your child?"

"Not exactly." Frances began to twist her fingers. Don't, Molly begged in her heart. But Forte was relentless. Perhaps some things are better left unsaid, she thought, hating the spectacle before her.

"Mrs. Graham." Forte lowered his voice, appearing almost ingratiating. "Are you afraid that your father-in-law would do to Tray what you perceived he did to Tray's father?"

"You're twisting things."

"But it is a factor in your decision not to allow them to visit your son, their grandchild?"

"I don't think so. I'm not sure."

"You're under oath, Mrs. Graham."

He's only making it worse, Molly thought. What good was it to bring out all these secret antagonisms?

"Not only fear, Mrs. Graham. Perhaps there is also vindictiveness lying just beneath the surface." He paused. "Do you think so?"

"No, I don't," Frances said calmly. "You're making it sound like I'm deliberately hurting them to get even. And that's just not true."

"So, if you had not remarried, you might never have prohibited your former in-laws from seeing their grandchild?"

"Maybe not."

"Then this decision not to grant the Waterses the right to visit their own grandchild was more your husband's than your own. It was he who barred these visits."

"No, he didn't." She seemed to be genuinely confused by the questioning, totally unprepared for the tack Forte was taking.

Molly's heart went out to her. "Awful," she whispered. Charlie did not respond, and she wondered what he was thinking.

"But if you hadn't married, the subject might not have come up." Forte paused for a moment and looked up at the judge. "Certainly it was not the child who wanted to have these visits stopped. He enjoyed being with his grandparents. It didn't trouble him. Of course, nobody ever consulted him. So it must have been Mr. Graham's decision."

"No. It wasn't," Frances's voice rose. Her cheeks flushed. "It was a joint decision."

"Not the three of you. Not Tray?"

Peck stood up, obviously livid with rage.

"We are talking here of a minor child. It is precisely because of that that we are here."

"I couldn't agree more," Forte said smugly. The two lawyers faced each other silently for a moment. Then Peck sat down, and once again, Forte faced Frances.

"He, your new husband, didn't want to be reminded of your

past life, as if somehow it diminished him, made him second. Isn't that right, Mrs. Graham?"

"This line of questioning is ridiculous, your Honor," Peck said, as he rose to his feet once again.

"It's obvious to me that she was corrupted by an outside force," Forte said.

"Corrupted?" the judge said. "That's a rather harsh characterization."

"In a way, yes," Forte acknowledged. "But not as accurate as the term *brainwashing*."

"I also object to that, your Honor."

"Counselor?" the judge said.

"I'm simply trying to show, your Honor, that none of the motivations for barring my clients from visiting their grandchild have anything to do with the child's welfare per se. That adult concerns have interfered with what is a perfectly natural and life-enhancing relationship. I see no reason for an objection to that line of questioning. It was deemed appropriate by Mr. Peck to characterize my client's wish to see his grandson as therapy."

"He is deliberately confusing the issue, your Honor," Peck said, jumping up. "The issue is the right of custodial parents to make decisions for their child without interference from outside sources. This is the common law interpretation. The distinguished counselor is trying to characterize the child's adoptive father as an outside source, which is patently absurd. In the eyes of the law Mr. Graham is hardly an outside source. He is the father."

"But the common law is superseded by the Maryland statute that grants grandparents the right of petition for visitation."

"Petition does not mean the automatic granting of visitation rights."

"I'm fully aware of the law, counselor," Forte sneered.

"Not adoptive law. You're quite weak in that regard."

"The new statute does imply that grandparents' rights should be considered seriously."

"That is exactly why you are in this courtroom," Judge Stokes interjected. "And I wish you would stop your wrangling."

On the witness stand, Frances looked wilted, and for a brief moment, Molly was frightened that the aggravation would have some effect on the baby. She glanced at Charlie, who merely shook his head and muttered under his breath.

"It's round the bend, babe," he whispered.

"Out of control."

"Damned lawyers."

"Poor Frances," Molly said.

"Poor us."

"Poor everybody."

But the lawyers continued to argue, their words echoing through the cavernous room. Then, suddenly, Judge Stokes banged the gavel. It took several bangs to get the lawyers under control.

"I am in charge here," the judge shouted. She was visibly angry, and the cords in her neck stood out. She looked at Frances.

"You may step down, Mrs. Graham."

Frances walked back to her seat. She was obviously shaken, and her husband rose to embrace her. He looked at Forte with naked hostility.

Forte sat down, and Molly imagined that she could hear his heart beating in his chest. His breath came in gasps, and he tapped his fingers on the table. There were many things Molly wanted to say, but she was afraid she would lose control. Instead, she just held on to Charlie's hand and squeezed.

"I will not have these outbursts in my courtroom," the judge said calmly. She looked at each of them in turn.

"It would seem that the presentation of this case is missing a very important ingredient." In the long pause that followed, Molly felt her stomach do flip-flops.

"I could, of course, make it a court order. Under the laws of this state I have that right. Instead I am putting it in the form of a request." She looked directly at Peck. "You will see to it that Charles Everett Waters the third is present in this courtroom tomorrow at ten?"

"No," Frances cried. "I will not have that."

The judge looked toward Forte.

"Have you any objection?" he asked Molly and Charlie. But before they could reply, he said, "Really, folks, it's your only chance."

"I hate the idea," Molly said, "of putting a child through this."

"It's her prerogative," Forte said enigmatically. "She's the judge."

"You can't allow this," Charlie said.

"It's not my choice anymore, Mr. Waters."

"But he's only seven."

"I didn't want it this way, either," Forte said. "Now it's our only chance."

Then it dawned on her, and she remembered Forte's unarticulated idea in the delicatessen.

"You did it on purpose," Molly said accusingly.

"I only provoked her. It's her decision. Not mine. Anyway, it's done all the time."

"But it's wrong," Molly said helplessly. "He's a child."

"It's also his life at stake here."

"Can they refuse to bring him?" Molly asked.

"I could have brought a writ of habeas corpus. I deliberately avoided that action. They really have no choice. Except to bring the child." All three looked at Peter and Frances, who seemed very upset.

"No way," Charlie mumbled.

Peck stood up and sucked in a deep breath.

"Tomorrow at ten, your Honor."

"I think it stinks to high heaven," Molly said.

"Yes, it does," Forte responded. "But then nobody calls me until it does."

Chapter 14

FRANCES combed Tray's blond hair, defeated finally by the cowlick, which just would not stay put with water. Just like Chuck's. She had dressed him in a white shirt and striped tie, blue blazer with gold buttons, and gray flannel pants, a replica of Peter's outfit.

"My little man," she whispered, pressing him as close to her as her pregnant belly would allow. He giggled and turned, putting his head against it. She stroked his back, as if that might smooth away the impending horror. No matter how hard she had tried, she could not view the situation in any other light.

"I hear him, Mommy," Tray whispered. He had decided that when he did this, a loud response would wake the baby. "Like a whish sound." She had explained that the baby was asleep in water, which approximated the truth. He continued to listen until, finally, she tapped him on the shoulder blades, and separated him from her.

"We mustn't be late."

"Where are we going, again?"

"To a courtroom."

"Oh."

She wondered what kind of an image that word suggested. He had seemed somewhat vague, perhaps recalling some television setting.

"Do you know what a courtroom is?" she asked gently.

"A place where people go . . ." He shrugged, obviously not quite certain.

"A place where people go to"— she searched her mind for adequate definitions —"to sort things out." No, she thought, moved by the puzzled look on Tray's face. "It's a place where people go to settle disputes."

"What's disputes?"

"Fights. When people can't fight their own battles." She was still not satisfied with the explanation. Nor, obviously, was Tray.

"Are we going to see people fight?"

"Something like that."

Not quite like that, she thought. Why was she having such a

difficult time explaining it? "Because people can't seem to settle their differences," she began. "Other people have to judge."

"Do I have to fight, Mommy?" Tray asked, proving the inadequacy of her answer.

"Of course not."

"Do you?"

"Not in a physical sense."

She felt herself getting deeper into a verbal maze.

"Is it like a game?"

"A game?" Perhaps to some, she decided. It occurred to her suddenly that there could be no sane explanation. Could she tell him that he was the object of some kind of human tug-of-war? He'd think that was a game as well. Yet, she did feel compelled to prepare him in some way. "People will ask you questions, sweetheart. Questions about your life, about us." She hesitated. "And about Grampa and Gramma Waters."

"Are they coming?" he asked eagerly.

"They'll be there, of course."

"Will they ask me questions?"

"Not directly."

"What kind of questions?"

"Oh . . ." She tried to act casual and matter-of-fact. "Questions about school, about your daddy—"

"This daddy or my other daddy?"

"Maybe both."

He hesitated for a moment, frowning briefly, as if suddenly assailed by unpleasant thoughts. She wasn't sure how to interpret it.

"How come we don't see Grampa and Gramma anymore?"

"My God." She felt herself getting more agitated. "Talk about questions."

Sensing her tension, he shrugged and looked out of the window while she finished dressing.

Peter, too, was beside himself.

"There can't possibly be a legal precedent for this," he told Peck outside the courthouse, with Frances standing beside him. "You've got to put a stop to it."

"Sorry," Peck replied. "In the state of Maryland as well as many other states, the judge has an absolute right to do this either in court or in chambers."

"But he's only seven."

Peck sighed with resignation.

"It is becoming increasingly common for the child to have a say in the determination of his or her own best interests if the child is competent to make a reasonable choice."

"That's nonsense. He's still only seven."

"It doesn't matter. He can communicate. Believe me, it wasn't my idea. I never thought it would go this far. What Forte did was muddy the waters, get the judge confused. It's visitation. Not custody. It's her first domestic case. Maybe she thinks she's going to school, and calling your son is all part of her education."

"Can't you refuse?"

"Sure. But then you lose the case."

"But dragging a little kid through this. It's wrong."

"As I said, she's the judge and she has the power to do it," Peck said with an attempt at sympathy. He rubbed his nose. "She might choose to see him in her chambers. The law says that both lawyers have to be present. Also a court reporter."

"What about us?"

"That's the whole point. The object is to get the child away from the pressures of the antagonists."

"Antagonists? We're his parents."

"I told you the alternative."

"Imagine a little kid like that with all those strange adults surrounding him. He'll be frightened to death."

Frances had listened, letting Peter carry the argument. She could see it was futile. Having control over one's own life was not, under any circumstances, a simple chore, she thought, not without a tinge of bitterness.

They had been unable to sleep. Frances couldn't get comfortable. The baby was acting up, offering her own protestations. Finally they had put on the lights.

"She must be madder than hell," Peter had observed, watching the undulations of Frances's midsection.

"No madder than her mother."

"I should have never let this happen," Peter had said, threading his arm behind her neck, kissing her cheek. There was just enough wrist room to pat her hair. "Peck said we had them dead to rights."

"He was never really positive about the outcome."

"Well, we had no choice but to contest their action."

"Who would think it would ever come to this?" she mused. She hadn't enjoyed any of the interrogation in the courtroom, certainly not her own. Nor was there any satisfaction in the way Charlie had been quartered. "Had to be done," Peck had told her at lunch, brimming with optimism. "I took no pleasure in it either," he assured her. Now she resented not being forewarned about the possibility of calling Tray.

"These lawyers play their own dirty game. It's almost as if we didn't exist as human beings."

"Unfortunately, we're in their hands," Peter said.

He had turned off the lights again. Still, she couldn't sleep. Her thoughts churned as she relived her waking nightmare on the stand. She had been totally unprepared for Forte's onslaught. It had been relentless, without mercy. The vaunted protection of her pregnancy had meant little or nothing. All through the testimony she had kept telling herself that she must endure this. Forte deliberately twisted everything, especially that implication that she was taking revenge on Molly and Charlie. Was there any truth in that? Had he uncovered some dark and hidden motive? Was she really capable of that? Unconsciously? She turned the thought over and over in her mind. There was just enough of the hint of truth in the lawyer's accusation to disturb her, as if he had stripped aside layers of self-protection. And even if it was true— what had that to do with Tray's best interest?

"It makes no sense," Peter whispered, his voice seeping into her thoughts. So he, too, continued to wrestle with the problem. Who needed this aggravation? Opening her eyes, she looked at the red figures on the digital clock. It was nearly two in the morning. "Tray, especially, doesn't need the trauma," he said. She could almost hear the humming logic cranking in his scientific mind. "The question is, is it worth the pain?"

She did not turn to face him. Was he, as Forte had suggested, the culprit after all? Had he brainwashed her? Was he now, in a fit of guilt and remorse, asking for surrender? Why not? He had already proven his manliness, his fatherhood. His place as head of the family was assured. His children were about to outnumber Chuck's. Had the wounds of his previous marriage healed? Was there anything for him to fear now?

"Can they hurt us now?" he whispered.

It hurt to hear. And she knew it would hurt more to respond.

Was he thinking of what was best for Tray? Or for himself? And what was her first priority? Tray? An avalanche of questions cascaded in her mind. But no answers. Except one. This was one decision that she would have to make on her own.

"It's the risk of it that's worrisome," he sighed. It was not, she understood, the hour for decisiveness.

"Do you think I've been vindictive?" she asked. It was a question for him, for herself, and for the darkness.

"You see how they manipulate us," he said with resignation. "They make us unsure of our motives."

"But I was afraid that Charlie would take Tray away from me. Like he took Chuck."

"All the more reason for our doing what we did," Peter said. "The fear was real enough to make a difference."

"Maybe I also didn't want him to be exposed to"— she hesitated, trying to think it out clearly —"Dundalk, and all it stood for."

"Dig deep enough, and you'll strike salt water," Peter said, reaching out to touch her hand. "Next thing you know, we'll be blaming each other. Also part of the strategy. Divide and conquer."

"No," she said. "It won't work."

He kissed her cheek, and for a long time there was silence. Then he spoke.

"You think it's true about me being . . . insecure?" Now it was his turn, she thought, listening. "He made it sound as if I were jealous of your first husband, because . . . well, because he came before me. You know something, there's a grain of truth in that. But then he accused me of brainwashing you into rejecting Chuck's parents. Do you think there's a grain of truth in that, too?"

"No. I don't."

"That would make me kind of a rat, wouldn't it?"

"You're no rat."

Reaching out, she grasped his hand, put it to her lips, and kissed it.

"All this is beside the point," she said.

"What point?"

"What's best for Tray."

"What's best for us is best for Tray."

In the silence she thought about that a long time before they both drifted off to sleep.

"I wish this thing was tomorrow instead of today, Mommy," Tray said, standing behind her as she combed her hair. Peter was downstairs feeding Mark, who was cranky with teething. She listened for Maria's familiar voice, dreading the complication if she didn't arrive on time. In fact, a feeling of dread pervaded her every thought.

"Why is that?"

"Because today they have frankfurters for lunch at school."

"Frankfurters aren't really good for you."

"Then why do they have them?"

"Good question."

His remark suggested other interruptions in his young life. The day she had gotten word that Chuck had died, she had taken him out of the day nursery in the middle of a game of dodge ball. When she had gotten married, she had moved him away from his friends. Then there was Charlie's crazy visit to his school. Now this. She wondered what effect these things would have on him, how he would handle them in his memory. Would they resurface later as clues to maladjustments? She tried to shake away such gloomy thoughts, studying his beautiful face in the mirror.

"My little prince," she said, tears rolling down her cheeks. "Will you ever forgive us?" All of us, she thought.

"Does something hurt, Mommy?"

"Not really, Tray."

"Is Snowflake okay?"

"She's fine."

Wiping her eyes and nose, she forced a smile. "You just be very calm today and answer all the questions with great honesty."

Her remark triggered fearful images. Were they going to cross-examine this child, submit him to what she had had to go through? Never, she vowed. That she would never allow, law or no law, procedures or no procedures. If that happened, she would dash out of the courtroom with Tray and insist that they immediately leave the state, out of the reach of these people.

Tray began to play with her perfume bottles, opening them and sniffing. She let him. "Don't spill any. You wouldn't want to smell up the courtroom." He giggled and put the tops back on.

By the time they got downstairs, Maria had arrived and Peter was giving her last-minute instructions in pidgin English.

"You no worry," she said.

"No worry," Peter whispered. "That's a laugh." He looked down at Tray. "Ready, Buddy?"

"Yup."

She looked at the clock in the kitchen. Earlier, they had agreed to make sure they arrived a few minutes late to avoid any unnecessary confrontations with Molly and Charlie, which could only confuse Tray.

"We'd better get going," Peter said.

But before they went out the door, Peter kneeled and embraced his adopted son. Goldy came over and, jealously asserting himself, licked Tray's face.

"You're my boy, right?"

"I sure am, Daddy."

"Well then, prove it."

Tray pushed Goldy away and kissed Peter noisily on the cheek. Frances watched, engulfed suddenly by a great wave of indignation.

"He should not have to be going through this."

"No way," Peter said, releasing the boy.

"If they really wanted to do what's best for him, they'd drop the suit instead of putting him through this."

"That's about the long and short of it."

Outside, they got into the car. Tray sat between them in the front seat. Suddenly she embraced him.

"It's not your fault, darling," she whispered. He looked up, confused. "And I pray and hope we're doing the right thing by you."

"You're my mommy. You always do right," Tray said, kissing her cheek.

She hoped it was true, but she was no longer certain.

Chapter 15

CHARLIE punched out the last cigarette in the pack, then crushed the wrapper and flung it in the direction of the plastic waste bucket. He missed. Story of my life, he shrugged, lifting the mug of tepid coffee. It had a sour, metallic taste, but he swallowed a mouthful anyway.

Through the kitchen window, he could see the faint silhouettes of the trees. From one hung the tire swing, looking like some ominous big-eyed predator, waiting for its moment to spring and devour. It was not yet dawn. Beyond the trees, the sky was coal black, glistening with the afterglow of the setting moon.

Despite all the valiant efforts he had made to hold back the depressing thoughts, they still came. This thing with calling Tray to court had jolted him. What he needed, he decided, was a mental sump pump to wash away the gloom. Why was all this happening? Had it happened before? He forced himself to probe his memory, focus some light on those darker corners of his life. They were there. He was sure of it, but, somehow, he had repressed them, shut them out. Had there been other ways to deal with them? He wasn't sure.

A memory did bubble to the surface. He was on Iwo Jima, pinned down in broad daylight on a tiny stretch of beach. He had gone in on the second wave. Dead marines were strewn along the beach like seashells. Gritty sand hung on his tongue. Sweat poured from his body. Shells crashed around him. He could hear the whiz of the bullets as they sailed ominously over his head. Men shouted in agony and frustration. Yet, amid all that carnage, some mysterious collective will had infected those who lay there, and suddenly, in the face of this relentless incoming fire, they moved forward. He knew he could not accurately reconstruct the thoughts of a twenty-year-old boy, but he was sure that the spirit of the memory remained intact in his mind all those years. Only now, he was certain, could he assess the truth of it.

It was not a foolhardy myth of heroism that had spurred them on. Not a mad wish for martyrdom. Not a soldier's programmed reflex to barking orders. A mere shouted command would not have been enough to move them into the jaws of a cruel death.

What then? Of one thing he was now certain. There was nothing in it of gloom or depression or pessimism or doubt. He had crawled on his belly toward the enemy guns with absolute certainty that his role as a marine and a man had logic and meaning. Of course, he feared the potential pain and the dying. But what he feared most of all was that he would fall short of grace and dignity in the face ot it, that he would dishonor those values of courage, loyalty, and honor without which he could not fulfill his role.

What had happened to all those old roles? Time was when you could go to sleep and get up in the morning and everything would be the same. A father went to work and provided for his family. A mother watched over her brood and cooked and cleaned the hallowed nest where a man could rest his heart. Grandparents stood by, loving and content, passing along the lessons of time and experience. The young respected the old. The bond between the old and the young was sacred. Graying had a hallowing effect. Passing was properly mourned. Had times changed that much? A hand clutched and tightened around his gut. Where was the grace, the honor, in grandparents' having to go to court to secure the right to visit their own grandchild?

But even the light of memory could not reveal why he had put those shells in his rifle. He could barely remember doing it. Had he been seeking to end it, check out of life, put an end to frustration and pain? Leave Molly? Never! Could he have actually done something so cowardly and unworthy? Of course not. He caught the element of sham in his bravado. He pounded his fist into his palm. Then it came to him. Was that it? A mystery cracked? The end of mourning?

"That bullet wasn't meant for me. It was meant for Nasty Jake."

"What?" It was Molly behind him.

"Nothing," he said, turning. "I was talking to myself, I guess." He laughed. "We were having a go at it. Me and him."

"You and who?"

"Me and me," he said. "I was trying to figure things out."

"Tell me when you do."

"This thing with Tray being called to court. I can't live with it."

"It's awful. Just awful."

"Our fault?"

She looked at him in the quickening light, avoiding an answer. "I dozed off," she said, changing the subject. "But when you weren't there, I woke suddenly." She giggled nervously. "Did I ever tell you, Charlie, that when you and Chuck would go away, I don't think I ever had a good night's sleep?"

"Not once?"

"No. I never told you," she mused, looking out the window. "I never told you how lonely I felt, either."

"No, you didn't."

He wondered whether, as Frances had confessed, Molly, too, had felt excluded. Women were mysterious creatures. Didn't they understand that manliness required that they be shut out sometimes? Hadn't he tried to explain that long ago?

"You should have told me."

"Would it have made any difference?"

"Maybe."

"I doubt that, Charlie. Besides, I always felt that I was doing the right thing by staying home. You used to come back feeling, the two of you"— she groped for the right word —"content. As if you shared some deep, dark masculine secret. Sure I felt excluded. And I forgot my loneliness because I could see that you and Chuck were happy for being away together."

While he listened, he looked out the window. She did understand that, and he felt grateful.

"I had him a lot to myself earlier. I had him inside me. Then at the breast. It's different with a mother. I never felt deprived in that respect. It didn't mean that I wasn't supposed to miss both of you when you went away. That's what Frances meant when she said she felt abandoned. Of course, you knew that, Charlie. You knew it."

He nodded.

"The difference was that I always knew that it was more important for you to come home than it was to stay away," Molly continued. "For some reason Chuck didn't feel that way. Something inside of him was different, I guess. I don't know why. He didn't, either. It wasn't Frances's fault, Charlie."

"Suppose it was mine?" Charlie asked. "Was I too selfish about him? Too possessive? Like Frances said?"

"Too loving, maybe."

"Whatever. It didn't do him much good." He continued to look out the window. The shapes outside were becoming more distinct. "You really think that I could have kept him from going?"

"I used to think so. I'm sure Frances still does."

"She probably hates me for that. Hates me for a lot of things, I suppose."

"I don't think Frances hates. She's just scared. Afraid of losing Peter. Afraid for Tray."

"I might have stopped him, Molly. I might have. But I felt he needed it." Charlie felt a sob bubble in his chest. "He didn't have his war. What's a young man's life without adventure?"

"Always what a man needs. What about us?"

"I don't know what you women need. I don't understand the rules of your club, either." She sat beside him and rested her hand on her chin, reaching out with the other to touch his hand. "But I'm always willing to learn."

"I think sometimes that if Tray were a girl, Frances wouldn't feel so threatened."

"Then *you'd* be the heavy. She'd blame it all on you."

"Would it mean as much? A girl grandchild?"

"I think so," he said emphatically. "And I'd be like you and you'd be like me."

"You mean I'd be the one flying off the handle, and you'd be the one trying to hold it all together?"

"It wouldn't mean that we wouldn't love her with equal feeling."

"It would have been great to have a little girl," Molly sighed. She bent over and put her arm around his neck. "It's too bad I was so barren, Charlie. You needed lots of children. You had a lot to give."

"Sure I did. But you had more. Anyway, I'm not going to look back. It's you and me, babe. No matter what. Besides, what would you have done without your biggest baby to worry about?"

"So what do you want to be when you grow up?"

"If I grew up, you might find some other baby."

"There's nothing to worry about then. You'll never grow up."

She moved closer to him, and they were silent for a long time, watching the familiar shapes emerge in the quickening light.

"You've got to admit that Peter's been a good dad for the boy, a loving, caring father. What more could you ask for?" Her voice seemed to tighten with caution. "The fact is, Tray might not need us as much as we think we need him."

He stiffened, the old anger beginning to swell inside of him.

"What's wrong with us needing him? With anybody needing anybody?"

"The law doesn't see it that way."

"Then the law is not so smart." He got up and began to pace the room. When he looked at her, her frown told him she was once more worried about his state of mind. "What do they know? Bringing a seven-year-old kid into the courtroom. Putting him through that. Those lawyers may think they know something about the law, but they don't know a damned thing about human beings."

Outside the courtroom, the scene with Forte had not been pleasant. Charlie had been hopping mad about the judge's ruling.

"Your fault," he had accused the lawyer. "You went after Frances with a horsewhip."

"Isn't that what you wanted?"

"Not if it turned out like this. You should have known what would happen."

"It was the only card we had."

"My grandson should not have been brought into it."

"He *was* in it. From the beginning."

"Is there anything we can do to stop it?" Molly had asked. She was in total agreement with Charlie.

"We could withdraw the petition."

"And never see Tray again?"

"You can't have your cake and eat it, too, Mr. Waters."

"You did it deliberately," Charlie had mumbled. "Got your ego in it. Got your nose out of joint. You knew what she would do."

"I hoped she would, yes," he said. "Look what I had to contend with. Your wife's big secret and you with a loaded gun on your lap."

"She had it all wrong."

"Did she?" Suddenly the lawyer calmed down, grew pensive. "They made their point."

"So did you," Molly had said. "About her seeking to punish us."

"Maybe it was true. It sure looks like it."

"It doesn't matter anyway," the lawyer said. "An acrimonious relationship between the grandparents and custodial parents is definitely not in the best interests of the child. I took a chance on that one."

"You could have concentrated on making Peter the heavy. You made the point, but you could have hammered away at it instead of attacking her." Molly had tried to press the issue, but Forte only shook his head.

"That's what makes a domestic trial so fascinating. You start down one path, but you never really know where it's leading. What I had to do was shake up the issue, confuse things, muddy the waters, ascribe deep, hostile motives. People have all kinds of aggressive secrets. Usually they're kept under control and don't affect the norm of behavior. So your daughter-in-law was wary of you. That was obvious from the beginning. I just built on it. Most people are secretly wary of each other, somewhat less than trusting, thinking that someone is trying to invade their turf. I've seen such manifestations even in what seemed like loving relationships. People, in the end, are individuals. Once they're born, they're on their own."

"All right then," Charlie had asked. "Tray gets into the picture. Now give me the bottom line. Will it be worth the candle?"

"Toss a coin." When no response came, Forte continued. "The good news is that I think the judge is so damned confused she had no other alternative than to call in the boy. The bad news is that the law is really on the side of your daughter-in-law and her husband. But you knew that from the beginning. She wants to satisfy her conscience, to make sure the kid is what they say he is. Happy. Adjusted. Actually, he's probably just that. But maybe he'll set something off in her. Who knows?"

"The law stinks," Charlie had said, before turning away and walking toward their car.

Sitting down again, Charlie felt in his robe for cigarettes.

"Damn," he said, when he found none.

"That's not good for you," Molly said gently.

"What is good for me?"

"I am, and I want you around for a while." Again, she embraced him. "I need you for my old age."

"Looks like that's all we're gonna have."

"Each other. Is that so bad?"

Thoughts of losing Molly always chilled his bones. That would end it all for him. He shivered, chasing the idea.

"You and me, babe."

"Everybody needs everybody." He sucked in a deep breath. "Why can't people just be nice? Why can't I just love my grandson?" He lifted a palm. "Our grandson." He felt as if something was thrashing around inside of him. "Loving is a two-way street.

No sense loving anything from long distance. Loving means being together. Doesn't it?"

"I never found it good from far away," Molly said, cuddling closer, warming him. Outside, in the distance above the trees, he saw the first pink edges of dawn. The inkiness was disappearing. It reminded him more of twilight than of dawn. Everything nowadays reminded him of twilight. He knew what that meant.

"A man's time sure runs out quickly," he said.

"Men again."

"People. I meant people."

"I know what you meant, Charlie," Molly said, reaching out to touch his arm. But before they went up to bed, he picked up the crumpled cigarette wrapper that he had earlier thrown on the floor and again tossed it toward the trash can. This time, he didn't miss.

It was too bright a day for heavy hearts, he told himself, remembering the other bright days long ago that ended in riven flesh and rivers of blood.

"Good day for the nursery," he said to Molly, mostly to chase the morbid thought. Above all, he warned himself, he must be alert to fend off these depressing images of doom. "I told them I had private business for a couple of days. They were really damned nice about it. Said they liked a man who had a feel for growing things. Funny, I never thought I did."

"Shows how much you know."

"Live and learn."

"We're doing that, all right."

Without having to say it last night, they both knew that if Tray was denied them, they could not stay in Dundalk and would have to move on to somewhere else. Anywhere. New places meant new beginnings. Somehow they would have to learn how to excise the ghosts of the past.

They crossed the long, curving Francis Scott Key bridge. Over the railing, Charlie could see the great port, merchant ships at anchor, shooting water plumes from their bulkheads. At the south end of the harbor was Sparrows Point, the giant Bethlehem works, where he had spent the better part of a lifetime. The plant was quiet now, mortally wounded by time, obsolescence, and the old Japanese enemy.

"Won't say I'm not scared," he confessed grudgingly.

"No, don't say that. Actually I'm petrified. Do you think he'll know me?" Molly had primped and patted and pulled herself together with more care than she had taken in years.

"You're his Gramma. Nobody forgets his Gramma."

He hadn't told her that of all the horrors of that day at the school, the worst was the vague light of recognition in the boy's eyes. Time had eroded his memory. Not completely, of course. But they were there: the first unmistakable signs of obliteration. No point in telling Molly about it now, he thought. If, by some miracle, they did win the right to see him, it would be a long, hard road back to the easy joy they had taken in each other's company. Maybe they could never get back to that point.

They parked the car in the lot across from the courthouse, and he looked at his watch. It was ten minutes to ten. Yet neither of them made a move to get out of the car.

"What's wrong?" Molly asked.

"Will they let him say hello?"

"I hope so." She leaned over and kissed his cheek. "Do I look okay?" she asked.

"Not like a Gramma. I tell you true."

They got out of the car and moved slowly toward the courthouse. It surprised them to see the courtroom nearly empty, except for the clerk and the stenographer. The courtroom had a musty smell. They took their seats. Soon Forte arrived with Peck. Probably had breakfast together, Charlie thought with disgust. Conspiring to manipulate their lives. What did it matter to them?

"Are both of you all right?" Forte asked. Groomed to perfection, he offered a mouthful of white teeth in a shy conciliatory grin.

"Will she make her decision today?" Molly asked.

"Probably," Forte said, taking out his yellow pad. "After the boy—"

"I want your promise," Charlie said suddenly. He sensed Molly watching him with questioning eyes. "If it becomes too much . . ." He looked toward Molly and swallowed. "I mean if it gets hard on Tray. We call it off." Molly smiled thinly and nodded in agreement.

"I'll do the best I can."

"Nothing hurts my grandson. Understand?"

"Don't worry."

"I want a promise."

"You're the client."

"I know that, and this thing is out of control."

"I'll try—"

"A promise."

"A promise it is."

Molly gripped his hand. They heard movement behind them and turned. Tray came in looking like a man in miniature, the image of Chuck. Charlie felt his heart leap to his throat. The boy walked between Peter and Frances, holding their hands. They moved to their places quickly; the boy sat between them. He was so busy examining the high ceiling that he didn't notice them.

"He didn't see us," Molly whispered.

"He will," Charlie said with some trepidation.

The big courtroom clock read fifteen minutes after ten. Still there was no sign of the judge. No one said a word. They waited. Then Forte cleared his throat, and the boy looked toward where they were sitting.

"That's Grampa," he cried with excitement. Charlie lifted his hand and waved. Tray waved back and smiled, and Charlie pointed to Molly.

"And Gramma," the boy said.

"Hi, darling," Molly said, her eyes quickly filling with tears.

"See? He recognized you. There's nothing to cry about." He had all he could do to blink away his own tears.

At that moment, the door leading from the judge's chambers opened. "All rise," the clerk said, and they stood up. Judge Stokes breezed through the door, lips pursed, unsmiling, tight-faced. She had no visible soft edges, Charlie observed, looking for signs of compassion. There was a severity about her that he had not seen yesterday, and suddenly he was frightened for Tray. He turned quickly to look at the boy, but Tray was busily absorbed in assessing this phenomenon of a mysterious black-robed woman who sat high above them. To his eyes, Charlie thought, she must, indeed, seem awesome.

"Will counsel for the parties approach the bench?" the judge said after the ritual of her entrance. Both men rose and walked to the bench. Charlie strained to hear what they were saying in fervent whispers. Occasionally, one of the men would shake his head. Then the other would nod, and the scene would be repeated.

"What's going on?" Molly asked.

Charlie shrugged. Again, he felt overwhelmed by an acute sense of powerlessness. Other people seemed always to be deciding his fate. He looked toward Tray. Apparently, he had lost interest in the conference at the bench and was scribbling on a pad. Frances turned at precisely the same moment, and Charlie's gaze locked onto hers. He wasn't sure what he saw in her eyes. Confusion? Animosity? Concern? That was in his own heart. He couldn't tell what was in hers. I never knew you, he thought with regret.

Finally, the two lawyers returned to their seats.

"It's the best deal we could work out," Forte said.

"What is?"

"She'll take the boy alone in chambers," Forte said.

What did that mean? Charlie wondered.

Judge Stokes looked up from her desk and nodded, then coughed into her fist.

"Counsel has waived the right to be present when I interview the boy in my chambers," she began. She scrutinized the faces ranged in front of her. She stopped and looked directly at Frances. "There will be no court reporter present and no lawyers. Just the boy and myself." She paused and looked at the boy. "Charles Everett Waters the third," the judge said gently.

The boy, surprised to hear his name, leaned toward his mother.

"Would you bring the boy up here?" she asked Peter, who stood up. Taking Tray's hand, he brought him to the bench.

"Up here," the judge said. Peter brought him up to where the judge sat. From that height, the boy looked down at his mother. He was obviously confused, and Charlie thought he might be on the verge of crying. They watched intently as the judge talked to the boy in low tones, then made a gesture for Peter to leave. White-faced and tense, he came down from the bench and walked, stiff-legged, back to his seat.

Up there, Charlie thought, Tray looked tiny, alone, reminding him of a tiny piece of flotsam bobbing on a muddy puddle—powerless. Like him. A victim. Stop, Charlie protested in his heart. After a few moments of earnest conversation with Tray, the judge turned to the adults in the courtroom.

"Court is adjourned for an hour," she said, standing up. She took the boy by the hand and started to move toward the door of her chambers.

"No," Frances cried.

Startled, the judge turned. Frances had stood up. She leaned slightly over the table, balancing herself with her knuckles. So she, too, felt helpless, he thought. But it gave him scant comfort. Peter stood up beside her, kissed her cheek, whispered something in her ear, and eased her back into her seat.

Charlie felt something give way inside of him. The black-robed judge, boy in hand, turned and walked toward the door. He saw the scene in slow motion. An image, like a developing Polaroid picture, began to appear in his mind. The judge, the boy, moving inexorably away from him, levitating, space as well as time disintegrating. The pores of his body opened. He felt the sensation of melting. In the image he could see his own trembling hands, pleading more than reaching, trying to stop the movement of the judge and the boy. Then they disappeared and he heard the sound of the door closing, and the Polaroid image dissolved instantly.

"What is it, Charlie?" Molly asked. There was no hiding things from her, and she sensed what was going on in his heart.

"It's no good," he said. "Either way."

She nodded. He saw her lashes brush her cheeks and he knew what he must do.

Chapter 16

FOREWARNED was not forearmed. Now Annie knew what Sam Compton meant when he said everybody is innocent, everybody is guilty. Including herself. Too bad life didn't come with an instruction book at birth. The worst of it was that everybody was not only both innocent and guilty but right and wrong. Anguish had seemed to fill the courtroom, the way she imagined mustard gas must do, clinging to everyone. Burning everyone.

Back in her chambers after the first day of the hearing, she had fallen into her chair exhausted, slipped a rarely used pint bottle of scotch from her lower drawer, and poured herself a stiff shot in a paper cup. Tossing her head to help it down, she felt it burn as it plummeted. The muscles in her neck contracted and her face flushed. Carter came in just in time to see the effect.

"It looks easy on paper," she said, when her breath came easier.

"The written words, unfortunately, don't come with stage directions."

"Believe me, I have a working understanding of dispensing justice. I can understand insurance scams, robbery, confidence games, fraud, embezzlement, even murder. Nice and clean. Greed and violence. But this—this is an enigma."

"Nevertheless, the law is clear."

"That's easy for you to say. I was there."

"The law is the law."

"Now I know what the beadle really meant in *Oliver Twist* when he said that the law is 'a ass.' Remember?"

"Ass or lady, Justice still wears the blindfold."

"That doesn't stop her from hearing." She was about to say "feeling" as well, but she held her tongue. He'd see it as a female reflex, and even though she was his superior, it would, she suspected, somehow diminish her in his eyes. The conclusion made her testy.

"Will you need more case law and citations?" he asked.

"As much as I can get."

"I've got more. The key issue in all of them is—"

"I know." She waved her arm. "Best interests of the child."

"Mommy and daddy know best."

"That, too."

"You might want to read them tonight. I've stuffed them into your briefcase. I assume you'll want to rule tomorrow."

"After I talk to the child," she said, leaning over to put the bottle back in the bottom drawer. She could still taste the sour aftertaste.

"That difficult?"

"Very." She did not tell him that the young lawyer had hit a chord inside her. Despite all her own warnings, she had remembered Peggy's words that morning. "Why don't you ever do what I want to do?"

"Well, it is within the purview of the Maryland law . . . so long as both lawyers and a court stenographer are present," Carter said, a trifle arrogantly, she observed.

"I'm fully aware of that; also of the unwritten law around here that a judge, if he or she promises accurate reportage of the interview, may waive that rule and interview the minor child alone."

"It could be dangerous on appeal. A technical violation."

"I don't think I'll get any objections on that score. Both lawyers are worse than barracudas. They'll tear the child apart if they get at him. I just want to see what kind of a kid this is and if he's really as happy as they all make him out to be."

Besides, it was all she could think of. For some reason she felt that Carter had better be given a logical explanation. "Maybe we ignore too much what kids think in these matters. Maybe this business of mama knowing best is a myth." Take me, for example, she thought. Suddenly she found herself cataloguing her own relationships. With her own parents. They had been undemonstrative. No one had ever said how much they loved each other. And with her grandparents. On her mother's side they were the same stuff, scattering wisdom, advice, and aphorisms like rice at a wedding. The traditional view prevailed. Family was family, and family obligations were rigidly enforced by guilt and custom. On her father's side, they were all doctors like him, busy and self-absorbed, but the same conditions prevailed. Did they matter? Did they really matter?

Harold's parents, on the other hand, were on a totally different wavelength. They had been affectionate and demonstrative. Harold had been their pride and joy, and his death had been an unconsolable blow. And although she understood this, she could never shake the idea that, in their hearts, they somehow blamed her for his death. It made her uncomfortable to be around them, and consequently, she saw very little of them in recent years. Suddenly she caught herself up short. That was one more thing they hadn't warned her about in domestic law. It forced you to look inside yourself.

"If you'd like, I could give you a draft opinion."

"On which side?"

"Both if necessary. Pick one."

"Just like that?"

"You're the judge."

"I'm glad you remembered."

Peggy wasn't home when she arrived, which, while not ominous, was certainly questionable. Annie tried to make it a point to be home for dinner, if only to show her presence and mothering authority and illustrate the necessity of "quality time" shared between herself and her daughter. Lately, it had been an illusion. Dinner had been as trying as breakfast. At night, Peggy was only slightly less surly. Nevertheless, she had tried to linger over the table, forcing Peggy into conversation. Most times it was a monologue with Annie trying to engage her daughter's interest in the events of her day. Peggy, on the other hand, revealed little. For a time, she had volunteered to help her with homework, but that, too, had been rejected.

She had defrosted chicken breasts, but decided at the last moment on steaks instead. Steaks were Peggy's favorite, although when Peggy asked for them, Annie ordinarily complained that they were too expensive. She took out a carton of frozen asparagus, also a favorite of her daughter's. Hesitating, she reached for the frozen french fries, weighing the psychological implications. Something fattening might clear the air between them, she thought, act as a kind of peace offering. Her day's ordeal in the courtroom had, without her noticing, triggered a compelling reason to find the key to end her own domestic problems. The Grahams and the Waterses were tearing each other apart, and it frightened her to think of what venom could be stirred up in domestic relationships.

While she sliced fruits for dessert, she listened to old Beatles tunes on the radio. The station was having a retrospective, and it was shocking to realize how much time had passed since they had provided the background music to her life. Harold had loved the Beatles. Memories of her early life flooded into her mind. Her life was divided into two parts, pre-Harold and post-Harold. The first part was defined by Harold's struggle to succeed in what for him had become a hostile and alien world. The pain of it assaulted her. Everything he tried came to nothing, and this failure had taught her that the enemy of success was the inability to deal with initial rejection. Harold could never handle that. Rejection could be corrosive, debilitating, and, in Harold's case, an instrument of death. She had learned that lesson well, along with ways to cope with it, overcome it, defeat it.

From his early demise, she had also learned the precious value of time. She became compulsive about filling every moment with a useful, productive pursuit. Life, in the final analysis, was time. Living was the efficient use of that time. And achievement was based on high-quality use of that time. It was a philosophy that worked well for Annie, and somehow she had managed to pass it along to Laura. Yes, she had sacrificed for it, made compromises. Why couldn't Peggy understand? Why did they have such a clash of perceptions?

"You want to be a judge just so you can be boss, have other people under your thumb," Peggy had once told her during an argument. It was an observation that she had seriously considered.

"I want to be a judge so that I can help other people," she had countered.

"Help? A judge sends people to jail. A judge hurts people."

"That's not true. A judge is a kind of referee for civilized society. Someone has to be sure the rules are obeyed and punish those who break the rules."

"Punish. You're good at that."

"Not only punish, decide what's the best course of action for people."

"How can you decide when you don't know what's best for your own daughter?"

"Because with my own daughter I'm too emotionally involved. I can't see the forest for the trees."

"That's because you don't look."

These arguments always devolved into recriminations and, for her, guilt. Sometimes, when the guilt became too pervasive, she blamed Harold for leaving her alone, for killing himself, for saddling her with this burden.

"Why can't you understand?" Ultimately, that was always Peggy's final refuge. "Why can't you?"

Always the unanswered question, she sighed, which brought her thoughts back to the case at hand.

That morning she had been dead certain that, careerwise, she wanted nothing more in the world than this profession. It had nobility of purpose, called forth all her resources, presented exciting daily challenges. What she was doing truly mattered, changed lives. Now her resolve had been considerably reduced. It was not easy playing God.

Play it safe, she warned herself, another echo of old Sam's advice, further buttressed by Carter's comments that morning. "Don't take chances on getting these decisions rolled back at you on appeal," Judge Compton had cautioned. "It could hurt your chances in the election if someone got it into his mind to criticize your bench marks." She remembered that she had snickered at the pun. But she wasn't snickering now. She had already made a fatal error—she had become emotionally involved. Worse, she was coming up on both sides of the issue. Hadn't Carter offered to write an opinion for each?

Complicating the decision-making process was the element of politics so subtly injected by her young clerk. He was, she realized, only being a realist. He'd go far, that boy. A decision on the side of the grandparents might win her lots of support from older voters. In an aging population, that was no small consideration. Some might say she was pandering to a certain constituency, a disgusting thought that she instantly rejected. On the other hand, it had a practical ring to it. Unethical as well. What had he called it—grey power? Well, if they had the clout to get a grandparents' petition statute passed in forty-nine states, one had to sit up and take notice. Now she was sorry it had even entered her mind. She would have to bend over backward in her decision.

Peggy's absence was beginning to nag at her now. She set the table, placed the steaks and french fries in the broiler, began to heat the water for the asparagus, and laid out the fruit salad. She looked at her watch, checked it against the kitchen clock. It was after seven. Her vague panic was becoming more defined.

She went into Peggy's room. As always, it was sloppy, clothes were strewn around, candy wrappers were everywhere but in her wastebasket, records helter-skelter. It seemed to her more like the lair of some frightened and unhappy animal. Inspecting it now, under the pressure of anxiety, she absorbed the atmosphere of lonely desperation and abject fear.

"Peggy," she whispered into the anguished air, assaulted now by overpowering guilt. "Have I done this?" But what had she done? Had she set unattainable standards? Unrealistic goals? Made unreasonable assumptions?

But when she left the room, she began to think that perhaps Peggy was being deliberately spiteful, making her squirm for all the imagined injustices she had allegedly perpetrated. It made her angry, but could not dissipate her anxiety. Despite all the psychological posturing, Peggy was her child, her blood and tissue, her creation, and, therefore, her responsibility. Soon, she was searching among Peggy's things for notes, telephone numbers, clues. She found nothing. She toyed with the idea of calling the police. But she knew too much about police procedures and the negative value of publicity for someone in her profession.

Since she could barely remember the names of Peggy's friends, there was no one to call. In fact, she couldn't think of a single person to call except Laura. She dialed her number in Cambridge. A roommate answered.

"Sorry, Mrs. Stokes. Laura's gone to a concert."

"It's nothing important, Sue," she said quickly.

"I'll tell her you called."

By nine-thirty, she was frantic with worry, genuinely panicked. She called her parents in Washington.

"Did Peggy call?" she asked her mother. Background noises indicated that her mother was having one of her regular bridge evenings.

"Not here, dear." There was a brief pause. "Is everything all right?"

Despite her mother's lack of sentimentality, she was quick to pick up signals of anxiety. Mothers know their daughters. She had told Annie that often enough. Did they really? Not if Peggy was an example.

"She's not home."

"Maybe she's out with friends."

"Could be."

"Teenage girls are a problem these days," her mother said with dubious authority. "I'm sure it's nothing." In her mother's mind, only death and disease were "somethings." Everything else was solvable. On the surface, she was often right. No, she decided, Peggy would never have contacted them. She had had more than enough advice dispensed to her to seek out this grandmother's platitudes.

"You're right, mother. Probably nothing."

"I'm sure of it."

She hung up, wondering if the idea of her panic would linger in her mother's mind during the bridge game. She doubted it. Nevertheless, the call to her mother had helped take the edge off her worry. Now she had only anger to contend with.

In protest, she took Peggy's steak out of the broiler. The best way to handle this kind of teenage protest, she assured herself, was to ignore it. She went to her desk, opened her briefcase, and tried to concentrate on her papers. The words swam in front of her, incomprehensible. Yet she remained dogged and determined, forcing herself to try to comprehend, but without any good results. Indeed, the case had begun to take on an air of fantasy. Like a soap opera. Who needs this, she told herself? I've got my own troubles.

Too late, she discovered that the steak and french fries were burning. Smoke filled the apartment, and she had to open the windows to get it out. By then, anger had turned to fury, and she decided that, as far as Peggy was concerned, she had done her best. She was blameless, she assured herself. People were, in the end, responsible for themselves. Weren't they?

The telephone's ring stabbed into her agitated thoughts. She rushed to pick it up. The voice was vaguely familiar. It was Harold's mother.

"That you, Annie?" Mrs. Stokes asked.

"Yes."

It had been a long time since Annie had called the woman "Mother." Her voice was high-pitched, as if it were still distrustful of long distance.

"Peggy's here."

"In Philadelphia?"

"Would you like to speak to her?"

"Of course."

She would decipher her reactions later, she decided. The relief, unfortunately, had not quite dispelled her anger.

"Mommy?" The reversion startled her.

"I was worried."

"I'm sorry. But"— her voice dropped octaves lower —"it was Daddy's birthday and all."

Harold's birthday? She recalled the date. Yes, she had forgotten. But it hadn't been relevant for years. Not for years. And Peggy had been barely a month old when he had died.

"Are you all right? That's what counts."

"Yes, I am. I took the train." A sob bubbled in her throat. "Do you forgive me?"

"It's never a question of that between us, baby. Of course I forgive you. I love you. I can't stand to see you unhappy."

"I was just thinking of Daddy. And, even though I can't even remember what he looked like, I missed him. I just missed him. Can you understand that?"

"Of course I do." She wasn't sure. The human heart's a puzzle, she thought.

"I'll be home tomorrow."

"You can stay with Grandma and Grandpa Stokes if you want, Peggy."

"No. I'll be home."

"Is everything okay with them?"

"Fine. I bought a birthday cake."

"You did? I'll bet everybody had a good cry."

"It was nice."

"I'm sorry I forgot."

"I just needed to think about him today, Mommy."

"I understand."

"So I'll be home tomorrow. I'll go straight to school. I promise."

"Have you enough for the fare?"

"I'm sure Grandma will lend it to me."

"Well, most of all, I'm glad you're safe."

"And you forgive me?"

"Of course I do."

"And Mommy . . . I do miss you. And I'll try much harder—"

"And I'll try, too."

"Would you like to speak to Grandma?"

"Yes."

Mrs. Stokes came on again.

"She's fine, Annie."

"I really appreciate this—Mother." She grew suddenly hoarse and cleared her throat. "I'll send you a check for anything you've laid out." It seemed hard-edged, and she regretted it.

"No, please. We're happy to have her. At least she remembered." Annie heard the sigh of despair.

"Is she really all right?" Annie asked.

"She's fine."

"At least she had someone to come to . . ." Annie began, but she could not continue.

"Anyway, she'll be home tomorrow. I just thought you'd be worried." She was about to say good-bye, but she apparently interrupted herself. "And Annie—"

"Yes?"

The woman's hesitation was tangible.

"Some people aren't as strong as others—some need a little more loving care." She seemed to want to say more but didn't and hung up with a polite good-bye.

After she hung up, Annie felt relieved but somehow more troubled than ever. Her stomach churned, and she lost her appetite. Besides, she resented the implied lecture on loving care. Hadn't she lavished loving care on Harold? On Peggy? If you weren't judgmental, all human relationships were easy. Mindless, but easy.

She took a hot bath, and it calmed her somewhat, but by the time she slipped into bed, taking her papers with her, she found herself dealing with a new kind of resentment. Why had Peggy gone to them? What did they have that she could not provide? She could not concentrate on the case materials. Finally, she tossed the papers on the floor and shut off the light. Curling under the sheets, she began to thrash around restlessly. Her feet were icy.

She must have dozed. She wasn't sure. The sheets were twisted and, in places, moist from her perspiration. If she had dreamed, her dreams were too terrible to remember. Sitting up, she saw the papers on the floor, leaned over, picked them up, and tried reading. After a few minutes of incomprehension, she closed the file. Everybody is guilty. Everybody is innocent.

Knowing that only increased the agony of her indecision.

Before she left the apartment, she wrote a note to Peggy.

"I do understand," she began, wondering if it was the truth. "Let's make today a birthday celebration for us—Daddy, too. We'll look at each other with new eyes. Maybe we need to find our way back to each other. This I do know—when you hurt, I hurt. I love you. Mommy."

She tried not to think of the case again until she entered her chambers and saw the smug and knowing face of her law clerk. Muttering a greeting, she put on her robe and patched up her puffy face.

"I wrote down some suggestions on what to ask the boy," he said, handing her yet another file. She took the file, turned and looked at him, so cocksure and knowing, bloated with the arrogance of youth.

"Have you ever had a child?" she asked.

"Me?" He looked at her, squinting, as if he was trying to focus on her motive for saying this. Without giving him time to respond, she flung the file in her wastebasket and strode through the door of the courtroom.

In her chambers, she asked the boy to sit down on the leather couch, patting the space beside her. Moving over, he put his hands on his knees and looked around the office. Light from the large windows deepened the cobalt blue of his eyes. He was a beautiful child.

"I'm just as nervous as you are, Tray," she said, offering a tight smile. He looked at her with some confusion. "Do you know why you're here?" she asked gently.

"No."

"I thought not." Annie shrugged. "That makes two of us."

"What do judges do?" Tray asked. She put her arm around him.

"They judge," she said, her smile broadening. She berated herself for giving him such an inadequate answer. "They help people make decisions that are sometimes too hard for them to make themselves." He seemed to think about that for a long time, then nodded his understanding.

"Am I going away somewhere?"

"Now, whatever gave you that idea?" She shook her head. "Of course not."

They sense more than we think, she told herself.

"Do you know why your last name is Waters?" she asked.

"It's my other daddy's name."

"Your other daddy?"

"My dead daddy."

"Do you remember him?"

"A little bit."

"Did you love your other daddy?"

"Yes." He seemed tentative.

"And this daddy? The one with your mommy now."

"I love him, too."

"And your mommy?"

"Yes."

"And your gramma and grampa?"

"Which ones? Grampa and Gramma Graham or Grampa and Gramma Waters?"

"Both," she said cautiously.

He grew thoughtful and looked around the room, then shrugged his little shoulders.

"Yes."

"Have you seen much of Grampa and Gramma Waters lately?"

"No." He started to say something.

"Yes?" she prompted.

"Grampa Waters came to school and gave me my old wagon."

"He did?"

"He shouldn't have done that because it was in the middle of class, and I think the teachers were angry."

"Were you angry?"

"No. I was scared. I didn't want Grampa to get in any trouble."

"Were you happy to see him?"

Tray looked at her, puzzled.

"He's my grampa," he said, as if her question was ridiculous. He shook his head and looked at her in a childlike, reproachful way. She decided to change the subject.

"Do you get good marks in school?"

"I get very good marks. My daddy helps me." He giggled.

"And mommy?"

"She's busy with Baby Mark and soon Snowflake will be here."

"Who's Snowflake?"

"My baby sister," he said with a touch of petulance, as if Annie should have known.

"Do you like the idea of a baby sister?"

"A sister would be okay if she didn't act like a girl." He looked up at her. "Girls are dumb."

Annie laughed. "Why do you say that?"

"They tell secrets, and they always tease. And they think they know everything."

"I'm a girl," Annie said.

"You're a lady, not a girl. Like Mommy."

She looked at the boy and pressed him close to her. Adults, including herself, had intruded on his pristine world, had brought their conflicts and frustrations into his life.

"Are you happy, Tray?" she asked. It seemed like the inevitable, quintessential question, and yet she felt both foolish and humble asking it. He chuckled and looked at her as if she were crazy. It was as good as an answer. "Well adjusted?"

"What's 'justed?"

"It means—well—content."

"Not me," he said, obviously confused. What seven-year-old wouldn't be? she thought.

"Are there any people that you really miss?"

The boy thought for a minute.

"Like who?"

"Your other daddy."

"I told you. My other daddy is dead. That means that he went away and is never coming back. When I die, I'll see him again."

"Do you miss Gramma and Grampa Waters?"

"I just saw them outside."

"I mean miss seeing them, miss going to their house to play, miss having them take you out?"

"I see Gramma and Grampa Graham."

"But do you need—would you like to see more of Gramma and Grampa Waters?"

How was the child to answer? she wondered. She felt suddenly inadequate to the interrogation.

"When I grow up, Grampa Waters will take me hunting and we'll try to get Nasty Jake."

"Nasty Jake?"

"He's the baddest buck in the whole world."

"Is he?"

"He's going to get me a sailboat, too."

"And Gramma Waters?"

"She's a teacher."

Was there a want, a need, a regret? What more could she ask?

She thought of Mr. and Mrs. Waters, to whom this boy was apparently the only living, tangible symbol of the life they had lived. Was he aware of their anguish? Did it matter to him?

"Does your mommy or daddy ever talk about Gramma and Grampa Waters?"

The boy became thoughtful again. He frowned and seemed to be struggling with a response. Apparently he was having difficulty finding the words.

"It's all right," she said gently.

All this trial and angst on the part of the adults around him seemed extraneous to his life. She did want to probe further, but it didn't seem right somehow, a violation of this child's peace of mind. In the boy, she could see no hate or animosity, only the faint and ominous signs of needless confusion. All she could see now was a little boy, a piece of human clay. Then she thought of what Peggy had said, surprised at how it had stuck in her mind. "What about what I want?" What, really, in his heart and soul, did this little boy want?

The answer came to her, not as a cliché, not as an empty promise, not merely a word. To love. To be loved. Her eyes misted.

"Are you sad?" Tray asked.

"Oh no," she said quickly.

"Something hurt?"

"Just a little twinge."

She managed a smile and blinked away a tear.

"There. That's better now."

She sat for a while longer, not knowing what more to ask. She thought of her troubled daughter. Had she missed something? Then she looked at her watch. It was nearly time.

"You be a good boy," she said, offering him her cheek. He planted a noisy kiss on it. Soon he would consider such things unmanly. Most of all, their conversation had taught her what it meant to be a child again.

Standing up abruptly, she looked in the mirror, fixed her make-up, and patted her hair.

"Why do you wear a black robe?"

"To hide my feelings," she said, smiling, proud of her answer. "Only it doesn't always work."

The boy nodded as if he understood.

"We have to get back to the courtroom now, Tray."

He got up from the couch.

"Then what happens?" he asked.

"I think I know now."

She felt finally that her mind had cleared. In the end all the historical legal research, all the citations, all the printed words meant less than she had realized. In domestic matters, the answers could be found only in that most vulnerable place of all, the human heart.

Chapter 17

ARE YOU all right?" Peter asked.
"How can I be all right?" Frances asked. "With my child in there. He's scared to death."

"I don't like it either."

"We're so helpless. It's all out of control."

"I'm sure he'll be fine," Peter said reassuringly.

"How can you know?"

She wasn't reassured. She leaned against a marble pillar of the ornate lobby of the courthouse and nervously watched the clock. The minute hand moved with excruciating slowness.

"You should be thankful," Peck told her. "She's taking him in chambers alone."

"He has no business being there in the first place."

She was tired of Peck's pompous surety, disgusted by the entire process of law that had invaded her life.

Imagining Tray's discomfort, her own anger smoldered. The baby kicked, and she touched her belly. Don't be in such a rush to get here, she told the baby silently. She could see Molly and Charlie across the lobby, talking in hushed tones with their lawyer. Occasionally Charlie would glance her way. What was he thinking? she wondered. Was there any remorse on his part for starting this chain reaction of unhappiness? Or was it her fault? She looked at Peter, studied him carefully. Had she resisted because of Tray? For Peter's sake? Or because of some deep resentment of her own? It had become jumbled in her mind.

"I never thought—" Peter began.

"None of us did, I'm afraid."

Again her eyes jumped to the clock, and she pictured her little boy, her sweet, lovely Tray, and that severe, black-robed woman locked together in her chambers. She shivered. The very word "chambers" had ugly connotations. As in torture chambers.

In the past two years she had deliberately refrained from any references to Tray's former life, except when his curiosity demanded answers. Hadn't she always been forthright in telling him the truth? Now all her careful nurturing was being undone.

"We should have moved away to another state. At least we would have been out of the clutches of the law."

"But we were told the law was on our side."

"Tell that to my son in there."

"Our son, Frances. And our decision was a joint one, remember?"

"Was it?"

They were silent for a long time. But with each glance at the clock her agitation rose.

"I would have done anything to spare you this," Peter said. They had been together long enough to sense each other's inner tension.

"Only me?"

"Tray, too." He paused, averting his eyes. "I'm not having such a good time of it either. I can't believe it's gone this far."

"Believe it." Her tone seemed overly snappish, and she put out her hand and touched his arm. "It all looked so simple when we got married, but when you take on a woman with another man's child, you take on problems not of your making."

"Take on?" He seemed hurt. "If you love someone, you buy the whole package."

"Buy?" Like molten lava, resentment rolled over her. She felt suddenly alone, thrown back to her earlier life. Abandoned. Taking crumbs from Uncle Walter's table. Her nostrils twitched with the remembered smell of sugary cakes. A wave of nausea broke inside of her, and she clutched the marble pillar.

"Are you okay?"

"A little nauseous."

He frowned, and she saw his anxiety as he inspected her. Odd, she wondered, how she had gone from one extreme to the other, from being barely noticed to being microscopically observed. Better the latter than the former, she decided. Didn't loving mean protection? And possession? It was so simple to pass over boundaries, to move into dark areas, to be either too selfish or to lose one's sense of self.

"Maybe they have a point. Maybe I am to blame? Perhaps I did overreact to the trauma of my first marriage. But, you see, I was so afraid."

"So was I."

"I wasn't looking far enough ahead."

She wasn't sure what he meant. His quick glance seemed to take in her puzzled look. Watching his expression was like observing gears trying to mesh.

"What I mean is—" he stammered. It wasn't like him to grope for ways to express himself. "I wasn't able to see things from their point of view. To be a grandparent . . ."

She continued to watch him, pondering his meaning.

"There could be ties there so deep we just don't understand them."

"Then you think we overreacted?"

"I'm not sure." He seemed awkward and uncomfortable, deliberately evasive. She was beginning to understand.

"Is it about Tray? Or Mark?" She patted her belly. "Or Snowflake?"

"I told you, I'm not really sure."

"If it were Mark, or the new baby—ours—and you were the grandfather of their children." She hesitated, carefully weighing the words she would use. These, after all, were his natural children. "Would you be less confused?"

"Yes. I think I would," he said after a pause, wishing, as always, to be scrupulously honest with her. He lifted his eyes to meet her gaze.

She nodded, but she did not in any way feel challenged or upset.

"It doesn't mean that I love Tray any less," he said.

"I know that, Peter."

"It's just that, well, life isn't quite like a computer. There are different shadings—"

"I'm beginning to see that as well, Peter."

"Above all, we can't let any of this come between us," Peter said. "It musn't hurt what we have."

"It won't. I just don't want it to hurt Tray."

"Neither do I." He looked anxiously at the clock.

"But if it does hurt Tray, it will hurt us." She felt the raw edges of anger.

"Peck said she would be gentle," Peter said.

"Peck again."

"Judge Stokes is a mother."

"But not of my child."

She felt her anger continue to rise. My child is in there and I'm out here, she shouted within herself. She imagined herself standing outside of an operating room, waiting, her son's life in the balance. It wasn't fair. It was wrong to put him through this.

She wanted to scream out her protest. It is my life. My child. Suddenly her attention was drawn across the marble lobby. Charlie was watching her, standing beside Molly, hesitant and forlorn. Had she tormented him with her thirst for vengeance? Or was it Peter who had provoked him? What had all this to do with Tray? Watching Charlie, he seemed a tiny figure in the baroque vastness, not the formidable figure of the early days of her marriage.

She saw him move, start toward her. Peter, too, must have seen his movement.

"If he starts any trouble, he'll have me to contend with physically," Peter said with uncommon bravado.

Charlie strode toward them purposefully. Frances pressed herself against the pillar.

But as Charlie drew closer, his features seemed to reflect a benign calm. The pinched lines of anger that she had seen when he was on the stand had flattened. Through a quirk of memory and illusion, she saw Chuck moving toward her as well. In tandem. A forgiving Chuck. Not the enemy now. Had she heard his voice? He's my son, too. Goosebumps came up on her arms. Again the baby kicked.

"I'll get rid of him," Peter said, starting to move forward. She put her arm out to stop him.

"It's all right. Just stand by me, Peter," she said.

"Could you ever doubt that?"

"Never."

She was surprised how gray Charlie looked up close. A nerve palpitated in his jaw, and she could see he was struggling to smile. Once he had seemed so formidable. Dad! She heard the hollow echo of Chuck's voice and tried to see him through her dead husband's eyes. Caught in the web of memory, she struggled to untangle herself. He's my son, too, Chuck's voice said.

"I'll only be a minute, Frances," Charlie said facing her.

"Are you sure this is wise, Waters?" Peter asked.

"I don't know what's wise anymore."

"I don't either," Frances said. She inspected him, noting the leathery quality of his skin, weathered and blotched by the elements. Even in here, she could detect the smell of the outdoors. Just like Chuck.

In a long moment of helplessness, Frances felt herself floating in a vacuum, weightless, free from gravity and control.

"I don't like this business of Tray being in this," Charlie said with a vague nod of his head. "In there with her." He looked down at his hands. "It wasn't my idea."

"Nor your intention, Charlie," she said with surprising gentleness.

"I tell you, Frances, I never wanted this. I swear it." His Adam's apple shivered as it moved up and down the length of wattled skin. It struck her suddenly how much he had aged since the first time she had seen him.

"You could have avoided it all, Waters," Peter said.

"I know," Charlie replied, nodding. He looked down at his hands and shifted his weight from one foot to the other. "That's why I need to say what I have to." He paused. Frances watched him. *Was he in some way different than she had ever seen him?* Or was she really seeing him for the first time? Alone. Without Chuck.

"Just don't upset her," Peter warned.

"It's all right," Frances said, patting his arm. He would, she knew, slay any dragon that threatened her. But Charlie no longer frightened her. Not anymore.

Charlie shook his head.

"It was wrong," he said, his voice reduced to a whisper. Clearing his throat, he spoke again, finding more strength. "And I'm sorry."

"You're a little late, don't you think?" Peter said. His tone lacked the venom of his previous remarks.

"Please, Peter." She turned to her former father-in-law. "I'm listening, Charlie."

"You know that I wouldn't want anything to hurt that child. I or Molly. You know that."

She nodded. What was there to say?

"I don't feel good about any of this." He paused again. She sensed how difficult it was for him to find the right words. "What I'm saying is that I don't want any more of it. I know you're a good mother, Frances. And Peter here." He looked at Peter. "I know he'll treat the boy fine. Just like Tray was his." Again he paused and she could sense his determined effort to keep himself under control. "So I'm saying that it's your say all the way. We're the outsiders now, Molly and me. And if you don't want us around— it doesn't matter why—you've got that right, as far as we're concerned. I see that now. Only Tray counts here. And the law is right on target about that. So what I want to say, Frances—and Peter—Molly and me, we're not going to force ourselves on Tray. It's just no good any other way. No good at all."

"I don't know what to say," Peter said haltingly.

Frances was too stunned to respond.

"You don't have to say anything. We're just not going to interfere in your lives anymore. What we want"— he took in some deep breaths to clear his throat of emotion —"is not to give you or Tray, or any of your family, a minute's worth of pain. We've done enough of that."

She watched as he squared his shoulders, a portrait of a man relieved of a great burden. But he wasn't finished yet.

"I just hope that you'll find it in your heart to forgive us, Frances. I don't want this to sound like hearts and flowers. To put Tray through this was no good, and I hope when he grows up, he won't think too unkindly of us. He's too good a kid. Chuck would have been real proud of him. I'm sure of that. We did have some great times together, and I am going to miss him. What's it all about, anyway?" He stopped abruptly, as if he had suddenly determined that he had outstayed his welcome. "So we're going to ask our lawyer to withdraw our petition, to stop this whole rotten business."

For a moment it crossed her mind that this could be a ploy, a tactic to get her to soften her stand. Had she become that cynical? Quickly, she dismissed the thought.

"I appreciate that, Charlie. Don't think we both are oblivious to the pain of it for you and Molly." As she spoke, her knees began to tremble and the baby inside of her began to kick up a storm. But it reminded her that she had obligations and responsibilities that transcended this issue.

"So, that's it," Charlie said. She noted that he rubbed his right hand against his pants leg, a familiar gesture of his preparatory to a handshake. Only he did not follow through, stepping backward for a few steps, then turning and moving toward the other end of the lobby.

They watched him go. Molly waited for him at the other end of the hall and embraced him when he reached her.

"So it's over, then," Peter whispered.

"As you said, Peter, the ties are deeper than we understand."

"It took a lot of courage for him to do that."

"Not just courage, Peter."

"What then?"

"I think . . ." She paused. "It's a matter of honor."

"Honor?" He appeared puzzled. She let it go at that. There was too much to explain, too much to define about people in her past and the way they thought about life. She was in a different place now, but it didn't mean she could or would ever turn her back on the other. She glanced at the clock. The hour was nearly up. The baby kicked.

Chapter 18

THEY STOOD near a stairwell off the lobby. It was the only private place they could find. Molly, less for support than comfort, held on to the rail facing Charlie and Forte. People came and went, climbed the stairs, appearing oblivious to anything but their own thoughts. Occasionally, she heard laughter, which sounded incongruous and irrelevant. Mostly, her thoughts were on Charlie and what he had done. Although it hurt to think about it, she had agreed with Charlie. It was pointless to put Tray, Frances, and Peter through any more ordeals.

A court decree could not be the answer to this dilemma. You couldn't decree boundaries for human emotions.

"Yes, you do have the right to ask her to withdraw the petition," Forte said. He seemed annoyed and was quite obviously reluctant to do so. "Of course, she doesn't have to grant it."

"Why not?" Charlie asked.

Forte hesitated.

"It depends on how adamant Judge Stokes is on offering her ruling. She could be hung up on it."

"I don't care about that," Charlie said.

"It's over for us. Simply tell her it's over," Molly added.

Forte tapped his chin and inspected them both.

"I think you're being extremely foolish," he said tartly. "You've gone this far. You're yielding to the emotion of the moment. That's dangerous. My advice would be to hear it out."

"What for? Our minds are made up." Charlie looked at Molly, who nodded affirmation.

"That's just the point. You think your minds are made up. Then you'll walk out of here and the doubts will begin to set in. And the loneliness. You'll wake up in the middle of the night and wonder, did I do the right thing? Nothing is going to change. You were miserable being separated from your grandson before, and you'll still be miserable."

"Rather us than him," Charlie said. "We'll get through it somehow, won't we, babe?" He reached out and took her hand.

"Sure we will."

289

"What about all that stuff about it being unnatural?" Forte asked.

"It is," Charlie said without hesitation. "But the kid is happy. He's got a good life. A brother. Another one on the way. Why louse that up with tension he doesn't need? She's a good mother. I can't fault her there. And he's a good father."

"You realize that you're being a martyr. Both of you."

"Best interests of the kid. Isn't that what it's all about?"

"What about all the other grandparents faced with this problem? Maybe the issue might be clarified for them?"

"You guys," Charlie said, shaking his head. "Always looking for the glory of it. You're getting paid anyhow. If she rules in your favor, you'll be a hero. If not, you'll wait for another client to walk in the door just like us. We've done the right thing by Tray. That's all that matters for us. We're not guinea pigs, we're just plain people." He turned to Molly. "That's us, babe?"

"That's us."

"But you've gone this far—"

"Too far," Charlie muttered.

Observing him, she realized that although he was agitated, he was not faltering. She saw glimpses of the old Charlie, the good and strong and faithful, trusting man. My Charlie. Just you and me, babe, she told herself. Oh, she was sure there were dark moments ahead for both of them. You couldn't excise such deep emotions from the human psyche. But the old couldn't depend on the young for solace. Above all, they'd have to make it on their own. Her head spun with plans. They'd go away. She'd give up her teaching job. She was getting too old for those know-it-all young principals. Maybe Arizona. There was a lake there somewhere. . . .

Forte looked at the clock. It was getting late. Everyone would be seated now, waiting for them.

"I think we'd better go," Molly said. They started up the stairs. Before they entered the courtroom Forte paused.

"Remember this," he said. "If you change your minds, you'll have to start again from scratch. This way, you might have some insurance. If she rules against you, there's nothing lost. You've already decided that you won't press to visit the boy. But if she rules for you, then you've at least got an option. People change their minds all the time. We're all human."

"I've noticed that," Molly said. Hand in hand, Molly and Charlie proceeded into the courtroom.

The others were already seated, the judge in her place. Tray looked up and smiled from where he sat between his parents, who watched them move to their seats behind the table. Peck also observed them. He seemed disheveled, like an overgrown old bear without claws and teeth. No longer fearsome.

But when Peck turned away, Molly noted that Frances continued to look toward her. Her head nodded, and a smile formed on her lips. Molly nodded back. It's all right, she wanted to say. Can you forgive us? Their eyes locked, and she imagined that her look transmitted an affirmative answer.

"Court is now in session," the voice of the clerk boomed.

Judge Stokes raised her head and looked over her half-glasses. She had been making notes.

"I have reached my decision in this case," she said, clearing her throat, scanning the faces in the courtroom. Molly looked at Forte. He sat rigid, looking in front of him.

"As you are well aware—" the judge began.

"This is not what we discussed," Charlie said, turning to the lawyer. "You were to stop this—"

The young lawyer's expression did not change. The judge looked at them, frowning. Charlie turned toward Frances and Peter. "I asked him to withdraw this—"

Charlie stood up and turned to the judge. "You can't do this— I gave them my word."

The judge banged her gavel.

"Will you please be seated, Mr. Waters," she said.

"But he didn't do what he was asked to do."

A nerve began to palpitate in Forte's jaw. "Trust me," the lawyer said. "You have nothing to lose."

"You have no right to do this," Molly said.

"Will you please keep your clients under control, Mr. Forte," the judge said. "I have no wish to order contempt citations."

"It's all right. Just sit down," Forte said.

"No. I won't stand for it." Charlie looked helplessly toward Frances and Peter.

"You're trying my patience, Mr. Waters," the judge said.

"I want this case dropped," Charlie shouted.

Again, the judge banged the gavel.

"I want . . ." He looked around him, then at Molly.

"It won't matter, Charlie," Molly said, conscious of his embarrassment. She turned toward Frances, noting tears running down her cheeks. Tray looked troubled and confused. "Let it alone, Charlie."

He looked at Forte with contempt and slumped back into his seat. Molly leaned over and kissed his cheek. "It won't matter either way," she said.

"As you are all well aware," the judge began again, "the law in this state is not explicit on the point being argued in this courtroom. This is not a custody battle. Nor is there any decision required on a division of tangible assets. The issue here is and has always been the best interests of the child. This is the centuries-old common law.

"What *is* in the best interests of this child?" She paused and took off her glasses. "We had a nice little chat in my chambers. Now, it is difficult to assess the state of anyone's mind and spirit in the brief space of one hour. Certainly, it is doubly difficult in the case of a child." She looked toward Tray and flashed him a broad smile. "But since I am charged with such a judgment, I have concluded that this particular child is a well-adjusted, bright, cheerful, quite happy boy. This is a child who is obviously loved and cherished by his mother and his adoptive father."

"What's the point? It's only words," Charlie whispered. Molly put a finger on his lips and he quieted.

"The question then is, does this well-adjusted happy child need the visits of his natural paternal grandparents to enhance the quality of his life? Could those visits be disruptive, inimical to the child's welfare? Would they, in some way, debilitate the child's emotional state? Will they create problems that are disruptive to the Graham family unit and, by a kind of emotional fallout, have adverse consequences for the boy? I suppose that each of the opposing sides might have brought expert testimony by psychiatrists and social workers to this courtroom, each contradicting the other, which might have influenced my judgment." In a nervous gesture, she put her glasses on again, but they slipped to the tip of her nose, and she pulled them off. "The inclination of the case law is to leave well enough alone." She paused and seemed to be wavering. Molly wondered why it was taking her so long to get to the point. She looked at Tray, who had apparently gotten bored and was now busy drawing pictures on a yellow pad. Enough, she thought. She wanted to go home.

"What we are dealing with here is not a science." Again, the judge paused, her gaze wandering over the people in the court-room. "We are dealing here with the most volatile and unreliable of human characteristics—emotions. It seems to me that in all human endeavors there is not exactly an overabundance of love—genuine, unselfish, honest, and caring. And when you find it, you should never ever deprive it of its natural outlet. A child, in my opinion, needs as much of it as he or she can get." The judge shook her head for emphasis. "It is obvious to me that the boy in question has been blessed with a cornucopia of caring and affection, to which his grandparents have been copious contributors. How can a child lose by being the recipient of such caring?"

"See what I mean? We've won," Forte whispered. Molly felt a brief stab of elation, which quickly passed.

"Doesn't mean anything to me," Charlie muttered.

"I am, therefore, granting the petitioners their right of visitation on a basis of time and access to be worked out between the parties, but not to be less than once a week."

Charlie turned to Molly, obviously confused, but said nothing. Peripherally, she saw the big lawyer begin to rise, then sit again when the judge continued to speak.

"Naturally this decision can be appealed." She looked directly at Peck.

"I fully intend to," the lawyer replied, jumping up from his chair. Molly saw Frances tug sharply at Peck's sleeve. The lawyer looked at her and sat down abruptly.

"No point in staying," Charlie said, getting up. Molly rose with him. The judge continued to speak, but Molly did not fully comprehend what she was saying. They moved past the seated young lawyer, ignoring his upturned face. Nor did they pause for a last look at Tray, although Molly could feel his eyes watching them.

"It wasn't really his fault, Charlie. He believed in it from the beginning. Remember?"

"He forgot who was the client."

"Say what you want. He won our case."

"His. Not ours."

He brooded for a moment, pausing in the aisle.

"How can she judge how we should conduct our lives?" Charlie asked.

"That's her job," Molly responded as they walked slowly out of the courtroom. "And it was a wonderful speech. I'll give her that. It turned out that she has a lot more feeling than I thought."

"She was right about Tray," Charlie said. "He is a happy kid. And that's what counts. He sure doesn't need us."

"But we need us. Right, Charlie?" And the truth is, we need Tray, she told herself.

"You and me, babe." She heard the catch in his throat. Deliberately, she did not turn to see his tears.

Holding hands, they walked down the stairs, finding themselves once again in the ornate marble lobby, dominated by the large statue of the blind lady of justice.

"Maybe she should take that blindfold off and see life as it really is," Charlie said.

Molly did not respond. Behind her, she heard a persistent tapping, a light step descending stairs, then a click-click growing louder on the marble floor as it moved toward them. Before they could get to the entrance, they heard his voice.

"Gramma! Grampa!"

Turning, they saw Tray, who was moving fast. Arms out, they caught him jointly and hugged him against their bodies.

"Mommy said "— he was out of breath —"Daddy, too."

She smoothed his hair and touched his cheek, finding Charlie's fingers already there.

"They said I don't have to go back to school today so maybe we could do something—"

"Sure . . ." Charlie swallowed, turning to flick away tears with his sleeve.

"Not a bad idea," Molly managed to say.

"We could go back to the house," Charlie said, clearing his throat. "That tire swing is still there." He shook his head. "May be broken."

"I can make some fried chicken, the way you like it."

"Gee." The boy hesitated.

"And maybe you can help me fix that swing."

"But we have to make it higher, Grampa," Tray said, straightening, calling attention to his recent growth.

"Lots higher, I'd say," Charlie replied.

Across the lobby, Molly saw Frances and Peter watching them. Charlie was too busy with Tray to notice them. Molly took a step forward, hesitated, watching them through a mist of tears. She saw Frances move toward her, equally hesitant. When they embraced, Molly was certain, it was not only a mutual contact with the body, but with the spirit as well. What passed between them was beyond words. Then they parted, looked at each other briefly, deeply, knowing that what they shared needed no articulation.

When Molly returned to Charlie and Tray, they were still deep in conversation.

"Then maybe someday we can go together and see if we can get Nasty Jake," Tray was saying.

Charlie looked suddenly at Molly.

"We'll have to ask your mother about that, Tray. Besides, somebody else got Nasty Jake."

"Oh." He seemed disappointed. Then he brightened. "Then he's up there with my other Daddy."

"Probably is. I never thought of it that way."

He took Tray's hand. Molly took the other. They started to walk toward the entrance. But at the door, they stopped and turned, as if the idea had occurred to all of them at the same time. Across the lobby, Frances and Peter watched them, smiling.

Without unlocking their fingers, all three lifted their arms and waved.